Also by Juliet Lyons

Bite Nights

Dating the Undead

Drop Dead Gorgeous

DROP DEAD
Gorgeous

JULIET
LYONS

sourcebooks
casablanca

Published by Sourcebooks Casablanca, an imprint of Sourcebooks, Inc.
P.O. Box 4410, Naperville, Illinois 60567–4410
(630) 961–3900
Fax: (630) 961–2168
www.sourcebooks.com

Printed and bound in Canada.
MBP 10 9 8 7 6 5 4 3 2 1

Chapter 1

Mila

TURNS OUT THAT WHEN YOU DATE THE UNDEAD, THERE is a whole host of conversational faux pas you must avoid. You can't talk about death, for example, or use the phrase *what's at stake*, and don't get me started on the garlic breadsticks debacle. This probably explains why I'm on a date with a vampire and babbling about rats.

Not love rats—cheating ex-boyfriends whose names occasionally fall into first date conversation—no, the real kind that hang around sewers and restaurant kitchens. Long tails, pointy noses, beady eyes. I'm prattling on about *rats*.

"And I've heard," I say, wagging a finger like I'm some kind of expert on rodent activity, "that they're developing immunity to traditional poisons, which means they'll probably take over the whole planet someday." I lift my oversize wineglass to my lips before realizing it's empty, a sticky crimson glaze clinging to the rim along with most of my lipstick.

I shake the glass, frowning. It appears I've been gulping large mouthfuls of red wine instead of drawing breath. Being drunk would explain how this conversation got to the rise of the super rodent in the first place. I must be way more nervous than I thought.

Setting the glass back onto the table, I meet the

vampire's eyes. To his credit, if he's disappointed by my lack of conversational finesse, he doesn't show it. He's been eyeing me all evening with bemused fascination, as if I'm a rare and exquisite jewel he's discovered in a trash bag. There are worse ways to be looked at, let me tell you.

"So," I say, sucking in a deep breath, "what was London like in the good ole days?" I virtually have to glue my arm to my side to keep from making a Doris Day–esque fist swing.

His dark eyes flash with amusement as he signals at a passing waiter to bring more wine. "Actually, there *were* a lot of rats."

I chuckle, sitting up straight on the stool and swiping a stray lock of hair from my eyes. He made a joke. He's normal. Everything is going to be fine.

"But you're not British?" There is a definite accent to his soft voice—French or Italian maybe.

He ducks his head. "Originally, I'm from the North of Spain, the Basque region. I was born there in the eighteenth century."

My heart skips a beat, which is ridiculous because it's not like I don't know what he is. I sweep a glance around the busy London bar, at all the sleek city workers in their well-cut suits, the occasional trendy type in ripped jeans dotted among them. Even if they knew a vampire was sitting just feet away, no one would care. No one does anymore.

After declining his dinner offer, I figured drinks were the safest option. Of course, the *really* safe option would have been daytime coffee at Starbucks, but if you're going to date a vampire, why not go the whole hog and do it under the cover of darkness?

"The world must have changed so much," I muse, meeting his steady gaze. I've been fascinated by his eyes ever since I arrived. They're dark—deep brown and ringed with violet—but they glow like burnished gold. I watch as his pupils dilate like a cat's before I look away. Although he's handsome and looks exactly like his photo on V-Date, I'm not attracted to him in the slightest. Still, things are going a lot better than my last date, the one where my Australian boyfriend announced he was married with two kids. Compared to that, this is like an indoor Mardi Gras.

"The world has changed," he says, eyes fixed on my face. "But people are the same as ever—greedy, materialistic, selfish." He pauses while the waiter sets down two more large glasses of wine. "Don't you ever feel disappointed with all life has to offer, Mila?"

I frown, picking at the hem of my too-short skirt. My best friend, Laura, and I have indulged in this conversation since we were teenagers. It's a dark place to venture and not one I care to visit when I'm supposed to be out having fun.

"Sometimes, but we're here for such a short while, it's pointless to dwell on it."

His brows shoot skyward.

"At least, some of us are only here for a short while," I mumble.

He leans back on the stool, toying with the cuffs of his crisp white shirt. When I walked in earlier and saw him sitting here, my first thought was that he looked a little like a Spanish matador. With his olive complexion and inky black hair, all that's missing is one of those

gold brocade suits. To some women, he'd be the ultimate pinup, so I'm not quite sure why I'm so uninter-
ested. Maybe I secretly prefer blonds.

I allow my gaze to linger on the explosion of dark
hair peeking out from the front of his shirt. A pair of
giggling young women sitting a couple of tables over
keep whispering and checking him out, and I try hard to
see him through their eyes. I'm not ready to sacrifice my
sex drive as well as my faith in men just yet.

Taking a small sip of wine, I ask, "Do *you* ever
feel disappointed by life? Or is living forever one big,
crazy adventure?"

"Oh, there are plenty of disappointments. But I find
ways to keep myself amused." The corner of his mouth
twitches. For the first time all evening, I feel a little like
a mouse being batted between a cat's paws.

"Are you a regular on V-Date?" I ask.

He smiles, and although real vampires don't go around
baring their fangs like they do in old movies, it's easy to
imagine how they might look—sharp and pointed, protruding over his pink lips like spiky, white pearls.

"I've only been on a couple of dates besides this
one," he says. "What about you?"

"You're my first."

He arches a thick brow. "You're curious, I take it?
About what we're like?"

I shrug. "I like trying new things, and I've recently
come out of a relationship. So I thought, why not?"

He tips his head to one side, as if trying to suss me out.
"Don't you think you might be better off on Match.com?"

"Maybe someday," I say, beginning to wish I were

sitting with the giggling girls in the corner—or, better still, at home with that party-size bag of Doritos I bought at Tesco's earlier. I stifle a withering sigh. If life were a movie, he'd be the soul mate I always longed for. He'd say, "I've waited three hundred years to feel this way, Mila," not "Don't you think you might be better off on Match.com?"

If there's one thing I've learned in my twenty-six years on Planet Earth, it's that life is nothing like the movies. Life is waking up and finding out that the man you've spent the last two years with is a compulsive liar with an ex–lingerie model for a wife.

If I'm honest, the ex–lingerie model bit stings the most.

He leans across the table, forcing me to make eye contact. "I hope I haven't offended you, Mila."

"Nope."

Then something odd happens. When I try to look away, I can't. Not because I've suddenly realized how hot he is, or because there's some gigantic blemish on his face commanding my attention, but because I literally *can't*. I'm locked in time, the bar's chatter and music muted as I watch my own startled reflection in the depths of his bright, gold-brown eyes.

"You look flustered, Mila." His voice comes from far away, as if I'm hearing it from the other end of a tunnel. "Maybe we should step outside. Get some air."

The words should be enough to set alarm bells ringing, but to my horror, I find myself nodding in agreement. It's like the real me is locked up, hidden and helpless, in a tiny part of my brain. As if I'm a puppet, and he's the master.

I drop down from the stool, body and mind no longer connected, and reach to accept the smooth, olive-skinned hand he extends toward me. A gold signet ring on his middle finger catches the light from the spotlights in the ceiling. In the middle is an engraved coat of arms, a tiny dove at the tip of its crest.

"You'll feel much better once we're outside," he says in slow, honeyed tones. "I'll look after you. Don't worry."

I gaze up into his face as he leads me from the noisy bar to the dark London street. *What are you doing?* I ask myself. *Stay in the bar.* But my robot feet follow his lead, my vocal cords frozen in my throat.

Outside, a misty drizzle is falling. Droplets cling to his black hair like cobwebs. The road is still busy with commuters dashing home, an endless string of buses and taxis moving slowly through the night. I shiver, goose bumps prickling my bare arms, remembering I left my jacket on the stool inside. I try to speak, but again, the words won't come—as if the connections between my thoughts and actions are severed.

He glances over his shoulder as he pulls me around a corner into a side street. The road here is empty, shadows hugging the edges of the pavement. There are no bars or shops, only back entrances used for deliveries. Several streetlamps cast a dull orange glow onto the shiny pavement. When we reach a gap between the buildings, his hold on my hand tightens into a viselike grip.

Just when I thought dating couldn't get any worse.

Inside I'm petrified, but like the rest of my thoughts, the fear is contained, my heartbeat as steady as the clip of my heels on the concrete.

He stops abruptly in front of me, pulling me into a narrow brick alley lined on one side with steel dumpsters. A whiff of kitchen waste and urine hits my nostrils.

"I'm sorry it had to be my profile you clicked on, Mila," he says. My stomach twists with fear when I see his fangs are out, hanging over his lips in sharp, needle-like points, just like I imagined.

I watch mutely as he lets go of my hand and shoves me viciously against the wall.

"I have to say," he continues, his voice rougher than the bricks and mortar cutting into the skin on my back, "I found you to be a lot more entertaining than the other girls. It's a shame the world has to lose you."

My eyes widen as he brings his face closer, his strange eyes burning like wildfire. The scent of his strong cologne—a dark, spicy musk—crawls into my brain, overpowering my senses. But despite this hold he has over me, this *invasion*, a strangled scream rips from my throat.

"I'll make it quick," he whispers, undeterred, fangs scraping my cheek, "and I'll wait until after you're dead to taste you."

His hands move to my head, gripping me around the temples as I close my eyes, waiting for the deathblow. But as his fingers tighten around my skull, a crashing noise shatters the silence, sounding like a heavy object falling onto the steel bins. Somewhere out on the street, a siren begins to wail.

His hands fall away, and all at once, the drugged sensation leaves me. My body is mine again. The coppery tang of fear floods my mouth as my knees buckle. But before I hit the filthy, litter-strewn ground, a strong pair of arms wrap around my middle, holding me up.

I scream, thinking for a second that he's returned. But when I look up into the face of my assailant, I see a pair of storm-washed-blue eyes, coiffed blond hair, and a chiseled profile that could make a grown woman weep.

Perhaps I've died and gone to heaven.

"Please don't be alarmed, Miss Hart. I'm Inspector Ferrer from the Metropolitan Police. You're quite safe now."

"Wh-where is he?" I stutter, darting frantic glances around the alley. "Where did he go?"

The man grimaces. "He fled as soon as I showed up."

I stare up into his face, suddenly aware that my dress has somehow rucked up around my ass in all the drama. I must look like a hooker, and yet I feel like Marianne Dashwood in *Sense and Sensibility* when Willoughby finds her slumped on a hillside with a twisted ankle. Something about this man exudes the same gentlemanly concern.

"I couldn't scream," I say, feeling the need to explain. "I tried to, but I couldn't."

His eyes soften, and for a wild moment I think he's going to stroke my hair. "He put a glamour on you. Vampires can—we can do that."

Oh, great. He's a vampire too. My gut reaction is to push him away, but beneath the handful of cotton shirt I grabbed on my way down, I feel the hard outline of a fine set of abs—and as every single girl worth her salt knows, good abs do not just fall from the sky. Maybe there's hope for my sex drive yet.

I'm still staring into his eyes when the alley fills with

flashing lights. The sirens reach a fever pitch, forcing me to release his shirt and cover my ears.

The noise cuts out and two police officers resembling a pair of middle-aged Columbo impersonators in long beige overcoats burst into the alley. One is lanky with a thinning mop of mousy hair, and the other is short and balding, not dissimilar to the used car salesman that sold me my dilapidated VW Golf a few weeks back.

"Oh, thank God," the shorter man says as soon as he claps eyes on me. "She's alive."

His colleague barges past, a shiny police badge held aloft. "I'm Superintendent Linton Burke. Are you injured?"

I shake my head, putting the weight back onto my wobbly legs. "I don't think so, psychological damage notwithstanding."

To my bitter disappointment, Inspector Abs releases me. "I think we should take you to the hospital anyway, just to be on the safe side."

"How did you know where to find me? Did someone at the bar call the cops?" I watch as they all stare at one another, their mouths set in the same grim line.

Burke clears his throat. "Miss Hart, I think it might be wise if we discuss this further in a more private setting."

Then it hits me. They aren't regular policemen— they're detectives.

I look between the three of them. "He said there were other girls…"

Inspector Abs nods. "There are. I mean, there were."

A violent shiver rips through me, and Inspector Ferrer removes his suit jacket, draping it discreetly around my shoulders. If it wasn't for a delicious waft of eau de hot man enveloping me, I mightn't have noticed it at all. I pull the surprisingly warm blazer tight across my chest to cover my cleavage, tugging my skirt down self-consciously. "Are you saying my first vampire date was a *serial killer*?"

Their faces tell me everything I need to know. I sway, the ground moving beneath me, as if the damp concrete has turned to water. A sound like waves rushing up a beach roars in my ears before everything turns black.

When I next open my eyes, I'm back in the hottie's arms.

"You're making a habit of this," I mutter.

"It appears so," he says quietly. "Put your weight on me. We need to get you to the car."

"You know," I say, leaning against his broad shoulder as we follow the two beige trench coats out of the alley, "I'm going to ask V-Date for a full refund after tonight." Hearing the tiniest snort of laughter, I crane my neck to see his face. "You can write me a note as evidence," I continue. "*Please give refund: date tried to kill her.* I think I'll treat myself to a spa day with the money."

"I can call them myself if you'd prefer," he says dryly.

"That would be fabulous, thank you."

The two Columbos open the car doors and I duck into the vehicle. Another police car is parked in front of us, and several uniformed police officers stand nearby. "They'll stick around," the short detective says from the front seat. "Take evidence from the crime scene."

"But I'm alive—aren't I?"

Inspector Vampire, who has climbed into the back-seat next to me, says, "Yes, but it's still a crime scene. Kidnapping and assault are very serious."

My thoughts wander back to the way I left the bar, completely under my date's control. "Wait!" I erupt. "I left my new jacket in the pub."

But Superintendent Burke is already accelerating away from the curb. "It'll still be there in the morning, Miss Hart," he says disinterestedly.

"It's Ralph Lauren," I say. "I doubt it."

"I can call them," Inspector Ferrer says. "What was the name of the bar again?"

"The World's End," I say grimly, staring into his chiseled face. "Please, no smart comments."

His eyes crinkle around the edges as he smiles, and I stare openmouthed. He's so gorgeous, it burns my eyes to look at him—like watching a solar eclipse without protective glasses. He says the name of the pub into his phone and hits a button. After someone answers, he says, "There's a Ralph Lauren jacket left on a barstool."

"Table six," I interject.

"Table six. Can you please hold it behind the bar? Someone will collect it tomorrow. Thank you."

He hangs up and puts the phone away. "Crisis averted."

Having surpassed the level of staring that is considered socially acceptable, I drag my gaze away. "Thank you."

"You're welcome."

When I dart a look back, he's still watching me, his jaw clenched. I tug my skirt down some more and he looks away. Though it's difficult to see in the low light of the vehicle, I swear a flush creeps up his neck.

Can vampires blush? I wonder, admiring his angular profile in the yellow light of the passing traffic. In any case, I've learned at least one thing from tonight's events.

I definitely, without a doubt, prefer blonds.

Chapter 2

Vincent

"It still doesn't make sense," Sergeant Lee Davies says through a mouthful of half-chewed pizza. "Why use his real photo?"

It's shortly after midnight, and the three of us are hunched around a table in a conference room at Scotland Yard, amid an explosion of crushed coffee cups and half-empty pizza boxes. Mila Hart was escorted home an hour ago by a squad car—shaken and tired but still making quips about the sorry state of London's dating scene.

I swallow a smile, remembering her reaction after we explained the killer had been using V-Date to target victims. Her pretty hazel eyes cast to the heavens, she said, "What a world, when you can't even trust the dead ones."

The room grows silent, two sets of eyes drilling into me.

"Don't you think it's a possibility, Vincent?" Linton Burke asks. From his weary tone, I can tell this isn't the first time he's asked the question.

Truth is, I was too busy thinking about Miss Hart's shapely legs. *Again*. "Sorry?"

Linton emits a heavy sigh. "That the killer put his own picture on the fake profile this time, thinking he'd throw us off the scent. After all, his other pictures were all taken from genuine profiles on the site. Maybe he hoped the confusion would buy him some time."

I loosen my tie, narrowing my eyes in thought. "It's a little farfetched, but it's a possibility. I'll call Catherine Adair first thing in the morning and see if she's found anything of interest on her client database."

"Excellent," Burke says, his tired eyes darting to the clock above the door. Unlike me, he has a wife waiting for him at home—a wife who, judging by the number of times his phone beeped during Mila Hart's extensive witness statement, is not at all happy about being left home alone.

"The other thing I don't get," Davies says, picking at an empty polystyrene cup with a fingernail, "is why the other two women didn't react faster to a complete stranger meeting them instead of the vampire in the pictures."

"We've been over this," Burke snaps. "He would have glamoured them straightaway."

"But why didn't he glamour Mila Hart until halfway through the evening? Why take the risk? Sitting there in the middle of a busy bar, seen by dozens of people. If Miss Hart died, we'd have been in that bar the next day with his photo. There'd be plenty of witnesses to testify the man they saw her leave with was the same as the one in the picture. Which blows your *throwing us off the scent* theory out of the water." Lee Davies smooths a hand over his shiny bald head and leans back in the chair, looking pleased with himself. Unlike Burke, he and his wife are going through a rough patch. He relishes late nights.

"Unless he wants to be caught," I offer, though I'm

not at all surprised he didn't glamour Mila Hart until halfway through the evening. There is no denying her obvious charms. I zone out, remembering slender thighs, an ample swell of cleavage, and her mesmerizing hazel eyes—large and intelligent. In the car and all through her interview, I was horrified by my inability to stop *staring*. I just hope she didn't notice. There's nothing like being kidnapped and assaulted and then having a police officer leer at you. I cringe shamefully as my trousers tighten. The cold setting on the shower will get a thorough workout tonight.

Burke fans out the V-Date photos. "You're sure you've never met him, Vincent?"

I lean across the table, peering intently at the dark-haired man in the picture before shaking my head. "I don't think so, though sometimes it's hard to recognize people with modern haircuts and clothing. There's always a chance Cat might know him, but even if she doesn't, someone will."

"Well, I say we break here, lads," Burke says, shuffling the pictures and copies of Mila Hart's statement back together and dropping them into a manila envelope. "Let's reconvene in the morning. What time did we ask Miss Hart to drop by tomorrow?"

"Three o'clock," I say without hesitation.

Linton raises an eyebrow, as if he knows full well why I've memorized the time. "Right-o." He pushes up from his seat. "Night, lads."

As soon as the door clicks shut behind him, Davies grins, spinning around on his swivel chair so we're face-to-face. Having worked in each other's pockets these

past years, I know what he's going to say before the
words pass his lips.

"Blimey, that Mila Hart is a bit of all right, isn't she?"

I close my eyes briefly, and when I open them, Lee is
wagging a finger in my face. "Don't pretend you didn't
notice either. I clocked you checking out her rack at
every given opportunity."

"Lee," I say, frowning, "don't say *rack*. She's our
witness. Have some respect."

Lee puts on a posh accent. "Oh, terribly sorry, Holy
Father. I meant to say she was an absolute delight."

I shake my head, trying not to smile as I adjust the knot
in my tie. Lately, I wonder if Lee's having some sort of
midlife crisis. He seems to be spending an awful lot of time
making inappropriate comments about the opposite sex.

"Seriously though, mate, isn't it time you had a
woman in your life?"

I snort incredulously, reaching behind to pull my suit
jacket from the back of the chair. At the last second, I
remember Miss Hart took it home with her. The vision
of her curvy frame swamped by my jacket, blond hair
spilling over her shoulders like a golden waterfall, is
enough to induce another dangerous wave of lust. I need
that shower. Fast.

"Lee," I say, "I'm a professional. End of."

He begins swiveling his hips on the chair, twisting
like he's performing a sit-down samba. "Christ, if I were
in your shoes, I certainly wouldn't be going back to a
cold, empty flat every night."

"I have a feeling you're going to tell me what you'd
be doing," I say dryly.

"I'd be down in the West End," he continues, ignoring me and staring wistfully off into space, "wining and dining a different bird every night. I mean, what's the point in owning a Porsche and looking like you do if you don't make the most of it?"

"All that is in the past," I mutter. "Besides, none of that means anything. Not really."

"Who cares what it means? Enjoy it. I mean, I get that you have integrity by the bucket load, Vince, and I admire you for it. I do. But these days, women are usually only after one thing themselves. With vampires being *out* and all, you wouldn't even have to lie about it. Look at Mila Hart—birds like her are dying to hook up with the likes of you. Unless…" He trails off, a devious glint in his eye.

"Please don't ask me if I'm gay again, Lee, and stop referring to Mila Hart as a 'bird.'"

Lee snickers. "If you are gay, Vince, you should be out and proud. I'm sure Barry down in narcotics would happily show you all the bars."

"Lee, stop." I push myself up from the table, signaling my intention to leave. "Go home to your wife. Treat her well."

He sighs, the life going out of him faster than helium from a burst balloon. "I'm pretty sure she's shagging the UPS guy."

That stops me in my tracks, one hand on the door handle. "*The UPS guy?*"

Lee sinks farther into his chair, his once-jubilant smile reduced to a grim line. "First she lost all that weight at Weight Watchers, and now she's ordering all these new clothes."

I release my grip on the door. The cold shower will have to wait. Lee may behave like a randy schoolboy when Burke isn't around to keep him in check, but he's still a good friend. "Isn't that what people do when they lose weight? Because their old clothes won't fit them?"

Lee picks at the edge of table, top lip quivering. "At first that's what I thought, but when I leave the house every morning, she's dolled up to the nines, even though she claims she's just popping around to Rosemary's for coffee. Then when I get back, there's always another parcel. Even if I wasn't a detective, I think I'd have figured it out by now."

"So why not confront her?"

"If I do, our marriage is over. We've been together since we were fifteen. UPS guy or no UPS guy, I can't imagine life without her."

Modern marriage is obviously a lot more complicated than I thought. I always assumed things were simple these days, what with everyone being so financially independent and all. "So is this why you don't want to go home lately?"

Lee breaks my gaze. "You noticed."

I nod, perching on the edge of the meeting table. "If you get divorced, wouldn't you be happier? 'Wining and dining a different woman every night,' like you said you'd like to?"

He sputters in disbelief. "I meant I'd do that if I were *you*. Who's going to want this"—he gestures to the portly stomach, rounded beneath his tightly stretched shirt—"a middle-aged, bald bloke with a potbelly? Let's face it—I'm no Hugh Jackman. Never was either."

I suppress a smile. "Looks aren't everything, Lee."

"Easy for you to say, *Brad Pitt*."

"It's true," I say, staring out the window at the milky-blue London skyline. "If they were, matters of the heart would be simple. You can't fall in love with someone just because they're beautiful. It goes deeper than that. A lot deeper."

"Is this why you never bring a plus one to the Christmas ball?" Lee asks, putting his feet up on the table and crossing his legs. "You're still waiting for Miss Right?"

"That ship sailed long ago."

"Oh, come off it. I know they say you only get one true love, but surely if you're three hundred years old that means you get at least three, right?"

I continue to stare into the night, not speaking. It's not that I don't want anything to do with women—au contraire. Though I'm not about to divulge my sexual history to the likes of Davies, I've had more than my fair share of meaningless, sexed-up encounters over the years. I've even had girlfriends, both vampire and human, who I've seen on a regular basis. But *love*—the real kind—takes a commitment I'm not prepared to make. I gave my heart once, hundreds of years ago, and I'm not willing to do it again. Falling in love is like leaping naked headfirst from a tall building. Life is far simpler and safer without it.

Finally, I meet Lee's probing gaze. "I'm just not interested in having that complication in my life again."

Lee nods slowly. "If I do get divorced, Vince, you and me should hit the clubs together. You can draw them in with your looks, and I'll dazzle them with my sparkling wit."

I laugh, patting my trouser pocket to make sure I have my car keys. "It's a deal. Come on. I'll give you a lift home."

After dropping Lee in the leafy suburbs of Muswell Hill, I drive back toward Chelsea, to the scene of Mila Hart's attempted murder. The streets have almost emptied out, but the odd red, double-decker bus hurtles along, sending litter and dust skittering in its wake. A few pedestrians, mostly workers on their way to or from a night shift, bustle past, rucksacks flung over their shoulders, desperate to be out of the chilly night air.

I park on the street where we found Mila Hart, opposite the damp alleyway that's now cordoned off with black-and-yellow crime tape. It was a heart-stopping moment for the three of us when we found the matching profile on the V-Date website—the exact same details given by the previous killer. Height, interests, and personal information—*verbatim*. Then enduring what felt like a hundred-year wait while V-Date's owner, Cat, pulled out all the messages from her system. I can still hear her gasp of horror from the other end of the phone line when she discovered that "Jeremiah Lopez," as he called himself, was meeting his date in Chelsea at that very moment.

I flew straight to the pub, leaving Scotland Yard in such haste that, stupidly, I didn't stop to pick up a copy of his picture. When I eventually tracked them down to the street around the corner, I was so relieved to see her alive, I let him slip away. If I hadn't behaved like such a pathetic Romeo by catching her midfall, I might have caught up to him. I release a slow hiss of frustration between my teeth. There's something about this case that irks me, something that goes beyond the fact that innocent women are being targeted.

Innocent and *sexy*, a voice in my head reminds me.

Turning away from the silent alley, I head onto the main road, to the bar where Mila met the killer. The trend these days seems to be for upmarket bars to masquerade as olde-worlde pubs. This one is no different. The exterior is painted a pristine shade of royal blue, the windows buffed to a mirror shine. There are several large, carefully tended hanging baskets on the walls overflowing with pansies, but the real giveaway we're not in Victorian England is the scent. Bars smell like cleaning fluids these days, not like tobacco and stale beer and body odors. Thank goodness.

I check my Rolex and see it's a little after one in the morning. Though the windows are dark, there are lights on behind the bar. A young man loads pint glasses onto a shelf above the beer taps. I push open the wooden door and step into the warm glow of the room. Inside it's furnished with expensive distressed tables and chairs. I can tell it's one of those places fond of serving food on wooden boards and shiny slate tiles. Plates and bowls seem to be a thing of the past in London's eateries of late. The other day at lunch, Lee Davies's portion of french fries arrived in a metal flowerpot.

The lad looks over his shoulder. "Closed, mate."

"I'm not here to drink," I say, wondering if I should take out my badge. Though I loathe being one of those types to play the police officer card, I have to admit it comes in handy at times. A bit like having a magic wand—at least where speeding tickets are concerned.

"I called earlier about a jacket that was left behind. A Ralph Lauren one."

The pimply youth looks me over, wiping hands on the front of his black apron. "Oh yeah. It's in the back." He grins. "No offense, but I'm not sure it's your size."

Smart-ass. "It's my girlfriend's." Using the word *girlfriend* about Mila Hart leaves me more than just a little hot under the collar. I loosen my tie as he chuckles, ducking through a door behind the bar and emerging a few seconds later with a black blazer.

"Thank you," I say, taking the soft bundle from him.

"No worries."

"I don't suppose you saw her earlier, did you? Blond hair, yea high?" I wave a downward palm level with my chest. "She was with a dark-haired gentleman?"

He shakes his head. "Nah, sorry. We were rammed tonight."

I flash a smile. "Never mind. Thank you anyway."

"My ex cheated on me too," he pipes up as I turn away. "Bitches. All of them."

Deciding not to dignify that sweeping statement with a response, I beat a path to the door, stepping back out onto the King's Road.

It's only when I'm back in the Porsche that a mortifying thought strikes me—tomorrow I'll have to hand the jacket back to her in person, probably in front of my work colleagues. If she possesses an iota of common sense, she'll know collecting lost property isn't in my job description. She'll *know* I'm attracted to her. Big time. Muttering a curse, I lift it, burying my face into the soft material. It smells like perfume and fruit shampoo, and with my heightened senses, I pick up a deeper scent—floral, sweet, and perfectly intoxicating. *Her*.

A tingle zips through me, and I impulsively fling the coat onto the backseat of the car. I must have fallen victim to some bizarre phenomenon where a man projects displaced feelings onto the woman he saves. I sigh, turning over the ignition. Maybe tomorrow I'll leave her jacket with the others, make an excuse not be present at her interview. She'll think I've just been kind, picking up the lost coat for her. Perhaps Lee can say he did it. I'll never have to see her again.

With a heavy heart, I push the car into gear and make a neat U-turn on the deserted street, heading home to an empty flat.

Chapter 3

Mila

"HE WAS A *SERIAL KILLER*?" LAURA ASKS IN DISBELIEF, crashing her coffee mug onto the table and sloshing dark-brown liquid everywhere. "Are you taking the piss?"

It's the day after my would-be murder, and I'm sitting in my best friend's kitchen in Richmond. Needless to say, I didn't get an awful lot of shut-eye last night. Being targeted by London's most wanted can really mess with a sleeping pattern.

I shake my head. "I wish I were."

"And he tried to murder you in an alley?"

"Yep."

After I've told her the full story, she sits back in her seat, staring at me across the table with a curious mixture of awe and horror. "Only you, Mila," she says finally. "Only you."

"I know," I say, pulling a cookie from the tin. "If they're not cheating, they're trying to kill me. It's gone beyond a joke."

"So what happens now?" Laura asks, eyes wide. "He won't come after you, will he? He doesn't know where you live?"

I shake my head, reaching across the table to pat her hand. "Don't worry. He didn't even have my telephone number. We arranged it all through V-Date. There's no way he can trace me."

Laura nods, some of the tension leaking out of her shoulders. "And the guy who rescued you was a vampire too?"

"Yeah." I pause, remembering his strong arms around my waist. "He was totally hot."

Laura's dour face brightens. "Really? What was his name? Did you see a wedding ring?"

This is one of the things I love most about Laura. She sits through a dramatic account of my near-death experience on a date and still believes there's a chance I might get a boyfriend out of it.

"Inspector Ferrer," I say, biting off a chunk of chocolate biscuit. "I can't say I was really in the frame of mind to be looking out for a wedding ring though. He just sort of fell from the sky."

"When you say hot, how hot?"

"Superhot. You know that guy on the billboard as you drive along the M40? The one frolicking in the surf? That hot."

Laura's jaw drops. "Jesus."

We don't speak for a few seconds, silent in our worship of the billboard hottie.

"He was nice too—he loaned me his jacket. Too bad I'll never see him again."

Laura frowns. "Why won't you see him again? Don't they want to question you some more?"

I glance down at my wristwatch, vaguely aware I was supposed to be there half an hour ago. Sometime during my sleepless night, I decided wild horses wouldn't be enough to drag me back to Scotland Yard today.

"I've already told them everything," I say, taking

a sip of tea. "I just want to put the whole sorry mess behind me."

"But what if they catch him?" Laura says, her blue eyes wide. "You would have to do one of those lineup things like they have on *CSI*. Then afterward, Inspector Hot Guy would ask you for coffee. He'd say something like"—she adopts a deeper voice—"'In a way, I should thank that psycho for bringing you into my life.'"

Despite my weariness, I chuckle. "Didn't we make a pact to quit pretending life is like the movies?"

"Yeah, we did," she says, a pink glow appearing on her cheeks. "Until I met Tom."

I narrow my eyes, pretending to scowl. "Yeah, thanks again for leaving me alone on Bitter Island."

Up until a few years ago, Laura had been in the exact same situation as me—building an impressive collection of douchebag ex-boyfriends and wondering if there was such a thing as happy ever after. Then the stars aligned. She met her now-husband, Tom, and experienced one of those miraculous moments when both timing and attraction come together in perfect harmony—the holy grail of dating.

Of course, I wasn't the least bit jealous.

Well, okay, maybe a tiny bit.

"I reckon something good will happen for you soon. Your days on Bitter Island are numbered," she says, gazing dreamily out the window at her gardenias. She opens her mouth to add something, but then thinks better of it, pursing her lips shut instead.

I wave an accusing finger in her face. "Were you about to say what I think you were about to say?"

She shakes her head vigorously before breaking into a devious smile. "It'll happen when you least expect it."

I snatch up a dish towel dangling from the back of a chair and fling it at her. If there's one thing that drives me mental, it's hearing that phrase.

"But actually," Laura says, picking up the cloth and refolding it, "maybe it's true this time. I bet you weren't expecting to meet the gorgeous inspector in that alleyway."

"No, Laura, at that point, I was more focused on the hands about to break my neck than meeting the love of my life."

"Exactly. So this could be it."

"With a vampire?" I ask incredulously. "Even if he swept in that door right now with a diamond engagement ring, it's completely pointless. There's no future in dating a man forever trapped in youth. I mean, it's tough enough trying to keep a regular man faithful for a lifetime. Think what life would be like with some model sort who remains eternally young. Look at Demi Moore."

She frowns. "So why were you using that site in the first place if you didn't want to seriously meet someone?"

I shrug, running a finger around the edge of my mug. "Because it interested me, that's all. I wanted to meet one. After Scott and that whole *oh, by the way, I'm still married to someone and we have two kids together* fiasco, I felt like dipping a toe in foreign waters. See what the other species are like. Now my curiosity is sated—the end."

Laura throws me a smug grin and raises a dark brow. "We'll see about that."

We both lapse into silence as I cast an admiring gaze around Laura's recently remodeled black-and-chrome kitchen. Lucky for her Tom is not only a sweet husband who remembers anniversaries, but he's also a dab hand with a power drill. "Are those tiles Laura Ashley?" I ask, pointing at the dove-gray-and-white mosaic pattern behind the sink.

When she doesn't answer, I glance back to see the color drained from her face. There's a knot in her forehead and she's twisting a strand of brown hair anxiously around her index finger. "Mila, they will catch this guy, won't they?"

I reach across the table to pat her arm. "I'm sure they will. I mean, look how fast they showed up last night. It's only a matter of time."

She twists her hands nervously. "Maybe you should stay here until they do. Tom won't mind. You're not going to work tonight, are you?"

I've already called in sick to my day job, temping at a large corporate firm as a receptionist. But my evening job, teaching English to a bunch of newly arrived immigrants at London Metropolitan University, is harder to wriggle out of—mainly because I enjoy it.

"I'm going," I say. "Some of them travel all the way from Essex. I don't like to let them down."

"Mila, you were almost murdered. I'm sure they'll understand."

I flash a smile. "Well, they barely speak English, so I doubt it."

"Oh, ha-ha."

"Besides, it'll be good to take my mind off stuff."

"Well, if you get home later and feel like you need me, drive straight over. I'll make up the spare bed just in case."

I nod, draining the last of my tea. "I'll be fine. Don't worry."

I leave Laura's around six in the evening and drive straight across town to the university. It's still light outside, a weak sun filtering through a mist of streaky-gray clouds. Though it's supposed to be spring in London, there's an icy breeze in the air that chills to the bone. Hard to believe that just a few short months ago, I was living in Australia, waking up each morning to a sun so dazzling, I practically lived in a pair of Ray-Bans. Those days already feel like a million years ago.

Climbing out of my car on Holloway Road, I'm hit by a blast of cold air. I wish I'd thought to bring a jacket. I'm still wearing the same clothes I flung on this morning—slouchy jeans, a frayed gray sweater, and a pair of Converse sneakers. My hair is pulled back off my face in a messy bun. Still, the best thing about London is that you can dress however you like and no one bats an eyelid. Hell, I could saunter along Holloway Road in a Mickey Mouse costume and no one would give a toss. It's one of the things I've missed most about living here.

Perhaps this blasé attitude is why so many vampires have migrated to London since their exposure. I still remember seeing the headline all those years ago: *Vampires Exist!!* I was about seventeen at the time and in high school when a super-famous Hollywood actress, no doubt exhausted by having to shoot down plastic surgery rumors, announced via her publicist she was, in fact, a vampire. For years, she and others like her had been casually milling around among us, minding their own business—*not drinking our blood*. It transpired that most vampire myths are utterly ludicrous—they don't need blood to survive, the sun doesn't kill them, and they absolutely *do not* sleep in a coffin filled with dirt from their motherland. Like most things in our world, people soon lost interest. A week later, we were back to Justin Bieber hating on his fans and the size of Kim Kardashian's butt.

My point is, in London, a city where grown men can and do waltz down King's Road in eight-inch glitter platforms, many vampires found their spiritual home. I guess that's why V-Date has proved such a huge success. Last I heard, there are similar dating sites branching out across the globe. This time next year, we could all be dating ghosts or something.

By the time I make it to my classroom, a cluttered, dusty little room in the basement of the languages block that smells of moldy books, my students are already waiting.

Most of them break into smiles by way of greeting. There are a few hellos. No one asks why I'm wearing jeans and not carrying any books.

Karolina, a stunningly beautiful Romanian woman with huge ebony eyes and an artfully curled mane of obsidian hair, is the first to break the silence.

"How was the date, Mila?" she asks.

In case it isn't already obvious, I share too much. Apparently in Tuesday's lesson, when we were all practicing our polite English conversations, I must have let it slip out about my date.

Karolina is waiting for my answer, head tilted to one side. This evening she's dressed in tight white jeans and over-the-knee patent boots, a huge pair of gold hoop earrings dangling from her earlobes. She looks like an exotic princess. The pair of brothers from Ghana, who never speak unless forced to, stare at her, mouths open, like she's queen of the Nile. I'm fairly sure she's the only reason they're still coming.

I make a face.

"Oh," Karolina says. "Bad."

I nod, snatching up the eraser from the desk to wipe away some leftover French verbs from the whiteboard. A guy at the back—Axel, a Norwegian Hells Angel—smashes a fist into one of his fingerless leather gloves. "If he gives you trouble, tell me. I sort it." He sounds a lot like Arnie in *The Terminator*.

"That's okay, Axel," I say, taking out the class list from my handbag. "It's nothing I can't handle."

After I've ticked off their names, I get them to start in the usual way, by turning to the person beside them and asking about their day. After that person's had their turn, they turn to whoever's next to them and so on, until everyone's had a go. After that, we get down to the nitty-gritty of today's agenda, which is simple past tense.

What I love most about this job is how quickly the time goes. Before I know it, it's nine o'clock and class is finished.

Usually, I'm last out the door, as I have all my books and things to pack away. Tonight, with only a handbag,

I leave with the rest of them. Karolina falls into step beside me as we spill into the corridor, talking about Marco, her wealthy Italian boyfriend who she mostly refers to as "asshole."

"Asshole call me up and say he no take me to Milan because uncle die and he must fly to Guatemala. I say, 'Fuck you, asshole. I go anyway. Fernando take me.'" She pauses to suck an angry breath through her perfectly white teeth. I'm gazing at them, wondering if she gets them professionally whitened or uses a special tooth-paste, when she freezes mid-rant. Her massive black eyes lock on the space a few inches past my head, dark eyelashes fluttering wildly like a pair of moth's wings.

I whip around to see what she's staring at and almost suffer heart failure when I find myself gazing directly into a pair of flame-blue eyes. There, standing in the hallway, immaculately dressed in a gray, tailored suit and looking like he's fallen straight from the pages of a men's clothing catalog, is Inspector Abs.

Before I can get a grip, my heart begins to thud like a hammer in my chest; my palms slicken with moisture. I tell myself it's because I'm remembering the horrors of my murderous date, but who am I kidding?

I must have been suffering from shock last night because I don't recall him being this beautiful. Hot, yes, but the man standing in front of me is nothing short of a vision. I half expect a crack to open in the ceiling and a white beam of light to shine down on him. That's not to say he's a pretty boy or anything. Far from it. His features are *rugged*—a square jaw peppered with stubble, thick brows, and dirty-blond hair so perfectly swept off his forehead that I wonder how it looks after sex—all *mussed*, pearls of moisture clinging to the silky strands.

I'm so utterly locked into my sex-hair daydream that several seconds pass before I realize my jaw is hanging open and my eyes are bugging out. I must look exactly like the Ghanaian brothers in class when Karolina walks into the room. Karolina herself stares between us in confusion before muttering something in Romanian and slipping away along the corridor with the others.

"Miss Hart," he says finally. His brow furrows, two vertical lines denting the space between his eyes. I'm suddenly all too aware of my shabby clothes. A couple of times last night I got the impression he was checking me out, but now he's staring at me like I've sprouted another head. Probably wondering how he got it so wrong.

Though I feel like slipping through a crack in the corridor floor, I pull myself to full height and meet his burning gaze. "Am I under arrest, Inspector?" To my horror, the words sound provocative, as if I'm speaking to some bachelorette party policeman and not the real deal. Then again, maybe it's impossible *not* to say anything provocative to a man his level of sexy.

"No," he says. "But we were concerned when you didn't turn up at Scotland Yard today, and I need to return this to you."

At this point, I notice my Ralph Lauren blazer is draped across his arm.

"Oh," I say, reaching to take it from him. "Thanks."

My hand brushes his, and I flinch as a tingle shoots up my arm, a ripple of warmth radiating through my body.

His frown deepens. "It's no trouble. We had to speak

to the bar staff anyway, so…" He trails off into silence, raking beautifully tapered fingers through his hair.

I nod, wasting no time slipping the blazer on. "How did you know where I work?"

"Huh? Oh, we ran a search on your National Insurance number. I went to your apartment first, thinking you might be there. When you weren't, I figured you would be at work."

The idea of him at my apartment affords me an adolescent thrill. "Oh, well, it's a shame I wasn't there—I still have your jacket. I was going to return it by courier in the morning."

"You mean you have no intention of helping us further with our inquiries?"

I shrug. "I've told you everything I can. If you catch him, I'll testify, but other than that, what more can I do?"

His blue eyes burn into mine as his gentle tone drops an octave. I get the feeling he's using his *serious policeman* voice on me. "With all due respect, I don't think you understand how serious this is. A serial killer is at large, and not just any serial killer, Miss Hart—a *vampire*. I'm not sure how much you know about our kind, but we are stronger than the average human in every way imaginable. You are at a much greater risk than you would be if he were human."

I scowl, folding my arms across my chest. "Yes," I say tartly. "I am aware of your strength." My eyes, with a life of their own, flicker to his chest, to the visible lines of muscle swelling beneath his white pinstripe shirt. The memory of how they felt beneath my fingertips sends heat soaring into my cheeks.

"I'm not an idiot," I say, tapping a foot on the tiled floor. "But I've given you my statement already, and if it's all right by you, I'd like to put this sorry mess behind me."

He stares at me, mouth agape. "I didn't mean to suggest you were an idiot, Miss Hart. I don't think you're an idiot—I mean *we* don't think that. Myself and my colleagues. I only wanted to point out that I'm concerned for your safety. That is to say, *we* are concerned for your safety. Very concerned."

It's my turn to goggle at him. There's something about his little speech that reminds me of my rat babbling from last night. "I appreciate your concern, Inspector, but until there's a development, I'd like to carry on as normal, you know? If that's not against the law."

"No, it's not against the law," he says, gazing at me with an unreadable expression. "Will you at least allow me to walk you to your car? I take it you have one? If not, I can drive you home."

I snatch a look at my watch. There are no windows in the basement, but it's bound to be dark outside by now—not that I need an excuse to go with him, of course. "Okay. I'm parked around the corner on a side street."

He motions for me to walk ahead, and I wonder how old he *really* is. There's an antiquity to his mannerisms, a courtliness that suggests Old World breeding. Once I start walking, he falls into step beside me, an awkward silence pressing down on us. For the life of me, I can't think of a single thing to say.

"So, how long—"

"Did you get—"

We both start speaking at the same time.

"You first," I say. My face burns so fiercely you could fry an egg on it.

"I was going to ask if you got much sleep last night," he says.

"Not much," I say. "Unsurprisingly."

He nods, another deathly silence dropping over us like a cloak. I feel about sixteen years old, having a conversation with the hottest guy in school.

When we hit the end of the corridor, there are two options: elevator or stairs. Not liking the idea of staring mutely at a pair of sliding doors, I lead him into the stairwell, my sneakers squeaking noisily on the linoleum as we trudge up the steps.

"Have you worked here long?" he asks.

"No." I stare up at his chiseled profile. "I was living in Australia until a few months ago."

"Australia? What took you there?"

"I went traveling after university and ended up living there for two years. My boyfriend was Australian. Ex-boyfriend," I add quickly. Just in case there's any doubt.

His jaw clenches. "And the ex-boyfriend stayed in Australia?"

I arch a brow. "Is this another one of your police interrogations?"

He smiles. "No. Just chitchat."

"Oh. Well, actually, he went back to live in Brazil. To be with his wife and kids."

Mr. Vampire does a double take before his features drop back into repose. "Ah, I see."

"I didn't know about it, of course," I say, not wanting

him to think I'm of one of those women you read about in *Take a Break* magazine who only date married guys. "He just dropped it on me one day over dinner."

We reach the top of the stairwell, and he holds open the door to let me through. "Hence your venture into vampire dating."

"Yes, and look what a great idea that turned out to be."

"We're not all killers, Miss Hart."

I grimace. "No, just the ones I pick."

He looks at me sideways, eyes dark with speculation. I get the impression he's trying to suss me out.

Outside the sky is navy blue, the chilly wind whipping loose tendrils of hair across my face. Strains of salsa music drift across the street from the Cuban restaurant on the corner, soothing amid the rush of traffic. When we reach my car, I turn to him. "This is me. Thanks for seeing me back." I click the doors open but make no attempt to move, transfixed as I am by his heavenly body. "I'll return it by courier first thing tomorrow."

Waving a hand, he says, "Keep it."

I wrinkle my nose. "But it's Prada."

He frowns and smiles at the same time, thrusting hands deep into his trouser pockets. "Is it? I have a lot of suits."

"Well, it's definitely a look that works for you," I say, noticing how the material stretches over his broad shoulders.

He averts his gaze. "Thanks."

Another thick cloud of tension settles around us until finally, I wrench open the door of the VW. "Good night."

"Miss Hart?"

I sling my bag onto the passenger seat before looking up. "Yes?"

"I think it would be a good idea if you took my number."

I swallow my excitement, trying not to act as if all my Christmases have come at once. "Oh?"

"Just in case you need me. I mean, us—myself, Superintendent Burke, and Sergeant Davies."

A wave of disappointment washes over me as I reach back into the car to pull my phone out. "Sure. Here you go."

He takes it from me and begins tapping. "It's under Vincent," he says passing it back. "Because that's my name."

For some reason that seems to amuse us and we smile. "Thank you, *Vincent*. I mean, Inspector Vincent."

I climb into the car, and he closes the door after me. I wind the window down.

"Remember, you can call me anytime—day or night," he says, ducking down to eye level. "Sleep is not something we vampires do an awful lot."

"Okay. That's kind. Thank you." I start the engine, wondering how I'll ever go on with my life knowing his number is programmed into my phone.

"Oh, and, Miss Hart?"

I take one last look up into his handsome face. His eyes are the color of a warm summer sky.

"That Australian ex-boyfriend of yours must be the biggest moron on earth."

My heart somersaults in my chest. "He is."

Before I can ruin what is quite possibly the best moment of my romantic life, I push the car into first gear. My hand trembles on the gear stick. "Bye, Vincent."

"Good night, Miss Hart."

Chapter 4

Vincent

As if I hadn't behaved creepily enough with the whole *your ex-boyfriend is a moron* line, I stand on the pavement and watch as she drives away, waiting until her battered VW Golf turns the corner, onto the main road, and disappears into the throng of traffic.

I cast my eyes to the star-speckled sky in disbelief. First jacket sniffing and now turning up at her place of work.

Although, technically, I was only returning her coat. When she didn't show up at Scotland Yard this afternoon, I suggested it might be a nonaggressive way of checking on her. I have a sneaking suspicion, however, that even if Burke and Davies hadn't agreed to the idea, I would still be standing here, hanging around like some lovesick dog whose owner just ditched him on the street. In short: pathetic.

I tighten the knot in my tie. Maybe cutting off my circulation will also sever the uncomfortable stirrings of arousal going on in my trouser department. Last night, after a cold shower failed to dampen my ardor, I decided it had been too long since I had sex, that lusting after Mila Hart was merely a primal reaction to seeing her sexy body so beautifully displayed in that tight black dress.

So I did what any red-blooded man in that situation would have done: I went through my phone, found the least emotionally needy woman who'd be willing to sleep with me at short notice, and called her. An hour later, I was at her place, pummeling into her as if my life depended on it. Except I didn't feel better—not during sex and certainly not afterward. I felt *empty*. For the first time in years, a pit of loneliness seemed to yawn open, dragging me and my resolve down into it. I couldn't get away fast enough.

When I got back to my apartment, I did something even more desperate. I went to bed with Miss Hart's jacket on the pillow beside me, lulled into a blissful daze by the floral scent of her perfume.

I officially need therapy. Or maybe locking up. Whichever comes first.

Taking my car key from my pocket, I cross the dark street to the Porsche and slip inside its shadowy interior.

Over the years, a woman occasionally would get under my skin. There was a Prussian countess back in the mid-nineteenth century, and then Magda, an Italian prostitute, during one of the world wars. Sex solved the problem back then, but I'm not sure that would work with Mila Hart. Seeing her today, all disheveled in jeans and sneakers without a scrap of makeup on her pretty face, should *not* have sent me into a tailspin. I should not be sitting here in my car practically salivating as I remember the way several strands of blond hair worked loose from her messy updo, moving against the slender column of her neck as she spoke. Nor should I be picturing what it might feel like to brush those strands to one side, rake fingers through her hair, and trail hot, feverish kisses from her jaw to the curve of her breast.

I ball my hands into fists on the steering wheel. This is even worse than last night. At least then there was still hope these carnal cravings could be laid to rest by a cold shower. Now I know the only thing that will fix this is *her*.

But it's hopeless. Even if she were here beside me right now, buck naked and begging me to make love to her, I couldn't. She's our witness. I can't screw the witness, can I?

I'm deep in thought, trying to recall if my contract says anything about having sex with witnesses, when my phone vibrates in my pocket. Taking it out, I almost believe it'll be Mila Hart, as if I've somehow conjured her up by thinking of her so intensely. The name flashing on the screen, however, reads *Catherine Adair*.

"Cat," I say smoothly into the phone, not sounding at all like a man who has spent the last few seconds deliberating if he could bed a crime victim.

"Vincent. Sorry I'm only just getting back to you."

"It's not a problem. Did you get a chance to go through your database yet?"

"I did. As far as I can tell, there is only one profile for Jeremiah Lopez. I've emailed you the IP address and credit card information, though I'm guessing that'll turn out to be a false trail like the other two." Cat sighs into the phone. "I'm considering suspending the V-Date site until you've caught this guy. I feel as though I'm putting lives at risk. Plus, once the press gets hold of it, my good name will be in tatters."

She is right, of course. This is exactly the type of case that would trigger a media feeding frenzy.

"I take it you don't recognize him?" I ask hopefully.

"No, which means he's new to London and, therefore, most likely new to the British Isles too."

Unlike me, Cat is a born and bred Londoner. She has traveled, of course, but she's always lived in the city. If he were from around here, she would know about it.

"You know what I'm going to say, don't you?" she asks.

I grimace. "Ronin McDermott?"

"Yes. If anyone can tell you who this guy is, it's Ronin." There's an odd mixture of admiration and disdain in her tone.

"Things aren't exactly civil between the two of us at the moment."

Not only is Ronin McDermott the city's vampire overlord, he is also an *ancient*—one of an elite group of vampires who are considered the oldest on earth. Ancients are different from the rest of us; more demon than vampire, they are both faster and stronger, and the only ones who can turn humans. All vampires spawn from this one elite group, so it stands to reason that one of them must know the killer.

"If Ronin wanted you dead, Vincent, you would be dead by now," Cat says. "Besides, I get the impression he's going soft in his old age."

I let out a hearty chuckle. Ronin McDermott may be old in years, but he's far from *soft*. He wouldn't be so feared if that were the case. "I'll take your word for it," I say. "But I can't see how he would be interested in helping me. Unless—"

"Oh no," Cat cuts in. "Forget it. I'm not going anywhere near that man."

I frown, wondering what the deal is with her and Ronin. He isn't her ancient, so there can't be any bad blood between them. "You could email him," I suggest.

She is resolute. "Absolutely not. Sorry. It's one thing to allow the police access to my database. It's quite another to expect me to liaise with a megalomaniac."

"No, it's fine. I'm sorry I asked. I'm going to have to face Ronin one of these days, I suppose." I pause, watching a group of students traipse by, laden with books and chattering noisily. "Why do you think he used his real likeness for the photograph?"

"I've been thinking about that since you called last night. He's either really stupid or he's playing some kind of game. If your department is trying to arrest vampires for historic crimes, maybe he's someone who's committed past atrocities."

"True," I say. "But I'm not sure how he would know what the police are up to. It's not exactly common knowledge."

Cat sighs again. "Lives as long as ours are complex webs of secrets and lies. You can't take anything at face value."

"I agree," I say. "Thanks for your help with this. I'll look over those emails when I get home."

"You're welcome, Vincent. Bye."

"Bye."

After hanging up, I toss the phone onto the passenger seat and push the ignition key, the Porsche jumping to life. I am about to pull out of the parking space when my phone begins buzzing again, an unknown mobile number flashing up on the screen.

"Hello?"

For a few seconds there is silence on the other end of the line. I hear the sound of shallow breathing. Then a familiar, sweet voice erupts with "Vincent? It's Mila Hart. I'm calling because someone's been in my apartment."

If my heart still beat, it would have stopped. "Mila, where are you?"

Her voice is fragile, like broken glass. "Outside. On the street. I didn't know what else to do. I—"

"Go to a neighbor," I cut in, "or to a bar or public place. I'll be there in a few minutes. Don't wait on the street alone."

"Okay. Do you remember my address?"

How could I forget? "Yes. Don't worry. I'll find you."

"Okay," she says again. "Please hurry."

"I will."

Heart in my mouth, I leap out of the car and onto a nearby roof and, for the second time in as many days, take off into the night after Mila Hart.

Mila

Perhaps for the first time all day, I wasn't thinking about the killer when I pushed open the door to my tiny flat in Finsbury Park. I was thinking of Vincent Ferrer and the way his voice sounded when he delivered that line about Scott being a moron—all deep and throaty and come hither.

Engrossed in the memory of his beautiful eyes gazing deeply into mine, I didn't notice the mess in the living room at first. Then it hit me—I hadn't left the coffee table upturned like that when I left this morning to visit Laura, and neither had I swept a row of photos off the shelf above the hearth, leaving glass sprinkled around the room like a deadly layer of confetti. I froze, my heart pounding in my chest. The window on the opposite side of the room hung wide open, my IKEA voile curtains billowing like sails as an icy gust of air blew into the flat.

Thinking the intruder might still be inside, I started to panic. All day I'd been waltzing around in some bizarre posttraumatic denial, but in that second, it hit home that a certain someone probably wants me dead, particularly now that I'm the sole witness. I stepped back into the hall on wobbling legs and half stumbled, half ran down the stairs to the street. Maybe I should have called the police directly or rang Laura to send Tom around, but standing there on the cold pavement, a fine misty drizzle starting to fall, I had the ultimate Lois Lane moment: I called the hot guy.

Sue me.

So here I am, hunched in a corner of the Chinese restaurant across the street, drawing suspicious looks from its owners. When I arrived, I told the waiter I wouldn't be ordering because I'm waiting for the police to show up, but their English is limited. When I tried to explain about the break-in, they only seemed to understand the word *police*.

Luckily, just a few minutes later, the door flies open, and Inspector Hottie lands in the restaurant. Even though it's only been half an hour since I left him back on Holloway Road, the sight of him—tall, blond, and now disheveled to boot—is enough to take my breath away. Judging by the number of female eyes swiveling to the doorway, it appears I'm not alone in my admiration.

"Miss Hart," he says with visible relief, cutting across the restaurant floor. "Thank God you're okay."

I stand up, my face flushing more scarlet than the red papier-mâché dragon hanging from the ceiling. "I'm okay. I'm sorry I called you. The window was open and I thought someone might be in there."

"Is it still open? Your front door?"

I nod. "Yes. I freaked and left without shutting it."

Out of nowhere, he reaches across and gently brushes my elbow. "Stay here. I'm going to check it out."

I try to ignore the warm, tingly feeling of his fingers burning through my flimsy gray sweatshirt and slump back into the seat as he retreats out the door.

A waiter puts a glass of water in front of me. "He is police?"

"Yes," I say, pointing out the window toward my building. "Break-in."

The man nods and leaves me.

When Inspector Ferrer returns, he looks fraught. Tension is set in his broad shoulders, and a pulse twitches in his angular jaw. I stand up so fast I bump the table with my knees, water slopping onto the garish orange cloth.

"What is it?" I demand. "What did you find?"

"Nothing. At least, whoever broke in has left. I've called the station for you. Forensics will come to take fingerprints."

"Oh."

He stares at me, lips pulled into a tight line, brows low over stormy, blue eyes. "Miss Hart, I think it would be in your best interests if you packed up some belongings and came with me." His voice isn't as smooth as it usually is. It sounds croaky, as if he doesn't want to say the words.

I frown as his gaze flickers to the window. "Really? Why?" But of course, I know why. I'm in danger. To think I believed it would fade away if I ignored it. Since when have I ever been that lucky?

Vincent tears his gaze from the window, and we share a tense, knowing look. For a few strained seconds, neither of us speaks.

"He's going to come after me, isn't he?" I ask.

When Vincent gives a curt nod, my knees go weak. Shivering violently, I sink down onto the chair. Even the thought of Inspector Hot Man catching me in his muscly arms again isn't enough to quell the fear trickling through my veins.

Inspector Ferrer slips into the seat opposite. "We don't know anything for sure, but I think it's wise to err on the side of caution." He pauses. "When I say come with me, I mean stay at my apartment tonight. Just until I've spoken with my superiors."

I glance up into his beautiful blue eyes. They are rounded with worry, though whether it's because of my break-in or because he's suggesting we spend the night under the same roof isn't clear. Attempting to lighten the mood, I smirk. "Are you in the habit of inviting victims back to your apartment?"

His eyes widen. "No. No, that isn't—" He breaks off, chuckling. "No. This is the first time, and the last too.

Hopefully. I would suggest you stay with a friend or family member but…" He trails off midsentence.

"But what?"

"I'm trying to think of a way to say it that doesn't sound arrogant." He narrows his eyes, worrying at his bottom lip.

Oh Lord, to be that lip.

Finally, he holds up his hands in surrender. "There is no way, actually. The fact is, no one can protect you like I can."

I sit back in the seat. "Wow," I tease. "Is this the part where I'm supposed to swoon?"

His cheeks turn decidedly pink. It's a good look on him. Though let's face it, *everything* is.

"I did try putting it differently."

"How about *he's a vampire and I'm a vampire so our strength is equal?*"

He leans back on the chair, flinging an arm across the seat beside him. Our conversation has gone from *CSI* to *Dinner Date* in seconds. "That does sound better, doesn't it?"

"Yes, Inspector Big Head, it does."

His twinkling gaze meets mine, a smile that could— and probably does—break hearts lighting up his face like sun through rain clouds. "I'll remember that one in the future."

We're silent for a few seconds, eyes locked. The restaurant's sounds—the hum of chatter, the rattle and clink of cutlery—fade into the background. I look away, forcing myself back to reality. So he has a nice smile. So what? I'm sure beneath his white-knight-in-shining-armor act, he's a dog the same as the rest of them.

"Shall we?" He flicks his eyes toward the door. In some alternate reality, we're on a date and he's suggesting we skip dessert to go home and bang each other's brains out. In that faraway land, *he* is the vampire I hooked up with online, not the psychopath from last night. But as usual, I'm stuck in the realm where I unwittingly date married guys and murderers.

"Okay. But first, I have to go back for my things." I push back the chair, and it scrapes noisily on the wooden floor, like nails down a chalkboard. The flirty vibe dies.

As we make our way across the busy street to my flat, I begin to feel nauseous at the memory of my belongings strewn around. The rain is heavier now, spattering onto my face and hair, and suddenly I'm so bone-tired I want nothing more than to crawl inside a dark hole and sleep.

"I'm not sure going back to the apartment is a good idea," Vincent says, scanning the street. "Are you sure there's no way you can manage with what you have?"

I shake my head. There is no way I'm willing to stay a night in this man's apartment without my toothbrush, killer or no killer. "I'm quite sure," I say.

When we reach the entrance, Vincent takes off his suit jacket and drapes it around my shoulders. An enticing aroma of musky man hits my nostrils, soothing my nerves.

"I can't keep taking your jackets," I say, looking up at him. The wet weather has done marvelous things for his appearance. His dirty-blond hair is damp, sticking to his forehead as if he's just stepped out of the shower, droplets of rain clinging to his eyelashes.

"Vampires don't really feel the cold much," he says.

Then he looks toward the narrow flight of stairs that leads up to my flat. "Are you ready?"

With him by my side, I'm ready for anything. "Yes."

"I'll go up first, if that's okay. Just in case."

He leads the way along the narrow passage and begins climbing the steps. "What's the shop below?" he asks, glancing over his shoulder to make sure I'm following.

"A hair salon," I say, trying unsuccessfully to drag my eyes away from the sight of his steely butt and long legs moving in front of me at eye level. "I came back to London in such a rush, it was all I could find that wasn't infested with rats or miles away from the tube. Where do you live?"

"Farringdon."

Of course he does. Farringdon is prime living for rich city dwellers like him, and trust me, he's rich. No one throws Prada suit jackets around like they're picnic blankets if they aren't loaded.

"Do you have a flat?"

"Yes. But to be honest, I barely seem to spend any time there. I have a house in France too."

At this point, it hits me—he has a girlfriend. There is no way on God's Earth a man who looks like him, owns property, and holds down a steady job cannot have a girlfriend. I decide to tear off the Band-Aid. Get the disappointment over with while I'm already at my lowest ebb. "I hope your girlfriend won't mind me staying at your place—or your wife, I mean."

He pauses for a brief moment, and I almost stumble into him. "Oh, she won't mind," he says slowly. Even though I can't see him, I get the impression he's smiling.

There it is. My heart crashes into my scuffed Converses. I can picture her already: her name is Lucinda and she's a dancer with legs up to her eyeballs. She probably even looks good in gym gear.

Bitch.

"She won't mind," he continues, "because she doesn't exist."

"Well, it'll only be for one night anyway, so—what?"

We reach the top of the stairs and he waits for me to catch up—both physically and mentally. "I live alone. I don't have a girlfriend."

"You mean not one that lives with you?"

"No, I mean not at all—no girlfriend, no wife, either in London or Brazil."

When he says the bit about Brazil, I go weak at the knees. It's the sort of comment that seems loaded with hidden meaning, and yet, when I repeat it tomorrow on the phone to Laura, it won't seem of any importance. Life will be a lot easier when there's an app that picks up on potential flirting and records conversations for later dissection. I mean, they send people into space and they can't manage a simple voice recorder—*puh-lease*.

All I say is "Oh."

Though I feel his gaze on me, I eyeball the door instead, trying to hide the fact this is the best news I've heard since, well, *ever*. Then a sudden panic grips me. *What if he's gay?* Please, Lord—no.

Luckily, he mistakes my inner conflict over his sexuality for anxiety about going inside. He ducks to make eye contact, his blue eyes soft and calming. "If it's too much, you could call a friend to come and get your things."

"No, it's okay. You're coming in, aren't you?"

"Of course I am. I'll be right here."

"Okay, E.T. Let's do this."

"E.T.?" he asks in an uncertain tone.

"The movie? E.T. says to Elliott, 'I'll be right here,' at the end."

"Never seen it."

I lay a flat palm on the door, feigning horror. "You've got to be kidding me."

With him close on my heels, I push open the apartment door and flick on the light. I must have expected everything to have magically tidied itself in my absence, because I recoil in horror at seeing my stuff flung about everywhere.

"Sweet mother of fuck," I whisper.

Considering I don't have many belongings, what with abandoning most of my clothes to avoid hefty excess baggage charges on the way back from Australia, the person who broke in did an admirable job of screwing around with everything I do own. Aside from the smashed photos and the upended coffee table, the TV is lying facedown on the carpet and my books are scattered about like leaves after a hurricane. I ditch my handbag on the carpet and weave through the mess to my bedroom. It's in a similar state, only instead of books strewn around the room, it's clothing.

Vincent knocks gingerly on the open bedroom door, feet firmly the other side of the threshold. He seems to fill the whole frame with his broad-shouldered body. It's a sight to behold, let me tell you. "Are you okay?"

I swallow a sob, sniffing loudly. "Yeah. It's just weird, knowing someone's been here, touching my stuff."

He nods, running a hand through his rain-damp hair. "You should probably pick up your personal items first—passport, ID cards."

I glance up at him, realizing he's still not coming in. "Why are you out there?"

A pink glow climbs his cheeks. "It's your bedroom, Miss Hart. It wouldn't be right for me to enter."

"Exactly what year did you say you were born in?"

"I didn't. But it was the eighteenth century."

I grin. "Ah. You're worried about my reputation."

He laughs throatily, the sound rumbling like a distant clap of thunder. "Old habits die hard."

I eye his perfect frame—the ridges of muscle visible through his white shirt, slim hips, long, lean legs. "Evidently," I mutter.

Vincent takes a tiny step into the room, staring around him. "When I came up, it didn't look as if they'd taken much, but you should probably check your valuables."

I pick up his gray jacket, hung on the back of my chair, and toss it to him. "There, now we're both wearing one."

He catches it one-handed, fixing me with a smoldering blue gaze. "They look better on you."

I spin around, unable to maintain eye contact, a blush creeping up my neck as I yank open the little drawer in my bedside cabinet to take out my passport and other documents. My hands tremble as I hold them aloft. "Still here." How on earth am I going to cope with a whole night under the same roof as him? I'll have to tie myself to the bed to keep from slipping into his room and licking his face. "I'll just pack some clothes and things." I still can't meet his eye.

"I'll wait in the lounge," he says, and I breathe a huge sigh of relief as he steps out of the room.

As I'm hauling my suitcase from under the bed, I get a whiff of something unpleasant, a tart odor, like spoiled meat. I sniff again and impulsively wrench back the duvet cover, sending clothes sailing through the air like ghosts. I scream as loudly as I wanted to last night in the dark alley, when Jeremiah Lopez was bending over me and my vocal cords were frozen. Because there, lying beneath my covers, a sticky splatter of congealed blood clinging to its mottled-brown fur, is a large dead rat.

I'm so horror-struck by the rodent I barely notice the note beside it, torn from the pad on the refrigerator, the cupcake motif obscured by a dark, spiky scrawl. It's only when Vincent bursts into the room that I absorb what's written:

Sorry I missed you today.

Chapter 5

Mila

VINCENT DOESN'T STOP APOLOGIZING THE WHOLE way over to his apartment in Farringdon.

"I should have smelled it," he repeats for the hundredth time. "I don't understand why I didn't."

I glance across the car at him. The streetlights illuminate his features, accentuating the exquisitely carved lines of his profile. There is a tiny bump on the bridge of his nose I haven't noticed before, an imperfection that only heightens his masculine looks.

"I only smelled it because I was under the bed pulling out my suitcase," I explain again. After noticing the rat and reading the note, there had been an awkward moment when Vincent stepped forward to put his arms around me. He froze, hands midair, as if realizing what it was he was about to do. The alarming thing is, I was going to let him.

When we stop at a traffic light, he turns to me. "I'm a vampire. I should have realized it was there."

"Even if you had, there wasn't a lot you could do. Besides, I'm sorry to say it's not the first rat I've had in my bed."

Vincent lets out a hearty chuckle. "Are you always like this?"

"Like what?"

He drums slender fingers on the steering wheel. "Prone to making light of serious situations."

Of course, I'd been absolutely terrified—and still am—after seeing that dead creature rotting away on my fifty-quid Egyptian cotton sheets. Even without the note, I would have known it was left there by Lopez.

I shiver, a cold dread settling around my shoulders like a fog. "I think maybe it's a defense mechanism."

He nods, tearing his eyes from me as the traffic lurches forward again. "It's incredibly lucky you stayed out all day."

We lapse into silence, each of us contemplating what would have happened if I *had* been home when he showed up. I begin to wonder what happens from here. Will they shut me up in some witness protection program? Change my name to Mandy and ship me off to Scotland? Laura is right—this could only happen to me.

I sigh, sinking low into the buttery leather of the seat. "This car really doesn't suit you," I say suddenly, staring out the window at the shuttered shop fronts.

He glances across at me. "How so?"

"You're too young. In looks anyway," I add, as his brows shoot up with amusement. "Usually men who drive cars like this are middle-aged and bald, and they've ditched their wives for some younger woman. Trust me, every time I see a fancy car and check out the driver, that's what they look like. *Every time*."

His eyes twinkle. "So I'm an anomaly, is that what you're saying?"

"A total anomaly."

Somewhere between the dead rat and the Porsche, I'd

lost my shyness around him. Now it's full steam ahead on the babble front. He doesn't look like he minds too much though.

"What car *should* I drive, Miss Hart?" he asks.

"An Audi," I say, not missing a beat. "A black or dark blue one. And there should be a space for your suits to hang in the back."

He laughs. "I'm a cop, not a traveling salesman. What about you?"

"What about me?"

"Have you got the right car for your image?"

I look down at my frayed gray top and jeans. I still haven't had a chance to change since this morning. "Considering how I'm dressed now, I'd say it suits me to a T. Not that I dress like this all the time," I'm keen to point out. "I was too traumatized to coordinate clothing this morning."

"That's understandable," he says, pulling off the main road onto a deserted side street. We roll to a stop beside a metal barrier. "This is where I live."

I glance up at the building. It's one of the newer ones, all sharp angles and gunmetal-gray panels with glass balconies jutting out of huge oblong windows. In the glow of the city lights, the whole building glistens like iron. An iron home for an iron man—well, an iron vampire.

Though I've never hankered after one of these serviced places myself, I know enough to appreciate that living in one costs a small fortune. I'd put money on it that inside there is a range of luxurious facilities—gym, spa, pool. It's an unusual choice for a Met Police inspector who claims not to be home much.

Vincent maneuvers the Porsche down a spiral ramp into a low-lit parking garage and pulls into a space. The other cars down here are just as impressive—Maseratis, Ferraris, and Lamborghinis line the concrete walls.

"Oh, how the other half lives," I mutter as he shuts off the engine before slipping from the vehicle in a gray blur of movement.

Before I know it, he's beside me, opening the passenger door and offering me an outstretched palm as if we're courtiers arriving at a ball. Not needing to be asked twice, I give him my hand. His warm, rough fingers briefly curl around mine as he helps me to my feet. I stand on the concrete, slightly dazed, while he lifts my suitcase from the tiny trunk and pulls up the handle.

"The elevators are that way," he says, motioning across to a pair of red double doors. It takes a few seconds to catch on that he's waiting for me to walk ahead. I'm not sure I'll ever get used to this good-manners thing. Scott's idea of gentlemanly behavior had been occasionally closing the door while he was on the toilet. But then, that's to be expected from a total douche.

Vincent follows me through the door to the elevators. "Which floor?" I ask, jabbing the call button.

"Top," he says.

I shake my head, smiling.

"What?"

"Like in *Pretty Woman*—it's the best."

He narrows his eyes in confusion, murmuring "Pretty woman" under his breath.

"The movie," I explain. "Julia Roberts is a call girl and Richard Gere is this rich but lonely man she falls in love with, and he stays in a penthouse suite even though he hates heights, because *it's the best*."

"Never seen it," he says, shaking his head.

"You really need to stay in more."

He chuckles. "I don't own a TV."

I widen my eyes dramatically. "Oh my God. No wonder it took you people so long to be accepted into society."

The elevator pings its arrival, clashing with his burst of laughter as the steel doors slide open. He steps aside again, politely waiting for me to step in ahead of him. As the doors close and the elevator begins to climb, my stomach rumbles loudly. All I've eaten today is a sandwich at Laura's.

Vincent obviously hears the growl because he says, "You're hungry. I'll order you something when we get upstairs."

"They even have room service in these buildings?"

A corner of his mouth lifts. "No, but there is a set of takeout menus in my kitchen drawer."

"What about you? Do you eat?"

"Sometimes, though we don't need food or drink to survive. I guess you could say I'm a social eater."

"How about blood? Do you have a fridge lined with bags of the stuff?"

He looks horrified. "Christ no. That's pure fantasy."

I snort with laughter. "*You* were pure fantasy until a few years back."

His blue eyes soften as he smiles. "A fantasy to you, maybe."

The atmosphere turns awkward again. Something about the word *fantasy* brings blood flooding into my cheeks. I stare up at the digital counter, waiting for my face to return to its normal color and trying not to imagine how it might feel if he were to suddenly fling me against the elevator walls and shove his tongue in my mouth. I'm pretty sure it would be epic.

When we reach his apartment, he digs a key card from his pocket and holds it up to a small white square on the door. There is a soft click as the lock opens and he steps aside, waiting for me to enter. When I step into the spacious lounge, I'm rendered speechless by the beauty of his flat—floor-to-ceiling glass spans the entire front of the room, offering a breathtaking view of the city.

"Wow," I say, cutting swiftly across the polished oak floor to get a better look.

Despite the fact it's dark and the skyline is obscured by low-hanging clouds, the River Thames winds through the shadowy buildings like a ribbon of molten steel. Light from surrounding buildings flickers on its surface like fireflies. In the distance, I can just about make out the ghostly white dome of Saint Paul's, and beside it, like a silver dagger pointed at the stars, the glassy spike of the Shard jutting high into the sky. Though I lived in London before I went to Australia, and I've been back for a few months, it's a rare treat to see the city in this way. I'm so mesmerized I don't hear Vincent until he's standing beside me.

"It's a good view, isn't it?" he says, hands shoved deep into his suit pockets.

I nod. "It really is the best."

"The view is what swung it for me," he admits, gazing out at the glimmering city below.

I turn away from the window to take in the rest of the apartment. The decor is minimalist—fawn-colored walls, black leather sofas, dark, wooden floors. The style is open plan with a shiny chrome kitchen and seating area tucked neatly into one corner. He wasn't exaggerating about not being at home much. The whole place is perfectly unlived in, like a swanky hotel room before check-in. There are no personal effects lying around, no half-eaten boxes of cereal on the countertops.

"I have a cleaning lady," he says.

"No shit."

"Shall I show you to your room?"

I'd rather he showed me to his room, but beggars can't be choosers. "Yes, okay."

I follow him to a door on the opposite side of the apartment, which leads into a wide hallway. He turns the brushed-steel handle of a door to our right and leads me into another space decorated in neutral tones. Again, it looks like it belongs in a hotel. There is a neatly made double bed with cream covers and a desk with a green reading lamp on it.

He gestures to a beech wood door in the corner. "The bathroom is through there. Hilda, my cleaning lady, always leaves towels, but let me know if there aren't any."

I suddenly realize my suitcase is already parked beside the bed. He must have sped in with it while I was busy fawning over the view.

"Thank you," I say with sincerity. Standing there looking at the bed, I'm hit by an overwhelming urge to climb between the sheets right away. I'm drained in every sense.

"It's my pleasure," he murmurs. "Now, what shall I get you to eat?"

I lay a hand on my empty stomach, glancing up into his warm blue eyes. "If it's all right with you, I think I'll go straight to bed. I'm exhausted."

"Of course. I'll order breakfast in the morning instead." He takes a step back, hand lingering on the door handle. "I should go make some calls anyway, see that the forensics are on the case at your flat. If you need anything, just shout."

"I will, and thanks again for tonight."

He makes a little bow. "You're welcome, Miss Hart." He turns to leave.

"Wait," I say. "You can call me Mila. If it isn't against your policemanly oath or anything like that."

His eyes crinkle at the edges as he smiles. "I'm pretty sure it isn't." He pauses before finishing with a quiet "Mila."

Ridiculously, my stomach flips, the way he rolls my name around his mouth shooting a warm flutter of desire to the pit of my tummy. When he steps out of the room and closes the door after him, I collapse in a heap on the bed, wondering how this evening turned out to be even more bizarre than the last. I pull my phone from my jeans pocket and consider texting Laura to tell her what happened, but if I do that, she'll end up calling me. How can I possibly explain where I am without referring to Vincent as "the hot guy"? With his superhearing, he'd be sure to overhear.

Ditching my phone on the bedside cabinet, I jump off the bed and yank open the bathroom door instead. Like the rest of the place, it's smart and modern, tiled from floor to ceiling in slate gray, with a shower cubicle you could probably fit a rugby team in. As promised, there is a generous stack of fluffy, white towels on a chrome shelf in the corner near the toilet. I pluck a medium-sized one from the pile and set about seeing how the shower works. I'm fiddling around with the dials when I hear the rumble of a voice through the wall. I turn the trickle of water off and listen. The bathroom, I realize, must back onto his bedroom, or at the least the room he's in. An office, maybe.

I should really carry on with my shower and ignore it, but truth be told, I'm nosy, and even more so when the conversation undoubtedly involves me. So rather than undress, I twist the shower dial to off. I grab a glass from beside the sink before pressing it against the tiles and holding my ear to it. The voice becomes clearer.

"It's definitely him," I hear Vincent saying. "He left a note. Though how he's found her is anyone's guess."

My heart begins to thud in my rib cage, but I don't pull away. Hearing the panic in Vincent's voice kills the delusion I've been harboring that this nightmare could be over by breakfast. I squash my ear against the glass.

"The traditional witness program won't work in this case, Linton. She needs around-the-clock protection from a vampire."

There's a long pause before he says, "No. Absolutely not. That's not my job. My role is to catch this guy, not babysit the witness. I don't mind helping out tonight— God knows I'd hate for anything to happen to her—but we'll need something in place by tomorrow and it can't be me."

My breath catches in my throat, a crushing weight of disappointment bearing down on me. I pull away from the wall and sink down onto the white toilet seat, gripping the edge with sweaty fingers. I'm such an idiot. Who do I think I am? Whitney Houston in *The Bodyguard*? He's a professional doing his job. What planet am I on to entertain the notion he's acting from anything other than a sense of moral duty?

The rumbling continues through the wall, but I don't bother to listen anymore. I turn the shower on instead and step inside. When the water is pummeling me like hot needles and I'm confident that not even a vampire will be able to hear, I sit down in the gigantic cubicle and cry until my face all but explodes under the pressure.

I cry for going on a date with a serial killer and nearly getting killed. I cry over Scott and his ex–lingerie model, until eventually I'm crying about never being able to pick a decent guy, for being so screwed up I constantly go for the ones with emotional attachment issues. It's a total pity fest. By the time I stop, I've even cried for the dead rat in my bed. I mean, what did he ever do?

Crying is usually cathartic, but when I step out of the shower and see my swollen, blotchy face in the mirror above the sink, I don't feel any better. In fact, I feel worse, because there's no way I'm going to look remotely normal at breakfast in the morning. Not that it matters, because after tomorrow, I'll almost certainly never lay eyes on Vincent Ferrer again.

Chapter 6

Vincent

THE FIRST THING I HEAR WHEN I HANG UP ON BURKE is Mila sobbing in the shower. I drop the phone onto the bed and ball my hands into fists, fighting the urge to check on her with every ounce of willpower I possess. This is exactly why I can't do as Linton Burke suggests and act as her protector. I'm already too involved.

Earlier, when she found that dead rat between the sheets, I came dangerously close to letting my guard down. I almost hugged her, for Christ's sake. I've been a lot of things over the centuries—nobleman, soldier, lover—but never a hugger. When it comes to Mila Hart, though, I yearn to fold her into my arms. If I agree to Burke's plan, become her bodyguard until the killer is caught, there is no way I'll remain objective.

In some way or another, one of us will get hurt.

Besides, she's only been here a few minutes and already the thought of there being only a thin wall between us is melting my brain. I keep fantasizing about her naked body in my bed, her soft, creamy thighs snug against mine as I plunge into her sweet warmth.

"Fuck," I mutter as my length becomes unbearably stiff inside my trousers.

In an effort to rid my nostrils of her sweet, soapy scent, I take off the suit jacket she returned to me and toss it onto a chair already strewn with clothes. My bedroom is messier than the rest of the apartment, mainly because I tell Hilda not to bother cleaning in here. Over the decades, I've deliberately kept my homes as minimalist and impersonal as possible, so when the time comes, I can move on without sentiment. But like any vampire who's been around for hundreds of years, there are certain things I like to hang on to. A large family portrait, painted before the French Revolution, when we were still considered one of the finest families in France, hangs above the antique medicine chest in the corner of my room—a relic from a long-dead world.

Often, I wonder if vampirism isn't some unnatural form of reincarnation. That, instead of casting off our old bodies for new ones, we keep them. Living again as different people in the same outer shell.

The phone rings again and I sigh, knowing it will be Lee Davies calling to inquire about my mental health after refusing the job of the century.

Sure enough, it's him. I almost decline the call but realize at the last second that if anything will ease the aching throb in my underwear, it will be talking to him.

"*Vincey*," his shrill voice echoes. "*Burkey* boy just told me you said no to taking care of our witness."

Here we go. "Yes. Go on, get it over with. Tell me how mental I am and how I make Barry in narcotics look like Bruce Willis in that *Die Hard* movie you're always going on about."

Lee snickers. "Oh, come on. I mean, she's pretty easy on the eyes, isn't she?"

"That's not the issue," I say wearily, wishing I'd never taken the call in the first place.

"Just saying, having her around 24–7 wouldn't exactly be a hardship. She might even wander about in a pair of those silky pajama things women like to wear."

"Lee, how on earth did you rise through the ranks of the Metropolitan Police? She's a witness."

"Chill out, Mother Teresa. I'm only messing. I'm not suggesting you actually go there—merely pointing out how cushy it would be to have her around for a few weeks. Beats stale coffee and late nights poring through internet records with two doddering old gits like us."

A thought occurs to me. "Are you still at work now?"

"Course I am. I came straight in when we got the call about the break-in. I'm waiting on a DNA and finger-print match from the windows to the ones left on Miss Hart last night."

I decide to take the wind out of his sails, cruel though it is. "I take it you still haven't spoken to Sian about this UPS guy?"

There is silence before a weary sigh breezes down the line. "I haven't had the chance. She was at her spin class this evening—don't even ask me what that is—but she wore her new leopard-print yoga pants. The ones *he* delivered yesterday."

I loosen my tie, sinking onto the edge of the mattress. "What other evidence do you have of her infidelity? Other than taking more interest in her appearance?"

"Well." I hear crunching down the line, like he's eating a packet of nuts. "She's gone off sex for starters, and then there's the issue of her phone—it's never out of her sight these days. Superglued to her hand, it is. Trust me, I know the signs."

He would because he very nearly had an affair himself a few years back. "Are you just going to wait it out? Not say anything?"

"All's fair in love and war, Vincey. Although it's killing me, I'm no angel. If I want to stay married, I'll just have to sit tight until it fizzles out or maxes out our bank accounts—one or the other."

"Lee," I say, "do you think this might be a sign your marriage isn't meant to be?"

"Nah. We were made for each other. This is just a blip on the road to old age. Now, are you sure you're not going to take Miss Hart on? Burke's talking about outsourcing her, paying some other vampire to keep her safe."

I almost drop the phone. "What? No way. How can he even consider that? *Who?*"

"For a vampire *and* police officer, you are surprisingly out of the loop when it comes to current affairs. All the big stars and royal families are hiring vampires as bodyguards these days. Think about it—sharp reflexes, heightened senses, speed. There are companies who specialize."

The idea of some strange vampire protecting Mila Hart for money pierces my heart like a knife. "What if I ask Catherine Adair?" I say, the idea only just popping into my head. "We trust her and she's female, so Mila might feel more at ease."

"I don't see a problem with that," Lee says, still crunching.

"I'll call her now, let you concentrate on finishing whatever it is you're eating."

"Pork rinds," he says, the words muffled by further chewing noises.

"I won't even ask."

I hang up and hit Catherine's number. There is no way I can let Mila be outsourced. No way.

Catherine answers on the third ring. "Vincent, what can I do for you? You're not going to ask me to talk to Ronin McDermott again, are you?"

I let out a nervous laugh. "No, but I do have a favor to ask." With that, I launch into the events of this evening, about how Mila is in danger and Burke is considering outsourcing her.

"And you can't help because you fancy her, right?" Catherine asks bluntly.

I leap off the bed, checking the door is closed before hissing, "What?"

Catherine laughs. "Oh, come on. Why else wouldn't you do it? I've gotten to know you quite well over the years—you're practically the last surviving knight of the Round Table. The only reason you wouldn't offer to protect a lady is if her honor is going to be compromised in some way—in this instance, by you."

I'm silent. What's the point in denying it? "Will you do it or not?" I say finally.

"No," she says.

My shoulders sag with disappointment. "I understand. It was a big ask."

"It isn't that I don't want to help—God knows it might even be fun to have a roomie for a while. It's just

I can't get involved in all this right now. I have my business to think of. I hope you understand. I'm done with all that dark vampire crap. I don't mind passing on some information here and there, but harboring your witness is taking it a step too far."

Strange, I thought I was done with it all too. "I do understand, Cat. I'm sorry I put you in this position."

"What are you so afraid of anyway? That you'll fall in love with her and she'll die?"

I suck in a short, sharp breath as if punched in the gut. Funny how it often takes another person to show you the truth you've been running from for the past three hundred years.

When I don't answer, Cat says, "Oh shit, Vincent. I'm sorry."

"Don't apologize. None of this is your concern, nor should it be. I'll let you get back to your evening."

"My evenings involve feeding the cat and watching Netflix. Trust me, you're not interrupting anything."

I smile. "Thanks anyway."

"Wait—I know it's none of my business, but if you do like her, even a smidge, don't push her away. Love is messy, but it's always worth it."

Not if someone dies, it isn't.

"I'll bear that mind. Speak soon." I hang up before she has a chance to go all Freudian on me. Not only am I decidedly *not* a hugger, but I'm also not a fan of heart-to-hearts.

Dropping the phone on top of my jacket, I open up my hearing to the next room. The shower has stopped running, and there is a soft rustle of sheets, a creak of bedsprings. Before my overzealous libido begins feeding me more smutty images, I do something I haven't needed to in a long time. I jerk open a drawer in the ancient walnut dresser beneath the window and remove the miniature portrait I keep hidden beneath a pile of yellowed, old papers.

Although the once-velvet frame is now threadbare, the picture itself is as vibrant as if it were painted yesterday. But the reason I need to see it is not to conjure up the memory of the sitter's inky midnight hair or the delicate buttermilk hue of her skin. Time has crumbled that infatuation like waves against a cliff. No, I take it out because I need to remind myself why love is dangerous for my kind, why passion has no place in my life, why it does and always will end in disaster. I stare at the portrait long and hard, remembering the birdlike weight of her body as she took her last breath in my arms; her amber eyes, ordinarily as bright as dawn, dark with betrayal and loathing. With that image secure in my mind, I slide the portrait back into its hiding place and slam the drawer shut.

Because no matter what anyone says about love being worth it, I know firsthand that when it costs a person her life, it isn't.

Not by a long shot.

~~~

In the middle of the night, I'm jolted from my half doze by the sound of a woman screaming. *Mila*.

I bolt out of bed and burst into the guest room, ready to pounce on whoever has managed to find a way into my apartment. Only there isn't anyone in the room but her, thrashing around beneath the cream duvet and screaming like a banshee. For a split second, I stupidly wonder if she's seen a spider, but in the light from the hall, I notice her eyes are closed and the words spilling from her lips are the nonsensical mumblings of someone trapped in a nightmare. I leap onto the other side of the bed and grip her gently by the shoulders, trying not to admire how soft her skin feels beneath my rough fingertips.

"Mila," I say, shaking her. "Mila, you're dreaming. You're safe. It's just a dream."

She shudders as her eyelids flip open, her eyes sweeping rapidly from side to side before finally resting on my face. It occurs to me I've never been this close to her before now.

I'm mesmerized, like I'm seeing a painting I've always admired from afar up close for the first time. There is the tiniest smattering of freckles across the bridge of her nose, a small dimple of a scar in the hollow of her cheek, a hint of laughter lines around her hazel eyes. I gulp heavily. "You were screaming," I whisper, my fingers still squeezing into the satiny flesh of her shoulders. Though she is no longer yelling, I can't seem to bring myself to let go.

"Was I?" she asks, frozen in my grip. "I was dreaming about an alleyway and rats."

I nod, not daring to take my eyes from her face. One of her hands rests limply across my thigh, and if I were to look down at it—at *her*—for one second, I fear I'd lose my mind, slam my body and mouth into hers, and exhaust all the passion that's been building to a crescendo for the past day. But while I can avoid looking, her touch is impossible to ignore, like a red-hot poker burning my skin.

"It was just a dream," I say, my gaze still locked on her face.

She blinks, dark lashes sweeping her pale cheeks. Now that she's fully conscious, her eyes wander over my body, widening like saucers when they reach my bare chest. I suddenly remember I'm wearing only a thin pair of boxers. My eyes flicker to my naked torso and then inevitably land on her body.

Unlike Davies's prediction about her night attire, there are no silky pajamas. She wears a cream-colored tank top and pink-and-white candy-striped shorts. With her shapely legs twisted beneath her and messy blond hair all over the place, she's just about the sexiest thing I've ever seen. My eyes fall on her breasts, swelling against the tight Lycra of the top. I fantasize about cupping them, rubbing my thumbs across the beaded nipples until they stand rigid beneath my fingertips, begging to be sucked.

I release her as if stung, fighting the rush of my blood to my stiffening length and forcing my gaze to meet hers. I pull back on the bed, feeling the weight of her hand drop from my thigh as I strategically position myself to hide the bulge in my briefs.

"I'm sorry I woke you," she says.

"It's nothing," I assure her. "Like I said before, vampires don't really sleep in the traditional sense."

I rise from the bed, hoping the half-light disguises my erection. It's either move or wait for it to go down, but if

I remain sitting beside her a moment longer, drowning in her delicious scent of spring flowers and soap, I'll probably stay hard forever.

She watches as I step back into the shadows at the bottom of the bed. "Wait. Would it be totally pathetic if I asked you to stay until I fall asleep?"

I'm silent for a few seconds. Cat Adair is right; I'm the last damn knight of Camelot. "No, of course I can."

I sink into a tub chair in the corner.

"Don't stare at me or anything though," she says. "I'm not one of those attractive sleeper types. There's drool and snorting—or so I've been told."

Envy, pure and true, rises within me. I'm suddenly jealous of every man, and even close relation, who has ever seen her drool and snort. "I won't stare," I promise, trying not to smile. "I'll just sit here and count sheep."

She twists around to plump the pillow. "Good. There might well be some snoring too. When that starts, feel free to leave."

"Why, thank you, Miss Hart. I'll be sure to take that as a cue for dismissal."

She flashes a wry smile before turning to face the opposite way. "Night, Vincent."

My heart gives out a little. I love the easy sound of my name in her mouth. "Good night, Miss Hart."

"Mila, remember?"

Like I need reminding. "Mila."

After a few sniffles, the lump under the duvet goes still and I sit for a while, trying to think unsexy thoughts. Unsurprisingly, they mostly revolve around Lee Davies. I'll have to buy him lunch to say thank you.

Using my razor-sharp vampire hearing, I detect the exact moment her heart rate slows, her breathing steady and regular. I ease out of the chair, smiling to myself as a snorting noise erupts from her nose. She was right about the piggy noises.

I'm about halfway to the door when she flips over. "Vincent."

I freeze like a cat burglar on a drainpipe. "Yes?" I whisper.

Silence. I take a few steps toward her.

"Vincent," she says again, my name low in her throat.

"Yes? Are you okay?"

No answer. I lean over, trying to see if her eyes are open, though it's hard to tell because several strands of hair cover her face like a cobweb. I'm reaching across to brush it aside when she lifts a hand and drags her nails down the length of my arm, from my shoulder to wrist, leaving a trail of tingly sparks in their wake. This close, I can smell another lingering scent beneath the soapy freshness—arousal. She writhes under the covers. I'm fairly sure she's asleep. I should leave, but the sight of her blond hair splayed across the pillowcase like sunbeams, the aroma of feminine sweetness, draws me in like a siren's song.

I sweep silky strands from her eyes, and as I do, she reaches up again, her fingertips stroking my arm.

"Vincent." Her voice is little more than a moan.

I'm so close I can practically taste her—mint and summer rain. I groan deep in my throat. It's a good thing she's not conscious, because right now my resolve is shattered. I want nothing more than to press my lips to hers, caress her hot tongue with mine, and devour her like a starving beast.

Then just as quickly as it began, she stops writhing, her arm falling limply back onto the bed.

The dull thud of her hand hitting the duvet is enough to bring me back to my senses. I spring backward, landing like a cat on the other side of the room and making hastily for the door.

To my utter shame, my fangs are protruding over the edges of my lips, my cock straining against my underwear.

I take one last glance at her before leaving the room, vulnerable and small in the bed, knowing without a doubt that I'll be the one who guards her until the killer is caught, that I will do everything in my power to protect her—not just from him, but from the selfish desires of my own heart.

Chapter 7

Mila

FOR A SECOND WHEN I WAKE UP THE NEXT MORNING, I forget it's Saturday. I sit bolt upright in bed, staring around at the sun-streaked room in confusion as the events from last night come tumbling back.

Apartment break-in, Vincent, the phone call through the wall, my nightmare…

Oh God, my nightmare. My eyes flick to the squishy plum-colored tub chair beneath the bright square of the window. I asked him to stay until I fell asleep. Could I get any needier? Especially after overhearing him complain about having to babysit me. Christ, why didn't I have him sing lullabies and be done with it? I cringe as mortifying images of my sleeping face flash behind my eyelids. No wonder he wants me out of his expensively gelled hair.

Thoughts of his hair set me thinking about the rest of his body, namely all the parts on display last night when my shrieking dragged him out of his man cave in nothing but a pair of boxers. The image of his ripped chest glistening like polished steel in the half-light of the hallway, a thin trail of downy hair disappearing into the promising bulge of his underwear, is branded onto my brain with the permanency of a cattle rancher's iron. I couldn't forget if I tried.

I stumble out of bed and flip open my suitcase, rummaging around for something suitable to wear for breakfast. Pulling on a pair of black leggings and a shirt, I experience my first twinge of homesickness. Usually on Saturdays, I stay in pj's all morning, watching crap on TV and eating bowl after bowl of muesli, while telling myself that any minute I'll get my act together and leave for the gym. What will Saturdays be like now that I'm Mr. Psycho's number one target?

Without bothering to brush my hair, I take a deep breath and make my way to the lounge. Vincent is up and fully dressed—not a sinewy muscle in sight—and sitting at the kitchen island with a laptop open in front of him. He is as crisp and bright as the sunshine filtering through the windows.

"Morning," I say, fiddling with the cuff of my red flannel shirt.

His eyes flick up briefly to meet mine. In the early morning light, they glitter like sun on a tropical sea. "Good morning, Miss Hart."

"It's a beautiful day," I say, motioning to the window. In daylight, the view is even more spectacular, London's sprawling landscape spread out like a concrete forest as far as the eye can see.

Vincent ignores the sentiment and continues to stare at the screen. "There are breakfast things in the fridge and cupboard," he says, pointing over his shoulder. "Please help yourself."

Clearly I've pissed him off with the nightmare thing. As I step past him into the kitchen area, he barely makes eye contact. Maybe the way I gawped at his pecs last night made him feel violated. Though to be fair, how could I not gawp? I'm a moth to the UV light of his heavenly body.

I pull open one of the steely cupboard doors. The shelves are almost bare, but at the bottom there is a selection of breakfast food—jam, marmalade, a couple of loaves of bread, and two boxes of the exact brand and flavor of muesli I have at home.

"You have my favorite," I say, grabbing the cardboard box.

He flicks a glance over his shoulder. When he speaks, his voice is distinctly less tight. "I noticed a box of it on your kitchen counter last night when you were packing. There are bowls in the cupboard by your knees."

"I guess they don't call you detective for nothing," I mutter. In the cupboard, I find a shiny, white bowl that looks as if it's never seen the scratch of a spoon and set it on the counter. I turn around, wondering whether to make another stab at awkward conversation or let it go. The *tap-tap* of his typing fills the air.

"Listen," I begin, "I'm really sorry about last night."

Awkward conversation it is, then.

His broad shoulders tense beneath his shirt, planes of muscle straining through the material. His fingers freeze, hovering above the keyboard.

"I'm aware I've intruded in your personal space and treated you like you're my..." I struggle to find the right word. I want to say boyfriend or lover, but I don't want to make my obvious attraction any more obvious. "My... bed toy isn't conducive to a healthy, working policeman-victim relationship." *Bed toy*. Seriously. I need to sew my mouth shut. "By 'bed toy,' I mean like a teddy bear or blanket, not a sex toy like a vibrator. Because, I mean, I don't own a vibrator. I never have. I'd be too embarrassed to even order one online. In case there's a bomb scare at the sorting office and they have to open it, and then when they realize it isn't a bomb, the postman delivers it with all the packaging torn and from then on you can't look the guy in the eye and it just becomes a nightmare, especially at Christmas when you want to order presents. So no, I've never owned one." I stop and a long silence ensues. "Was I just talking about vibrators?"

He flips the lid of his laptop shut, the hollow snap cutting through the tension in the room. When he spins around on the stool, he is smiling, his beautiful eyes creased at the edges with mirth. "Yes, Miss Hart, you were talking about vibrators, and there's no need for an apology. If anyone should apologize, it's me."

"You?" I ask, baffled. "Why? You're not the one discussing sex toys over breakfast. You can probably understand now how I ended up prattling about rats on my date."

He ignores the question, staring at the breakfast things on the counter. "I think we need to discuss where we go from here. Professionally," he adds quickly.

"About the killer and all that jazz?"

His luscious lips form a thin line. "Yes. I've asked Superintendent Burke and Sergeant Davies to drop by this morning so we can discuss the situation, but in the meantime, I'm sure they won't mind my disclosing that the fingerprints we took from your neck and face two nights ago match those taken from the window in your apartment."

"No surprise there," I mutter grimly.

He offers a weak smile. Now that he's closer, I notice faint half-moons of shadow around his eyes. If he were human, I would guess he had a sleepless night.

"I know the situation might seem desperate, Miss Hart," he continues, "but we've never been closer to catching this guy. His picture will go out on the news tonight. It's only a matter of time before he's caught."

"But in the meantime, I'm screwed."

A hint of pink climbs his neck, warming his pale cheeks. "In the *meantime*, you will remain under police protection. That's what my colleagues will discuss with you when they arrive."

I nod. "I'll just get on with breakfast, then."

He slips down from the stool, and a breath catches in my throat as he stands, looming over me, a chiseled Greek god in a suit. A waft of expensive aftershave with a hint of freshly laundered clothes radiates from his body. This man is my nemesis. Every woman has one—a man who strips you of rational thought and action, and leaves you with nothing but base sexual desires. Just standing here, one hand on an unopened box of muesli, I can already sense myself tilting toward him, a flower reaching for sunlight.

Feeling brave, I glance up into his handsome face. He opens his mouth to speak but then closes it again, his Adam's apple bobbing against the smooth column of his neck. "I'll leave you in peace to eat your breakfast," he says.

I turn back to the muesli. "Okay."

When I look up, he's already left the room.

〜〜〜

Before the Columbos arrive, I jump in the shower and wash my hair. Though I'm not particularly bothered by what they think of me, I don't want to give off the impression I'm flaky or that I'm not taking the case seriously. Of course, it doesn't do any harm to look your best when staying with the hottest vampire in London either. No harm at all. I blow-dry my hair straight, adding a couple of waves with the straightening iron, before tugging on a knee-length, collarless, cream-colored shirtdress. I give myself the once-over in the long mirror on the back of the door before leaving the room—apart from the dark circles around my eyes, I've looked worse.

Out in the living room, I'm surprised to find the two police officers already sitting on the leather sofas by the window. Davies, the short one, is cradling a mug of coffee in his hands, while Burke, who is tall and gaunt with a schoolmaster's air of authority, is poring over a laptop. Vincent stands as I saunter in, his gaze dropping from my face to my legs and back again. For a split second, I swear a flash of fear sparks deep within his eyes. Which is ridiculous, because why on earth would he be afraid of me?

"Ah, Miss Hart," Superintendent Burke says in a flat voice, without looking up from the computer. "Do take a seat."

Vincent, if anyone, should be the one inviting me to sit, but he seems busy waging some inner battle, his gaze fixed on the glass coffee table, brows low over his eyes.

I sink onto the edge of a sofa. My throat feels dry and I don't know what to do with my hands. It's like being dropped headfirst into a job interview.

"We're sorry you couldn't make it over to Scotland Yard yesterday, Miss Hart," Davies says, taking another gulp from his mug.

My eyes flick to Vincent, who shakes his head, intimating he hasn't told either of them about my reasons for not going. I decide it's best to say nothing, so I just nod and smile, crossing and uncrossing my legs.

Then Burke snaps his computer shut and fixes me with a level gaze. "Vincent has told you about the fingerprints from your apartment matching those taken from your person two nights ago, I take it?"

"Yes. I gather it's not safe for me to go home until Jeremiah Lopez is caught."

All three nod soberly.

"Did you give Lopez your address, Miss Hart?" Burke asks. "Either before or after your meeting?"

I picture our date, my nerves and the copious amounts of wine I consumed. I definitely spoke about living in Finsbury Park because that's how I ended up on the whole super-rat topic. I was describing a house I'd been shown around the corner that turned out to have a rat infestation and got carried away on the subject. But did I go as far as to give him my actual address?

"I'm pretty sure I didn't give the details. I know I said Finsbury Park. It's possible I might have mentioned living on the high street. But I wouldn't have said a number or anything like that."

"Miss Hart," Davies says, "the flat is above a hair salon. Is it likely you mentioned that?"

I rack my brain as they wait for my answer. It's hard to remember with them all watching. My stomach feels queasy all of a sudden, the large breakfast I wolfed down churning about like clothes in a washer.

Vincent slides into the seat beside me. "Why is it important how he found her? We're supposed to be discussing where to go from here, not dredging up that night all over again."

I glance up at him, but he doesn't return my gaze. His jaw is tight as he surveys his colleagues.

Burke nods. "Very well. Miss Hart, as Inspector Ferrer has already explained, we are insisting you remain under police protection. Ordinarily, this would involve little more than a squad car outside your home or wherever you choose to stay, but dealing with vampires is trickier." He takes a breath, rubbing the bridge of his nose with his forefinger and thumb. "In short, to offer you adequate protection, we are assigning a vampire to look after you."

"Who?" I ask, staring between them.

Vincent clears his throat. "Me."

Davies's eyes flick up at Vincent, wide with surprise. "But—"

"It's easier all around if you stay here with me, Miss Hart." Although Vincent is addressing me, his eyes remain fixed on Davies's face.

My cheeks burn as a mixture of emotions stampede through me all at once—relief, confusion, fear. "But won't I annoy you?"

He shifts his gaze from Davies to me. His eyes are soft, his voice throaty. "No. Why would you think that?"

We remain, eyes locked, until Burke coughs loudly. "Well, that's sorted, then. Miss Hart will stay here for the time being."

"Wait a minute," I say, breaking away from Vincent's limpid eyes. "What about work? My family? I have a cousin's engagement party in a few weeks' time."

"You must carry on as you normally would. Daytimes are less risky. Sunlight has a negative impact on a vampire's speed and other reflexes. Vincent can escort you to work each morning and be there to pick you up afterward." He throws a glance to the pastel-blue sky outside the windows. "Lucky for us the evenings are light this time of year."

"What about seeing friends? Can I tell them what's going on?"

"Close friends and family are fine. But try not to announce it over the staff intranet," Davies says, smirking.

I cut him a scowl. "Of course not."

Burke leans forward, the leather sofa squeaking. "I don't want to dramatize things any more than necessary, but the fewer people you tell, the safer you will be. Whom you confide in is ultimately a matter of your own judgment, but I would tread carefully if I were you. People are horrendous gossips."

"Folks love nothing more than other folks' problems," Davies continues. "Makes them feel better about their own lives."

"Don't worry. I'll probably only tell Mum and my best friend."

I hadn't really thought about Mum until now. How will she react when she discovers her only daughter is the target of a serial killer? Maybe it would be kinder to lie and say there is a gas leak at my apartment and I can't go home. I could say I'm staying with Laura until it's fixed. Besides, if she finds out I've been dating vampires, she'll think I've lost the plot. It was bad enough telling her about Scott being married. Mum is from a generation that doesn't do personal drama. If there's even a hint of it, it's brusquely swept under the carpet and never spoken of again. At least, that's how she dealt with Dad leaving when we were kids.

A thick silence settles over us as I contemplate how I'll cope sharing a flat with London's answer to Chris Hemsworth. All that looking and not touching surely can't be good for a woman in an already fragile state. What if I turn into a randy sex pest and have to be forcibly removed and Vincent ends up in the witness protection program himself?

"Next week," Vincent says, breaking into my thoughts, "I have some important business to attend to in Soho."

Sergeant Lee Davies winces. Even Burke looks mildly disturbed, rubbing his chin and frowning. It's obvious they know exactly what *business* Vincent will be attending to.

"Is that wise?" Davies says.

Vincent toys with a shirt cuff. "I believe the person in question is our best shot if we want a quick answer to Jeremiah Lopez's real identity."

"I see your point," Superintendent Burke says darkly. "But it's still a bit of a risk. Wasn't there some sort of threat against you on his part?"

My eyes flit between their faces. Now they have my attention. Why would Vincent be threatened?

"There was," Vincent affirms casually. "But that was

several years back. Besides, I doubt he'd risk harming a police officer. It wouldn't exactly go unnoticed. My point is, someone will need to watch Miss Hart while I'm gone. I can hardly take her with me."

"Why not?" I ask. "From the sound of it, you may need someone to call for an ambulance if this mysterious meeting goes wrong."

Vincent quirks a brow. "Where I'm going is no place for someone like you."

"Someone like me?" I repeat incredulously. "I know I'm no Buffy the vampire slayer, but I'm hardly Olive Oyl."

He frowns.

"Oh for God's sake, it's a cartoon."

"Right." He smiles down at me, turning my insides to mush. "More TV shows. But anyway, I didn't mean weak. I meant wholesome—a wholesome woman like you."

"Wholesome? Like a loaf of bread?"

"That's whole wheat. 'Wholesome' means—"

"All right, bloody hell," Davies cuts in. "Miss Hart can be dropped at Scotland Yard during the visit. She'll be as safe as houses with us." He shakes his head, muttering something unintelligible under his breath. "Are we all done here? I've got a round of golf to get to."

Burke fixes him with a disapproving stare. "We all have places we need to be, Davies. Eve and I are supposed to be at a wedding in Ipswich by two."

Vincent snatches a look at his Rolex. "In that case, you should probably get going."

They stand up. Although they ooze professionalism with their starchy suits and formal speech, there's an easy familiarity between the three of them. It's clear they like each other immensely.

Before they leave, Lee Davies says in clipped tones, "Vincent, I'd like a word outside before I go."

"It's okay. You can stay here." I jab a thumb in the direction of the bedrooms. "I'm going to go and unpack and call my mum."

We exchange farewells, and full of relief, I make my escape. While Vincent is out of earshot, I take advantage by calling Laura.

"Jell-O," she says, panting.

"Jell-O." My eyes widen. "Please tell me I haven't interrupted you and Tom doing the nasty?"

She laughs. "It's fine; I'm out jogging."

What is it with jogging these days? It's an epidemic. Folk aren't happy unless they're training for a charity run.

"Phew. And for future reference, never answer the phone if any of that other business is happening."

I take a deep breath before telling her about the break-in and having to stay here with Vincent. She is deathly silent. I hear ragged breathing down the line.

"Laura, are you crying?"

It takes a good ten minutes to talk her out of booking me on a flight back to Australia and a further fifteen to convince her not to show up in Farringdon. After I hang up, I decide I'll call Mum tomorrow. I've had my fill of emotional meltdowns for one day.

Tossing the phone onto the duvet, I pad out into the living room, immediately doing a double take when I find Vincent crouching by the coffee table, surrounded by cardboard and bits of polystyrene, fiddling around with wires at the back of a large flat screen TV.

When he glances up to find me watching in bewilderment, he smiles shyly. His tie is off, abandoned over the back of the sofa, and his shirtsleeves are rolled past his elbows, revealing inches of smooth, golden skin.

Clutching a cord in one hand, he says, "I figured it was about time I reconciled myself with popular culture. Plus, I don't want you to get bored." We both stare awkwardly at the lump of plastic for a few moments. "It said online it has Freeview," he continues. "I wasn't sure if that's a good thing or not, so I subscribed with an online provider too."

Just when I think a man can't get any sexier, he buys me Netflix.

I edge closer, heart racing, cheeks burning hotter than Mount Etna in a heat wave. For the life of me, I can't remember anyone doing anything so nice.

But rather than drop to my knees with gratitude, I blurt out, "Will we get *Game of Thrones*?"

He frowns, snatching a leaflet from the coffee table and flipping through it, muttering "*Game of Thrones*" under his breath. "It doesn't list it here. Is that a show?"

I don't process the question. I'm too busy gazing at him like he's Superman and the Messiah all rolled into one. In that moment, I decide that if he's gay, I'm joining a convent, because then I'll know for sure the world is conspiring against womankind.

"How did it get here?" I ask.

His cheeks glow pink. "I ordered it this morning. Turns out if you pay extra, they deliver it the same day."

"The world is good like that." Blushing fiercely, I meet his soft blue eyes. "Thank you."

He nods, gazing down at the television. "It's nothing. Like I said, it's high time I ventured into the modern world. Davies is always quoting some movie called *Die Hard*."

I nearly groan. "We'll start with *E.T.* I don't think *Die Hard* will be your bag, and by that, I mean it's not *my* bag."

He chuckles. "Ah, no romance, is that it?"

"No," I say, grinning. "Just because I'm a girl doesn't mean I crave romance. There's no romance in *E.T.* Merely the love between a boy and his alien."

"Aliens," Vincent says, shaking his head. "What will they think up next?"

"Says the vampire," I point out.

His smile widens, more dazzling than any sunset. "Touché, Miss Hart."

"Didn't we agree you were going to call me Mila?"

He rakes slender fingers through his blond hair, a frown replacing his smile. "We did. But maybe, considering the new circumstances, we should keep things formal."

"So, we'll sit and watch *E.T.* together, and then afterward, you'll turn to me and say"—I adopt a deep, husky voice—"'Would you like to watch *Die Hard* next, Miss Hart?'"

He narrows his eyes playfully. "I don't speak like that."

"Yes, you do."

He smiles, shaking his head. "Fine, Mila it is."

"Meee-lah," I imitate in a baritone voice.

The dent that appeared between his brows when he

mentioned keeping things formal disappears completely. "I don't speak like that," he repeats.

I smirk, flicking through the shiny instruction booklet. "Hey, if you have a drill, we could hang it on the wall."

"I do have a drill."

My eyes flit to the front of his trousers. Yeah, I bet he does.

"Which position do you think would provide optimum viewing?" He picks the TV up as if it weighs no more than the leaflet I'm holding and balances it against the wall with one hand.

I gulp, wishing it were me he had pressed up against the wall instead of a forty-inch plasma. "That's no good," I say, eyes glued to his pecs. "We'll get the glare from the sun through the windows. I think on the table with its back to the window."

He drags the table backward and plonks the TV on top of it. "There?"

I chew at my lip. "More to the left."

He scoots it over several inches. "How's that, your ladyship?"

"Perfect."

Later, after we've set up the TV and are sitting watching the opening credits to *E.T.*, I ponder why being here with him feels so natural. He sits with his legs apart, elbows resting on the cushions at his back, blond hair— minus the gel—flopping over his forehead. Peering at him from the corner of my eye, I realize this is a man who could rip out my heart and feed it to the wolves, and even though my life is in danger, it's this thought alone that sends an arrow of cold fear shooting through my heart.

Chapter 8

Vincent

STANDING OUTSIDE THE BLACK DOOR ON BROADWICK Street, Soho, it's impossible not to remember my last visit to Ronin McDermott's notorious vampire nightclub. Back then, I didn't particularly care what happened to me. I was exhausted from all the "dark vampire crap," as Cat describes it, worn ragged by a struggle to reconcile the demands of London's vampire overlord with those of my job. In many respects, I was ready to die. Perhaps that's why Ronin didn't kill me. Maybe he saw it was a far greater punishment to keep me living in misery than enjoying the sweet release of death. Tonight, all of that feels like a million years ago.

I'm afraid.

I sigh, inhaling a lungful of stale city air. It's a little after nine o'clock and daylight is leaking out of the sky. An inky blue darkness presses down between the buildings, casting long shadows onto dirty pavement. People bustle past—workers and tourists. A girl wearing gym clothes smiles. I smile back, but only because she reminds me a tiny bit of Mila and how she's wearing her hair today—golden strands that started the day coiled and pinned on top of her head but have since worked loose, messy tendrils falling around her neckline. Over the past few days, I've noticed tidy hair is an impossible task for Mila. Somehow it always ends up in her face. I wasn't aware I found this look so sexy until I met her.

I shiver, not from the draft cutting through gaps in the tall buildings, but because Mila is the reason I'm afraid to meet with Ronin tonight. Who will protect her if I'm gone?

The club's facade has undergone a facelift since I last saw it. The door, which used to be battered and flaky, paint peeling off around the edges, is now buffed and preened to a deep, shiny black. A gold plaque reading *66 Broadwick Street* is screwed into the brick. It appears the club is no longer the big secret it once was. I'm lifting a fist to hammer on the door when I spot a fancy chrome intercom button just below the gold sign.

I hold my thumb to it before shoving my hands into my pockets, my stomach a tight knot of nerves. A dial tone erupts from the speakers and static crackles before a female voice says, "Sixty-six Broadwick."

Leaning a wrist against the jagged brick wall, I stoop to speak into the microphone. "This is Vincent Ferrer. I'm here to see Ronin McDermott."

There is a long pause on the other end. "There's nothing in the diary."

"I don't have an appointment. I'd be grateful if you could let him know I'm here."

The intercom goes dead. I stand up straight and wait. A few minutes pass, enough time to witness a drunk man pee into a trash bin on the other side of the street and hear a taxi driver hurl abuse at a pedestrian for crossing the road in front of his cab. London at its finest.

"It's open," the same crackly female voice says as the door swings forward beneath my palm.

A few years ago, a burly doorman could be found lurking on the other side of the entrance, but tonight the corridor is empty. This part too has had a makeover since I was last here. The walls are now papered in deep gray. Crystal light fixtures are dotted along their length, illuminating my path. The once-stagnant whiff of beer and sweat is replaced by the musky, perfumed scent of lilies. But beneath the fresh paint and shiny furnishings, the faint metallic odor of blood persists. As I near the end of the narrow corridor, it grows stronger. I'm struck by the realization that I haven't been so exposed in years. Like an ex-smoker, I'm comforted and repulsed all at once, my lungs itching both to repel and absorb the sharp iron tang. I'm sorely tempted to ditch the whole venture. But I can't. For Mila's sake.

So far, the photo we sent out to the news channels has brought us zero genuine leads. The press vultures pick over their meat carefully, and for some reason, this story seems to receive only a small amount of coverage. I wonder if there's a vampire high up in the media world who doesn't care for cases that give off the wrong impression of our kind. That, or the killer is protected.

When I reach the end of the corridor, I pause for a few seconds, my fingers splayed against the black inner door. From the other side, I can hear strains of a piano and a low hum of chatter. The club never used to get going until midnight, so it's unlikely I'll be entering a den of vice at this hour, but I need to gather myself before meeting with Ronin. As an ancient, he's as sharp as an arrow, and although mind reading is a myth, he can read body language like humans read lunch menus.

I try to put myself back into my frame of mind of several years ago—depressed, lonely, exhausted. I'm surprised by how difficult a task this proves to be. Mila coming into my life is like a window opening onto a dark, abandoned room—sunshine and fresh air filtering into long-forgotten corners, illuminating everything.

I open the door and step through onto a small square of landing at the top of a flight of winding stairs. The decor of the club, once purple, is now the same shade of gray as the hallway, the velvet booths replaced by black leather sofas. The UV strip lighting in the ceiling is gone, traded for plush chandeliers that bathe the room in a soft golden glow. I scan the shadows for any sign of Ronin. A man dressed in evening clothes sits at the piano, playing an instrumental version of "Autumn in New York," while a few people—vampires, as far as I can tell—sit around chatting among themselves. It's a far cry from how it will be in a few hours, when a pulsating techno beat will rattle the furniture and pound the eardrums. When the blood begins to spill.

As soon as I reach the bottom of the stairs, a petite, dark-haired woman with a pixie crop and a tight silver dress steps out from behind a podium with a clipboard.

"Mr. McDermott will be out in a few minutes. If you would like to follow me." There is a hint of contempt in her voice, and I wonder what Ronin said to make her act so snooty. Ronin rules his employees with an iron rod, and for her to behave impolitely means he must have indicated his dislike. Perhaps she caught him sharpening his machete in the office.

Miss Snooty gestures to a round walnut table

surrounded by hard-backed chairs. Evidently I'm not to be offered any comfort during my visit. I thank her before pulling out a seat and sinking into it, wondering how long he'll keep me waiting.

A barman with eyes the shade of liquid gold hovers over me. "What can I get you to drink?"

Obviously he didn't get the *make Vincent Ferrer suffer* memo in time.

"Malt whiskey and soda," I say, hoping alcohol will ease the tight band of fear squeezing my chest. If it doesn't, at least I'll have something to do with my hands.

A few minutes pass. The amber-eyed barman brings me the whiskey and I drum fingers on the polished wood. After throwing a glance at a raucous couple laughing their heads off at some unheard joke in the corner, I turn back to find Ronin McDermott lounging in the chair opposite, as if he was there all along.

His hair is longer, russet strands curling over the tips of his ears, but aside from this, he looks the same as ever—broad shoulders, steely blue eyes, cheekbones like sharpened knives. He wears a well-tailored dark-blue suit with an open neck. Though his accent is mellow, there's a definite whisper of Scots to his dialect. It's thought he was once an ancient Scottish warrior, though of course, no one knows for sure.

"Vincent," he says in acid tones. "You wanted to see me."

I try not to shrink beneath his unflinching stare. "Ronin. How have you been?"

His Celtic features are hard as he skims me with a cold glare. "Why are you here?"

I sigh, reaching into my jacket pocket for the photos of Jeremiah Lopez. "I was hoping you could enlighten me as to who this man is."

As I'm unfolding the page, Ronin's hand shoots out, closing around my wrist in a viselike grip. A sharp stab of fear rips up my arm, chilling me to the bone.

"Correct me if I'm wrong, Vincent, but this sounds a lot like you need a favor," he says through gritted teeth.

Meeting his icy blue gaze, I nod.

He drops my arm and shakes his head, his deep voice rattling in his throat like thunder. "You dare to come to my club after all these years, after you betrayed my trust and honor, and expect me to do you a *favor*?"

Keeping my face impassive, I say, "It's in your best interests, Ronin. This man has killed two women already. Think of the impact it might have on our kind if humans begin to see us all as bloodthirsty monsters."

He leans back in the chair, eyes narrowed. "What do you care for *our kind* these days, Vincent? I'd have thought you'd be too preoccupied playing detective with your new friends."

A spark of anger flares within me. "You asked me to be your spy, Ronin, and I tried to put aside my misgivings because I owed you. But doing so put lives at stake. We were lucky no one was seriously hurt."

"How was I supposed to know Anastasia would get involved? Or that Logan Byrne would go gooey-eyed over a human? Besides, it all worked out. Anastasia is wiped from the face of the earth and Logan got his happy ending. They're married now, you know? With a baby son."

A stab of regret pierces my heart. Although I'm pleased for Logan, a vampire friend who met the love of his life and regained his humanity, the sentiment is tinged with envy. There will be no happy ending for me.

"I know," I say, gazing into my drink.

"Who's the woman?" Ronin asks.

Damn.

"What woman?"

Ronin leans back in his chair, a smug glint in his eye. "There is always a woman, Vincent." He wags a bony finger across the table. "I don't believe for one second you would be sitting here if there wasn't some Lady of Shalott metaphorically tied up somewhere needing your help. The last time I saw you looking this forlorn was the French Revolution. There was a woman involved then too, if I remember rightly."

Without taking my gaze from his face, I unfold the picture and slide it across the lacquered tabletop, trying not to let my emotions get the better of me.

Ronin reaches down, grasping the photo between his index finger and thumb. I take a sip of the whiskey, feigning indifference, though I'm fairly sure if my heart still beat, it would be pounding out of my chest.

"He's been here," Ronin says, tossing the picture back across the table.

My voice catches in my throat. "Who is he?"

"No idea. But he likes to drink, I can tell you that much."

I shudder. Ronin doesn't mean alcohol. Alcohol, though soothing, has no real effect on a vampire's nervous system. By *likes to drink*, Ronin means from the arteries of human beings. Blood.

Although it's true enough vampires do not need blood to survive, some crave its sweet taste as dangerously as if they did. We call it *bloodlust*, and much the same as human alcoholism, it destroys lives. Unfortunately, in this instance, it's not just vampires who suffer from its ill effects.

"When was he here?" I keep the questions short, a ploy we use often in the police. The idea is that there's little time for the interviewee to conjure up any mistruths.

Ronin shrugs. "A couple of months back. I only saw him the once. I assumed he was just passing through." He pauses to stifle a yawn. "Will there be anything else?"

We eye each other suspiciously. I want to ask him to put the photo out among the other ancients in his circle. At least one of them would claim him for their own. But this is Ronin. He could well be playing me. Deciding to cut my losses while the going is good and my head is still attached to my body, I stand up, scraping the chair on the dark, wooden floor.

Tucking the folded square back into my jacket pocket, I say, "Thank you, Ronin."

One brow quirked, he drops me a nod. As I turn to leave, he says, "Wait."

My shoulders sag. It was all going so well. "Yes?"

"I'll circulate that photo, find out who he belongs to, if—"

I brace myself, waiting for some devilish bargain. More spying on my colleagues, perhaps the release of some locked away ex–vampire buddy of his.

"If you put in a good word for me with Catherine Adair."

"Cat Adair?" I ask in disbelief.

He nods. For the first time since he sat down, his blue eyes shine a little less coldly. "Get her to come here if you can."

"I can't do that."

Ronin rolls his eyes. "Oh relax, I want to do the opposite of kill her, if you get my meaning."

I frown. "She despises you."

For some strange reason, this seems to please him. He smiles, chuckling to himself. "Yeah, she does, doesn't she?" he mutters. "Don't you love it when women get all riled up?"

"Not if it means they hate me."

Ronin chuckles again. "What can I say? I'm centuries old. I like a challenge. Get her to see me and I'll find out who Bloodthirsty Bill is. Do we have a deal?"

I sigh. Suddenly, spying on my colleagues seems entirely more doable. "I wouldn't say we have a deal, but I will certainly pass on your request to Cat."

With a flick of his wrist, Ronin dismisses me. I waste no time in getting out. Within a few seconds, I'm back on the street and clicking open the Porsche, relief rising inside me like an air bubble in a hot spring. It's over and I'm alive. I can pick up Mila from Scotland Yard and take her home. The thought fills me with warmth. Spending these past few days with her has made me more content than I've felt in decades.

The TV had been a whim. I told myself it was to keep her occupied during her stay, but really it was to make her happy. I knew that as soon as I saw her face that morning, when she smiled at me over the empty boxes and polystyrene, and the ice in my heart melted. Ice I hadn't known was there until that moment.

Loneliness is a curious thing. Often, we don't realize it's crept up on us until the void is suddenly filled. It's like in winter, when we forget to miss the sun's warm rays. Then when summer returns, we wonder how we ever coped without it. Mila is that sunshine. A bright, pure-white summer's day. But those days never last, and the cold always returns.

But not tonight. Tonight I will pick her up and take her home with me, sit beside her on the sofa—an ever cautious twelve inches apart—and pretend that I'm not secretly learning by heart the soft lines of her profile, or the way she twirls a strand of honey-colored hair around her index finger when she's bored. With her intoxicating scent—wildflowers, fruity shampoo, and fresh air—I'm an addict in my own home.

Nighttime is just as difficult. Knowing there are only a few thin walls between us, I lay awake remembering that night she said my name in her sleep, the way she touched my arm. I daren't ponder the possibility she might return my ardor. Because that would be terrible— both the best and worst thing that could ever happen.

Davies of all people is the only one with the slightest clue about how I feel. He clocked the way I was staring at her that morning at my apartment and read me the riot act out in the hallway. While it's fine, in his opinion, for me to date multiple women at the same time if I choose, it isn't okay to form a forbidden and clandestine attachment that might result in deep feelings of affection. As Burke would say, it just isn't cricket.

At Scotland Yard, I park underground and head upstairs to our offices to collect Mila. As soon as I step out through the steel doors of the elevator, I hear her animated voice drifting along the corridor. It appears that while I've been gone, she and Davies have bonded over his marriage problems.

"You *have* to talk to her," Mila is saying. "How can you think this will all just go away? Every time she's online shopping you'll always wonder: Is she ordering those guest towels because we need a new set? Or is it solely to ride the UPS man again?"

"Maybe he'll be moved to a different route," Lee pipes up.

"Oh yeah, like that's going to stop the sex bunnies in their tracks."

I push open the door, my eyes darting about until they land on Mila. Is it me, or does she look pleased to see me?

A slow smile unfurls from the corner of her rosebud mouth. She sits up straighter on the swivel chair she's slumped in. "You're alive."

She doesn't get up, but like that night at her flat when I almost hugged her, the urge to greet her with more than just words coils within me like a dangerous snake.

I grin like a buffoon instead, momentarily losing myself in her eyes—the shade of early autumn leaves. "I'm alive."

"Any joy on Psycho Sammy?" Davies asks, stuffing a Dorito into his mouth and crunching it loudly. It's then I notice they're sharing a party-size bag of Doritos, a jar of dip between them on a pile of brown files.

I cross the room and perch on a chair opposite them. "Nothing groundbreaking." I will, of course, share what Ronin said about him *liking a drink* and all the rest, but not in front of Mila.

Davies clocks the raised brow I give him and nods. "Mila here has been giving me marital advice," he says, changing the subject.

I use this as an excuse to allow my gaze to linger on Mila for a little longer than necessary. "So I heard." She looks as pretty as ever, the tiny smudge of sour cream at the edge of her mouth doing nothing to divert my attention from her plump lower lip. If only she knew the secret fantasies I have about that lower lip of hers, it would make her toes curl. I tear my gaze away, turning back to Davies before my brain connects to my groin again. "So, will you take Miss Hart's advice and ask your wife what's going on?"

He sighs, wiping a splodge of dip from his gray trousers. "I'll think about it."

Mila looks at him, head tilted, like he's an injured puppy.

"Did you also tell Miss Hart about how you almost succumbed to temptation yourself a few years back?" I ask, stifling a smile.

Mila's face transforms from sympathetic to disgusted in a millisecond. "Lee! I shared my Doritos with you."

Lee holds up his hands. "That was different, and besides, nothing ever happened. Not in the end."

"Who was she?" Mila asks, frowning.

"Her name was Anita, and we were working on a case together," Davies explains. "One of those really intense ones where the bodies are piling up faster than poker chips at the Casino Royale. We were a little like those two off the TV show—Mulder and Scully. The Mulder and Scully of Essex." He pauses to stare off wistfully into the distance, before continuing. "But like I said, nothing happened. We didn't even kiss. But nevertheless, I came clean to Sian about it. Told her I was attracted to another woman. We had some marriage counseling and I transferred here to Scotland Yard. That was the end of it."

Mila, who almost choked with mirth on her Doritos when Lee mentioned the Mulder and Scully thing, licks her fingers. I try not to drool. I've never wanted to be a woman's fingers so badly.

"This explains everything," she says, eyes narrowed. "Even though you claim nothing ever happened between you and Scully, Sian has been insecure ever since. So much so that when her own temptation came knocking, quite literally, she didn't think twice before taking the plunge."

Several lines appear in Lee's bald head. "Do you think?"

"There's been a power imbalance," Mila continues, leaning forward. "You're out at work all day, meeting God knows how many women, and she's at home wiping down surfaces and potting marigolds. It's no wonder she's trying to readdress the situation."

There's a long silence while Davies processes this new information.

"Did you also tell Mila about your urges to wine and dine the women of London?" I tease.

Lee cuts me a look of daggers. "Hadn't you two better

be on your way before you miss one of your favorite TV shows?" Davies retorts smugly. I told him about buying the television and he wasn't fooled for a second that I did so for any other reason than to please my attractive new guest.

Mila screws the lid onto the dip. "We should make it back in time for *Housewives of the Home Counties* if we leave now."

Davies's grin widens. "Yes, Vinnie, you don't want to miss *Housewives of the Home Counties*."

Throwing him a scathing look, I stand up. "After you," I say to Mila. "Be sure to take the Doritos. Davies is supposed to be on a diet."

Davies flips me the bird. "Yeah, well, we can't all be Brad Pitt, can we?"

"Vincent doesn't look like Brad Pitt," Mila says, shaking her head. "He's more Chris Hemsworth."

Davies rolls his eyes. "Same difference."

"Who?" I ask.

Chapter 9

Mila

"Is Hunk O'Rama picking you up this evening?" my colleague Janice asks.

We're both in our usual morning positions—sitting, bored out of our brains, at the front desk. Matters have escalated to the point where we get excited when the plant guy comes around to water the displays. Having his freshly cut grass scent wafting around reception reminds us of what it's like out in the real world. That, and he usually has gum.

"Yes," I say, avoiding her laser gaze. "He's picking me up. As usual."

As far as my work colleagues are concerned, Vincent and I are in the midst of a whirlwind romance. The only valid excuse I could think of under such short notice and one, I have to say, I'm enjoying a lot more than I should.

I feel Janice's gaze on me. "He's very keen, isn't he?" she points out for the hundredth time.

"And why shouldn't he be?" I challenge. "Do I not deserve love?"

Janice chuckles nervously, patting her sleek, black bob. "Of course, Mila. It's just…"

"What?" I demand.

She begins pecking at an imaginary thread on her

Marks & Spencer trousers. "Well, he's not one of those controlling types, is he?"

I stare at her blankly. Knowing Janice, anything could be going on inside that brain of hers. For a fifty-something woman who crochets bobble hats in her spare time, she has a surprisingly sordid imagination.

"A dom," she says, turning pink. "I've read about them in the *Daily Telegraph*. They're usually rich and go for women of a lower social status."

"Janice," I shriek. "Are you asking me if I'm his *submissive*?"

"Well, the *Daily Telegraph* says—"

"No, Janice," I cut in. "I'm not in a sadomasochistic relationship."

Though if I had to be, I could do worse than Vincent. A lot worse.

"Sorry. I had to ask. Some of the girls in marketing put the idea in my head."

"I wasn't aware my private life was such a hot topic."

If only they knew the truth. Still, I'd take catty glares from marketing over pity any day.

Just then, Paul O'Geary appears out of the lifts—or Leery O'Geary, as we refer to him behind his back.

"Looking radiant as ever, ladies," he says in his smarmy voice, slithering over to the desk like a serpent.

Janice releases a high-pitched giggle, which nearly makes me gag. Though in her defense, it's not like he's entirely hideous to look at. Some might even say good look-ing. Not to me though. I'll never find another man attractive again after living with Vincent. It'd be like existing on cold gruel and dirty water after a diet of oysters and champagne.

"How are things up in sales, Paul?" Janice asks brightly.

Being far less tolerant than my reception buddy, I pretend I've just received a fascinating new email and stare at my computer screen instead.

"Sales is awesome, thanks, Janice," he says.

I feel his gaze drilling into me, but I refuse to look up. Once, while I was making coffee for a client in the little kitchenette off reception, he accidentally-on-purpose pinned me against the counter and tried to feel me up. Then, when I shoved him off, he had the nerve to pass it off as a big misunderstanding. Asshole. I should have reported it, of course, but it was only my third day on the job and I panicked about what might happen. Since then, I've studiously ignored him.

"Are you ladies attending the office spring party this evening?"

I frown into the screen. I vaguely recall hearing something about a staff social at some fancy bar in Leicester Square.

"Not me," Janice says. "Bob's away, so I have to get home to let the dogs out."

Dog owners and parents always have the best excuses. No one ever argues with canine care or kids. No one.

The door swings open again and one of the bosses who hired me, Joel Peters, waltzes into reception.

"Ah, O'Geary, there you are," he says, adjusting shiny gold cuff links. "Ready?"

Leery O'Geary tears his gaze from me at last, and I breathe a sigh of relief.

"We were just discussing the spring party this

evening," he says to Mr. Peters. "Janice can't go because of her dogs. Mila, what was your excuse again?"

I look up to meet Mr. Peters's eyes, going completely blank. "Er—"

Mr. Peters frowns. "It would be great if you could make it, Mila. I don't think I've seen you at one of our social functions before."

Drat. Think of an excuse. Fast.

"I'd love to," I say, smiling, "but I've just, um, got a new kitten and I don't want to leave him alone in the evenings."

This stuff always works for pet owners. Always.

"Nonsense!" Mr. Peters says, deflating me like a balloon on a spike. "My wife breeds kittens from our Burmese, Shona. Just lock him in the kitchen with some water, food, and warm bedding. He'll be quite all right for a few hours." He grins, looking pleased that he's just solved all my problems. "See you there." He drops Janice a nod. "Sorry you can't make it. But dogs come first, eh? Bye, ladies."

I glower at their retreating backs as they exit through the revolving doors.

"A new kitten?" Janice asks. "Is that a euphemism for your boyfriend?"

"No, Janice," I mutter through gritted teeth. "It's not."

Later, over dinner, Vincent asks why I'm so quiet.

We're sitting at his kitchen island eating the carbonara he cooked for us and I'm fretting about the office party and how it will affect my job if I don't show up. Will they even notice?

"Oh," I say, pushing my pasta around the plate. "There are these work drinks tonight that my boss wants me to go to."

"Do you want to go?" he asks.

I glance up to meet his gaze. In the fading sunlight from the windows, his eyes shimmer a glassy blue, tiny flecks of silver at the center flickering like stars. He is a vision—shirtsleeves rolled up to reveal golden planes of muscle, blond hair falling all over the place. For some peculiar reason, his hair never looks quite as immaculate as it did when I met him. Perhaps messy hair is catching.

"No," I say, forking a pasta tube between my lips. "I'd much rather stay in and watch Dr. Quinn."

Of all the slick, high-class drama I've shown Vincent these past few weeks, the only one he's shown interest in is *Dr. Quinn, Medicine Woman.* "Now this," he said, when Sully and Michaela were involved in a face-off between the prejudiced townsfolk and the Cheyenne Indians, "is entertaining."

Men. Go figure.

"If you don't want to go, what's the problem?"

I sigh. "My boss thinks I'm going. I've not been out socially with them yet."

"So we'll go."

I frown. "Won't that be dangerous?"

"Not if I'm with you."

I chuckle, putting on a deep Arnie voice. "Come with me if you want to live."

He wags a tapered finger across the island. "*Terminator*? With the cyborgs, right?"

Slapping a hand to my chest, I feign a look of motherly pride. "He's learning. He's truly learning."

Vincent flings the dish towel from his shoulder through the air in a perfect arc, where it lands on my head. "Yes, Yoda, I'm learning."

I smile, tossing the cloth aside, resisting the urge to hold it over my nose and mouth and inhale his manly scent. The struggle is real.

"We'll go then," he says. "It'll be good for you. Can't be much fun being cooped up in here with me all the time."

How wrong can he be? I think I'd happily live holed up in this apartment with him for the rest of my life if he allowed it.

"My colleague asked me today if you and I are enjoying a sadomasochistic relationship," I blurt out.

He almost spits out his orange juice, a line furrowing his brow. "Jesus. Do you think it's the suits?"

I shake my head. "No, it's Janice's perverted mind. Your suits are perfect." I wrench my eyes away before he notices. "So I guess we're going. There'll be a free bar for your troubles."

He chuckles. "Alcohol doesn't really do a lot for me. But you go ahead. I'll carry you home."

The idea of being hoisted into his strong, capable arms sends fire soaring into my cheeks. "I might hold you to that."

When I look up, he's gazing at me intently, his eyes burning like blue flames. He opens his mouth to say something before closing it again. It happens a lot, I've noticed. As if there's something he wants to say but is never sure how to word it.

He rakes a hand through his tousled blond hair instead, before reaching across for my plate. "Finished?"

I nod, pushing it toward him across the tiled countertop and enjoying a peek into the open neck of his shirt. I still fantasize about the night of the bad dream—catching a glimpse of those satiny smooth muscles rippling his chest. It's getting harder and harder to fall asleep each night knowing there's a god lying in bed next door.

"I'll go get showered," I say, sliding off the stool.

Cold showered.

—⁓—

When I return to the living room an hour later, wearing a simple black skater dress with tiny stars emblazoned across it, I almost suffer heart failure to find Vincent *not* wearing a suit. Apart from *abs night*—which doesn't count, as he wasn't dressed at all save for a pair of briefs, thanks be to God—I've never seen him wear anything but a suit. Truth be told, I was beginning to assume he didn't actually own anything else. Yet here he is, dressed in dark-blue jeans that hug his lean legs like a second skin, and a thin navy sweater that accentuates every line of bulging muscle. The blue in the material picks up the light in his eyes, turning them the color of the sky after sunset.

I blink uncontrollably.

"No suit," I squeak.

He glances down at his clothes, mussed blond locks falling in his eyes. My knees almost give out there and then.

"I'm trying for a less sadomasochistic look," he teases.

"Hey, don't knock sadomasochists. They know a thing or two about tailoring."

He grins, eyes crinkling around the edges. Standing there, outlined by the amber glow from the windows, I struggle to remember ever seeing a man look so beautiful.

"You look lovely," he says, waving a hand at my outfit and frowning deeply.

My cheeks instantly alight. I do the thing I always do when paid a compliment. Babble. "This is old," I say, plucking at the material. "I don't have many clothes because I had to leave so much behind and of course, most of my stuff is still in Finsbury Park. Did you hear anything about my flat, by the way?"

"It's all locked up and secured," he says, eyes still pinned to my dress. "Nothing for you to worry about."

"Good."

I stand, swinging my arms like an eleven-year-old waiting to be asked to dance at a school disco, until he jerks his head toward the front door. "Shall we?"

I reach down to snatch my clutch bag from the sofa, grateful to at last have something to do with my hands. "Let's."

—⁓—

The office party is held at Ruby Green's, an imposing six-story building wedged on a corner of Leicester Square. I've been a couple of times before, so I know it well enough to lead Vincent from the loading-only parking spot around the corner where he parks the Porsche.

"This is your one vice, isn't it?" I ask as he clicks the doors locked.

He grins. "The parking? Fines always seem to miraculously disappear when you're a cop."

I shake my head in mock disapproval. "What about the poor guy with the two hundred crates of bananas who can't make his delivery on time because of some wanker with a Porsche? His words, not mine," I add quickly.

Vincent laughs. "I have a job to do too: escorting Miss Mila Hart safely to a work party. The bananas will have to wait."

"Smooth," I say, as we cross the street into the hustle and bustle of Leicester Square.

The front of Ruby Green's is a lot like a mausoleum, its tombstone-white facade lit up purple and green. Before we walk up the carpet to the entrance, Vincent hangs back. "Don't feel you have to hang out with me when we get upstairs, Mila," he says, hands thrust deep into his pockets. "I'm more than happy to fade into the background."

I open my mouth to tell him not to be silly, that I don't even *like* half the people I work with, but then it occurs to me: he's probably sick of the sight of me and would relish a couple of hours without me glued to his side like a spare tire.

"Uh, okay. If you're sure," I mutter. Then, for some bizarre reason, I lightly punch his arm, as if we're buddies heading out for a night on the prowl. "And feel free to chat up as many women as you like, because when the killer is caught and I move back home, I'm going to have to pretend we broke up. Lay as much groundwork as you can, partner."

A look of confusion flits across his chiseled features,

but before I can even begin to figure it out, it's gone and he gives me a small salute. "Chat up lots of women. Got it."

Inside, I'm pretty sure a part of me just died.

"Let's go have some fun," I say almost too brightly.

The party is taking place on the third level, the piano barroom. I have to hand it to corporate—it's a pretty cool venue. The floor is polished marble, the walls paneled in lacquered dark wood. The man tinkling the keys of a grand piano at one end of the room adds to the 1920s vibe.

A waiter with a tray of champagne ambushes us immediately. "Drink?"

Vincent surprises me by snatching two from the silver platter.

"Well, what kind of future dumped boyfriend would I be if I didn't drink too much?" he says, smirking and handing me a tall flute.

I take a sip. Usually, I drink the cheap stuff—carbonated paint stripper, as Laura calls it—so I'm surprised by the delicate tang of bubbles, smooth on my tongue. I hold it up to the light appraisingly. "This," I say to Vincent, "is good poison."

He grins, whipping another from a passing tray faster than I can blink. I don't think the waiter sees it go either. "Here, have another."

"You might live to regret this, Vincenzo," I say, taking a gulp of bubbles, "when you're carrying me to bed later."

I freeze in horror, glass halfway to my lips. "M-My bed," I stammer. "Alone, with you next door. Obviously."

He ducks his head in agreement. "Obviously."

I never thought I'd be so relieved to be landed on by one of the marketing girls, Layla, the dark-haired one with slanted cat's eyes. The relief is short-lived, however, when she says, in a voice that may only be described as a *purr*, "Mila, aren't you going to introduce me to your friend?"

I ache to say no, but my mouth has other ideas.

"Sure," I say with a hint of smugness. "This is Vincent. My boyfriend. Vincent, this is Layla. She works in marketing."

Layla smiles a sickly sweet grin. "What is it you do, Vincent?" she asks, tucking a tendril of inky black hair behind an ear and batting her eyelashes so rapidly I'm surprised she doesn't get whiplash.

"I work in sales," Vincent says smoothly. "I sell upmarket vehicles to London's rich and famous."

I stare up into his perfectly impassive, handsome face as the lies pour forth. Hard to believe this is the same man who blushes a violent shade of hot pink during Dr. Quinn and Sully's chaste kissing scenes.

"Fascinating," Layla says, head tilted to one side, as if he's announced he sends farm animals into space. "Do you get to take them home?"

"Excuse me. I'm going to go say hi to Mr. Peters," I interject, the words *before I vomit in my Moet* dangerously close to my lips.

They ignore me as I slip across the room. I know Vincent is acting, but it still cuts like a rusty knife.

"Hi, Mr. Peters," I say when I reach my target.

"Mina!" he says jovially. "You made it."

I let out a nervous chuckle. "Mila, actually."

"Right. My apologies. How's the cat?"

My eyes flicker across to where Vincent and Layla are deep in conversation. "Oh, you know…hard to keep tabs on."

"Excellent," he says. I can tell by the glazed look in his eyes that he's not in the least bit interested in my fake feline problems—or me, for that matter.

He then employs the age-old trick of palming me off onto a huddle of people next to us. Why I came tonight when I could be at the apartment eating snacks with a blushing, blond hunk and watching middle of the road nineties drama is already beyond me.

Luckily, ten minutes into my small-talk torture, my lunch buddy Faith materializes at my side.

"Let's hit the bar," she says, brown eyes flashing as she steers me away by the elbow.

"Thank God you're here," I hiss as we cut through the sea of waiters and schmoozers. "All they talk about is work and money. It's so boring."

"What are you doing?" Faith demands when we reach the safety of the bar. "You left your hunk of a new boyfriend alone in the shark pit." She spins me around to face the spot across the room where Vincent is now talking to not just one, but four of the marketing girls.

I shrug. "You know what they say, Faith. If you love someone, set them free. If they come back, it's meant to be."

Faith grips me by my shoulders. She isn't normally this assertive. In fact, she's one of the nicer people I've met since I started working for Wilkin Morris.

"You're crazy." She leans in closer. "When you showed up with him that day, you gave me hope karma is alive and well, that sometimes the nice single girl gets the hot guy. And now you're on the brink of letting those rich, *I don't really need a job but I've got nothing better to do*, Sloane Square upstarts take him away? Why would you do that?"

I'm sorely tempted to tell her the truth. That karma is as cold as ever in its grave. That the only reason I have a guy like Vincent escorting me to work parties is that he's paid to do it. But staring down into her round, wide-eyed face, her brown cheeks flushing violently, I can't find it in my heart to destroy the dream.

"He's into whips," I blurt out.

Faith's expression turns from concerned to horrified in a millisecond. "I'll fetch us some drinks."

As it turns out, lying about being in a sadomasochistic relationship is surprisingly easy. Also, if I'm completely honest, the idea of being tied up by Vincent is far from harrowing. By the end of the conversation, I'm convinced I'd thoroughly enjoy it. Mind you, that probably has a lot to do with all the free cocktails I'm swigging.

"By submitting to his needs," I say, staring wistfully into space, "I'm transported to this strange sexual plane of nirvana."

Faith sighs. "Maybe I should give Tinder another go."

I nod. "Just promise me you'll avoid V-Date."

"Why?"

I slide my empty glass onto the bar behind us. "I need the ladies' room," I say, ignoring the question. "I'll be right back."

The swell of people has grown considerably since we first arrived. As I weave a wobbly path to the bathroom, I crane my neck, trying to distinguish the broad-shouldered frame of Vincent from the other revelers, but he's nowhere to be seen.

A dark clutch of fear seizes my heart. What if he's outside somewhere, in a clinch with a marketing girl? I've drunk way too much alcohol to be able to hide my true feelings. If that happens, I will throw up. Pure and simple.

After visiting the ladies' room, I look for him on the balcony. Outside, the sun has already slipped below the horizon, a glowing moon visible through silvery wisps of cloud. The busy street below has been thrust into shadow, and from up here, the chatter from the street is muted and dull. There is no one about, but I sink into a bistro chair anyway, trying to clear my muzzy head. I really shouldn't have mixed all those drinks.

"I thought I saw you come out here," a voice says behind me.

Even though I know it isn't Vincent's deep, soothing tones, I whip my head around expectantly, only to find Leery O'Geary loitering in the doorway with a half-empty pint of beer.

"If you're looking for the bloke you came with, I think he's still flirting with Layla near the piano," he drawls.

There's a slur to his voice that tells me he's had a lot to drink. That and the way he's swaying like a wheat stalk in a breeze.

I rise to my feet, ignoring both him and the wave of nausea sweeping over me at his words.

"Of course," he continues, a smirk plastered across his smarmy face, "if he does hook up with Layla—which looks likely, by the way—I'd be more than happy to escort you home."

"Paul," I say, "even if he's hooking up with Kim Kardashian in there, I still wouldn't want anything to do with you."

He sways again, a spark of anger igniting within his dark-gray eyes. "What makes you think I'd want to fuck the likes of you anyway?" he sneers, beer slopping onto the deck as he steps closer.

What happens next is a bit of a blur. I move to leave, but he blocks my path, forcing me backward until the backs of my knees hit the chair. One of his hands seems to move in slow motion toward me. It's like that day in the kitchen all over again. Then the hand is gone, and Leery with it, and Vincent is standing in his place, staring down at me with the same gentlemanly concern as that night in the alleyway. He grips me gently by the shoulders. In my tipsy state, I ponder if he's about to kiss me.

Instead he asks, "Did he hurt you?"

I shake my head, wondering how Leery disappeared so fast. I don't have to wonder for long though. I catch a scuffling noise from the other end of the balcony and when I glance over, he's picking himself off the deck and swearing under his breath, beer splattered all over his face.

"Did you throw him?" I ask.

"Of course I did," Vincent says. "I heard what he said to you. Did he touch you?" His fingers squeeze harder into my flesh. A lick of flame ignites at the contact.

I shake my head. "Not this time."

He does a double take. "You mean he has before?" Without waiting for a reply, Vincent releases me. "Mila, go and wait inside, will you?" A pulse in his jaw pounds like a hammer.

"Why?" I ask.

Short of cracking his knuckles, his intense stare tells me everything. Leery O'Geary is about to get his just deserts.

I place a hand on Vincent's arm, feeling the solid bulk of muscle through the sleeve of his thin sweater. "You're not going to kill him, are you?"

Vincent flashes me a terse smile. "Mila, I'm a police officer. Of course not. This won't take long."

Still unsure of his meaning, I step back into the noisy bar. I barely have a chance to sit down before Vincent returns.

He jerks his head toward the exit. "Shall we leave?"

I nod. He doesn't look like he's just punched a man's lights out. He is as cool and calm as a politician on *News Time*.

"After you," he says, waving me ahead.

As soon as we're out on the dark street, I ask, "What did you do to Leery O'Geary, exactly?"

"Nothing overtly physical, I assure you."

"So what did you say?"

"I didn't really say anything."

I stop dead in my tracks. "Just tell me. I still have to work with the weasel."

Vincent shakes his head, jaw clenched. "If he touched you, Mila, you should have reported him."

"It was my third day on the job. I could hardly waltz

into the CEO's office and say, 'Hi, I'm Mila. I started two days ago, and I'd like to sue the company for sexual harassment.' Besides," I continue, "it was awkward. He made it look like an accident, like he'd only been reaching for a coffee mug."

Vincent's hands ball into fists. He mutters an expletive. "Don't fret about work. I doubt he'll come near you again."

"Tell me what happened."

He sighs, staring over my shoulder into the distance. "I showed him my fangs."

I screw my face up. "That worked?"

"Yes, it worked. I can be pretty menacing when I want to be."

"Well, go on, then."

"Go on what?" he asks, frowning.

"Show me your fangs."

"Mila, no." He looks faintly appalled, as if I've asked to peek inside his underwear. "Now, you've had a fair bit to drink. Will you manage walking back to the car?"

"Oh, please. Of course I can. I should be asking you if you're okay, considering the number of pheromones you were drowning in back there."

"Those women?" he asks with a baffled expression as we cut back across the square. "I thought I was supposed to act like a bad boyfriend."

"You were."

I should probably stop speaking soon, but the alcohol and the O'Geary incident has made my tongue looser than the dodgy exhaust on my rusty Golf. "But you didn't have to look as if you were enjoying it quite so much."

He exhales sharply. "You were having quite the time of it too, if your talk of sexual nirvana is anything to go by."

My stomach drops like a stone, my heart freezing in horror. "What?"

He cocks a brow and says nothing.

"Hang on. Were you listening to my conversation?"

A middle-aged man and woman holding hands pass us on the street and throw us knowing smiles, clearly thinking we're a couple bickering after a night out.

I give them a look of daggers before saying in low tones, "Unbelievable."

He laughs, shaking his head. "That's some imagination you have, Mila."

I'm grateful the street is dark, so he can't see my face burning. "You shouldn't have been earwigging," I point out.

He shrugs. "Probably not."

For the entire drive back, neither of us speaks. I sit, arms folded, staring out the window, wishing my cocktail buzz hadn't packed up and left so soon.

We don't talk in the parking garage either. All the way up in the elevator, I stare at the numbers, lips pursed. It's not so much that I'm angry with him for listening in—it's more that I'm angry with myself for always getting into these situations. My life is nothing short of ridiculous and now he knows it. My pride is wounded.

Inside the flat, I kick off my heels and turn the cold tap on full blast, grabbing a glass from the cupboard. "Do you have any aspirin?" I ask, breaking the silence.

Vincent shakes his head, face glum. "I'm sorry I listened to your conversation," he says, picking at the edge of the kitchen island with a finger.

"It doesn't matter," I say quietly. "Thanks for sorting out O'Geary for me."

He nods, frowning. "Mila—"

"Look," I say, interrupting him. "I know what you must think of me."

His frown deepens, eyes dark. "What do I think of you?"

"That I'm totally flaky and pathetic. What with dead rats in my bed and going on dates with serial killers and getting felt up my first week at work. If you think I don't know how ridiculous my life is, Vincent, you're wrong, because I do, and the truth is, I don't know why I told my work friend you like to be tied up with silky scarves. Maybe I've watched too many dodgy French movies. But my point is, I know I'm not like you, with the fancy view and the starch spray in the cupboard and all *this*." I circle a finger wildly in the air. "So I'm sorry that you're stuck with me, and I'm sorry you had to show your fangs and lose your chance at a hookup with Leggy Layla from Marketing. I am *sorry*."

I suck in a deep breath and take a gulp of my water. I must be drunker than I thought.

When I finally summon the courage to meet his eye, I jolt in surprise. His eyes are dark, tortured. He leans against the counter, hands gripping the edges so tightly his knuckles are whiter than bone.

"That's the second time you mentioned those girls." His voice is husky, throaty, as if the words are coming from some dark, forbidden place deep inside him.

"Yeah, well. They irritate me. Add that to my list of faults. I'm jealous of a group of women who wear double the recommended amount of mascara."

"Jealous," he repeats.

Jesus. What is up with him? He looks like a four-year-old trying to figure out an algebraic equation. "Yes. Jealous. Not usually. Just tonight. Because you were speaking to them."

Inside, I'm well aware I've more or less just announced I have an enormous crush on him. But on the outside, the half-drunk, cocky Mila is still running the show.

He continues to stand, frozen. I snatch up my glass of water and slip past him into the lounge.

"Mila," he says loudly.

I turn around at the same time he does.

"I don't enjoy *Dr. Quinn, Medicine Woman*."

"Yes, you do."

"No. I don't." He runs a nervous hand through his dirty-blond hair. "It's the only show where I can sit and not have to pay attention to the plotline to know what's happening."

I sigh. "Fine. I give up. We'll hire a harpist for our evening entertainment." I continue stomping toward the bedrooms—as much as it's possible to stomp in bare feet.

A gust of air lifts the hair from the nape of my neck and, in an instant, Vincent is filling the doorway with his luscious frame. "I can't pay attention to the plot," he says, "because I'm too distracted."

"Why? Because I'm here messing up your apartment and getting in the way? It won't be forever, and I'll tidy up before I go—"

Before I can finish the sentence, he cuts the short distance between us in a single bound, placing hands on my hips. The heat from his fingers burns through the material like red-hot flames. My heart thuds beneath my ribs. Without my heels, my head is level with his chest—his perfectly sculpted, chiseled-from-rock chest—rising and falling as if something is fighting to get out. I lift my gaze, and as our eyes lock, he bunches my dress in his fists. The relaxed look he wore when he lied to the marketing girls and threatened Leery is gone, naked anxiety assuming its place.

"Ask me to stop," he says, his voice breaking.

I gulp. The only sound is my heart pounding against my rib cage. *Is this really happening?*

"I can't," I say at last. "Because I don't want you to."

He releases my dress, looping strong arms around my waist, and lifts me onto my tiptoes until our bodies press together, torso to torso. I drop the glass of water onto the rug at our feet, hearing the loud slosh of liquid as it soaks into the carpet. The water is swiftly forgotten as he leans closer, brushing warm lips over my jawline. He tightens his grip, anchoring me to him as a tremor of pleasure rips through my body.

When his mouth finally fastens onto mine, I mold myself into him like clay, my breasts pushed up against the steely ridges of his chest, my hands twisting into his hair like vines around the branches of a tree. I part his lips, and he responds intensely. He tastes like champagne—warm and fruity—and I devour him like a woman who's been living carb-free would a loaf of bread. My tongue slides over his, a low, animal groan erupting from my throat.

He cups my face in his warm hands as he begins

feverishly whispering my name between kisses. "Mila, oh God, Mila."

He wants me, I realize in surprise, knowing from the way my name sounds in his mouth—hard and spiky as barbwire—that this is no whim, no spur-of-the-moment fancy. All the times he's blushed suddenly make sense, those intense stares I mistook as him thinking I'm an idiot.

I stop kissing him, leaning back to gaze into his drowsy, silver-dappled eyes. His face is slack, his mouth half-open, lips moist.

"It's true, isn't it?" I murmur, dragging my hands down his muscled back. "You haven't really been enjoying *Dr. Quinn* at all."

"No. But I've been enjoying watching you—or being tortured by you, depending on how you look at it."

We gaze at each other in silence.

"So you're not really such a Good Samaritan after all? The TV, letting me stay—all just part of the seduction."

His face drops. "No, I never meant for this to happen. It's wrong, Mila. You're a witness and I'm a police officer, which makes it—"

My eyes flash. "Forbidden."

The arms around my waist loosen. "You're right. We should stop."

"Vincent, I was kidding."

He shakes his head, blond hair flipping into his eyes. "I've been fighting this ever since we met. The last thing I want to do is to complicate an already terrible situation."

"Vincent," I say, brushing the hair from his eyes. "This situation is far less terrible because of you."

He takes a step backward. "You've had a lot to drink,

Mila, and I wouldn't want to take advantage, particularly when I'm supposed to be taking care of you."

I drop my arms to my sides, my heart crashing in disappointment, but as soon as my touch leaves him, he lets out a low hiss of frustration, drawing me back into his arms and running his fingers through my hair.

He slowly releases a deep breath as he rests his forehead on mine. "How drunk are you?"

I shake my head. "I know what I want—what I've wanted for weeks now."

He kisses me again and I drown in it—his warm lips opening onto mine, the scent of aftershave and fresh linen pulling me under like a dangerous current. I push the front of his sweater up, exploring the hard, satiny ridges of his abdomen, curling my fingers into the soft downy hairs that lead a tempting path into the waistband of his underwear. He moans as my hand drifts south, brushing the bulge straining against the front of his jeans.

"Mila," he growls. "I can't let anything happen tonight. You might wake up in the morning and regret everything."

I take his hands, threading my fingers through his. "I won't regret anything, I promise. Now get those trousers off."

He holds my wrists to keep me from pawing at him. "I'm not going to get any rest tonight."

"Not in my bed, you won't."

"We can't. Not only have you had a lot to drink, but you should also sleep on it. Not me," he adds, as I flash a mischievous smile.

"Fine," I say with a sigh. "But you should probably lock your door."

He grins. "Because you'll be doing what, exactly? Prowling around the hallway in your nightie?"

"Maybe without a nightie."

He groans. "Stop."

I lay my hands against his hard chest. "So I guess I should go to bed then, wait to be sober."

He nods, grimacing. "I think it's for the best."

"Okay." I've never regretted drinking as much as I do right now. Not even the time when I was sixteen and threw up all over the next-door neighbor's prize-winning chrysanthemums.

I let go of him, walking backward into the hallway toward the bedrooms. My fingers have just gripped the door handle to my room when he's on me again, spinning me around and pinning me to the wall with his hands and mouth. I liquefy as rough fingertips skim my breasts, his tongue tangling with mine. When we finally break apart, his sweater is rucked up and I'm panting like a dog, my nipples hard as bullets from where he touched them, a throbbing ache between my legs.

"Don't stop," I whisper.

"I have to," he whispers before placing a soft kiss on my bottom lip, making me shiver. "Good night."

He steps away and I see resolve in the tense set of his shoulders, his fists clenched tight.

Somehow, I extract myself from the wall and cross to my room on wobbling legs. I push open the door, taking one last look at him—eyes dark in the low light of the hallway, blond hair all over the place from where I ravished him.

I will not be sleeping well. Probably not ever again.

"Good night."

Chapter 10

Vincent

THERE ISN'T ENOUGH COLD WATER IN THE WORLD TO dampen the desire rampaging through my veins.

Standing beneath the icy jets in the shower, I'm consumed to the point of madness by the lingering aroma of Mila's sweet scent, the rub of her skin against mine. No amount of scrubbing can loosen the feel of soft fingers under my shirt or the taste of her hot, wet mouth. She is buried deep inside me, locked in a place I can't reach, too far under my skin to wash off with soap and water.

Outside the bar, when she punched my arm and told me to chat up women, I was sure my desire was one-sided, that any hint of mutual attraction I felt was a mere figment of my imagination. Then she made those remarks about the women I was chatting with, mentioned the word *jealous*, and suddenly all my resolve packed up and flew right out the window. I wasn't thinking about her being our witness or that I've long sworn to never love again. All I could see were her magnificent tawny eyes narrowed in anger at me for listening to her conversation, and the way her legs looked in that dress that kept sliding up every time she fiddled with her hair. All I could think about were the nights I've sat beside her on the sofa, watching that daft period drama, when really all I wanted to do was lean across and kiss every inch of her soft, curvy body.

"Dammit," I growl as blood rushes to my groin.

Accepting my erection is here to stay and that no amount of jerking off is going to relieve me, I towel off and step onto the mat. Maybe I should have agreed to her locking her door. How will I get a moment's peace knowing that not only is she in bed in the next room, but that she also wants me to join her? Possibly do all the dirty things I've been fantasizing about since I first clapped eyes on her?

A single moment of weakness and my resolve is shattered. Because tomorrow, if her feelings are unchanged, I won't be holding back any longer. I can't. Not now that I've felt her lips on mine, held her in my arms.

I usually sleep in my underwear or naked, but tonight I pull on a pair of track pants and a T-shirt, hoping the extra layers will smother the sensation of her touch. It doesn't work, of course. All night long I stare at the ceiling, tenting the covers with my arousal and extending my hearing into the next room to listen to the steady drum of her heart. I fantasize about how good it would feel to have her nestled up against my chest, our limbs tangled up like vines, my fingers wound into her hair.

By the time the first gray needles of light filter through the blinds, I already have a plan of action for the day ahead. I will visit Catherine Adair after I've dropped Mila at work and beg—or pay if I have to—for her to visit Ronin for me. I already asked her over the phone, of course, the day after my visit to Ronin's club, and she responded in the way I expected, repeating *no* like a toddler in a shopping center. Now the stakes are higher for Mila and me. Before last night, I was happy to bumble along in our new routine. I was enjoying it. But now, the thought of someone wanting to harm her is eating at me like acid. Catherine *will* go to that club, if I have to drag her there myself. If she doesn't, then I'll have to beg Ronin instead, or track down another willing ancient. Either way, the killer must be found.

I get up, dress, and walk past her door to the lounge, trying not to think about how her slender body will look under the covers, her blond hair a spill of sunshine on the pillow.

In the lounge, bright daylight streams through the windows, casting its rays over the now-messy room. There are DVD boxes scattered over the glass coffee table, a hairbrush on the back of a sofa, and a dozen other tiny pieces of Mila everywhere, from stray blond hairs clinging to the cushions, to clothing items shed and forgotten.

I'm so deep in thought I don't hear the door from the bedroom hallway creak open.

"Well, if this headache is anything to go by, I'd say I'm sober now."

I turn around to see Mila standing sheepishly in the doorway, her hair stuck up, wearing the same tank top and pajama shorts as that night she had her nightmare.

I shove my hands into my pockets, a familiar gesture I've acquired to keep myself from wrapping my arms around her. "We really need to buy some aspirin."

She nods, cheeks pink. I notice a faint ring of mascara

beneath her eyes. In all her dishevelment, I have never seen her look more beautiful.

"I'll make you some breakfast," I say, crossing to the kitchen and busying myself in a cupboard.

When I turn around with her bowl of cereal and spoon, she has slipped onto a stool. One of her tank top straps has fallen down her arm, drawing my eye to the outline of her nipples beneath the thin material. The memory of how they felt—hard beneath my fingertips— makes my length stiffen.

"So," she says, a corner of her mouth quirked.

I grin, handing her the dish and shoving my hands back in my pockets. "So."

We continue to gaze at each other, tension swirling palpably in the air.

And then we both start chuckling like buffoons.

"I can't believe you faked *Dr. Quinn*," she says.

I nod. "I hate it. Don't get me started on the anachronisms."

She shoves a spoon of Rice Krispies into her mouth and my length hardens a little more. I can't help but muse about the various parts of my body I'd like to see disappearing between those soft, pink lips of hers.

I wait until she's eaten her cereal, and when I pass her a glass of orange juice, I ask, "Do you regret it?"

She arches a brow. "What do you think?"

"I know I don't," I say in a low voice.

Flashing a wicked grin, she says, "I don't either."

Relief and fear course through me like warm air.

"So, it's Friday. What would you like to do tonight? Shall I ask around about a harpist?"

She laughs. "No. I'm not sure I want a third wheel in the room. Are you still taking me to my cousin's engagement party tomorrow?"

I nod. "Yes. Will you be drinking again?"

She shakes her head, eyes sparkling mischievously. "No. After last night, I'm considering never drinking again." She pauses as our eyes lock. "I'm well aware this morning could have started very differently if I'd only kept a tighter rein on the cocktails."

I gulp, moving closer to the kitchen island to disguise the bulge in my trousers. "I'm not against drinking," I say, my voice rasping with barely concealed lust. "I wanted you to have a good time last night. But I can't take advantage when you might not be thinking straight."

Her eyes narrow and she tilts her head to one side, as if she's figuring me out. "What did you used to be, Vincent? Before you were a vampire policeman?"

The change of topic is enough to subdue my trouser stirrings for a moment. I don't often talk about the past. I break her gaze. "That's a story for another time."

Or never, preferably.

"Were you a musketeer?"

I laugh. "No, I wasn't a musketeer. I was the son of a French duke."

She screws up her pretty face. "You're not French."

"I am," I say, smiling. "A long time ago. I just lost the accent."

"I knew you had to be something like a nobleman. I can tell by the way you're always opening doors and waiting until I'm seated before you sit down."

She wouldn't be calling me noble if she knew the

kinds of fantasies I'm having right now about those
sweet lips of hers.

"Say something French," she demands, grinning.

I snatch a glance down at my watch. *"Nous allons
être en retard."*

"Which means?"

"We're going to be late."

"Sexy," she mutters. "But I get the hint. Give me
twenty minutes, Your Highness."

I watch her scurry across the room. At the door, she
skids to a halt, a devious twinkle in her hazel eyes. "You
can practice your sword fighting while you wait."

"I wasn't a musketeer," I yell, laughing, as she twirls
a wrist, pretending to lunge.

"It's all the same," she yells back, disappearing into
the hallway.

———〰———

We manage to make it all the way down to the parking
garage without touching, but when we climb into the
car, the tension is so thick it's like wading through tar.

I glance across at her in the dim light, her features
half-hidden by shadows. She's wearing her work clothes,
an ivory blouse pulled tight across her full breasts and a
charcoal pencil skirt that shows off her shapely thighs.
The material has ridden up and I can't help but stare
longingly at the gap between her knees.

"Be sure to put your seat belt on," I say, voice trembling. Though to be frank, safety harness or not, having
her in the seat beside me brings dangerous driving to a
whole new level.

When she doesn't move, I lean over for the buckle, her smell all around me, blinding me like sea mist. I freeze as she slowly turns her head.

Our eyes lock, and for a few crucial seconds, neither of us moves, time standing still. I should end this, right here, right now, either by looking away, or pushing the ignition key and driving her to work. But I don't.

Eventually the invisible string of tension snaps—one second we're apart, and the next her warm lips are on mine and my hands are roaming all over the place, one curving around her cheek, the other resting in the enticing space between her legs.

"Mila," I whisper as she cups my face, dragging me closer. "I'm out of control."

"Me too," she says between deep kisses. "Put your hands on me. Wherever you like. Please."

I groan, sliding my hand farther up her skirt, rubbing a thumb into the soft, silky flesh of her leg. I don't want the first time I touch her intimately to be inside a car, but at the same time, I can't stop. I trace the line of the juncture between her panties and inner thigh with my fingertips, feeling warmth radiating from the spot between her legs. Then I give in, gently pushing aside the moist strip of lace and rubbing an index finger into her delicious heat. She moans, her legs opening, urging me deeper until my whole hand is inside her panties, teasing her wet bud with my thumb, sliding a finger around her tight walls. She feels even better than I imagined.

She shudders, tipping her head back onto the headrest, one hand around the door handle in a white-knuckled grip. "Vincent," she gasps, and the way my name sounds in her mouth, as wild and out of control as I am right now, drives me on. I increase the pressure on her clit, her ragged breathing coming out in short, sharp pants. With my other hand, I turn her face, pulling her open lips roughly to mine, my tongue in her mouth, mimicking the movement of my finger exploring her core.

"I want to watch you come," I say, my voice as jagged as broken glass.

"I am," she pants. "I'm going to."

I push another finger inside her, swirling my thumb around her nub. My dick is so hard in my trousers I can practically hear the seams groan under the pressure.

Her thighs begin to shake, a breath catches in her throat, and then she unravels, jaw slack, chest heaving, animal cries erupting from her lips. In all my centuries on earth, I've never seen anything so beautiful.

I pull my hand away, wishing we weren't in a car so I could lie beside her, encircle her with my arms.

She closes her eyes until her breathing slows. I leave a trail of soft kisses along her jaw.

"How am I supposed to go to work after that?" she asks, opening one eye.

"I'm not sure how I'm supposed to go on living after that," I say, nuzzling into her warm neck, burying my face in her hair.

The air in the car is humid, a fine mist now clinging to the windows, but I shiver as she brings shaking fingers to my face, slowly working them down over my chest, stroking me with languid caresses until she reaches the straining bulge in my trousers.

I encircle her wrist with my fingers. "Mila, you don't

have to." And although I mean it—I would happily stay hard forever if it meant watching her fall apart like that every day—my length twitches almost painfully at her touch.

She frowns and then smiles, her pretty eyes glowing in the gloomy light of the car, the tiny smattering of freckles across her nose standing out dark against her flushed, rosy skin. "Don't you realize that I've been dying to do this since the first time I set eyes on you?"

The zip of my fly being yanked down may be the sweetest sound I've ever heard. My erection springs out like a trapped beast from a cage. A breath hitches in her throat.

"So, how does the reality compare to the fantasy, Miss Hart?" I tease.

She chuckles, flashing me a coy smile. "Let's just say I'm far from disappointed."

I groan as she takes my length in her hand, closing my eyes briefly as she begins to stroke the shaft with soft, velvety caresses.

"It's perfect," she murmurs. "Is there any part of you that isn't perfect?"

"I could say the same about you," I whisper.

My eyes widen as she leans over, her long hair tickling my groin, sparks of pleasure shooting through me like tiny electric shocks. I gather her blond locks up, coiling the length around my fingers like a thick rope. When she licks my glistening tip, my whole body jerks as if I've been shot. I brace myself, placing my free hand on the ceiling of the Porsche as she wraps a damp palm around the base of my cock.

"Mila," I say, my voice raspy.

It's usually at this point I wake up.

Then her lips are around me, sliding down my shaft, my whole length disappearing into her hot, wet mouth. I cry out, a tide of ecstasy immediately threatening to spill as she pumps me furiously. In a tiny corner of my brain, I acknowledge that the sight of her swollen pink lips and blond head bobbing up and down in my lap will haunt me forever. A hiss escapes my lips as she increases suction, her tongue swirling against my sensitive skin, and when her hand slips lower to cup my balls, I'm done for. Screaming her name, my head lolls forward as an earth-shattering climax rolls over me, cutting me adrift until I'm nothing more than a loose bundle of nerve endings exploding in pleasure.

The sound of her sweet voice pulls me back to earth and into the car. "Do you think we should call in sick?" she asks innocently as if she didn't just give me the most intense orgasm of my life.

I splutter with laughter, opening my eyes to find her beautiful face inches from mine. "I don't even think it would be a lie," I say, carving my hands through her long hair and sighing with contentment. In all honesty, this feels like an illness—a consuming sickness that's running through my veins, transforming me the same way I did all those centuries ago when Ronin's venom flooded my system. I'm not the same man I was two weeks ago. I'm not even sure if I'm the same man from two *minutes* ago.

I draw her toward me, loving how she knots her fingers into my shirt, the gentle moan that escapes her throat as I kiss her deeply. I want to carry her upstairs and spend the rest of my days ravishing her in my bed, exploring every nook of her beautiful body. But at the back of my mind is the constant, gnawing awareness that every moment we spend kissing is another moment the vampire who wants her dead walks free.

I pull away. "There's some work I need to do on the case today," I say, remembering Catherine Adair. "But I'll pick you up at the usual time. We can come straight home."

She frowns, worrying at her bottom lip. "I've got my English classes at London Met after work, remember? I don't want to let them down."

"I'm not sure I can wait," I say in a low voice.

She places a long, simmering kiss on my mouth. "Me neither. But it is Friday, so we'll have the whole weekend."

I smile. "That does sound promising."

We spend a few moments straightening our clothing, fastening buttons, smiling shyly at each other in the dim light of the car, before I reluctantly start the engine.

"Ready?" I ask, taking the handbrake off.

This evening can't come soon enough.

Catherine Adair's office is out east, near Hackney, on a tiny cobbled street lined with brightly painted artist studios and trendy boutiques, sandwich boards thronging the pavement. In the early days of the V-Date website, I assumed Catherine chose the area because it was cheaper rent than central London, but she's since revealed that she was born around the corner in a poor neighborhood in the nineteenth century. For us vampires, it isn't unusual to circle back to a place that meant something to us as humans. It's mostly why I keep the chateau in France—not that I would ever live there permanently.

I hum a little tune to myself as I park the Porsche on the double yellow lines, grinning like a buffoon when my phone vibrates with a text from Mila.

I'm a mess. You're a bad man, Vincent Ferrer.

Leaning against the car, I reply, I am a bad man. Practically a sadomasochist. P.S. You're not exactly innocent yourself. I have a tear in my pants to prove it.

I lock the car and stride across to Cat's building, pressing a buzzer on the panel beside the door and straightening my tie in a bid to recoup a sense of professionalism. Though I'm fairly sure professionals don't go to third base with witnesses whose lives they're supposed to be protecting. A chink of guilt opens in my brain, eating up some of the endorphins. This time yesterday, Mila and I were buddies at best, awkward cohabiters at worst. One night out in a bar and we've turned into something entirely more intimate. Something that makes me feel less *lonely*. I push the thought from my head as the door clicks open and I make my way up the narrow, rickety spiral staircase to Cat's office on the second floor.

Inside, the building is bright and airy, the walls painted brilliant white. The contrast after the mottled-gray sky outside is jarring.

Whoever it was that buzzed me indoors, it wasn't Cat. When I knock on the glass door to her office, she looks up from her massive white computer screen and jolts in surprise to see me standing in her doorway.

Like most vampires, Cat is undeniably a beautiful woman—the change when an ancient gives their blood reverses all dying processes in the body. If a person had damaged their skin in the sun as a human, turning vampire would reverse the effect, leaving it unblemished. And yet, Cat is so far removed from Ronin's usual type that I can't help but muse why he's so desperate for her company.

Ronin is always surrounded by beautiful women—vampires and humans, showy model types with perfect hair and white teeth who never appear to be overly fond of clothing. Cat is more down-to-earth. Her cloud of black, curly hair is pinned up today, a yellow pencil shoved through the middle. The huge black glasses she wears for show—no vampire would need a prescription—magnify the intelligent, brown-green eyes behind them. She is wearing an oversize blue shirt with tiny dogs all over it and tight black cigarette pants. Her fashion sense isn't unlike Mila's. She too, I've noticed, has a thing for animal patterns.

Cat's lip curls. "Didn't I say no a thousand times already?"

I evade the question by pretending to examine some of the art on the walls. "Is that a real Andy Warhol?" I ask, motioning to an iconic image of an old movie star.

She folds her arms across her chest, swinging in her swivel chair. "I didn't even say you could come in."

Next, I feign fascination with the gloomy street outside the big sash windows on the opposite wall. "It's a nice office," I say finally.

"Yes," she snips. "You've been here before, remember?"

I frown. "Yes, but you've done something with the blinds since then—"

"Oh, for God's sake, Vincent. Do your pathetic begging so I can get on with my morning."

Ordinarily, Cat isn't the sort to lose her temper, but Ronin always manages to bring out the worst in people.

I inhale deeply. The office smells like air freshener and perfume. Again, I think of Mila. I still have her scent all over me. "Please, Cat," I start. "I really, really need you to see Ronin. I'll pay you if necessary, or if you feel the visit would put you in danger of some kind, I could go with you."

At the mention of the ancient's name, Cat's perfectly shaped brows pull tight. "Vincent," she says slowly, "has there ever been a person you just want to forget? Who you never, ever want to set eyes on again as long as you live?"

Oddly enough, there hasn't. When you spend your existence not getting close to people, you shut yourself off to hate as well as love. "Yes," I say anyway.

"Then you'll know why I categorically do not want to see Ronin McDermott. As for danger, well, I know I won't be in physical danger. It's mind games with him. He loves messing with people. I hate him."

I remember Ronin's smile when I told him as much at the club. How pleased it made him. He clearly relishes the challenge of a woman like Catherine Adair.

"I know that as well as anyone, Catherine, and I wouldn't ask if there weren't lives at risk."

"You mean your witness," she says, quirking a brow. "How are those repressed feelings going, Sir Lancelot?

From that twinkle in your eye, I'd say you've been caving in to those illicit desires very recently."

I fiddle with my shirtsleeves, a flash of Mila's blond head in my lap popping into my mind. After throwing a guilty glance about the room, I slip into one of the floral tub chairs near her desk. "The truth is, Cat, I'm out of my depth, professionally and emotionally. I know you might think I'm some Romeo, but I'm not. I'm terrified. She terrifies me."

Cat leans back in her chair and steeples her fingers like she's some kind of love guru. "How? Tell me."

I clasp my hands in my lap, avoiding Cat's eye. "I've only ever been in love once, when I was human, and it ended badly. She died." To my horror, my throat tightens. I haven't spoken about it in so long I'm unable to keep the emotions from spilling into my voice. "I never had any intention of feeling that way again. Ever."

"You mean you haven't fallen in love since?" Cat asks, eyes wide.

I shake my head. "I haven't let myself. Why? How often do you fall in love?"

Cat smiles. "I fall in love every day in London. Today, it was a green-eyed busker singing a Beatles tune outside Starbucks."

I cock a brow. "Seriously."

Her eyes roll behind the thick, black frames. "Okay, fine. Love is difficult for our kind. Why do you think I started V-Date? We could all use a helping hand." She pauses. "What's so terrifying about her?"

Looking up, my eyes fall on a massive canvas above Cat's desk. Some die-hard, trendy street artist has daubed *All you need is LOVE* in graffiti-style lettering. There can be no doubt—Cat is a believer.

"Because in one way or another, I'm not sure my world will ever be the same again."

Cat frowns. "Go on."

"Everything is a mess since she came into my life," I continue. "My apartment, my career, *me*. I'm a mess. I was so organized before. I had it all under control. Now everything hinges on her and her well-being. As if my life is no longer my own. I should be miserable, but I'm not. It's like a window opens in some dark place whenever she's around, as if she's oxygen itself. I feel human again." I lapse into silence, picking at a corner of my thumbnail, feeling Cat's gaze drill into me from across the desk.

"You're falling in love, Vincent," Cat says, her voice filled with surprise.

I flinch at the word *love*, a stab of regret plunging into my heart like an icicle. "I know," I mutter darkly.

Cat releases a heavy sigh. "I'll go and see Ronin this afternoon."

Chapter 11

Mila

THE WORST THING ABOUT GIVING YOUR SECRET VAM-
pire protector a blow job in his Porsche is you can't tell
a damn soul about it. Especially not Janice, who keeps
asking questions about last night's party and why Leery
O'Geary showed up to work sporting a black eye.

It is this nugget of information that finally grabs my
attention. Since arriving at work this morning, I've been
wandering around in a lust-fueled haze.

But I guess that's normal for a woman who's just
enjoyed the most explosive sexual encounter of her life.
I mean, my God, the things he did with his *hands*.

A day ago, I considered myself to have a thorough
understanding of the word *orgasm*. But now, the truth is
as plain as the stars on a cloudless night: I didn't have a
clue. No one, in my whole nine years of sexual activity,
has ever managed to push the buttons Vincent did. No
one has ever given me pleasure like the avalanche of
ecstasy that rained down on me in the car. He is ruining
me in every sense possible—ruining me for the rest of
my life.

Jerking back to reality, I turn to face Janice. "Paul
O'Geary has a black eye?"

"A real shiner," she announces, clucking her tongue.
"He said he fell over a table."

Remembering the speed and ease with which Vincent flung him aside, a warm feeling of pride flutters in my chest.

"What a shame," I mutter sarcastically.

For about the zillionth time today, I reach into my bag and pull out my phone to see if Vincent has sent any more texts. Nothing.

"No word from lover boy?" Janice asks nosily, peering over my shoulder.

"I was checking the weather app, actually," I snap.

Janice gives a smug smile, letting me know she isn't fooled. "Why don't you go in the kitchen and call him? It's a slow day. I can handle everything. You can make us a cuppa while you're in there."

I'm on my feet before she has a chance to change her mind, although I can't call Vincent. By now, he'll be too busy saving lives or whatever he does all day at Scotland Yard, but I can call Laura. She's still the only person who knows anything about what's been going on.

As soon as I've made sure the kitchen is empty, I hit her number. She answers in the normal manner of late, a rattle of panic in her usually calm voice. "Mila, are you okay? Where are you?"

In spite of her worry, I smile. It's nice to have at least one person from my old life fully aware of what's going on in the new, crazy one. "Relax. I'm fine. I'm at work."

"Oh, thank goodness. I'm so jittery lately. I'll feel better tomorrow when I see you."

"Tomorrow?" I ask, puzzled.

"Anna's engagement party? Tom and I are invited. I can't wait to see Officer Hottie for myself."

My stomach lurches. Suddenly, introducing Vincent

to a room full of people who will forever ask after him seems nauseatingly real.

I take a deep breath. "Something happened between us."

She squeals louder than a kid at Disneyland. "What? Did you tell him how you feel?"

"Well, sort of. We kissed…and stuff."

"What stuff?"

I lower my voice. "Third-base stuff."

"Oh my God. You're so marrying this guy. I feel it. I knew it from the first time you mentioned him. It's so exciting! We can go on couples cruises."

"Laura," I hiss. "Firstly, I think you're forgetting he's a vampire, and secondly, you better act way cooler than this at the party tomorrow."

She ignores me, asking, "Is he a good kisser?"

I sigh, falling into one of the metal chairs next to the coffee machine. "The kind of kisser who makes you feel it right down to your toes."

Laura gasps. "Better than Shaun Whitby?"

"Way better than Shaun Whitby. I'll never think of Shaun Whitby again."

"Oh boy, are you in trouble."

"I know," I say, grimacing. "As if my life isn't complicated enough."

We lapse into silence. The only sound is the drip of the broken tap and the distant drone of Janice's voice in reception.

"Do you think he might think I'm cheap for giving him a blow job *before* we've had sex?" I ask suddenly.

Laura catches her breath, coughing down the line. "Oh, so it was that kind of third base."

"Yeah," I say, twirling a loose strand of hair around my finger. "It just felt right. He's so beautiful, I couldn't help myself."

"Okay," Laura says. "Too much information. I'm hanging up. Just be sure to use protection if you go all the way."

"Vampires can't procreate in that way, remember? Now, tell me the truth—will he think I'm cheap?"

"I'll know tomorrow when I see you together," she says. "This is going to be one awesome engagement party."

<hr />

The rest of the day drags by at a snail's pace. When the digital clock on my monitor finally creeps to five o'clock, a mixture of nerves and excitement begin to swirl in the pit of my tummy. Every time the revolving door spins and a gust of air wafts into reception, I pop my head over the desk so fast I almost pull a muscle. Eventually I'm rewarded with Vincent's tall, broad-shouldered frame sweeping through the entrance. My breath hitches in my throat. His dark-blond hair is all over the place—it doesn't look as if he's made any attempt to smooth it down since our encounter in the car. His shirt still bears the creases of our fumble.

I rise from my seat like a courtier greeting a king, unable to stop a massive grin from spreading across my face. With the light through the glass outlining his muscled frame, he's nothing short of a Greek god.

"Hello, Mila," he says, his voice deep in his throat.

Janice fussing around in the background and the group of clients waiting on the other side of the lobby may as well be on a different planet. It's as if it's just me and him in the whole universe.

I reach down to grab my bag. "Hi, Vincent."

"Ready?" he asks, gaze locked on mine.

"Yep," I say, blushing. I'm beginning to feel more than just a little hot under the collar at the prospect of getting back into a car with him.

I wave a casual goodbye to Janice as I step around the desk and take his hand, my heart fluttering as his warm, rough fingers close around mine.

Janice mutters, "Christ, get a room," under her breath and Vincent chuckles. He drops her a nod as he leads me across the shiny floor to the exit.

Once we're outside in the Porsche, the tension returns, the memory of what happened just a few hours ago as thick and consuming as quicksand.

"So, here we are again," Vincent says, eyes crinkling around the edges.

Without thinking, I reach over, brushing strands of blond hair from his forehead. His Adam's apple bobs visibly in his throat.

"Mila," he whispers, rubbing a bristly cheek against my palm. "I'm not sure I'll be able to stop this time."

I drop my hand, and he quickly covers it with his. Long, tapered fingers curl around my wrist, a callused thumb tracing lazy circles across my knuckles.

Trying to ignore the ache pulsing between my legs, I say, "My evening class. I do have to go."

"I know," he says. "Which is why I brought you some dinner to eat on the way."

He releases me, reaching behind him to pluck a

Harrods bag from the backseat and handing it to me. "I figured if there's food in your mouth, then nothing else will be."

My jaw drops in mock horror. "Vincent!"

He bursts into a deep rumble of laughter. "I'm kidding. Can't a musketeer make a joke these days?"

"You would make a good musketeer," I say, eyes narrowed. "God knows you're sexy enough." I slap a hand over my mouth. "That was supposed to stay in my head."

"After what transpired this morning, I was kind of assuming you find me sexy anyway, so…"

"We should stop saying the word 'sexy,'" I say, leaning closer, practically drowning in the scent of expensive cologne and fresh linen that rolls off him in waves.

He cups my face in his hands and I hold my breath as he presses his lips to mine, forgetting that we're parked on a street in rush hour, forgetting everything but his gentle kiss, the rasp of his stubble on my skin.

"What? No tongues?" I tease when he draws back.

Smiling, he starts the engine. "Later, there will be plenty of tongues. For now, we should concentrate on getting you to job number two on time."

I pull a pasta salad out of the bag. "Fine. I'll just eat my sexual urges."

He chuckles, shaking his head as he maneuvers the car into the traffic. "Mila," he says, "never stop being you."

―⁂―

Although the offices of Wilkin Morris aren't far from the university, it takes ages to crawl through all the early-evening commuter traffic. The sun has broken through the clouds, turning the smog-filled air hazy with sunlight and exhaust fumes. I wind down a window as we pass the Gherkin, getting an unpleasant lungful of black belch from a taxicab in the lane next to us. This relentless traffic usually makes me irritable and ratty as hell, but sitting here, eating Doritos next to Vincent, enjoying the play of muscle and tendons beneath the skin of his smooth forearm every time he changes gear, I'm filled with contentment.

"I haven't brought any books with me," I realize aloud, as we merge into the busy stream of cars and buses thronging the Holloway Road. "What will you do while I'm teaching?"

Vincent glances over, a breeze from the open window lifting the hair from his forehead. I stare into his chiseled face, marveling at his otherworldliness. He belongs on some exotic mountain road, driving an open-top car beneath an azure sky. Not here, ferrying me around a smoke-clogged city.

"I'll make some phone calls, surf the Net. I won't be bored," he assures me, reaching across to squeeze my knee. The touch sparks the memory of his fingers between my legs, and when he moves his hand, I cross them in a bid to stem the steady ache building at my core.

It's as if a million years have passed since I last walked through the university halls with him. We were awkward strangers then. Now...well, I'm not sure what we are, but it feels nice when he opens doors for me, smiling and ghosting a hand on my waist as I step through ahead of him.

When we reach the door of my damp-smelling

classroom in the basement, most of the students are already seated. I whip around to Vincent. "Don't listen to me teaching, will you? I won't be able to concentrate if I know you're out here listening."

He grins, holding his laptop up. "Internet surfing, remember?"

I smile back. This lesson can't go quickly enough.

My students greet me warmly as I scurry inside and shut the door. Ten minutes into our introductions, Karolina arrives. The Ghanaian brothers immediately straighten in their seats. One produces a small comb from his top pocket and jabs it at his hair a few times. Karolina, as always, is oblivious. A person at her level of beautiful must be used to making waves each time they enter a room.

Despite my constant awareness that a sex god willing to do dirty things to me is waiting outside in the corridor, the lesson moves at its usual speedy pace. The only difference this evening is Karolina. She keeps gazing at me with a frown on her face, as if I'm a caterpillar she's just found in her salad. When the lesson ends and everyone says their goodbyes, she hangs back, watching me with a mixture of disappointment and confusion.

"Is everything okay, Karolina?" I ask, meeting her black, limpid-eyed gaze. "How was Milan with Fernando?"

She flicks a wrist dismissively. "So-so. Asshole still in Guatemala, so I no happy."

I nod in sympathy. "I'm sure he'll be back soon and then you can—"

"The guy outside," she cuts in.

I jerk a little, not because she is about to broach

the subject of the hot blond waiting outside the door, but because for the first time since Karolina has been coming to class, she looks nervous. She doesn't meet my eye, fiddling with the brown leather strap of her designer shoulder bag.

"What about him?" I ask, a knot forming in my stomach.

"Do you know he's a vampire?" she asks, eyes flashing like black, burning coals.

"Yes," I say slowly, wondering where she's going with this. "I know."

She nods, her perfectly French-manicured nails still toying with the bag strap. For the first time, I notice a brightly polished silver ring on her left hand—a five-pointed star, its lines interwoven like a Celtic knot.

"Humans and vampires," she continues. "They are not good mix. Too much sacrifice. You are better off seeing nice, normal man."

The trouble with that is, there are no nice, normal men.

Not wanting to be rude, I say, "Thanks for the advice."

She nods before throwing her bag onto one of the desks and rummaging inside. When I look down, I see a tiny purple card clutched between her elegant fingers.

"Here," she says, handing the card to me. "I don't tell the others what I do, but if you ever need anything, call me, okay?"

"Okay," I say, smiling.

It's only after she's swept from the room that I read it. There, emblazoned on the front, is the same five-pointed star as her ring. It reads *Karolina Dobrescu, Witchcraft & Psychic Services*.

I'm still standing, frowning, when there is a soft knock at the door. Vincent is there, a shy smile at the corners of his mouth. "Is the prettiest teacher in town ready to leave?" he asks.

I grin, slipping the card into a front pocket of my bag. "I think she works up on the second floor, but I'm sure if you hurry, you might be able to catch her."

His smile widens and we stand for a few seconds, staring at each other.

"Did you know you have a vampire in your class?" he says finally.

"Really?" I ask, my thoughts immediately going to Axel. If Axel isn't a vampire name, I don't know what is.

"The tall, dark-haired woman who arrived late," he continues.

I screw my face up in disbelief. "Karolina?"

Vincent nods. "I noticed when she arrived. The absence of a heartbeat, you see? It's something I always pick up on. Though I didn't the first time I was here. But then, I was too distracted to see or hear anything but you that night. I even missed the smell of a dead rat."

My heart thuds beneath my rib cage, a blush climbing my neck. "I couldn't exactly think straight either. I still can't."

"Me neither," he murmurs. "Shall we go?" He pulls the key fob to the car from his pocket, spinning it expertly around his index finger.

My stomach flutters as we trail out into the corridor. Now there's nothing but a car journey standing between us and the empty apartment. Feeling nervous, I wipe sweaty palms on my work skirt.

Vincent flashes me a reassuring smile. His eyes are

rounded, as if he can read my thoughts. "So you had no idea about this Karolina?"

I shake my head. "She gave me a card tonight that reads 'Witchcraft and Psychic Services.'"

"That's interesting," he murmurs. "If she's genuine."

"Are there genuine witches and psychics?"

He holds the door to the stairs open for me. "I believe so, though I've never met one myself."

"A vampire witch," I mutter as he falls into step beside me, our jacket sleeves brushing as we climb the stairs.

"It's an interesting concept. When a human turns vampire, any special gifts or talents from the human life are magnified. A person with that kind of gift could become quite powerful."

"What were your special gifts and talents?" I tease. "Excellent cooking and good manners?"

He throws me a sideways glance, smiling. "Is that all I'm good for?"

I blush, thinking of what happened in his car earlier. "No. I can think of something else."

"I can think of something you're good at too," he says, splaying his fingers and lacing them through mine.

I stop at the top of the stairs, our fingers still entwined, a tingly warmth radiating from his touch. "I don't usually go around doing that in cars, you know? In fact, the whole morning was out of the ordinary."

A shadow of anxiety flits across his handsome features. "I hope I didn't make you do anything you didn't want to, Mila. I—"

"No," I interrupt. "I didn't mean that. I liked it. All of it." I prod his shoulder with an index finger. "How could

I not?" Sensing his moral compass is spiraling over our delicate situation, I jerk my head toward the door. "Shall we talk about this at home—I mean, at your home?"

He squeezes my hand. "Yes."

All the way back to Farringdon, the tension builds, as if the oxygen has been sucked from the air. He stalls the car twice at traffic lights, apologizing and looking flustered, raking nervous hands through his messy hair. I always thought confidence was sexy in a man, but watching him falling to pieces over the idea of us being alone leaves me longing to rip his fly down and bury my head in his lap all over again. By the time we pull into the parking lot, my whole body and every nerve ending is thrumming with want.

I'm almost considering making a move in the elevator up to his apartment, but a woman in gym gear gets in on the first floor and rides all the way up with us. While we're standing there, politely staring up at the floor indicator, I slip a hand under his suit jacket, hooking a thumb into the belt at his waist. He flinches, staring down at me with burning topaz eyes. Naked fear and desire swirl together in his gaze, instantly robbing me of my cocksureness. My knees tremble beneath my skirt.

When the apartment door slams behind us and Vincent has performed his usual sweep of the apartment to make sure there are no serial killers lurking, we turn to face each other. He shoves his hands deep into his pockets, a tiny pulse throbbing in his angular jaw. I slide my gaze over him—the suit jacket stretched tight over his broad shoulders, the planes of muscle visible beneath his shirt, the perfect V of his torso.

I gulp. "I think I'm going to go and change," I say, jabbing a thumb over my shoulder. He nods, watching me leave. I get so flustered I yank open a closet door instead of the one leading to the bedrooms. I blink in confusion for a few seconds, staring into the gloomy space at the vacuum cleaner and mop bucket.

"I didn't think overalls were your thing, but if that's what turns you on, I'm sure Hilda won't mind you borrowing them," he says from behind me.

My face on fire, I turn to find him smirking. "You make your cleaning lady wear a uniform?"

He laughs, deep and satisfying. "No, I think she wears it so she doesn't get her things dirty."

I shut the closet door and open the right one. "Aha! Got it. I'll be right back."

I take the fastest shower of my life, scrubbing at my skin with fruity bodywash and lathering my hair into a frenzy with the shampoo and conditioner. After rinsing, I wrench a comb through the tangles and wrap myself in a towel, stepping back into the guest bedroom.

Now I have a dilemma. Do I slink out there in pajamas or wear a full set of clothes? I stand with my pajama shorts in one hand and a pair of jeans in the other, weighing my options. In the end, I ditch both and settle for a gray sundress I used to wear on Sundays in Australia. Only this time I wear it with ultra-expensive La Perla undies, hidden like secret weapons beneath the soft cotton.

After a quick brush of my teeth, I give my lashes a swipe of mascara and blast my hair with the dryer. This is precisely why a person isn't supposed to hook up with a housemate. They know exactly how long you're spending getting ready for them. I take a deep, shaky breath before stepping out into the lounge.

Vincent is in the kitchenette, stirring a teapot. His hand stills as I step into the room, eyes lingering on the hem and neckline of my dress. My heart lurches in my chest. I'm not the only one who's had a change of clothes, it seems. He's wearing a faded green T-shirt that strains against his bulging biceps, with a pair of blue Levi's slung low on his slender hips. His blond hair is damp from the shower, dark and falling in messy waves over the tips of his ears. My insides melt.

"I thought I'd make some tea," he says.

I don't want tea. I want him.

I take a few steps closer. "Are you always this domestic?"

"No," he says, pouring dark-brown liquid into a mug. "But it's different having you here. Don't tell Lee Davies or he'll tell me I need to relocate my balls, but it's nice having someone to look after."

"Like a pet?" I ask, smirking.

He shakes his head. "Not like a pet. Like a beautiful woman I'm rapidly becoming a slave to." He speaks with a twinkle in his eye, but the words are prickly in his throat, as if beneath the joke, he means it.

"Vincent," I say, my breathing growing faster. "Put the teapot down."

It lands with a clunk on the countertop.

"See?" he says in a hoarse voice, his eyes piercing mine. "I'm a slave."

I don't see him move, not even a blur, but suddenly

I'm in his arms, my body pressed tight to his, my toes barely brushing the floor as his lips hover over mine. "Mila," he whispers. My heart is racing, pulse pounding through every inch of my body, coming alive at his touch. "If there is any part of you that thinks this is a bad idea, you have to tell me now."

I press my palms into the hard ridges of his back, as if my fingers might sear through the thin material that separates his skin from mine, and inhale his intoxicating scent—aftershave, mint, fresh linen. How can any of this be a bad idea when I feel this way?

"This isn't a bad idea," I say, losing myself in the silvery flecks of his eyes, the exquisite angles of his face. "Trust me, I've had plenty. I would know the signs."

"I'm scared, Mila," he says, running his hands through my hair. "This. You. It scares me."

My chest tightens. "I'm afraid too."

Because the ridiculous truth is, the idea of Vincent catching the killer and me going back to my old life scares me more than anything else.

He lifts me off my feet and carries me effortlessly across the room to the sofa—the place we've spent so many hours *not touching*. The spot where I made him watch all those romantic dramas, the movies Laura and I thought real life could never live up to. As he lays me down flat, a knee on either side of my hips, and peels off his T-shirt, I can only think how wrong we were. Real life has played its trump card.

I reach up, tracing fingers across the ridges of his sculpted muscles, satin stretched over steel. His skin is warm beneath my fingers, hot and hard as burning iron.

"You're beautiful," I say, resting my hand on the waist of his jeans and twisting open the top button.

He shakes his head and smiles. "No, *you're* what's beautiful in this world, Mila."

As he reaches down to the hem of my flimsy dress, a wave of insecurity rolls over me. I grab his hands. "You should know, there are marks and lumps and parts that mean I'll never be Playmate calendar material."

"You don't get it, do you?" he says, placing a kiss at the corner of my mouth. "To me, you're perfect. Even if there were fish scales under this dress, I will never see you as anything less."

Jack. Pot.

I arch my back from the sofa, allowing him to lift off the dress, saying a silent prayer of thanks to La Perla and all its lacy magic as he leans back on his haunches, sweeping a drowsy, heavy-lidded gaze over my body.

"This is beauty," he says, placing burning hands on my hip bones, slipping thumbs beneath the string of my panties and sliding them down over my legs.

I writhe under his touch, the need for him burning away my insecurity. I reach behind my back to undo my bra, and he peels it off, tossing it aside. Hooking an ankle around his hip bone, I drag him close, running my hands over the firm, silky skin of his shoulders and chest.

My hands trembling, I undo the rest of the buttons to his jeans, smothering a gasp of delight as his erection springs out, thick and hard, from an explosion of soft, downy hair. I hungrily stroke its satiny length, eliciting a moan from deep inside his throat as he thrusts against my hand.

With a growl, he grasps my wrist. "If you keep doing that, I'll lose my mind again," he says in a raspy voice. "And I have plans for you before that happens."

I sit up to slide his jeans down his hips, and he stands, wriggling out of them and tossing them aside. He leans over me, hands on either side of my shoulders, tendons cording the length of his strong arms. Outside, the sun has almost disappeared beneath the horizon, the light from distant skyscrapers casting his body in a soft, burnished glow.

I gulp, staring into the gap between our bodies, trying to memorize his perfectly sculpted shape—long, muscled legs, lean hips, a firm swell of buttocks. I spread my legs the width of the sofa, inviting him in, wanting nothing more than the feel of his rough fingertips inside me, the bristle of stubble against my thigh.

Lowering himself into the nook of my body, he kisses me on the mouth, hands tangling into my hair, tongue sliding over mine in lazy rhythm.

I meant what I said to Laura about feeling it down to my toes. It's the kind of kiss that suspends time, scattering every thought like leaves on the wind. I melt in his arms, my core blooming hotter and wetter with every gentle thrust of his tongue, until I'm nothing but a puddle of simmering desire.

By the time his hand works its way between my thighs, I can barely remember my own name. I break the kiss and emit a low hiss of pleasure, my head tipping backward as he glides expert fingers through my soaking folds, rubbing my clit in torturous circles with his thumb.

Then his lips nudge their way down my neck, burning into my skin with the heat of a thousand suns. I twist my body, my hands burying themselves in his damp hair as I guide his mouth onto one of my hardened nipples, moaning as he sucks the tip between his lips, flicking at it with his rough tongue.

When he slides a finger inside my core, my breath catches in my throat. I tug at his hair, a stream of incomprehensible words erupting from my lips. It's like my brain is living solely at my nerve endings, at all the places his hands and lips and tongue are connecting with my body, abandoning speech and rational thought in pursuit of greater things.

I cry out, feral and wild, as he thrusts his fingers deeper, lapping at my nipples. Unable to take any more, my core spasms around him as I climax, tipping me into an abyss of ecstasy.

"Vincent!" His name explodes from my throat as waves of bliss pour over me. Just when I think it's slowing down, he moves lower, hooking my trembling legs over his shoulders and licking my soaked opening, his tongue pushing against my sensitive walls until I'm rocked by another white-hot orgasm.

When I return to my body, I fall back against the couch, hands on my head, a sweaty mess of spent pleasure as he ghosts kisses between my hip bone and up over my tummy.

"Wha—" I gulp, unable to recall the English language. "Why—how—oh God."

Vincent extracts himself from my legs and stares into my face. "Are you okay?"

I laugh crazily at the absurdity of his question, my breathing ragged. "Vincent. I'm ruined."

Smiling, he circles a thumb into the underside of my breast, brushing wet lips across my nipple. "Then prepare for further ruination, Miss Hart."

He lifts me up so I'm sitting in his lap, nose to nose, my knees either side of his muscular thighs, his arms wrapped around my waist.

"This is what I was really thinking about all those times we sat watching television," he whispers, wriggling so that his hard length springs up between us.

I smile. "Even in the middle of *Dr. Quinn*?"

He grins. "Especially during *Dr. Quinn*."

With one hand resting on his chest, I reach down to stroke his velvety length, mesmerized as his jaw slackens, his eyelids fluttering.

"Mila," he murmurs, his hands moving to grasp me beneath the buttocks, his mouth working its way along my collarbone.

I push myself onto my knees, teasing the glistening tip of his erection along the wet slit of my entrance.

"Yes," he says, the word coming out like a hiss of steam. "Please, Mila. I need to be in you."

Pushing up higher, so that my chest is level with his face, I position myself over his hard length. He presses warm fingers into my lower back, his mouth latching on to a nipple, before thrusting deep inside me.

Stars explode behind my eyes. We both cry out. The feeling of him, hard and thick, is the most perfect thing that's ever happened to me. This time when I come, I shatter, as if I'm a piece of glass hitting the ground from a great height, fragments scattering like debris after a blast. Then I hear Vincent's groans clashing with my own as he pours into me, his head collapsing into the space between my shoulder and jaw, the hard swell of his body going limp.

How is it possible to go from being Netflix buddies to *this* in the space of twenty-four hours?

We don't make any attempt to move for a long while. His face remains buried in my neck, his moisture mingling with mine, beads of perspiration clinging to our skin.

I'm the first to break the silence. "Hilda won't be happy we stained the couch."

Vincent is quiet for a second before bursting into laughter. He sits back, gazing lazily into my eyes. "It's about time she earned her keep."

I take a playful swipe at his shoulder. "Beast. I hope she's in the union."

He smiles, his gaze never straying from my face. He brushes damp hair from my eyes as I run my fingertips along his jaw. I explore his face with my hands, the exquisite lines of his face—a bump in his otherwise straight nose, the sweep of lashes on his cheek. He is perfect. Like a statue brought to life. A fairy-tale prince.

"So, what shall we watch on TV tonight?" I tease.

He chuckles, leaning forward to brush a kiss against my lips. "Nothing. I'm taking you to bed and we're not leaving for *many, many* hours."

"Is that a police order?" I ask, wide-eyed.

His eyes flash in amusement. "It's a police command."

I smile. "You might have to carry me. I'm not sure I'll ever walk again."

He rises off the sofa, keeping my jelly legs wrapped tightly around his hips. "Your room or mine?"

Chapter 12

Vincent

"Vincent? How come you haven't bitten me yet?"

Several hours have passed since making love on the sofa, and we're lying on the guest bed. Her peachy body is nestled into the nook between my knees and chin, our limbs knotted up like vines. I've been drawing lazy circles around her belly button with an index finger, my face buried in the tousled hair at the nape of her neck. She smells incredible, like honeysuckle after a rainstorm mixed with good, clean sweat. Though we've been making love for hours, I'm hard and ready to go again.

My hand stills midstroke. The truth is I've gotten good at controlling my fangs over the years. The last thing I want to do is scare her off.

"I would never bite you," I say gently. "Not unless you asked me to."

I try to keep my tone neutral, as if I'm telling her it doesn't matter what kind of pizza we order, because of course I want to bite her—the urge comes from the same place as wanting to slide my tongue inside her core, to suck her nipples until she screams with pleasure. But those are human urges, whereas biting and drinking blood are entirely vampiric.

She turns over, resting her head in the curve of my arm and tracing a line through the ridges of my chest with her finger. "So you'd want to if I asked? I mean, it couldn't turn me into a vampire, could it?"

I sigh, twirling tendrils of her honey-colored hair around my fingertips. The idea of her seeing me fanged is as terrifying as it is arousing. It could change everything between us, bring back memories of the night she was almost killed. It would also reveal me for what I truly am—a freak of nature who can never give her the life she deserves.

"No, it isn't possible for me to turn you or anyone into a vampire," I say, frowning. "That's not the issue."

"Then what is?" she asks, wide-eyed.

I take a deep breath. "Often when a vampire bites a human, the human loses consciousness for a few moments. There's this thing we call a life essence. It's like an exchange: as the vampire absorbs blood, the person he or she is biting sees a vision—a montage of moments in the vampire's life that are important to them."

She frowns. "I see."

"But more importantly, I'm supposed to be protecting you. I've already crossed the line."

Her frown fades as she smiles. "That's putting it mildly. We're so far over the line it's on a different hemisphere."

I chuckle, dropping my hand to her breast and brushing a thumb over a silky tip. It hardens at once and I groan, pressing my lips to her open mouth and kissing her deeply. She clings to me, small moans of pleasure escaping from her throat. The last of my resolve disintegrated to dust during that moment on the sofa, when I slid inside her tight, hot sheath for the first time and felt the whole world turn on its axis. There is no going back now.

I roll her over, spreading her legs wide with my knees, her burgeoning heat beckoning me in.

"Mila," I groan between kisses. "How will I ever live without this?"

"I've been asking myself the same question," she whispers, her head tipped back against the pillows, exposing the satiny, white column on her neck.

My fangs prick at my gums, but I fight them back.

"Do it. Bite me," Mila hisses. She writhes around beneath me, rubbing her soaked core against my skin and sending my erection into overdrive. My cock twitches as if it's on the end of a string.

"No," I whisper, beginning to pant. "You have your party tomorrow night. You won't heal. Please, Mila. Don't tempt me."

She brings her hands up, holding my face steady above hers. "Then at least let me see them. I want to know all of you. It won't change the way I feel, Vincent. Nothing will."

This time when my gums prickle, I let the fangs slip out, watching her face in silence.

She holds a finger up to them, as if she's Sleeping Beauty touching the spindle of a spinning wheel.

"They're sharp," she murmurs.

Her eyes retain their drowsy look of lust, and when she coils a hand around my head and draws my lips toward hers, I sag in relief. She places a kiss on each fang. "They're sexy. You're sexy."

Some of my anxiety melts away. "You don't know how relieved I am to hear you say that."

"If you won't bite me, use them on me. I want to feel them on my skin."

Staring into her shining eyes, I release a sigh of pure happiness. I lean down to her breasts, round and heavy with need, scraping my fangs gently around the sensitive skin of her nipples before sucking one between my lips.

Her back arches, a breath catching in her throat. "Keep going," she urges.

I dip lower, the sweet aroma of her arousal filling my senses. My cock is so hard it's verging on painful as I graze the soft skin of her inner thigh.

"Lick me," she says desperately, as if it's been hours and not just minutes since her last orgasm.

My tongue sweeps through her core, the prow of a ship parting the ocean, and she bucks her hips, forcing me deeper into her glistening, pink flesh. Just when I feel her start to contract tightly around me, I pull out, guiding my bulging length into her entrance and burying myself to the hilt inside her. She comes at once, her sheath tightening around me, sucking me in. If only we could stay in this moment forever, our two bodies merged as one. This is how immortality should be lived.

Though I'm about to explode, I manage to hold back, watching as she climaxes, her eyes half-closed, her pink lips parted in a perfect O. Her body shudders, her heart thumping as the waves of pleasure hit. She repeats my name over and over.

I have lived for over two hundred years, have watched the sun rise and set on every continent, in almost every country known to man, but I've never been so moved as

I am by the sight and sound of this woman falling apart beneath me.

When she reaches up and twists her fingers into my hair, tugging at the ends, I plunge back into her, enjoying her gasp of surprise. A few seconds later, my own orgasm takes hold—powerful and even more satisfying now that I don't have my fangs to control. I spill into her, not just with my body but with my mind as well. Anything she wants is hers. I would give her the sun and the moon if she asked.

After, we lie tangled together in a tight knit of limbs, my head buried in her soft breasts, her arms wrapped tight around my neck and shoulders. I lost track of the time hours ago, but it feels past midnight. The city is dark and silent outside the window.

"Do you make all women feel this way?" Mila asks suddenly.

I lift my head from the swell of her cleavage to meet her tawny-eyed gaze. "Which way?"

She averts her eyes, worrying at her plump bottom lip. On impulse, I push myself up onto my elbows and draw it into my mouth, sucking on it the way I've been longing to since we met.

She sighs, raking fingers through my hair. "I mean with the orgasms and stuff. Is that one of those special gifts you were talking about earlier? Exceptional lover?"

"I'm not sure. I mean, there have never been any complaints, but nor have there been any medals of honor."

She chuckles, flicking my shoulder. "It's just I've never felt like that before. During sex, I mean."

"Like what?"

Her face turns a vibrant shade of pink. "You're going to force me to say it, aren't you?"

"No. Not unless you want to."

She slaps a hand over her face. "I never had an orgasm before you."

I grin from ear to ear, my heart bursting with joy. I've never been the possessive type, but the idea that I might be able to give her something no other man can fills me with an inflated sense of pride.

"Am I pathetic?" she continues.

I move her hands away from her face. "No. It's different from anything I've ever experienced too."

"You've lived for centuries. How can that be?"

I trail the back of a hand over her flushed cheek. "It just is."

She searches my face, her hair splayed across the pillow like a shot of spun gold. "Are you sure you're not just being a gentleman?"

Shaking my head, I say, "I'm not convinced there's a gentlemanly bone left in my body after the kinds of things we've gotten up to tonight."

"Vincent?"

I lean forward, pressing a kiss to her soft lips. "Hmm?"

"Were you ever married?"

The words hit me like a gust of cold air. We were always going to discuss the past eventually; I'd just hoped it would be later rather than sooner.

"Yes," I say. "A very long time ago. When I was human."

"Was it happy?" There is a tinge of regret in her voice, as if she's sorry she asked.

I shake my head, pleased that on this occasion the truth will not hurt her. "No, it wasn't happy. There has to be love for a marriage to be happy and we never loved each other."

She visibly brightens. "Why did you marry her, then? If you didn't love her?"

I roll off, turning her on her side so we're nose to nose, my arm coiled around her waist, her sweet breath warming my skin. "It was arranged between our families, before we were born. That's the way it worked in those days within nobility. Marriage was a business contract, each family getting something out of the union. My family needed her money and her family needed our good name. It was the perfect match for them."

"Didn't you mind? Marrying someone you didn't love?"

"Yes, I minded a great deal," I murmur. "Particularly as I was in love with someone else at the time."

Her face drops. I know how she feels—punched in the gut. I feel the same whenever she mentions anything to do with Australia or that scumbag ex of hers.

Lips turned down at the corners, she says, "Oh. That sucks."

I smooth hair away from her beautiful face, urging her to meet my gaze. "It was a really long time ago, Mila. I was a completely different person in those days. If you went back in time and we met, you might not even recognize me. My hair was long and I wore tights."

"Tights?" she repeats, grinning.

I smile back, relieved to lighten the mood. "Personal hygiene wasn't so hot in those days either."

We both chuckle. I rub lazy circles into the peach-soft skin of her lower back.

"Tights and long hair can be pretty hot," she says. "In a *Dangerous Liaisons* sort of way."

"Is that another movie?"

She nods. "I'll add it to the list."

I narrow the tiny gap between us and kiss her, loving the way she moans deep in her throat, her hands burning a trail over my chest and torso.

"Stop trying to change the subject by kissing me," she whispers breathlessly, drawing back.

"I wasn't," I murmur.

"Tell me how you became a vampire."

That takes the wind out of my sails. My shoulders droop. Like most vampires, I'm not overly fond of telling the tale. An immortal life means always moving forward, and in truth, most of us would rather forget.

"Unless you don't want to. I understand if it's too painful," she says, her hazel eyes rounded.

I stare into her pretty face, but this time, I see only the miniature portrait hidden in my bedroom drawer, the amber eyes and ink-black hair of its sitter. If I tell Mila about how I turned, chances are I'll have to tell her about Adrienne and how she died. Will she look at me the same way when she knows the truth about that night? How I was responsible for the death of the only woman I ever loved?

I swallow heavily. Unflinching honesty has always been my curse, but she has a right to know. If we carry on in this vein, someday she will need to decide if I'm worth the sacrifice of a normal life.

"I wish you hadn't asked." My voice is hoarse as I rake my fingers through her hair. It's too soon to lose her.

She grips my wrists. "I'm sorry. Forget I said anything. I'm too nosy for my own good. My mum always says I'll grow old and be one of those women twitching behind their net curtains."

"No, it's okay. I want to tell you." I press a kiss onto her forehead before reaching down to draw the sheet over us. She laughs as I plump the pillows.

"Geez, how long will this story take?" she asks.

"I just want you to be comfortable," I say, dropping back onto the bed beside her and weaving my legs through hers. I figure I might as well make the most of being able to touch her. She mightn't want anything to do with me before long.

She yawns, stretching out like a cat. "Tell me."

I take a deep breath, wondering if, like Scheherazade of *The Thousand and One Nights*, I could spin the story out for a few years. At the very least until morning.

"Like I mentioned before, I was born in France in the eighteenth century. As the son of a duke, my family was well connected, friends to the court of King Louis XVI. I grew up with every privilege." I pause, remembering our large chateau in the South of France: sharp-edged lawns sloping down to the sea, the scent of lavender and roses mingling on a salty breeze.

"It was a happy childhood. My mother and father were almost never around, but my siblings and I had good nursemaids. We wanted for nothing. There was a girl I grew up with—she was the woman I mentioned being in love with when I married my wife." I take a deep breath, my throat tightening as I swallow her name. "Her father was our gamekeeper at our chateau in the South of France. She was not of my class, so marrying her was out of the question. If I had, my father would have disowned me and no doubt evicted her family from their home. She had several brothers and sisters—a dozen lives would have been ruined. Besides, I was extraordinarily pragmatic back then and felt a great duty toward my family."

Mila gives a little snort. "You haven't changed so much."

I grin, tickling her sides. "The old me would never have relinquished my police duties to fraternize with the witness, no matter how sexy and alluring."

She narrows her eyes playfully. "I'd have managed to seduce you somehow."

I try my best to ignore the pulse of arousal I feel at her words, but gazing into her pretty face, her complexion soft and dewy from our lovemaking, it's hard to believe she doesn't have a point.

"But you didn't marry her? You married someone else instead?" she asks.

"Yes, a daughter of another aristocratic family. Then after we wed, shortly before the French Revolution, an unusual gentleman arrived at the court of Louis XVI."

"Wait," she interrupts, holding up a hand. "You were in the king's court?"

I nod. "My wife was a lady-in-waiting to Marie Antoinette."

Mila's jaw drops. "But isn't she that famous woman who died on the guillotine and said—"

"'Let them eat cake.' Yes. That's her. Though I'm not convinced she used those exact words."

I see a faded image of the lady herself in my mind's eye—ivory skin, silvery-blond hair the hue of gossamer. She was more faerie than human. Born into such extravagant wealth she truly held no notion of anything less.

"If you were the son of a duke, why did your wife have to work as a maid?"

"In those days, ladies-in-waiting weren't servants. They were companions, handpicked from noble families. They lived at the court, away from their husbands. Like I said, our marriage was arranged and we didn't love each other. Aside from our wedding night, we slept separately, so the arrangement suited us."

Her brows knit together. "Love or no love, she must have fancied you. Was she gay?"

I chuckle, leaning forward to land a quick kiss on the end of her nose. "Not all women find me irresistible. As I recall, she had a bit of a thing for her father's Master of the Horse. She held no interest in me."

"Oh, come on," she says, smirking. "I mean, you're sex on a stick."

My hand slips from her back to the curve of her bottom, my cock stirring as I massage her soft skin. "You're not so bad yourself," I say in a low voice.

Smiling, she reaches behind and moves my hand back to her waist. "There will be plenty of time for that later. Now, carry on. What did *you* do back then?"

I emit a lusty sigh. "I was a courtier to the king. Which was a sort of male version of a lady-in-waiting.

We hung out with him, hunted, drank, gambled. That was pretty much it."

"What was he like? The king?"

"He was a sensitive man. I got the impression he'd rather not have been king. That's the odd thing about power—the ones who can handle it don't want it in the first place."

"And you mentioned an unusual guy arriving at court. Who was he?"

"At court, he masqueraded as a Scottish laird banished from his lands by the English—the king and queen had a penchant for surrounding themselves with people of interest. In reality he was a vampire. An ancient."

"Ancient?"

"Yes. There is a group of old vampires. They're the only ones capable of turning humans. They're stronger and faster than the rest of us, and until recently, it was thought nothing could harm them. But then one was killed by an old curse. Afterward, all the vampires she'd made across the centuries turned back into their human selves. Which was handy for us at the Met Police because she was a psychopath, and her subjects were mainly killers. Most of them are now languishing in jail."

Mila pales. "What are you planning to do? If you catch Jeremiah Lopez? Would a prison hold a vampire?"

I shake my head. "No. He would be *disposed of*."

"How?"

I move a hand to cup her face. "There's only one way to kill a vampire, and that's decapitation."

She recoils in horror. I can practically see the cogs in her mind turning. "Who would do it?"

I drop my gaze to her hand, curled on my chest. "Me. I'm the only one fast enough."

"But that's dangerous! He could kill you."

"It's unlikely."

"Unlikely?" she echoes incredulously.

"Mila," I say softly, stroking her cheek. "I've faced worse than Jeremiah Lopez or whoever he really is."

The words do little to ease the crease in her brow. "What happens to a vampire when they die?"

"We go to our graves as if the vampiric life was never lived at all. In other words, the body decomposes. Fast. In a way, we're already dead."

Her fingers come up to my face, tracing the line of my jaw, making me shiver. "You're not dead, Vincent."

I cover her fingers with mine, touched by her concern—there's been no one who would miss me for many, many years.

She gulps, opening her mouth and closing it again, as if she wanted to say something but changed her mind. Then she says, "Carry on with what you were saying about the ancient in the king's court."

"Right. The ancient, Gregor McLaren, lived among us at court. No one suspected he was anyone other than who he said he was. They were hedonistic times— people lived to excess, and Gregor fit right in. He was there many months before I saw the first sign of what he was. By that point, the French Revolution was in full swing. The king and queen were sent to Tuileries Palace to be kept under surveillance. I think it was the revolution which drew him to court. He'd been around so long, lived through so many monumental moments in history, that he liked the thrill of a front row seat. He certainly got one with us. We were all there when an armed mob stormed the palace and began killing people."

Mila sucks in a breath. "Oh my God."

"The royal family were led out through the gardens, but I was one of the last to leave. I noticed Gregor was in no hurry. Everyone else was in a state of pure panic, but Gregor seemed amused by all the chaos. At the time, I thought he must have seen worse in the barbaric Highlands. As I fled after the others, I called to him, but he hung back, as if waiting to be caught. Then the door to the lounge burst open and a group of men appeared, brandishing swords and other weapons. I was halfway out an open window in the corner of the room at this point. I froze as the men landed on Gregor, expecting him to be murdered and mutilated in front of me. Instead I saw a blur of movement and heard screaming. When the calamity was over, the lifeless bodies of the men were piled in a bloody heap at the center of the room. Gregor was laughing, as carefree as if he'd just won at faro, sharp fangs the same chalk white as his powdered wig, spilling from his lips like shark's teeth. It was at that moment he spotted me, still half hanging from the ground floor window. In all the excitement, he hadn't even realized I was there."

Mila gasps, squeezing my hand. "Oh shit. Is that when he turned you?"

"No, he merely stared at me across the heap of torn flesh with a glare as cold and hard as diamonds. Like a coward, I fled."

"That's not cowardly, Vincent. That's common

sense. I would have been screaming and fainting all over the place."

I smile. "I never said I wasn't screaming and I certainly felt like fainting. Afterward, I told myself I had hallucinated and imagined the whole thing, especially when Gregor showed up later like nothing happened."

"What did he say to you?"

"Oddly enough, we didn't talk about it—there was so much going on at the time—but I started to watch him closely. I noticed how fast he moved, and then one afternoon, after losing at cards, he crumbled the stem of a goblet into dust."

"When did you find out for certain?"

"After I was arrested. They were rounding up nobles on charges of counterrevolution. My parents, myself, and most of the court were flung into prison. Gregor McLaren came along for the ride. One night, he approached me. He told me what he was—an ancient vampire, a demon, undead."

Mila frowns. "Wasn't he afraid you would tell everyone?"

"He must have had an inkling most of us wouldn't live to tell the tale. And after I hadn't said anything about that day at Tuileries, he'd developed a high regard for me." My throat tightens, though this isn't the worst part of the story. Not by a long shot. "He offered to turn me and I accepted."

"Just like that?" she asks in disbelief.

I loosen my grip on her waist, staring over her head toward the dark square of the window. I gaze at the same stars that looked down on me back then, in an airless cell crawling with rats and filled with the stench of human waste, the same stars that will continue to shine long after the beautiful mortal in my arms is dead.

No matter what happens, life isn't fair. It never will be.

"I knew we were going to die," I say, my voice a whisper. "The guards spoke of nothing but the revolution with each other, all through the night. There was no way I would be leaving that cell. Yet I wasn't afraid to die. That isn't why I accepted his offer. I accepted because of the girl back home. If I died in Paris I would never have seen her again. I acted from my own self-ish desires—the desire for a new life. One without constraints. A life where I could be in control, marry whomever I wanted to marry, be rich and free at the same time."

Mila goes quiet, staring off into space. Like a coward, I silently pray she doesn't ask about the girl. Though I owe her the truth, I suddenly can't bear the idea of losing her so quickly.

"Did you manage to break out?" she asks, brow knotted.

"Not right away. New vampires are susceptible to daylight, as well as silver, crucifixes, holy water—all the clichés are true in those first few weeks. After the transition period is over, nothing can hurt us."

"I wondered where all that stuff came from," she says. "What happened after you were free?"

"The first thing I did was break out my mother and father. After a couple of months, I could bend metal—new vampires are exceedingly strong. I helped as many as I could to escape. My mother and father were horrified at the change in me—they didn't fully understand what I'd become—and after they were free, I never saw them again. I remember the look in their eyes the last time we were together—pure horror, as if I were a stranger and not their own flesh and blood. I've felt like a monster ever since. A freak of nature."

Mila brushes hair from my face, tangling her fingers into my hair. "You're not a monster, Vincent," she whispers.

I open my mouth, fully prepared to tell her what happened next, why she's wrong in more ways than she knows, but instead I lean in and kiss her softly, relieved beyond measure as she responds, pulling me closer, her warm breasts pressed up against my chest, sending a zing of arousal straight to the tip of my cock.

"If you were a monster, I wouldn't want to do this," she whispers, rolling on top of me, her blond hair falling around us like a curtain.

I brush strands of hair aside and gaze up into her hazel eyes. I should tell her now about Adrienne—there will never be a better moment—but my tongue will not form the words, my jaw wired closed.

I choose the present over the past, losing myself to the heat of her body on mine, my old life and all its horrors slipping away like a bad dream, into the furthest reaches of my mind.

Chapter 13

Mila

THE NEXT MORNING, I WAKE UP TO DAZZLING WHITE sunlight at the back of my eyelids and wonder if I dreamed it all.

But then I feel a warm, strong hand splayed on my thigh, legs intertwined with mine, and the unmistakable scent of musky man permeating my nostrils. I whisper a silent *amen* to the heavens. I'm not usually a religious person, but after this twist of fate, I'm convinced there is a God.

And He is good.

I stir, furrowing deeper into the mattress, smiling as Vincent's hand moves to my tummy, dragging me backward into the snug warmth of his chest, soft downy hairs tickling my spine.

"Morning," he says throatily, brushing my hair aside and pressing hot kisses into my shoulders.

I release a sigh of pure contentment. "Morning."

Part of me begins to grieve for a future when I will not wake up like this—a knot of tangled sheets, my bottom pressed against his stirring groin, expert hands torturing me with soft, circular caresses. If I could freeze time and live in one moment forever, this would be it.

I turn over, burying myself in his embrace, wanting to drown in the hard and soft lines of his body.

I want to know nothing more of the world than his touch and smell, his smooth skin golden in the light from the window.

"Let's never leave this bed," I murmur.

He chuckles, rough fingertips inching their way up my inner thigh.

"I'm serious. If we locked the door and closed all the blinds, how long do you think it would be before they broke the doors down?"

"A few days," he says, the words vibrating through me as he moves his lips against my neck. "I don't think my superiors would take kindly to our new situation."

A breath catches in my throat as his fingers probe the warmth between my legs. "Vincent," I gasp. "Keep going."

He smiles into my lips. "I have no intention of stopping."

———————

A couple of hours later, I'm wrapped in a towel at the kitchen island, watching a shirtless Vincent make me boiled eggs. He's saying something about French cooking, but I'm not listening. I'm too busy admiring the play of muscles and tendons under his satiny skin as he lifts a carton of eggs from the fridge. If men who looked this good never wore shirts, the world would be a better place.

"Don't put the eggs in until the water is boiling," I say, coming back to my senses as he flips open the carton.

"Yes, ma'am," he says, a wry smile on his lips.

"And throw some salt into the water. Otherwise the shells might crack. Have you seriously never made boiled eggs before?"

"I have, but they always end up too hard."

I lay a hand over my chest. "It's a good thing I'm here, Vincenzo—boiled eggs are one of the few things I can make without screwing things up. Now, the trick is, lower the eggs in carefully from the edge of a spoon. Then as soon as they're in, you put the bread in the toaster. The art is in the synchronization."

"Ah, so it's all about timing," he says, putting the first egg on a dessert spoon. "That makes sense."

"Exactly. Timing is everything."

He turns back to the bubbling pan of water and lowers the egg in, giving me a good view of his ripped back and fine ass. A slow, involuntary whistle of appreciation slips out from between my lips.

"Did you just whistle at me?" he asks, sliding the second egg into the pan.

"I think it was the wind," I say innocently. "It's drafty up here in the penthouse. You should consider closing a window."

He grins, shaking his head and taking another egg from the carton. In a flash, he pushes down the lever on the toaster. "Fast enough?" he asks, cocking a brow.

"Excellent. Now set the timer for three and a half minutes."

He snatches up a little egg-shaped timer and twists the dial around. "Are you always this bossy in the kitchen?"

"Only about eggs."

He chuckles, reaching into the cupboard and taking out an unopened box of egg cups. "So, what time does the party kick off this evening?"

My stomach plummets. I've been racking my brain

all morning for an excuse not to go to my cousin's engagement party tonight, but Mum is suspicious enough already that something is going on. If I don't show, she'll have a total meltdown and wind up at my flat in Finsbury Park. Where I won't be.

I sigh. "We can get there about six."

The party is being held at a village hall in Kent, where I grew up. Running my gaze over Vincent, it isn't hard to imagine what everyone's reaction will be when I rock up tonight with him on my arm. They will totally lose their shit, and I'll be asked about the hot blond man for the rest of my days. I gulp, staring at his handsome face as he rips open the packet of egg cups, doubts creeping into my head like rats at a door. What am I thinking, opening my heart up like this again? Playing make-believe that the kind, good-looking man before me could be my boyfriend?

Just then the timer goes off, ringing and bouncing on the countertop. "The eggs," I shriek. "Go, go, go!"

Vincent moves in a blur of speed. Within a few seconds, the eggs and two slices of buttered toast are on a plate in front of me. He holds out a cutlery knife. "Would you like to do the honors?"

"You do it," I urge. "I always burn my fingers."

He turns the knife and lops off the heads of the eggs in two neat flicks. A rich, yellow yolk oozes over the edges as we beam at each other.

"Perfect. They're not hard," I say, high-fiving him and taking a bite of toast.

"The eggs aren't, no," he mutters, ghosting a hand along my bare arm, almost making me choke on my bread.

My eyes flick to the bulge in his tracksuit bottoms, making me sway a little on the stool. "That's enough smutty remarks, Inspector."

He pulls out the stool opposite and slides onto the seat. "My apologies, Miss Hart."

Dipping a strip of toast into the creamy yolk, I quirk a brow. "There's nothing sexy about boiled eggs."

He leans across to wipe a stray crumb from my chin, blue eyes burning. "There is when you're around."

I'm considering putting the piece of soggy bread down and kissing him when the sound of someone pounding on the front door breaks the spell.

I frown as he slides off the stool. "Will that be Hilda?"

"I doubt it. It's Saturday, and besides, she has her own key."

I carry on eating as he disappears into the hallway, shutting the door behind him. After a few seconds, I hear the distant rumble of voices.

It isn't until the door is flung open like a loose screen in a hurricane and the balding head of Sergeant Lee Davies appears that I remember I'm wrapped in a towel. Not one of the large types either—no, this one barely covers my ass. Vincent jumps between us too late. Davies's wide eyes flit from the towel to Vincent's naked torso and back again. I wrap my arms around my middle self-consciously, realizing it probably looks like we were having sex right before he arrived. I mean, we kind of had been, give or take twenty minutes, but it's still mortifying.

I bounce off the stool, my face burning. "I'll go get dressed."

The short distance from the kitchenette to the bedrooms brings a new level of meaning to the phrase *walk of shame*.

As soon as the door closes behind me, I hear Davies's blunt cockney tones erupt. "What's going on here, then? Laundry day, is it? Both of you ran out of clothing?"

When I emerge a few minutes later, in black leggings and a long-sleeved sweater, Davies is slumped on the sofa like a broken puppet, rubbing the bridge of his nose and breathing heavily. At first I think he's having some sort of panic attack, but then as I get closer, I realize he's fighting back tears. Vincent looks up as I approach, his blue eyes round with sympathy.

"Mila, Davies's wife has left him."

I sink like a stone onto the sofa opposite. "Oh." As soon as my backside connects with the seat, Davies flips his head up, eyes swollen and red.

"She's kicked me out. I confronted her about everything, just like you said, and she admitted it all. Except it wasn't because of what happened in Essex. She says she loves him."

At the word *love*, his head lolls forward and he dissolves into tears. Vincent slips into the seat next to him, giving him a pat on the back.

I spring up from the sofa as if electrocuted. "I'll make a cup of tea."

Vincent glances up, flashing me a grateful smile as I scurry off to the kitchen, across the room.

"I saw Marjorie from three doors down on my way out," Lee says between sobs. "She says the bastard isn't even good looking. Says he has greasy hair and sideburns that need trimming, and once he left her husband's brand-new lawn mower outside the front door without even knocking. I mean, what kind of heartless bastard does a thing like that? He didn't even put a card through the letterbox—it got rained on."

"Bastard," Vincent agrees, patting at his shoulder again. "Shall we get Janie at work to have a dig around? See what she can get on him?"

After I've filled the kettle and flicked the switch, I have a good gawk at Lee Davies in turmoil. I've seen women crying over men a hundred times. Back when my dad left us, Mum took to her bed and cried for a month solid. But seeing a man in the same situation is strange. It's not something you see every day.

While watching the spectacle unfold, I notice a slightly worrying sight at the edge of the coffee table—a bulging, black suitcase that he wouldn't have brought from his car unless he plans to stay. Which would just about take the cake. I have plans for Vincent and me, and they most definitely do not require an audience. Or clothing, for that matter.

After adding two sugars and a gallon of milk to Davies's tea, I carry the mug back to the lounge and plant it on the coffee table in front of him. He snatches it up immediately and leans back into the sofa, eyes closed.

I seize the opportunity to widen my eyes at Vincent, jabbing a finger in the direction of the black suitcase.

Vincent shrugs before clearing his throat. "I guess you'll being staying with your mother for the time being, then?"

One of Lee's eyes pops open, flickering between us.

I know instantly he isn't fooled. "I was hoping it might be all right to stay here for a few days," he says. "I know the guest room is taken by Mila here, but I'll be fine with the sofa. Unless…"

"Unless what?" Vincent asks.

Lee's brows twitch, some of the twinkle returning to his gray eyes. "Unless there's suddenly another room available." He sits up straight in the chair, some of the tea sloshing onto his beige golfing slacks. "Or I could bunk in with you, Vince."

Vincent and I exchange fleeting and horrified glances.

"You snore," Vincent says quickly. "I'll take the sofa, you can have my room. I don't really sleep anyway."

Lee's eyes flicker to me. "I bet you don't. But anyway, the sofa is fine. I'm not sure I'd get much sleep in your bedroom. The soundproofing in these places is atrocious."

Heat creeps up my neck and I push myself from up from the sofa. "I'm going to get my outfit ready for tonight," I say, eager to escape Lee's knowing stare.

I've just made it into my room when Vincent appears. He wraps strong arms around me, thrusting me up onto the bedroom wall, his chest pressed tight against my breasts, the thick rope of his hard length digging into my groin. I melt into him like hot lava spilling down the side of a volcano.

"God, Mila, I'm so sorry. I'll call Burke right away. Maybe Lee can stay with him until he sorts things out with his wife."

"It's okay," I say, looping my arms around his neck. "He should stay. He's your friend. Do you think he's guessed about us?"

Vincent nods. "But he won't say anything. He'll just tease us mercilessly until one of us beats him to death with Hilda's industrial-size iron."

I chuckle, leaning my warm forehead against his cool one. "What will we do? I can't not kiss you or touch you. I'll explode into a thousand burning embers of lust."

He groans, grinding me harder into the wall. "I missed you. How is that possible? It's only been twenty minutes since we were last alone."

"I don't know," I say, panting slightly as he works a hand beneath my top and begins swirling a rough thumb around my nipple. "But I missed you too."

I knot my hands into his hair and mash my lips against his, groaning as he begins rubbing his erection against me.

The moment dies when Lee Davies's voice drifts out from the lounge: "Got any biscuits to go with that tea, Vince?"

Vincent and I freeze.

"Yep," I whisper, leaning out of the kiss. "Call Burke as soon as you can."

~∙∙∙~

"We're doing it all backward," Vincent says later as we weave our way out of the underground parking garage.

I straighten my dress. After restraining ourselves for the rest of the afternoon, things heated up when we finally made it out of the apartment. Vincent's carefully styled hair is now stuck up like wild grass, and I have pinpricks of stubble rash on my jaw.

"How so?" I say, pressing a button on the door to open the window. In true British style, the weather has turned on a pin. It is heavy and humid, yet the sun is nowhere to be seen. The sky is a deep lilac as clouds gather ominously on the horizon.

"We moved in together, then we slept together, and now I'm meeting your mother."

I smile, reaching across to smooth his mussed hair. "The first one won't be forever."

Though, God, I wish it were.

"Maybe when this is over, we can do things how people normally would," he continues.

"What, sleep with me and then ignore my text messages?"

He glances over, eyes dark against the backdrop of the lilac sky. "No. I simply meant go on a date. Maybe the opera. I have a box, you know."

"A box?"

"At the Royal Opera House in Covent Garden."

I wrinkle my nose. "Really? So that's what you did for entertainment before me and the Netflix premium package arrived."

He chuckles. "Yes, as it happens. Would it be your sort of thing?"

"Hmmm, let's see—a dark room, a private box, and you. I think I could handle it. As long as there are Magnums."

"Of champagne?"

"The ice cream."

"Ah."

The dense clouds disappear as we break away from the gray bulk of the city, a few silvery threads of light peeking through the clouds here and there. On one of the Porsche's tiny backseats is a large bunch of flowers. The stuffy air is filled with the rampant scent of lilies, roses, and gerberas. Vincent had them delivered earlier. Not for me, and not even for my cousin Elizabeth, whose engagement party we're attending, but for my mother. The guy buys flowers for mothers.

"It's the right thing to do," he said when I came out of the bedroom to find the ginormous spray covering most of the kitchen counter. "I'm your pretend boyfriend meeting your mother for the first time. Don't all young folks offer a gift when they meet a loved one's family?"

Davies snorted in derision from his position on the couch. He'd already made himself at home, cramming sour cream Pringles into his mouth with one hand and channel-hopping with the other. "Only if you've knocked up their daughter," he said cynically, shaking his head. "Jesus, Vince, this is the twenty-first century, not *Pride and Prejudice*."

"Well, I think it's really sweet," I said, glaring at Davies. "Plus, it might overwhelm her so she won't ask too many questions about how we met."

Vincent nodded, flashing me a secret smile, and I'd swayed a little toward him, unsteady in my heels.

Back in the present, I smooth down the full skirt of my two-tone dress. The bottom half is sugar pink and lacy, falling just below my knees, and the top half is white satin, the sleeveless style showing off the last of my Australian tan. I had worried it was too fussy and princess-like—it's not really a sexy dress—but Vincent's face when I'd stumbled out from the bedroom laid those fears to rest. For the first time in my whole life, a man looked at me as if I were the sun rising over the mountains. The cold beer he'd just retrieved from the fridge for Lee Davies slid through his fingers and smashed on the floor, and I couldn't help but wonder if it was a symbol of broken things to come. Things like my heart.

"Has Burke made any progress with the case?" I ask, thinking perhaps Lee Davies had brought information with him.

"Burke hasn't, no, but I'm waiting on some new leads. Going through the official channels is always time-consuming."

I nod, staring out of the car window as the hills roll by, moss green and endless. The notion of Jeremiah Lopez being brought to justice fills me with fresh dread now that I know Vincent will be the one dispensing his punishment.

I feel Vincent's eyes on me. "Mila, do you mind me asking something? You've never mentioned your father. Will he be at the party?"

My mouth goes dry. I get the same slapped-in-the-face feeling I always do when I'm asked about him. Most of the time I prefer to pretend he doesn't exist.

"No. He left us years ago when I was thirteen. He lives up north somewhere—with a new family."

A dent appears in Vincent's brow. "I'm sorry to hear that, Mila."

I wave a hand dismissively, the gesture I've been making since my teens. "It doesn't matter. I don't miss him."

Vincent's eyes are soft. "Were you very distressed? When it happened?"

"Yes. Particularly because I was always a daddy's girl. But I wasn't hit as hard as my mother. She was devastated. Luckily I'm the youngest, and we were all old enough to fend for ourselves."

He places a hand on my knee, as if his touch might melt away the hurt of the past.

Before Laura did interior design, she studied psychology at university. Once she suggested that my appalling dating history isn't bad luck at all; instead, I subconsciously pick unsuitable men as a way of replicating the pattern of my childhood—growing close to a man and then having him leave me. The conversation caused one of the biggest arguments we've ever had. But sometimes, I wonder if it's true. Maybe this relationship with Vincent is an extension of the pattern. After all, there's no future with a man who won't age, who can't give me a family.

Suddenly my mood is darker than the clouds on the horizon.

Vincent squeezes my leg. "I'm an idiot. I shouldn't ask you about it right before a party."

"No, it's fine," I say, covering his smooth, golden hand with mine. "I like sharing things with you."

He smiles, lifting his knuckles so our fingers lock together. "I like sharing things with you too."

When we arrive, the party is in full swing. A few people I've never met are hanging around outside the front doors, smoking and laughing as the strains of an acoustic guitar drift out from the hall.

Although the music doesn't stop when we walk in, what feels like a million heads swivel in our direction. I can almost hear their thoughts—Mila, romantic pariah, has a man on her arm at last.

The spacious hall is low lit and decked out in pink and white balloons, strings of heart-shaped fairy lights strung across the ceiling. It isn't long before Mum appears, cutting across the room faster than a puppy chasing a pork chop. She never got to meet Scott the douchebag, so she's hungry for this. And let's face it, Vincent is unlikely to disappoint.

Mum—who is five foot five like me—never wears heels, so she has to lean back to gander at the handsome man clutching the ridiculously large bunch of flowers. She is so mesmerized she completely forgets to greet me.

"Are you Vincent?" she asks, extending a hand. From the hopeful note in her voice, you'd think she's meeting Jesus Christ himself.

"I am," he says, taking her small, pudgy hand in his long, tapered fingers. "You must be Mrs. Hart, Mila's mother?"

Mum nods, her free hand resting limply at the base of her throat. "I don't think Mila's ever been out with anyone who wears suits before."

I roll my eyes. "Yes, I have, Mum," I mutter through gritted teeth.

But neither of them is listening. Vincent holds out the bouquet. "These are for you, Mrs. Hart. Mila already has a gift for the happy couple, but I wanted to express how sincerely pleased I am to meet you."

Mum eyes the flowers as if he's holding out a million-dollar check, her eyes glassy with moisture. "That is so kind," she says, patting her short bobbed hair and accepting the bouquet.

Then without so much as a nod in my direction, she grabs him by the elbow. "Come and meet the family."

Vincent pauses to flash me a brief smile before allowing her to manhandle him across the room. He disappears into a melee of elderly relatives who swoop like wasps around a candy wrapper.

So there it is. Now my mother will probably never get over him either. Maybe we can form a support group.

Someone taps my shoulder. "Ahem."

I whirl around to find Laura and Tom standing behind me. Judging by the bottle of champagne Tom is holding, they've only just arrived too.

"Laura!" It feels like years since I last saw her. We hug fiercely for a few seconds before she breaks away, her eyes sweeping the room like searchlights.

"Where is he?" she demands as I give Tom a quick hug.

"Over there," I say, jabbing a thumb in the direction of the table full of elderly relatives where Vincent is holding court.

I delight in watching Laura's jaw drop. "Holy mother of God, angels walk among us."

"Laura," Tom says, smiling awkwardly. "Your husband is in the room."

"Is he?" she says, her wide eyes fixed on Vincent. She smooths down her shiny, dark hair. "He's exactly as I pictured he would be."

Tom looks faintly appalled. "When exactly have you been doing this *picturing*?"

"Oh relax, Tom, you know I don't go for blonds."

Tom shakes his head and smiles, but when he looks away, Laura feigns a swoon, fanning herself with her hand.

"Seeing as my wife is incapacitated by another man's beauty, I'll go say hi to our hosts," Tom says good-naturedly, heading over to the table laden with gifts and depositing the champagne.

As soon as he's out of earshot, Laura's head swivels back around. "So tell me everything that's happened since we last spoke."

I drag her outside, where the smokers are puffing away, and tell her as discreetly as I can about our night of all-consuming passion.

"What did he say about the future?" she demands. "Would he be willing to adopt?"

I shake my head in disbelief. "Do you really think I'm going to ask him if he wants children when we haven't even been on a date?"

Laura quirks a smile. "Not even a date and you're shagging. So much for *The Rules*. Did he bite you?"

"No. But I wanted him to. I don't think there's anything I wouldn't do with him."

She sighs dreamily. "I love relationship beginnings."

"We don't know this is the beginning of anything. Besides, you're forgetting I'm usually about the endings. Lots and lots of endings."

But Laura isn't listening; she's leaning backward and peering into the party. "Geez, the old people still have him hostage in there. I'm going to go and introduce myself."

"What?"

But it's too late—she's already swanning confidently across the room. I didn't even remind her to play it cool.

As it transpires, I don't have time to worry about what she might be saying. I'm soon swept up into a million conversations with relatives I haven't seen since before I left for Australia. At one point, I briefly glimpse Laura sitting with Vincent. His eyes are creased at the corners, and he laughs as my best friend wildly gesticulates some unheard story. I dread to think what it's about. The time whizzes by—each time I try to seek out Vincent, another person accosts me. Laura and Tom make it back to me before he does.

"I like him," Laura says grinning.

I narrow my eyes. "What did you say?"

"I just told him a few stories about our misspent youth. Don't worry," she adds as my eyes widen. "Nothing about guys. He really likes you, Mila. He was lapping it up faster than an alcoholic at a wine tasting. Even Tom thinks he's into you."

Tom cocks a brow. "Men don't do family unless they're serious."

"Not even under duress?" I say, assuming Laura's told him about the police protection.

Tom shrugs. "He doesn't have to talk to them. He could protect you just as well from the sidelines."

I'm about to respond when the microphone on stage whines sharply and the singer of the band announces they're going to play the bride- and groom-to-be's favorite song. Instinctively I begin to shuffle backward. Our family occasions always seem to involve a slow dance. I've lost count of the number of times I've had to sway about with Great Aunt Eileen to "Lady in Red."

But tonight is different. I hear a deep cough, and when I glance over my shoulder, Vincent is standing a few feet away. He smiles at me through dark-blond lashes, eyes glittering beneath the fairy lights like blue diamonds.

"I thought I'd lost you," I say, unable to keep a huge grin from breaking out across my face. "What were you talking about for so long? Bingo tips? The merits of rationing during World War II?"

He lifts an index finger, eyes narrowed playfully. "Did you know your uncle Patrick thinks he was Napoleon in a past life?"

I burst out laughing. "I should have warned you about that."

The song begins and the people around us start swaying from side to side like pendulums.

"Shall we?" Vincent asks, holding out his hand, palm up.

It's the easiest question I've ever had to answer. I step toward him and lay my hand in his. "Don't expect me to be able to waltz, Mr. Son of a Duke. Because 'La Macarena' is about the limit of my dancing abilities."

"Isn't that a village in Andalucía?" he asks, curling warm fingers around mine.

"No, it's a dance song."

In my heels, my head fits perfectly into the gap between his shoulder and chin. I loop my arms around him, brushing the hairs at the nape of his neck, the skin at his collar velvety soft beneath my fingertips. His scent is both comforting and arousing—freshly ironed clothes and cologne, a hint of leather. He releases a faint sigh as he holds me lightly around the waist, the warmth from his hands searing through my dress.

Even though we spent the best part of last night and most of today naked in each other's arms, there is an intimacy, a vulnerability to dancing that seems distinct from all that. It feels a little like we're strangers again, staring at each other in the darkness of a police car. I blush as fiercely as I did that night as we begin to sway in time to the music, my heart pounding against his chest as our bodies inch closer.

Though it's true I'm not much of a dancer, I needn't have worried. He moves for the both of us, graceful and long-limbed, turning me so that the lacy skirt of my dress fans out around us in a frothy halo. I forget there are other people on the dance floor, losing myself in a sea of him.

"Vincent?" I whisper into the collar of his shirt.

He glances down at me, golden lashes feathered on angular cheekbones, his eyes glazed and drowsy. "Yes?"

"I was thinking how this party would have gone if what happened between us didn't happen. I might be dancing with Great Aunt Eileen by now."

He chuckles, his chest vibrating against my chin. "I still would have asked you to dance. Would you have accepted?"

"Yes. You know, for appearance's sake."

We smile and he slowly ducks his head, capturing my lips with his.

"By the way, I'm going to have to arrest you later," he murmurs into my lips. "Laura informed me about the stolen Pokémon cards racket when you were eleven."

"Oh," I say, eyes wide. "Well, be sure to use the handcuffs on me. I'll come quietly if you do."

Leaning down to my ear, he whispers, "There'll be no coming quietly if I have any say in the matter." He presses himself against me, making sure I get the meaning.

"Let's leave," I say, my whole body growing unbearably hot and heavy. "As soon as the song ends, we'll slip out."

"Okay. Though I'll have to say a quick goodbye to your mother."

I roll my eyes. "She has the flowers. You're already her benchmark of potential son-in-law perfection."

He chuckles. "It's only polite."

After the dance, it takes us a while to extract ourselves from the gaggle of relatives who gather around to say goodbye. I guess they think it might be another three years before they see me again and possibly a whole lifetime before I bring another boyfriend to a party.

When we finally make it back to the car, I'm surprised to discover it's still light out. A glowing blue sky shot with silvery streaks of cloud. "Do you think Davies might have fallen asleep by now?" I ask.

"I hope so. If not, go straight to my room—it's farthest away from the lounge—and I'll meet you there after ten minutes."

I smile. "Don't keep me waiting."

He leans in, fastening soft lips to mine. "I couldn't wait if I tried."

———∿∿∿———

Back at the apartment, Davies is sprawled out across the sofa in a bathrobe. The TV is blaring, the sound of machine gun fire erupting from the speakers. He barely rouses as we enter the room.

"Good party?" he asks eventually, eyes still glued to the screen.

"Yes, thanks," Vincent says, frowning at the TV. "Let me guess—*Die Hard*?"

"Back to back. I'm on *Die Hard 2*."

I stretch my arms in an exaggerated way. "Well, I'm beat. I'll leave you boys to it."

Vincent stares at Lee meaningfully. "I think I'll turn in too. Maybe I'll call Catherine and see if she has any information for me."

Lee ignores us. Another explosion erupts from the screen, casting Davies's plump face in a yellow glow. While the going is good, I make a dash for the bedrooms, Vincent hot on my tail.

Just as the door is about to click softly shut behind us, Lee says loudly, "Have a good shag, you two."

Vincent's broad-shouldered frame stiffens, but he keeps walking. We make it to his bedroom before dissolving into fits of laughter.

"So much for being subtle," I say, sweeping my gaze over Vincent's things.

The room is almost double the size of the guest room and painted in a soft shade of forest green. A huge rosewood bed with beautifully carved rolled ends takes center stage, white sheets and a diamond quilt coverlet stretched across it. Beneath the window is an ancient-looking chest of drawers, several black-and-white photographs in small frames arranged on top. Unlike the other rooms, thick and expensive gold carpet covers the floor.

I kick my heels off, feeling the springy fibers spread between my toes. This room is noticeably more lived-in than the rest of the apartment had been before I arrived—crisp shirts are hanging everywhere, empty coffee cups clustered on the bedside cabinets. My eye is drawn to a large portrait hanging on the wall above an antique cabinet. I step closer, tilting my head. Even if the group in the painting weren't dressed in old-fashioned clothing—frilly shirts, long-tail coats, the woman in a tight corset with an impossibly tall wig—I would know it's centuries old by the cracked paint and the chipped gold of the gilt frame.

Peering closer, I ask, "Who are they?"

"My family," Vincent says in a fragile voice.

"You mean... Are you in it?"

He nods and I step closer to examine the figures. The woman in the tall, silvery wig sits on a red velvet chair, a middle-aged man standing to her left, and around them are three children, presumably Vincent and his siblings. A little girl in the foreground kneels at her mother's feet in a white, lacy dress—she looks about twelve and has a pile of golden ringlets cascading around her soft, pale face.

The other two siblings are young men. One sits on a red chair similar to his mother's, his father's hand resting on his shoulder. The other stands beside him, a hand on the hilt of a sword at his waist. They each have the same build—tall and strapping—but the one sitting has dark eyes, a heavy jaw. The one with the sword, however, is undoubtedly Vincent—the angular bone structure, a tiny bump on the bridge of his nose. The only physical difference is the long hair tied back at the nape of his neck. Steely arrogance lurks behind the blue eyes of the

Vincent in the portrait, a superiority that seems to shine from the depths of his ivory face.

"Do you recognize me yet?" Vincent asks, standing beside me.

"Yes," I say, smiling. "But you look a bit mean."

He grins. "Like I told you, I was a different man back then."

I glance between Vincent and the painting, trying to reconcile the pair—to get my head around the fact that in another few hundred years, he will still be alive, whereas I'll be long gone, fragments of bone and dust lost on the wind. His immortality strikes like a blow to the chest. There will be no growing old together, no pushing our grandchildren on the swings at the park. All the things you're supposed to have with the love of your life can never happen with Vincent Ferrer. I bite the inside of my cheek to keep a sob from rising up my throat. The last few nights have been magical and perfect, but they were bubbles: beautiful but temporary.

"Mila, say something. What are you thinking?"

I turn to face him. "Nothing. It's just—you really are a vampire, aren't you?"

He nods sadly, brushing my jaw with the backs of his fingers. "I'm sorry. I wish it could be different."

"No." I hold a finger to his lips. "Don't be sorry. There's no need to apologize for who you are."

He takes my wrist and turns me around, his fingers threading themselves into my hair. "Mila," he whispers, "beautiful Mila."

I let him kiss me, but mixed with the passion and desire

is sadness, a broken dream. The kiss grows fierce—as passion always does when it's to be short-lived—and I cup his face, rubbing my thumbs along his stubbly jaw as my tongue slides over his, surrendering myself to him. When we break apart and he leads me over to the bed, I say, "Will you bite me tonight?"

His eyes widen. "Mila, I want you to know it isn't necessary. I don't need it in any way. You're enough for me. More than enough."

I shove him gently onto the coverlet, positioning myself between his legs. He may not need it, but I do. Tonight, I need a physical reminder of why I'll never get to keep him, so I can stop kidding myself, open my eyes to the reality lurking at the bottom of our situation.

"But I want you to," I whisper, leaning down to kiss him.

He groans and falls back onto the bed, pulling me on top of him, his hands dropping to the hem of my lacy dress.

"Take it off," I urge between kisses. I straddle his hips, my trembling fingers already working on the buttons of his shirt.

His fingers find the zipper, tugging it down, and he peels it over my head, his hands coming to rest around my waist, rough fingers rubbing circles into my skin. He gazes up at me, his blue eyes vulnerable, as if it's him about to get his heart broken and not me.

"Your turn," I say, finally freeing the last button. "I command you to disrobe."

He chuckles but makes no attempt to move. Instead he continues to gaze into my eyes, his hands moving from my waist to my hair, where he pulls it back at the nape of my neck, running an index finger along the line of my jaw.

"What if I refuse to bite you?"

I smile, moving a hand to the thick, hard bulge in his trousers. "You won't," I say, watching his eyes narrow, eyelids growing heavy with lust. "Now strip before you make me angry."

His eyes crinkle at the corners as he laughs. "I'm the one with the handcuffs, remember, Little Miss Pokémon Card Thief?"

"In that case, maybe you should take control."

In the blink of an eye, he shifts our positions, rolling on top of me. I push the shirt off his muscled shoulders, digging my fingers into his satiny flesh, spreading my legs wide so he rests in the juncture between my thighs.

His belt rattles as he eases himself from his clothing. I unhook my bra, flinging it across the room, and then his bare skin is on mine, delicious, warm friction the only thing between us. He moans and I sigh, and we pause for a second, locked in a tight embrace, enjoying the warmth of our bodies pressed together.

"I'm not sure I'll ever get over this," he says hoarsely, burying his lips into my neck.

"That makes two of us," I murmur, as he kisses his way up to my mouth.

He places his hands on either side of my head, lifting his chest and torso to create a gap between our bodies, before running a flat palm over my breasts, pausing only to pinch a hard tip as he works a hand between my legs. When his fingers find my wet warmth, I cry out, arching against his hand as he pushes a finger deep inside me.

I writhe around like a woman possessed, an aching wave of ecstasy building as he explores my inner walls.

"Don't stop," I say, panting. "Please don't ever stop."

"Mila," he whispers into my neck.

I open my eyes and rake my hands through his hair. "Your fangs. I want to see them."

He raises his head and I lift a finger to the sharp, white canines. Without meaning to, I press too hard, a droplet of crimson beading on my fingertip. Vincent takes my wrist and sucks the blood off, moaning low in his throat.

"God," he says, his voice little more than a crackle. "You taste sweet. Like ripe fruit in the sun."

"Then have more," I say. "Take it."

Eyes burning, he trails kisses over my breasts and stomach, working his mouth lower and lower until his tongue reaches the slick folds between my legs. I moan loudly, all thoughts of Davies out in the lounge disappearing from my mind. There is only Vincent and me in the whole world.

My hands grab fistfuls of his blond hair as he buries his face in my heat. His tongue flicks at my bud, sending tiny electrical jolts of pleasure shooting through me as his hands knead my buttocks. When he pushes his hot, wet tongue into my core, I'm unable to hold myself together—my walls clench, my whole body shuddering as wave upon wave of smoldering ecstasy washes over me. No wonder the French word for *climax* translates to *little death*—it feels like I'm burning, shattering into a million pieces ready to be snatched away on the wind.

Just when I'm about to lose myself to the stars

exploding behind my eyes, Vincent's lips work a path back to my face. He positions his hard tip at my entrance and thrusts inside me, making me die all over again, contracting and spasming in white-hot pleasure as he plunges in and out in a glorious rhythm, my hips bucking from the bed. Then he stills, shouting my name before exploding in an orgasm of his own, oozing warmth mingling with mine.

"Bite me," I manage to say between ragged breaths. Even though he's inside me and we're as close as two people can get, I still need more.

Between my thighs, his body tenses. My back arches from the bed and I tip my head, exposing my throat. "Do it. Don't hold back. Please."

"Mila," he breathes, brushing tendrils of hair from my neck and pressing a soft kiss into the hollow at the base of my throat.

I lean back farther into the coverlet, my body still tingling from orgasm. "Please," I repeat, wrapping my legs around his hips and balling the quilt in my fists. "I don't care about the life essence. Just do it."

His fangs scrape my collarbone and then two sharp points slide into my skin. A hiss of satisfaction escapes my lips as they sink deeper, pleasure and pain intermingling, melting into waves of bliss. I hear my pulse, fierce like a drum, and then I'm falling, like Alice down the rabbit hole, fading into unconsciousness, to a place where I'm no longer Mila at all.

I'm standing beside a field of waving, yellow wheat, a golden sun hanging low in the sky. A woman emerges from the tall stalks, a beautiful young lady with waist-length, inky black hair and stunning amber eyes the same shade as the horizon. She calls my name by way of greeting—Vincent—and my chest is crushed by a fierce sensation of love. She beckons with one hand, walking backward into the field, inviting me after her.

The scene shifts and I'm hurtling through undergrowth. The sky is dark, the moon a glowing smudge behind silvery streaks of cloud. I erupt from the trees into a clearing. Beyond is a drop, the ocean stretching before me on the horizon, the light of the moon glinting off the water like broken glass. Then I'm plunging forward, long wet grass soaking through my shoes. A woman screams and I see the same girl from the wheat field, only this time her amber eyes glow with terror. I call to her as she backs away, trying to shorten the gap between us, but she only yells at me to keep away, grasping at her left hand and tearing a gold ring from her finger before throwing it to the ground. She is perilously close to the edge of the cliff, but as I take a step closer, begging her to be careful, she recoils in fear, plunging over the edge.

A shrill cry cuts through the air like a knife.

I fling myself after her, finding her on the jagged gray rocks where the sea hits, white foam spraying up over her broken, twisted body. I haul her into my arms but it is too late; her gaze is dark with loathing as she takes her final breath of air.

When the life goes out of her amber eyes, I rise up from the scene, out of the blackness and into reality where I am Mila once more.

Vincent holds me against him, exactly like he once

held the dying woman. Though my body still hums with pleasure, my mind is foggy. I blink up at Vincent, disorientated. "How long was I out?" I ask, lifting my head from his chest.

"Only a minute or so. Are you okay?" Fear swirls within the blue depths of his eyes.

I nod, too groggy to know what I feel. "Who was the woman?"

"I should have told you last night," he says, a knot forming in the middle of his smooth forehead. "That was Adrienne. Adrienne Moreau. She was the girl I grew up with. The woman I loved during the revolution."

My stomach clenches and I briefly close my eyes, remembering how she plunged into the darkness, her scream dying on the wind. I sit up in his lap, my gaze snagging on several spots of blood, bright red against the white cotton sheets. I put a hand to my neck, feeling two tiny puncture marks above my collarbone. "When did she die?" I ask, wanting to forget about what I saw but, at the same time, needing to know what happened.

Vincent blots the bite marks with his thumb, and takes a deep, shuddering breath. "After I freed my mother and father, I left Paris and headed south to see her. I was so naive, I had this crazy idea she might have the ancient turn her too, so we could be together for eternity."

I watch as his eyes darken with self-loathing.

"She was afraid of you," I say.

He nods. "I should have broached the subject gently, in daylight, when there were plenty of others around. But instead I went at night, appeared at her bedroom window like a deranged Romeo, and asked her to walk with me.

She came so willingly. Trusted me utterly. Back then, as a new vampire, I wasn't good at controlling my fangs. They slid out as I kissed her. I bit her—it was an accident, but I drew blood. When she pulled away and saw both the crimson stain on her skin and my fangs, she was petrified. I tried to tell her what happened, but she wouldn't listen. She ran away."

"She thought you would kill her," I murmur, remembering her pretty face contorted in terror. She'd been as afraid as I was that night Jeremiah Lopez almost murdered me in the alleyway.

Vincent lifts a hand to touch my face, but at the last moment thinks better of it, his gaze wandering to the droplets of blood on the sheets. "Yes. Before I knew where she was headed, we were at the edge of my father's estate, near the cliffs that dropped into the sea. I was pleading with her, but she was screaming at me not to touch her. She tore off the family ring I gifted her before the revolution and threw it to the ground, cursing me to an eternity in hell. I stepped forward to grab her—I was worried she was going to fall—but as I reached out, she sprang backward, tumbling over the edge. She died hating me, believing I wanted to kill her, when all I ever wanted was for us to be together."

A thick silence flows into the room, the distant hum of the air-conditioning unit the only sound. Vincent's features are twisted in torment; a tiny pulse throbs at the corner of his jaw.

"This has haunted you ever since, hasn't it?"

His blue eyes meet mine. "Always. I can never forgive myself. After Adrienne died I left France. I went south to Italy, fighting alongside the Italians in the war against Napoleon's army. Though I knew it was impossible, for years I hoped I'd be killed on the battlefields. I ran headfirst into every cavalry charge, threw myself in front of every weapon. I wanted nothing more than to die. After Italy came Russia. I followed a path of war across the globe, hiding among common soldiers from vampire society. It wasn't until I came to London in the twentieth century that I finally stumbled across Ronin McDermott again, the ancient who turned me. For years I'd avoided him. But when vampires revealed themselves and I secured my first official job with the Met Police, I couldn't hide any longer. Being part of society meant sacrificing my anonymity. Suddenly the whole world seemed to know what I was." He averts his gaze, focusing on the tiny bite marks on my neck, his brows pulled low. "The truth is, I'm a coward, Mila. A coward who's spent most of his life wanting to die. There's nothing heroic about me. Nothing at all."

I take his hand, threading my fingers through his, feeling him jerk in surprise as I lay a palm on his warm cheek. "What happened to Adrienne was terrible and desperately sad. But it was an accident, a tragic accident—one you've punished yourself over for too long."

He shakes his head. "I completely understand if you want nothing more to do with me."

"Vincent," I say, rubbing a thumb into his angular jaw. "This doesn't change the way I feel about you."

A crease dents the space between his brows. "It should."

I shake my head vigorously. "No, it shouldn't. No

one should be defined by their past. What matters is who we are today. Trust me, I've watched a shedload of Dr. Phil over the years."

"I caused the death of the woman I loved," he says grimly. "I'm a monster."

I screw my face up. "Vincent, you're the nicest guy I've ever met. Not every man would be willing to invite a stranger into his home and let her take over the place. There's a nail polish stain on the sofa, by the way," I say with a smile. "I hid it with a cushion but now seems like a good time to mention it."

He chuckles, some of the anxiety melting from his face. "You could blow up the Porsche and I wouldn't care." He toys with a strand of my hair. "I wish I could believe I haven't disappointed you."

I press a kiss into his stubbly jaw. "Believe it."

His lips curve into a smile as he draws me close, his mouth fastening to mine in a deep, consuming kiss.

Suddenly he breaks away, staring down at me with worried eyes. "The bite... I didn't hurt you, did I?"

My fingers drift to the marks. They feel bruised, as if I've had two tiny injections there, but they're not painful. "I liked it," I say. "Not so much the vision part, but the biting was *erotic*."

He smiles, leaning in to kiss me again but then pulling back at the last moment. "By the way—"

"Yes?"

"Who's Dr. Phil?"

Chapter 14

Vincent

MILA FALLS ASLEEP AROUND MIDNIGHT, TWO TINY RED bite marks visible on her slender neck.

As soon as she drifts into slumber, a powerful surge of regret rears up inside me—I should never have bitten her, should never have risked her witnessing the night Adrienne died. It was ridiculous to think that, after all these years, my essence might have changed. I'd stupidly hoped she might see herself, recognize in it the depth of my feelings. But alas, the past is inescapable. Now, having seen the beast inside me, it's only a matter of time before this ends.

I brush blond tresses from her sleeping face, coiling them beneath her chin to cover the puncture marks. With her spill of golden hair against the white pillowcase and dark lashes feathered against her flushed pink cheeks, she looks like an angel. A knot as tight as a fist squeezes my heart at the thought of a future without her.

After arranging the coverlet into a cocoon around her sleeping body, I slide out of bed and pull on my boxers, closing the bedroom door gently behind me as I slip into the lounge.

Davies is sitting up fast asleep on the sofa, a pair of headphones over his ears and his laptop open in front of him. I remove the headphones and prod his shoulder.

His eyes flicker open. "Oh, it's you," he says, stretching into a yawn. "What time is it?"

"About half past twelve."

Davies cuts me a disapproving gaze. "Have you been going all that time? What are you? A Duracell bunny?"

I laugh, heading for the kitchen where I flick the kettle on. "Coffee?"

He folds his laptop closed with a snap. "White with two."

I lift two mugs from the cupboard, waiting for his next wisecrack.

"So, what are your intentions toward the young lady?" he asks, crossing the room, hands shoved into the pockets of his tracksuit bottoms.

"Weren't you all for this a week ago?" I ask.

Davies looks sheepish, breaking eye contact. "That was before I got to know her—before I saw the way she looks at you."

"How does she look at me?" I ask, on a knife's edge of desperation.

"Like you're her knight in shining Armani."

I sigh. Even if that were true, after tonight she'll see me as anything but.

"Seriously," he continues. "When you mentioned the flowers for her mother, I thought she was going to swoon at your feet."

I hold up a hand. "Enough."

"Don't pretend you're not besotted either. Unless now you've slept with her…"

"Now I've slept with her what?" I snap.

"You've lost interest."

I'm just about to set him straight when my phone begins buzzing on the kitchen counter. I hold up an index finger to Davies and accept the call. "Vincent Ferrer."

For a short time, no one speaks. All I hear is a thud of techno music in the background. But then a familiar voice crackles down the line.

Ronin McDermott.

"I have the name for you," he says. "I'm at the club."

The line goes dead. Typical Ronin. He always had a penchant for the dramatic.

Davies frowns. "Who was that?"

"Ronin McDermott," I say tersely. I fire off a text asking him to send the name, though deep down I know there's no way I'll get a response. "He wants me to visit him at the club. He says he knows who our killer is."

Davies sways, looking as if someone's hit him. "Fucking shit."

We both lapse into silence, the kettle switch cutting through the tension like a gunshot.

"Could we send Burke?" Lee asks.

The thought of Linton Burke in Ronin's vampire club brings a smile to both our faces. It's like imagining a vicar in a lap-dancing bar. He would probably try to arrest people for indecent exposure.

"I wish," I say grimly. I glance toward the bedrooms, picturing Mila asleep in my room. With Davies here, she'd be fine if I left her. She would probably never even know I had gone.

Unless I don't come back. But that isn't worth thinking about.

"I can get there and back within half an hour," I tell Lee. "Will you do me a favor and sit outside my bedroom for me? Make sure Mila is okay? Sometimes she has nightmares."

"She'll get the shock of her life if she wakes up to find the likes of me hovering at the end of the bed. That'll give her nightmares, all right."

I shake my head, suppressing a chuckle. "No, I mean, she might wake and come looking for me. If she does, tell her I have an errand to attend to and I'll be back soon. I'll double lock the window in my room before I leave."

Lee makes a salute. "Guard the queen. Got it."

"You're a good friend, Lee."

He quirks a brow. "Is this the part where we man hug?"

"Only if you want to."

He shrugs awkwardly. "Nah, let's save it for a special occasion."

I flash him a smile. "Agreed."

I slink into my bedroom as quiet as a cat. Mila has turned onto her side, a long, bare leg half out of the sheet. Though the last thing I want is to wake her, I lean over and press a kiss to her cheek, trailing fingers along the soft curve of jaw. "I'll be right back," I whisper, and because there is no one to hear me, I finish with, "my love."

She snorts in response, her nose wrinkling. Even making piggy noises, she is the most beautiful creature I've ever seen.

God, give me more time with her. Don't take her from me yet.

After double locking the windows and throwing on my discarded suit from the party, I steal one last glance at Mila's peaceful face before slipping from the room.

Davies is nursing a mug of steaming coffee in the kitchen. "I was thinking. What shall I do if you're *not* back within the half hour?"

My stomach clenches. "Give it another half an hour. If I'm not back, send a squad car to the club."

Davies nods tightly. "Got it."

I pluck my keys from the kitchen island. "Be back soon."

The street outside the apartment is quiet, though not deserted. A group of drunk men stagger past, oblivious to me waiting in the shadows. They're having a loud conversation about a girl in a club as they sway about like bowling pins. In the background, the distant scream of an ambulance cuts into the balmy night air, fading as tall buildings smother its high-pitched whine.

When the lads have disappeared from view, I leave the shadows and become a blur of speed. Though vampires cannot fly, we can move fast, leap higher than any building. Sometimes it's a little like having wings.

The city lights merge into streaks of yellow and orange, the clamor of the street roaring in my ears like white noise. Before long I'm in Soho, the pavements still bustling with clubbers and tourists, the cloying aroma of restaurant kitchens—garlic, ginger, and cinnamon—spilling from open back doors.

The club on Broadwick Street is alive tonight, the thump of music pounding through the pavement at my feet. I push the shiny black door, not expecting it to give, but to my surprise it does, swinging inward beneath my palm. On the other side is a burly doorman, a vampire with a jet-black crew cut and a neck as wide as his head.

"Vincent Ferrer." His voice is surprisingly refined. "Mr. McDermott is in his office. Go straight through."

I drop him a nod and follow the gloomy corridor to the inner door. There is a tiny hatch open to one side of it, and a bored-looking human woman with white-blond hair sits on the other side, scrolling through her phone. Behind her are racks of coats. She sits up straighter when she sees me.

"Is this a coat check?" I ask.

"No, it's an ice cream parlor. What flavor would you like?" Her voice drips with flirtatious sarcasm.

I frown, baffled. A coat check seems so *normal*. Maybe it's not just the decor that's changed around here. "There never used to be one," I explain.

She raises a penciled brow, her gaze sliding over me. "I get off at two, if you're around."

I jolt in surprise, amazed at how it isn't obvious I'm utterly smitten with someone else. "I have a girlfriend," I say, a warm flutter unfurling in my chest as the word leaves my lips. "I'm crazy about her."

The girl rolls her eyes, muttering, "Whatever," under her breath. Her gaze flickers back to the screen of her phone.

I tug open the door to the club, but before the thump of the music blots out all other thoughts, I realize Cat was right. I'm falling in love. I'm probably already there.

I look down into the dark pit of the room, strobe lights slicing the dance floor like white blades, and realize the coat check has lulled me into a false sense of security.

A bloody orgy is unfolding before my eyes—a modern day William Hogarth drawing, only with blood instead of gin.

Every corner is crammed with writhing bodies, mouths clamped to various body parts as rivulets of crimson spill from red-stained fangs. Clothes, scarlet-splattered and torn, hang from limp bodies like rags. Other individuals are less reserved—a man lies sprawled across a table, three female vampires latched on to him, suckling like newborn lambs, blood smeared across his body like war paint.

Despite the heavy thump of the music, the pulse of beating hearts is deafening, the stale air thrumming with the scent of sweat and blood. There must be close to two hundred people crammed into the room and the only ones not participating in the frenzy are the staff.

Several stacked vampires, just like the one out in the hallway, patrol the floor, checking a pulse here, pulling a lusty vamp from a vital artery there. I wonder, in a detached way, what the body count will be by the end of the night.

Fighting the urge to flee, I force myself down the steps and into the fray. It goes against every fiber of my being not to wrench every human I see from the grips of the vampires attached to them. I torture myself with the notion that this could easily have been Mila's fate if Lopez had brought her here the night he tried to kill her.

Clenching my hands into fists, I push through the heaving bodies toward the light of the bar. A man and a woman are going at it on a stool. The woman's head tips back onto the stainless-steel countertop, dark-red droplets falling in a slow drip from the column of her neck. The barman—not the same as the one from the other day, but a tattooed youth with a lip ring—motions at the door next to the bar. I nod gratefully, following his pointed finger through the heavy door into a tiled hallway.

The corridor is empty, but I remember Ronin's office is last on the left. After clearing my throat and pushing the hair from my face, I rap on the purple-painted door. No response. Thinking he hasn't heard, I knock again. No answer. Remembering the doorman said to go straight in, I twist the handle and open the door wide.

At first all I see is his back, a well-cut suit stretched tight across his broad shoulders, as he stands before his desk. But then my brain clocks a pair of female legs parted around his hips and registers the moaning, writhing person spread over his desk.

I divert my eyes, face burning, and turn to face the door. "I'll come back."

The moaning stops. I hear Ronin curse under his breath and the sound of a zipper being pulled. "Vincent, stay. These ladies were just leaving."

Ladies. Plural.

"But we're not done yet," a woman's voice exclaims.

I hear a smack, like a palm hitting flesh. "Don't worry. I'll call you back when I'm finished," he says, his Scottish accent raspy.

"Your friend is handsome," the voice continues. "Does he want to join us?"

I briefly close my eyes. Jesus. Why the hell couldn't he have sent a text?

"Vincent?" Ronin asks, voice brimming with mirth. "He doesn't have a fun bone in his body."

I tense as not one but two partially dressed women, brunettes with slanting, dark eyes, trot out of the room, gazing over their shoulders into my face and pouting.

Once they cross the threshold, I slam the door after them, spinning to face my maker.

"They said they were sisters," Ronin mutters, staring at the door. "But they didn't taste related."

Resisting the urge to roll my eyes, I say, "The name, Ronin. I'm here for the name."

He turns a cold, blue glare on me, sending a chill zipping up my spine. "I'm sorry you had to see that, Mr. Monk-in-Training. Be sure to say some Hail Marys for me later, won't you?"

Shoving his hands deep into his pockets, he circles his desk and sinks into his leather swivel chair. "Take a seat," he says, gesturing to the space where he was pleasuring the two women only moments before.

Ignoring his smirk, I pull over a chair from the other side of the room to sit opposite him, wondering how long he plans to drag this out.

He runs a hand through his hair, russet in the low light of the room. "Cat came to see me," he says. "I thank you for that."

At the mention of her name, his eyes lose some of their iciness, the hard lines of his face softening. "She barely uttered two words to me the whole twenty minutes she was here. She sat where you're sitting now and stared at her watch. Then she got up and left. When I called her on it, she said the deal was that she visited me

at the club. It said nothing about actually talking to me."
He shakes his head, his expression a mixture of amusement and pride. "She's tenacious, that one."

"Which I'm guessing is the appeal," I say dryly.

His blue eyes narrow as he tilts his head to one side.
"What do you call that thing women do with their hair?"
He lifts an index finger, swirling it around his crown.
"When they knot it on top of their head?"

I smile, thinking of Mila and the hundreds of hair
bands I keep finding all over the apartment. "A bun or a
chignon, I think."

Ronin's eyes light up. "A bun, that's it. She was wearing her hair in a bun and she had this soy sauce stain on
her blouse." He brushes a finger over the shiny material
of his gray shirt. "She's a bit of a mess, actually."

"The best ones usually are."

"Aye," he says dreamily. "They are."

A silence falls. I stare at London's vampire overlord, trying to figure out the depth of his feelings for
Catherine Adair and wondering if he's ever going to get
around to giving me the name I came for.

"So, the name," he says finally, jaw clenched tight.

"The name," I concur.

"He comes to us courtesy of the lovely Esme, New
York's overlord. I don't have all of the details—you
know how contrary Esme can be—but she did give me
his name: David Moreau. She met him in the Basque
Country, northern Spain, in the early nineteenth century."

My heart freezes to ice in my chest, a cold drip of fear
trickling down my back. "Moreau?"

"David Moreau," he repeats.

It's a coincidence, my rational mind tells me. *Moreau is a common name in that part of the world.* Yet in some quiet corner of my brain, alarm bells begin to ring.

Ronin leans across the table. "You know the name?"

"Adrienne's surname was Moreau."

"The woman you loved back in the revolution?"

I nod, a hollow feeling settling in my stomach. "But it can't mean anything."

Ronin sits back, eyes narrowed. "Could it be a relation of hers?"

I swallow, a lump sticking in my throat. "She came from a large family. I can't recall all of their names." I get to my feet, the chair tipping backward and crashing to the floor in my haste. "I have to go."

Ronin holds up a hand. "Vincent?"

"Yes?"

"I'm going to find out where he's staying. I'll have someone call you with the details."

"Why would you help me?" I ask, stunned.

He shrugs, a devious smile quirking his lips. "Maybe when Cat hears of my chivalry, she'll realize what she's missing."

The intimate scene I interrupted when I arrived flashes into my mind. I really can't see how Cat would miss any of that in her life. She has never struck me as the ménage à trois type.

"How do I know I can trust you?" I ask, eyes narrowed.

He shrugs. "You don't. But what choice do you have?"

Good point. "Thank you, Ronin."

He dismisses me with a flick of the hand. "You'd

better be getting back to that woman I can smell all over you," he says. "I hope you left her protected."

"I did, but you're right. I have to go." I drop him a nod before leaving the room. Outside the corridor is empty, the two women nowhere to be seen. I emerge back into the dark carnage of the club, cutting through the writhing bodies as swiftly as I can before taking the stairs in a single bound. I'm so desperate to get back to Mila, I don't give a moment's pause to bid farewell to the coat girl or the doorman.

Once outside, I dart into a shadowy side street, away from the cars and late-night revelers, and take flight, the name Moreau turning over and over in my mind as I speed back to Farringdon. Is it merely an unlucky coincidence the killer has the same surname as my first love, or is there a more sinister meaning at play? All these weeks, working day and night on the case, is there a chance I've missed the obvious?

Outside the door of my apartment, the sound of Mila's soft breathing in the bedroom is music to my ears. I exhale in relief, deciding that there's no way I should tell her about the significance of the name or even that Ronin has agreed to help—it would only worry her. Besides, after tonight, seeing my life essence, relations between us will be different. A wave of sadness rolls over me. A couple of months ago, I'd never heard of Mila Hart. Now, the thought of going on without her is unbearable. A year from now, a hundred years, two—how will I be able to live in a world where I don't wake up to her every morning? Or even more unbearably, one where she no longer exists?

I check my watch as I push open the front door. Only twenty-five minutes have passed since I left. True to his word, I find Lee propped up against the wall opposite my room, his laptop on his legs.

"Did you get it?" he asks me.

I nod, motioning him through to the lounge, where I tell him the name and about the connection. "I'm not going to tell Mila about the link," I say, staring through the window at the twinkling city lights.

"Well, that's up to you," Lee says. "Though I'm told women appreciate honesty. Shall I call Scotland Yard with the name or will you?"

"Pass it to Burke, though he won't see it until morning."

I bid him good night and head back to my room. Mila is much as I left her, sprawled out asleep, golden and pure in the glow from the bedside lamp. I shed my clothes and put my watch on the chest of drawers before crawling under the sheets, wrapping my arms around her warm body. Her sweet scent, like roses after rain, draws me in. She stirs as I press a kiss into her neck.

"What time is it?" she mumbles.

"Time I let you get some sleep," I whisper, nuzzling her neck.

She moans before flipping over and pressing her lips to mine. As our tongues meet, the noise of the club and the scene in Ronin's office begin to lose some of their intensity. I glide a hand over her, savoring the soft contours of her body, pulling away as my cock stiffens.

Mila is undeterred. She smiles, scooting closer across the bed and stroking my hard length. Suddenly, Ronin's revelation is the last thing on my mind. Her breathing falters as I slide a hand between her legs, rubbing a finger into her wet nub, loving how she squeezes my shoulders, her nails digging into my skin. But before I can turn her sharp pants into animalistic cries of pleasure, she shoves me onto my back and climbs astride, pushing blond hair from her eyes. "Make me come while you're inside me," she whispers.

"Anything," I say, staring into her eyes as she caresses me, my fangs slipping out between my lips. "I'm yours."

She stops the stroking briefly. "Do you mean that?" Her voice is small, but a storm of emotions swirls behind her dark eyes.

I answer in a hoarse voice, my swelling erection rising higher, demanding her attention. "Of course."

Leaning over, she kisses me on the mouth, leaves a path of kisses down my throat and onto my chest. The sensation of her tummy brushing my rock-hard length, her swollen breasts nudging my abdomen, sends me wild with desire. With a groan, I wrap my hands around her waist and slide her down onto my pulsing cock. Her hips open wide as she takes me in, her warmth stretching around me to the hilt. The sweet honey scent of her wet arousal is as intoxicating as a drug. I sit up, sinking deeper inside her, a thin sheen of sweat breaking out as she rides me, gasping my name, her gaze never leaving my face.

"I love the way you feel," she pants.

Listening to the words fall from her parted pink lips unleashes an even darker beast within. I palm her breasts, twisting her nipples between my fingertips. "What else do you like?" I ask in a throaty voice.

She glances down at her breasts, her nipples red and raw from my caresses. "I like it when you suck them."

I groan, grabbing her buttocks and giving her several hard thrusts before lowering my head onto one of her hard nipples and taking it between my teeth. She cries out, wetness seeping out between her thighs. "Yes," she says, her head lolling backward. "Just like that."

Suddenly I'm hit by the overwhelming realization I will never get enough of her—of her body, her voice, her presence. My life is no longer my own. I lift her off me and slide out from beneath her, so she's left, her knees pressed into the bed. Then I push her gently forward onto all fours and grip her hips before thrusting into her from behind.

"How about this?" I ask, reaching around to circle her swollen clit. "Do you like this?"

"Yes," she gasps. "Oh God, Vincent, yes."

I arch over her, the slap of my flesh against hers filling the air as we pound mercilessly together. When she reaches between my legs to stroke my balls, I growl, scraping my fangs on the nape of her neck. I'm struck with the urge to sink my teeth into the baby-soft skin at the bottom of her hairline, the place that always smells so sweet, so floral.

With all rational thought obliterated, I've become the animal I never wanted her to see. But she doesn't pull away from my fangs—she presses back into them, moaning. Suddenly it's all too overwhelming—my length buried into her tight sheath, my fingers rubbing her dripping entrance, her hands stroking me. Before I know it, I've sunk my fangs deep into her neck and I'm sucking, drinking her in like she's the finest wine in the world, her blood flowing warm and sweet into my mouth. A part of my brain registers that I'm no better than those animals back at the club, yet I don't stop. For the first time since Adrienne died in my arms, I cave to the beast inside me, and God forgive me, it feels like heaven.

Mila cries out, her warmth clenching tight around me, her body shuddering as release takes her within its grip. Hearing her cries of pleasure, sensing the lick of heat erupt from her body, brings me over the edge. I pump into her, a flow of ecstasy surging through me like a tidal wave. I come harder than I ever have, pouring into her in an unending stream of pleasure. I withdraw my fangs from her neck, but my orgasm continues, my stomach and thighs trembling, hot juices dripping onto the sheets. I say her name, over and over. When the waves finally begin to calm, I sit up, pulling her into my lap.

I've made a mess of her. Her hair is knotted with sweat and blood, her body sticky with my release.

"Mila, did I hurt you?"

"No," she whispers.

Her voice is distant. I lift her up and lower her gently onto the bed before twisting to face her. I'm horrified to see tears glistening in her eyes.

Any remaining pleasure from the most powerful orgasm of my life is instantly crushed when I see hurt in her face. I cup her flushed cheeks in my hands. "Mila, I'm sorry. I should have asked if it was okay to bite you. I don't know what came over me—"

"Don't be silly," she says. "It's not the bite. I wanted it. I loved it. It's—"

"What?" Though really, I know what.

"It's Adrienne."

What did I expect? But before either of us can say anything else, we're interrupted by a furious pounding on the bedroom door.

"Vincent, get up now. Burke just called. There's been another murder."

Chapter 15

Mila

I FREEZE AS LEE'S WORDS REACH MY EARS, WATCHING as Vincent's gentle, blue eyes turn dark with horror.

He grips me by the shoulders. "Stay in the bedroom, Mila. Whatever Lee says, I don't want you to hear it."

I nod mutely. Maybe it's the shock, but I'm more concerned about where our conversation was headed right before we were interrupted. I swipe at my eyes, sniffing away unshed tears. The best thing he can do for both of us is leave before the ugly crying starts.

With a final worried look, he leaps off the bed.

"Wait," I say, as his hand closes around the door-knob. "What about your clothes?"

He glances down at himself in surprise. There is a thin sheen of sweat shimmering between the ridges of his muscles, his thick length purple and raw from our lovemaking. Golden strands of his hair stick up from his head like a toilet brush.

"Not that I don't think that's an exceptionally good look on you, of course."

He flashes a grin, plucking his underwear from the pile on the floor before grabbing the door handle again. "We will continue this conversation."

I nod as he disappears, pulling the door closed behind him. Without Vincent, the air in the bedroom turns cold.

I pull my legs up to my chest, wishing I were home in my flat above the hairdressers, watching *Britain's Next Top Model* with a tub of ice cream. Life might have been dull, but at least it was simple.

After a few minutes of self-pity, I decide to do something about the clumps of dried blood in my hair and the fact that I reek of sex. Not that smelling of sex with Vincent is a bad thing, but tonight there has been a lot of it.

The shower cubicle in Vincent's bathroom is huge, even bigger than the one in the guest room. The powerful surge of hot water feels heavenly on my skin. I take my time under the jets, using his body wash and shampoo to rinse the blood and sweat from me, watching the water turn from pink to clear as it disappears into the drain. When I finally step out of the steamy warmth, I wrap myself in a large towel before rummaging through Vincent's medicine cabinet for Band-Aids. The puncture holes on my neck are barely visible, but blood still spots from the ones beneath my hairline.

"You're an idiot," I mutter aloud. "Why would a vampire need Band-Aids?" Yet I find some underneath a couple of bars of soap. No doubt his cleaning lady likes him to be prepared. Unless, of course, they were left here by another woman.

I stick the Band-Aid on as best I can and towel-dry my hair, trying not to imagine how many women have been here before me, seen what I've seen in the inner recesses of his mind.

Out in the bedroom, the occasional high-pitched exclamation drifts through from the lounge, though it's too far away to make out who's speaking, let alone what's being said.

There's been another murder. For the first time since hearing the words echo through the door, I picture how it might have played out. A woman like me, perhaps also down on her luck with men, heading out for a date. Nervous about outfits and hair and whether she'll have anything in common with him, when all the while the jaws of death awaited. I shudder, dread worming its way into my gut, the night of my botched murder playing out in my head like a half-forgotten dream.

I'm recalling the strange shine behind Jeremiah Lopez's dazzling eyes as he sat opposite me in the noisy bar when my eye snags on Vincent's large family portrait. I'm struck by an odd sensation of déjà vu. I creep closer until I'm nose to nose with the crusty, age-worn paint.

On Vincent's right hand, the one holding the hilt of a sword, is a ring. It's made of gold and a coat of arms is engraved on the green background, a tiny silver dove visible at the tip of its crest. I suddenly recall Jeremiah Lopez as he led me from the bar—hand outstretched, the same gold ring on his middle finger, glinting beneath the spotlights.

My blood runs cold; my heart begins to thud in my ears. I back away from the painting and drop my towel before grabbing one of Vincent's freshly laundered shirts from the end of his bed and throwing it on. My hands shake so badly I can barely fasten the buttons.

Out in the lounge, Vincent sits on the sofa with his head in his hands, his long fingers threaded through his dirty-blond hair. Every sinewy line of muscle in his body is tense. Lee is on his phone with his back to the room, framed by the darkness of the window. Vincent's head flips up when he sees me, his face ashen.

"The ring," I say breathlessly. "It's the same."

Vincent is before me in a millisecond, grasping me by the arms, ducking his head level with mine. "Mila, did you hear us talking? Because I'm going to find him. No harm will ever come to you, I swear it."

His grip tightens, the heat from his fingers burning through the cotton of the pin-striped shirt.

I shake my head in confusion. "No. The ring you're wearing in your painting. Jeremiah Lopez was wearing one the night of our date."

In the time I've known him, I've never seen Vincent look afraid. But the words appear to hit him with the force of a fifty-ton juggernaut, life draining from his chiseled features like the glow from a snuffed-out candle.

His gaze wanders past me, staring into space. "Are you sure?" he whispers.

"Yes."

Past Vincent's head, I see Lee glance over his shoulder, clearly wondering what further drama can be unraveling across the room. He jabs a finger at his phone to indicate he's still speaking.

"Oh God," Vincent says, the words coming out in a gurgle of pain.

"What does it mean? It has to be coincidence, right?"

I'm unaware Vincent has moved until I'm suddenly pressed tightly into his bare chest, his arms gripping me around my back, his skin silky against my cheek and jaw. His lips are in the hair of my crown and he's muttering in a foreign tongue, his voice vibrating through my body. It sounds a lot like he's praying. For the first time since we met, I push him away.

"You're scaring me. What is it? Why does he have the ring?"

Before he can answer, Lee gets off the phone. He stares between us, shaking his head. "You'll have to tell her."

I screw my face up. "Tell me what, Vincent?"

Vincent brings a hand to my face, brushing the back of his fingers across my jaw, his eyes round and sad. Then he lifts me up and carries me to the sofa, setting me down on the cushions as if I'm a fragile china doll.

"This is all my fault," he begins, a tremor in his voice.

Lee moves to the kitchen, busying himself in the cupboards. The clink of mugs rattles around the otherwise silent room.

Vincent kneels before me. "I went to see Ronin McDermott again tonight. He procured the name of the killer."

I jolt in surprise. "That's good though, isn't it? To finally find out who he is?"

His mouth forms a grim line. "He gave me the name of David Moreau. Adrienne's surname was Moreau."

I frown, wondering where he's going with this. "So they're connected?"

"I thought it was a coincidence," he says, his grip on my knees tightening. "I didn't want to worry you about it. But now they've found another body and…" He breaks my gaze, trailing off into silence.

"What?" I demand.

He closes his eyes briefly. "The female, as yet unidentified, was discovered in the same alley where I found you that night."

Fear stabs at my chest like a thousand knives. "Do you think that's a favorite spot of his or something?"

Vincent shakes his head. "We don't believe the female was using V-Date. Cat has temporarily frozen new memberships anyway. The victim bears a startling resemblance to you—hair color, age, build."

My teeth start to chatter. Although I already know the answer, I ask, "What are you saying?"

Anything to delay the inevitable.

"I don't believe this was ever about random or even serial killing, or punishing the police for nosing into vampire crime. I think it's always been about me. David Moreau is some relative of Adrienne's, and he's out to avenge her death. This whole killing spree has been about taunting me. If he has that ring, it proves it."

My throat dries up. "The ring," I repeat.

"There's only one of those rings in existence. My family ring. If you remember, Adrienne threw it from her finger that night she went over the cliff. I never saw it again after that. Never even really thought about it. If he has it, he must have been close to her, known the link between us."

My eyes meet his. "You think this new murder was deliberate? That he's caught on about us and killing a girl who looks like me is his way of letting you know?"

Vincent nods, cupping my face in his hands. "He must have seen us together. He must realize how I feel about you."

I forget that Lee is across the room making tea and grab Vincent's wrists, wanting to finish our conversation from earlier no matter how inappropriate the timing. "It's okay, Vincent. I get it about Adrienne. I felt it in your life essence. I know you'll never be able to move on from the past—love me the way you did her."

His jaw clenches, and he rakes his hands through my hair, shaking his head. "No, Mila, you're wrong. God, is that what you think? I thought you were secretly repulsed by me. That seeing her in my life essence made you realize how dangerous I am."

I shake my head in disbelief. "You could never repulse me."

Pressing his forehead to mine, he says, "I know what's in my heart, Mila, and trust me, it's you."

Lee coughs loudly, breaking the spell. He slides a tray of tea and biscuits onto the table. "I think the important thing is not to let our emotions get in the way of this."

I look back at Vincent. I want to press the matter, ask him what he means by "in my heart," but Lee begins crunching a biscuit noisily.

Vincent throws him an irritated glare.

"I'm a stress eater, okay? It's not every day you find out your wife is screwing the UPS guy and a psycho wants your work colleague dead."

Vincent strokes my damp hair. "We'll sort this, Mila," he says. "I'll sort it. Ronin has agreed to help. He's going to find out where David Moreau is staying. As soon as I have the address, he's toast."

"But then you'll be in danger," I say, my stomach churning.

Lee snorts derisively, cramming another custard cream into his mouth. "Vincent can handle him, don't worry. He may act like an aristocrat, but trust me, he's a badass. Think Bruce Willis minus the dirty tank top."

For the first time in what feels like forever, Vincent and I both smile. I suddenly remember I'm wearing nothing but one of his shirts. Vincent, who is still crouching between my knees, is dressed only in a pair of boxers. We must make quite the intimate scene.

I swallow loudly. "So, what about the victim?"

"Burke's there now and I'm off in a minute," Lee says, slurping his tea.

"I'll stay here with you, obviously," Vincent says. "Until other arrangements can be made."

"What other arrangements?"

"We need to hide you until he's caught. I have contacts in France. The safest option is to move you."

My jaw drops. "I'm not leaving you."

"If it's me he's after, we don't have much choice," he says, swiping his thumbs across my cheekbones. "But I promise it won't be for long."

Great. More hiding. Only this time I won't have the consolation of being protected by a hot vampire.

"When will I have to leave?" I ask, darting a glance between them. The idea of having to leave Vincent so soon is giving me heart palpitations.

The pair exchanges worried looks.

"This place is as safe as any," Lee says, breaking the silence. "Strong locks on the windows and doors. Two security guards on the desk downstairs."

Vincent nods, deep in thought. "It would be dangerous

to try to move her tonight. I can protect her better here until we have everything in place."

"I agree," Lee says. "She stays here tonight." He drains his mug and slams it down onto the coffee table.

It's only now that I notice he must've gotten dressed while I was in the shower. He snatches his beige overcoat from the back of the leather sofa. "I'd better be off. I'll call first thing in the morning. Try to get some rest."

As soon as the door slams, Vincent stands up and pulls me into his arms, and I sag against him, weary down to my bones.

"Can we sleep in my room tonight?" I ask, nestled up into the hard ridges of his chest.

Somehow I don't like the idea of spending the night beneath that portrait—the ring watching over us like a bad omen.

"Yes, of course," Vincent says, placing a kiss on top of my head.

He pulls me close again, rubbing my back in comforting circles as I press a kiss into the golden skin of his chest.

We remain in the same position for a good ten minutes, locked together in silence, until eventually Vincent leads me across the apartment toward the guest room. He folds down the duvet, and I crawl gratefully between the deliciously cool sheets, my eyelids already beginning to droop, my body as heavy as lead.

"I'm going to take a quick shower," he says, tucking the duvet around me like a cocoon. "The door will be open the whole time."

I'm so weary, he could tell me he's going to Beirut

and I wouldn't flinch. "Uh-huh." My eyes fall shut. Everything will be okay in the morning, I tell myself. The last sound I hear before drifting off to sleep is water hitting the tiles, and the last image in my mind is Adrienne, her black hair whipped across her face as she disappeared over the edge of the rocks.

I dream of the dark landscape in Vincent's life essence. Like Adrienne, I'm running, sprinting through wet grass toward the edge of a cliff. Fear makes me clumsy, slowing me down until my legs stop working completely. I grind to a halt. Above, in the dark sky, is a blood moon, casting the trees and everything beneath it in an eerie, red glow. I turn to look over my shoulder, telling myself it's only Vincent, that he will never hurt me.

David Moreau—or Jeremiah Lopez, as he was on our date—steps out from the shadows. "You have something that belongs to me," he says in singsong tones, walking closer and smiling. Moonlight glints from his white fangs like sunlight on water.

I look down to my left hand and see Vincent's signet ring on my wedding finger. "It doesn't belong to you," I say, voice trembling with fear.

Moreau smirks. "It doesn't belong to you either. He'd have to marry you for it to be yours, and that will never happen."

I stare at the ring and back to Moreau, but he is gone. Karolina from my English class stands in his place, wearing her trademark white jeans, her designer brown leather bag slung casually over her shoulder. She extends a hand toward me. "I can help you, Mila," she says, her dark eyes filling with blood. "I can help both of you."

The blood in her eyes begins to spill over her cheeks like tears, dripping onto her jeans like red paint on a white page.

I scream.

When I wake up, I'm thrashing around like an eel, fighting the covers and gasping for breath. Vincent leans over me, his hands gently gripping my shoulders like he did my first night here.

"Mila, it's a dream. You're safe."

I stare into his face, heart thudding. His eyes glow like milky blue lagoons in the early morning light from the window. "I was dreaming about Moreau," I whisper as he draws me close.

He cradles my head between his jaw and collarbone, rocking me like a distressed child. "Do you want to tell me about it?" he asks.

I shake my head. "I just want to forget."

We lie still and silent. It feels nice to be this close to him without having sex—calming. I could lie here for the rest of my days and never want for anything else. Not that sex with him wouldn't be welcome, but my insides are feeling more than a little sore after the voracious session last night. I inhale, smelling apples in his hair and skin.

"Did you use my shampoo?"

He chuckles. "Yes, and the lemon body wash. Did you use mine?"

I smile into his neck, his stubble scraping deliciously against my skin. "Yes, and I'm still in your shirt."

"I like seeing you in my clothes," he says, pulling me closer. "It's sexy."

I grin. "Was I snoring when you came out of the shower?"

"A few snorts, and just the one trickle of drool this time."

I pinch his bottom hard. "You're lying."

He chuckles again, kissing the top of my head. "Do you remember the first night here when you had a nightmare?"

I groan. "The one where I made you babysit me? Yes, I do."

"God, it was like being tortured over a slow-burning flame," he continues. "I wanted you so badly."

"I wanted you too," I whisper.

He smiles, planting a kiss on the end of my nose and exploring my face with his fingers.

"I'm not sure what I would've done if you hadn't felt the same way."

"What woman in her right mind wouldn't feel the same way? And don't say your first wife. She was clearly a nutcase."

Laughing, he holds me tight against him. My eyes flutter closed in contentment.

"What happens after?" The words spill from me without thinking, a slop of liquid from an unsteady glass.

His hand stills in my hair. "After I've dealt with David Moreau, you mean?"

"Yes."

He continues to study me, his callused index finger drawing lines across the bridge of my nose. "Did you know these freckles right here make the constellation of Sagittarius?"

"Vincent." There is a hint of pleading to my voice. "What will happen with us?"

His fingers drop to my chin and he lifts my face to meet my worried gaze. "The future scares me, Mila. More than ever before." He pauses to brush his lips against mine. "Would you go away with me?"

My breath catches. "Where to?"

"Maybe to France for a while, to my house. Time moves fast and we won't have the luxury of being able to waste too much."

Though he doesn't say it, I assume he means the disparity between our life spans. Mine is like a leaf in summer, a victim of the seasons; his, as frozen as ice. "What about work?" I ask.

He shakes his head. "I'll quit. I'll never do anything that puts you in danger ever again."

"You can't quit your job for me," I say. "We'll end up having to sell mangoes on the beach or something."

"That wouldn't be so bad," he says, grinning. "Though I'm not sure there are any mango trees near my house."

We're silent for a few seconds, each lost in our separate thoughts.

"So, would you?" he asks after a time. "Go away with me?"

"Yes," I whisper, kissing him. "I'd go anywhere with you."

—∿—

I must have fallen back asleep because when I next open my eyes, bright light blooms around the edges of the blinds. I'm still lying in Vincent's arms, my cheek resting in the nook of his shoulder and arm. I feel surprisingly calm considering the turn of events last night, as if it were all a dream and the night ended with the party and not the discovery of a body.

"Morning," Vincent says, kissing my forehead.

I stretch, my bones creaking like loose floorboards. "Morning." His blue eyes are alert and clear. "Have you been awake since we last spoke?"

"Yes. How are you feeling?"

I wrinkle my nose. "A bit sore," I admit.

He chuckles. "Why don't I run you a bath and then make you breakfast? Take myself out of temptation's way." He glances between the gap in our bodies, where his rigid length prods my stomach.

I place my hand over the bulge. "Seems a shame to waste it."

Vincent scoots backward, away from my touch, smiling. "That's not going anywhere, don't you worry. But you need a break from my constant pawing."

"Do I?" I ask, sliding a hand into his briefs and stroking his erection.

In a flash, he leaps from the bed and stands by the door. I hear water pounding from inside the bathroom.

"That was fast," I say, cocking a brow. "Perhaps you're going off me."

Before I can even blink, I'm flat on my back, pressed deep into the mattress by his luscious body. "In what universe would that ever happen?" he asks, working a hand under my shirt and circling a nipple, his blond hair falling in my eyes. "When you're done with your bath, I'll have breakfast ready."

"Yes, Inspector."

He smiles before blurring from the room, leaving me with my shirt rucked up in a compromising position. He is right about one thing though—I'm aching in muscles and body parts I never knew existed.

I hobble into the bathroom and turn off the taps. Not only did Vincent manage to draw a bath in those few split seconds, but he also added some lavender bath oil. Stripping off the shirt, I sink into the deliciously hot water, letting it soothe my sore muscles.

After soaking for ten minutes, I step out and grab a towel, noticing a few dots of blood in the fluffy white fibers as I dry off. The Band-Aid covering the bite marks on the back of my neck has come loose, and it whirls in wild circles around the drain. I pluck it out and throw it in the trash before returning to the bedroom, wondering if there might be one in my handbag.

I'm rummaging around in the pockets when I stumble across the purple business card Karolina handed me after class on Thursday. I stare at the writing, *Witchcraft & Psychic Services*, remembering how she said to call her if I ever needed anything. Was it a coincidence that I also dreamed of her saying she could help us? Though how could she possibly help? The thing I want more than anything is for Vincent to grow old alongside me— that, and to ease the burden of his past. It isn't right for a good person like Vincent to go through life believing he's unworthy of love. Even if I'm not the person to give it to him, even if his heart always belongs to Adrienne, he deserves to be happy. His life essence should be joyous, not that terrible scene on the cliff top.

On impulse, I wrench my phone from my bag and tap in the number on the card. Then I write:

> Karolina, it's Mila. Can a vampire's life essence change?

Hearing a spoon banging a pot out in the kitchen, I guiltily drop the phone and card onto the bed. If I ask Vincent about the possibility of his life essence changing, he'll think I'm upset about what I saw and never bite me again. Besides, he has bigger things to worry about at the moment. We both do.

The door to the lounge opens and Vincent's smooth voice calls out, "Mila, your eggs are ready."

"Just coming," I call back.

Flipping open the lid of my suitcase, I pick out some underwear and a simple yellow T-shirt dress and throw them on before trailing through to the kitchen.

My scrambled eggs are waiting for me on the kitchen island along with a large glass of orange juice. I'm so entranced by the sight of food, the enticing whiff of toast, I don't notice that Vincent has turned pale as parchment, his whole body frozen in tension as he stares at the screen of his phone.

When his gaze meets mine, his blue eyes are dazed.

"What is it?" I demand, the eggs forgotten.

"It's Ronin," he says, his voice strangled. "He's sent me an address for Moreau."

Chapter 16

Vincent

UNTIL THE TEXT FROM RONIN, I'D BEEN TRYING TO keep things as normal as possible. Yes, there's been another killing and the horrific realization that all this is personal, but Mila is unharmed and still in my arms in spite of everything. For a few hours, I convinced myself all would be well.

The single line of text on the screen changes everything.

Flat B, 55 Francis St, N22.

A thin sheen of cold sweat breaks out beneath my collar. I set the phone down on the countertop as if it's a loaded gun.

"You should eat your eggs before they get cold," I say, motioning to the plate.

Mila is ashen. "When?" she asks in a hoarse voice. "When will you go after him?"

I glance quickly to the bright rectangle of the window. For once the gray mass of London is bathed in a watery, yellow glow. It will be well past nine before the sun dips below the horizon.

"Tonight," I say. "I can't go in daylight because it will impact my speed."

"You were fast enough just now when you ran my bath," she points out.

"It's different indoors. The light in the bedroom is dull. I'll need a fast approach."

She nods, chewing her bottom lip. I cut the short distance between us, cupping her face in my hands. "I'll be fine, Mila, I promise."

"Really? Can you be utterly, one hundred percent sure? Because while there's even the slightest chance you won't be, I'm sick with worry."

I lean my forehead against hers and close my eyes. Fearlessness brings power, an edge deadlier than any weapon and something I once possessed in abundance. Throughout my time with the police, I've never had anything to lose. I threw myself headfirst into every confrontation with the dogged determination of an ox.

I open my eyes to stare into her upturned face. "Did anyone ever tell you your eyes are the exact shade of early autumn leaves? When the sun comes low through the trees and turns them to bronze?"

She smiles. "I've dated men who think it's romantic to belch my name during dinner, so no, Vincent, no one has ever told me that before."

"You should be told a lot of things. Every day. Did I ever tell you about the night we met?"

"Vincent, stop. You just said everything would be okay and now you're acting like you're off to the trenches."

"There was a moment," I continue, "when I might have gone after him. A split-second decision I could have made. Burke and Davies were right behind me, and I knew you'd be safe. But I didn't because you were falling to the ground and I wanted to catch you. I wanted you in my arms. So he got away. That's what matters of the heart do, Mila. They cloud your thinking and put people in danger. I tried to fight it. I was determined not to be the one to protect you, because I knew I couldn't hold back. But the truth is, you're not the only one who fell in that alley. I fell too. I've been falling ever since. The odd thing is I always thought I had nowhere left to fall *from*. That's what you've done for me, Mila. You've drawn me from the ashes and brought me back to the living."

Mila's eyes are moist. "Brought you back to the living and now there's a chance you might…"

I shake my head vigorously. "I won't let it happen. I promised to keep you safe and I'm a man of my word."

A single tear slides from a corner of her eye, leaving a silvery trail as it rolls down her cheek. "I don't care about being safe unless you're here to be safe with."

I fold her into an embrace, wishing we could stay cocooned in each other's arms forever.

"Tell me something really terrible you've done, Vincent, so I'm not left here thinking you're the most wonderful man on earth."

I give her a wry smile. "You mean aside from driving my first girlfriend off the side of a cliff from fear?"

She shakes her head. "We talked about that. No, I mean something dodgy, like cheating or telling a woman she's too fat."

I chuckle, raking fingers through her hair. "I don't mind so much when a woman grows portly."

"Ah! I knew you were a secret feeder," she says

triumphantly. "But no, I mean an occasion where you've cheated or behaved dishonorably, and not back when you were rich and spoiled either."

"I've never cheated," I say truthfully. "But there is something."

Her eyes widen, the smile dropping from her shiny face. "What?"

I take a breath. "The night we met, I was so aroused by you I thought maybe it had been too long since I'd had sex. Lee was goading me about it. I called a woman I slept with once. I knew she'd be willing, and I did the deed. I used her."

Mila looks crestfallen. "Oh."

"Then afterward I went home and slept with your jacket on the pillow beside me. So, there, dodgy and creepy."

"Did you bite her?" she asks.

"No."

She sighs. "The jacket thing takes the edge off."

"When I went to the bar to collect it, I told the barman you were my girlfriend. And I enjoyed it."

She smiles. "Sick bastard."

I smile back. "I think maybe I bought that television so I could sit and stare at you unhindered."

"Strangely enough, I'm finding all this endearing rather than weird."

Before bringing my lips down on hers, I say, "Then it must be too late for us both."

Later when Lee returns, we call Burke for a conference call. Before any plans can be made to swoop in on the flat, the possibility that this is nothing but a ruse must first be addressed.

"What would Ronin get from providing a false address and colluding with this David Moreau?" Burke's voice asks from the speakerphone.

I shrug at Lee, whose eyes swivel in my direction. "Revenge for betraying him is the only motivation I can think of, but even that's unlikely. Ronin McDermott is a lot of things—womanizer, overlord—but he's no cold-blooded killer. He wouldn't put petty revenge over the life of an innocent woman."

"How did he get the address in the first place?" Lee puts in, eyes narrowed in suspicion.

I sigh, my eyes darting to Mila, who is over in the kitchenette making tea. I didn't want her to have to hear any of this, but the alternative—have her out of my sight and reach for any length of time—is too risky. "Ronin has a vast network of vampire acquaintances. Besides, he told me himself Moreau had been to the club. Someone must have spoken to him while he was there. I could call Ronin to find out, but if it's a ruse, he's hardly going to own up and yell, 'Gotcha!'"

Burke is silent on the end of the line as Lee nods in agreement.

"My main concern is Mila's safety," I say, briefly catching her eye across the apartment. "She needs ironclad protection while I investigate. I can ask Cat, of course, and I think she would be happy to help in this instance, but we need more and I think I have the solution."

"I'm listening," Burke says from the phone.

"I'm going to ask Ronin."

Lee screws up his face. "But if he is out for revenge, you'll be offering him Mila on a plate."

I meet Mila's wide eyes as I answer him. Her hand trembles as she spoons sugar into the mugs, her heart rate accelerating. "Like I said, petty revenge or not, there isn't a chance he'd allow the death of a young woman. But the real reason why I know, both that he'll agree to it and that Mila will be safe, is because he's half in love with Catherine Adair"—I fix my gaze on Mila's pretty face—"and we all know the kind of effect that can have on a man." She flashes me a smile and I glance back at Lee. "Either way it's a risk. But this way, Mila is protected while I'm gone. That's all that really matters. Agreed?"

Lee sighs and leans back into the sofa. "What do you think, Superintendent?"

"I think we should go with Vincent's gut instinct. After all, he knows these *creatures* better than we do. I can post a backup squad on the street near the flat and extra hands on deck at Scotland Yard for Miss Hart."

"Wouldn't it be safer to leave her here?" Lee cuts in. "Get some officers downstairs. I could stay with her. Make sure Dracula plays nice."

"No," Burke says firmly. "I insist she's brought in. Far safer for everyone."

"Agreed," I say, trying and failing once again not to make eye contact with Mila. I give her a tight smile as she lowers the mugs onto a tray, my stomach a knot of apprehension. In past situations like this, I've never felt nervous or uneasy. It's always been a case of getting the job done. But this is personal on so many levels. I can't even begin to imagine how it might feel to come face-to-face with a connection of Adrienne's—whoever he may be.

A few hours later, everything is set up. Ronin agreed to help as soon as he learned Cat would be there, and Cat... Well, by the time she finds out the freelance vampire bodyguard she's working with is none other than Ronin McDermott, it'll be too late for her to back out. Even without knowing the truth, she took a lot of convincing. In the end, I took Mila's advice, by referencing some movie named *The Bodyguard*.

Before we're due to drop Mila at Scotland Yard, Lee takes me discreetly into the hallway. Propped up next to the front door is a familiar black canvas bag. I unzip it and stare down at a glittering array of weapons, wrapped in plastic and tucked neatly into elastic loops.

I swallow loudly as Lee slaps me on the shoulder. "Better get down to business, eh, Vince?"

I nod, removing a black-handled machete and unwrapping the cover. The silver blade glistens like liquid metal beneath the spotlights in the ceiling.

"Your personal favorite, if I remember rightly," Lee says.

Turning it over, I frown. I meant what I said to Mila earlier about quitting the force. Something doesn't feel right anymore. Not the taking of life—Moreau deserves everything he has coming to him—but inside, a part of me has changed.

I rewrap the weapon in its plastic and take a smaller knife from the bag as backup, though the machete will do its job fine if all goes to plan. One strike, pure and true, to the neck. Forget about stakes through the heart—decapitation is the only way to destroy a vampire. Unfortunately, Moreau will be all too aware of this.

Not wanting Mila to see, I leave them by the door and follow Lee back into the lounge. Mila is staring out the window at the darkening sky, her shoulders stiff with tension, arms folded across her chest. She turns when she hears us approach, making a weak attempt at a smile. Her hazel eyes hold the weight of the world in their tawny depths.

"Is it time to leave?" she asks.

"Almost."

Her gaze slides over me. "Do you always wear a suit when you play assassin? Shouldn't it be a black balaclava?"

I pluck at my charcoal jacket. "I've ditched the tie, haven't I?"

She steps toward me and smooths the shiny material with her hands. "How are you even real?" she murmurs.

I hug her tightly, my face buried in her hair. Even though we both promised we wouldn't say goodbye, our actions do it for us.

"Thank you for saving my life, Vincent."

I hold her tight. "If it wasn't for me, it would never have been in jeopardy."

"But then we wouldn't have met. None of this is your fault."

Lee's coughing interrupts us. "Time to go," he says, lips set in a grim line.

Mila takes a deep breath and steps back. She's changed clothes from earlier, wearing tight gray jeans and a loose blue sweater that hangs off one shoulder. "I'm ready."

That makes one of us.

Taking her hand, I can only wonder if I will ever be ready again.

Lee drives his BMW to Scotland Yard as Mila and I sit in the back, hands clasped together so tightly our knuckles are white. When we arrive at the underground parking garage, I turn to Mila, her face lit yellow by the glow of artificial lights. Her hair is tied back in a messy bun and I reach across to tuck a wayward strand behind her ear.

"Not long now until it's over," I say, trying to smile but grimacing instead. My fingers linger on her shoulder, on the exposed triangle of skin. Forgetting about Lee Davies sitting up front, I lean in and kiss her there, inhaling her floral scent, willing my mind to remember the sensation of her skin beneath my lips—silky and alive. I'm tempted to grab her and run. Take her to France or somewhere else far away. Forget all about London and the force and David Moreau. But running never solves anything. I should know. I've been running for almost three hundred years.

Upstairs on the second floor, Cat is the first to arrive. She sits on a swivel chair alongside Burke, looking like she came straight from the gym. Her curly hair is piled on top of her head, hands thrust deep inside the pockets of a gray hoodie. She smiles as we walk in and I smother a frown. She won't be smiling for much longer.

Burke gets to his feet, a fierce look of determination shining behind his gray eyes. "Ready, Inspector Ferrer?"

he asks, chin in the air. In another life, he would have made an excellent army major.

I swallow heavily. "Ready."

As Lee makes the introductions between Mila and Cat, Ronin arrives, flanked by two officers. Cat's jaw hits the floor at the sight of the tall, broad-shouldered redhead, his piercing blue eyes going straight to her.

"What the fuck are you doing here?" she asks, glaring at him.

Ronin grins like the Cheshire Cat, glancing at the men on either side of him. "Don't mind her," he says. "We had a thing once and she's still hung up about it."

Cat spins around to face me, nostrils flaring. "I trusted you."

I hold up my hands. "I had no choice."

"Relax," Ronin says, smirking. "I think I can control myself for a couple of hours, especially seeing as how you're dressed like that." He rakes a disinterested gaze over her. "What is it? Laundry day?"

Cat looks as if she's about to burst a blood vessel, she's so angry. "One hour," she says, glaring at me. "Then I'm leaving whether you're back or not." Arms crossed, she drops back into the chair.

I give her a curt nod. "I'll be back." I clear my throat. "Mila? Can I have a word outside before I go?" The six pairs of eyeballs in the room swivel to stare at us.

"We should get going," Burke says, checking his watch.

"It'll take two minutes," I tell him.

Feeling their gazes on us, I steer Mila by the elbow into the corridor. As Davies closes the door discreetly behind us, I hear him ask, "Anyone watch the game last night?"

As soon as the door clicks shut, Mila and I fly at each other like magnets.

"Please be careful," she says, her voice cracking.

"I will," I say into her hair. "I promise."

I squeeze her so hard I must be hurting her, but she doesn't flinch or pull away. She presses against me until I'm not sure where I end and she begins.

When we finally break apart, there's a rock-sized lump in my throat and I notice Mila is trembling. I smooth hair from her face, my eyes prickling with tears, lifting her chin with my thumb and forefinger. "I'll be back within the hour, and then we can go home and order pizza."

She nods, her own eyes glassy and moist. "Good. I'm hungry."

We smile and I bend over, holding my lips firmly to hers. "I will see you very soon."

"Do you promise?" she asks in a tiny voice.

"Yes," I whisper, holding her to me again. "I promise."

I let go of her and step backward, trying to hold the memory of her in my mind's eye—flushed cheeks, messy tendrils of blond hair tickling the nape of her neck, eyes shining like sunlight on copper. More than anything, I want to tell her I love her, that having her in my life these past weeks has brought me back to life. But words are powerful and timing is everything. It isn't right to burden her with such a declaration when there's a chance I'll never see her again.

Also, I'd be lying if I said I wasn't terrified she doesn't feel the same.

With a strained smile, I open the door and follow her back inside the office.

Burke gives me a terse nod, slapping me on the shoulder. "Let's go, Inspector. In, out, and home in time for supper."

I salute him, nodding in turn to each of the others. After throwing Mila a last, loaded look, I follow him from the room.

All the way down in the elevator, I regret my silence. When we reach the parking garage, I almost turn back. But then Burke flings the car door open and barks, "Get on form, Inspector, get on form," and I know if I return upstairs now, I'll never leave her side again, will never kill Moreau.

It's only at this moment I realize just how much I have to lose.

———

As we head north, the concrete jungle of the city begins to thin out—trees appear, gardens and parks are dotted around modest streets, their pavements lined with shuttered storefronts and brightly colored doors. The buildings turn from shades of gunmetal gray and glass to red brick with sash windows. Net curtains shield the bright glow of front rooms from the street.

When we stop at a set of traffic lights outside Wood Green tube station, Burke finally speaks. He's been quiet the whole way over, not even giving me his usual sergeant major routine.

"Forgive me if I'm wrong, Vincent, but I get the impression you've grown rather attached to Miss Hart these past weeks."

I clear my throat. "I've enjoyed her company, yes."

I turn to stare out at the dark streets, hoping he'll drop the subject.

"Whatever your feelings, Vincent, you must put them aside and stay focused on the task at hand. It's like when I have an important golf match at the club, I never let Eve come to watch. She distracts me too much. Mostly because she keeps asking if I'm hungry and would I like a sandwich, but still, it helps to put a distance between yourself and those you, er, care about."

I look across at Burke. In all our years working together, this is the closest we've ever gotten to a heart-to-heart. Not that I've been waiting for one.

"Out of curiosity," I start, "what are the rules regarding fraternization with witnesses?"

"I have no idea," he says, taking off the handbrake as the lights turn from red to green. He smiles, shaking his head. "You know I met Eve *on the job*. She was a nurse in the ER department at Middlesex Hospital. I'd taken in a drunk football fan who'd been glassed in a bar brawl. It was love at first sight."

I stare at his weary, lined face, a smattering of silver hair at his temples. As my gaze wanders to the thick gold wedding ring on his left hand, I'm struck by a desperate stab of envy. Burke, who Davies and I often mock for his stern attitude and lack of humor, a man who has never strayed from the path of righteousness, has one of the greatest gifts known to man—a long life lived at the side of the woman he loves.

"You're lucky," I say, remembering the first time I ever saw Mila.

Burke's gaze doesn't waver from the road. "We make our own luck in this world, Vincent."

Francis Street is set deep in the leafy suburbs of Alexandra Palace, swaths of terrace houses with Victorian mosaic front paths and imposing bay windows lining the road. Parked cars sit bumper to bumper on either side of the pavement, packed in like sardines. The whole street is an embodiment of middle-class urban living.

If only they knew a serial killer is living in their midst.

Burke and the rest of the team spent the hours since the text came in discreetly surveying the house. On the first floor, overlooking the front garden, is a rusting wrought-iron balcony, off which is a sash window, open six inches. This is the spot through which I'll make my entrance. The house, like so many of its neighbors, has been divided into two separate flats—one up, one down. According to the floor plans Burke obtained from the internet, the window leads into a kitchen.

We drive slowly along the street without stopping the first time, giving me a chance to look at the window and suss out if he has company. I open my ears to the top level of the house, but there is no heartbeat, only the rumble of a television set coming from the rear of the property.

"Sounds to me like he's home alone," I tell Burke.

Burke gives a quick nod. "Excellent."

On our second loop of the street, Burke stops the car ahead of the house. My hand is already clenched tight around the black handle of the machete, the spare knife tucked into my jacket pocket. We don't have to worry about anyone seeing me enter the building because the darkness coupled with my speed means I'll barely be visible against the shadows of the night.

I reach for the door handle.

"Ready?" Burke asks rather pointlessly.

I nod, relieved the moment has come. A welcome rush of adrenaline surges through my veins. For the first time all day, I'm confident. "Ready."

I climb out of the car into the glow of a streetlamp, my eyes flicking upward to the star-spangled sky. It's still too early in the year to see the constellation of Sagittarius, but the bright dots comfort me somehow, reminding me of my goal—get the job done and get back to Mila.

Burke climbs out of the driver's seat. He will follow at a distance, and along with two other officers—who are parked farther up—kick the front door in. By that time, Moreau will hopefully be no more than a dusty sack of bones on the floor.

Tightening my grip on the machete, I give Burke a final terse nod before leaping onto the orange tile porch of the house two doors away from Moreau's. I land neat as a cat, legs bent at the knees, before diving onto the rusted rails of number fifty-five's upper story. Not landing feet first on the balcony itself turns out to be a good omen—the wood is rotten and splintered and would have undoubtedly caved under my weight. Without wasting any more time pondering the decorative state of the building, I slide the window open with my free hand and duck into the kitchen, machete held out ahead of me.

I stand on a tiny square of torn linoleum, next to a stove with scorch marks on the hob, waiting. A vampire would have heard the window opening, should be confronting me by now. But there is only the tinny sound of the TV from a room farther along the hallway and the slow drip of a leaky tap hitting the ceramic sink with a soft *plink*.

Something isn't right. Despite the open window, the air in the kitchen is musty, *unlived in*. I open a cupboard. Empty, though mine were pretty bare before Mila arrived with her junk food habit, so that doesn't necessarily mean anything.

I step into the dark hallway. On my right are the stairs, a wooden bannister stretching ahead. To my left, farther along the wall, is a half-open door. I hurl myself into the room, fangs out, but it's completely empty—not a stick of furniture.

Not bothering to turn on the lights, I enter the other rooms in turn, finding them all the same at the first one—empty, no furniture, a sour, airless musk swirling between the walls. Nearing the one with the television blaring, a cold dread begins to creep up my spine. I kick the door open so fiercely the whole thing comes loose from its hinges, falling flat onto the carpet. A cloud of dust, visible in the blue glow of the television, puffs out from the edges.

The TV is plugged in and propped up on a small plastic table, the bray of a noisy quiz show echoing off the walls. Downstairs, I hear the front door being rammed, the splintering of wood as Burke and the others pound into the flat. I scan the room, my hands trembling from pent-up adrenaline. I'm so pumped for action it takes a while for my head to clear, the implications of the empty flat beginning to sink in.

He knew we were coming.

In a fit of rage and aggression, I kick the television into the wall, the incessant babble dying instantly as the room plunges into darkness. I whirl around to face Burke, who despite his age and fondness for cream cakes is always the first to arrive on the scene. He holds his police badge out in front of him as if it were an AK-74.

He flips the light on, bathing the empty room in a stark white glow. "Inspector?"

"A trick," I say, looking around at the blank walls as if Moreau might still materialize before us. "I don't think he was ever here."

Footfalls echo along the corridor as the rest of the team finishes their search.

"Nothing, Superintendent," an officer confirms.

Burke sighs loudly. "Right-o. We'll send forensics in first thing tomorrow and dust for prints, make a proper search of the place."

They all file back along the hall, and I'm about to follow them, my gaze lingering on the smashed pool of glass beneath the TV, when I catch sight of a white envelope facedown on the faded blue carpet.

Frowning, I reach down to pick it up. I run my thumb under the seal, tipping the contents into my open palm. A familiar object hits my skin with a *thunk*, a white square of paper fluttering to the floor.

I open my fingers to stare at the object in my left hand, but even before the gold glints beneath the electric bulb in the ceiling and I turn it over to see my family's coat of arms—a diagonal strip of silver through a green background, a dove at the tip of the crest—I know what it is and what it means.

I stare dumbfounded at the ring, a token of everything I used to be, a reminder of the night my first love died, a symbol that no matter how many years pass or how far you run, the past always catches up.

My knees sag as I drop to the dusty carpet and unfold the thin white paper. It takes my eyes a moment to focus on the black spiky ink on the page.

You should take better care of your things.

A burst of horror explodes at the center of my chest as the meaning sinks in.

I drop the ring and the note, and without stopping to explain to a stunned-looking Burke, I flee the house, moving so fast, the night air cuts into my skin like a knife.

You should take better care of your things.

He is going after Mila.

Chapter 17

Mila

"FIGHT," I SAY TO LEE DAVIES, LEANING FORWARD ON the swivel chair. "Fight for her with everything you've got, and when there's nothing left, fight some more."

For the zillionth time since Vincent left, my eyes flicker between the clock on the wall and my phone on the desk. Though it's been roughly thirty minutes since he left with Burke, it already feels like hours.

Cat, who is sitting on my left, shakes her head. "I disagree. No disrespect, Mila, but I think you should go Buddhist on this one, Davies—do nothing."

Davies glances between us both in confusion, his brow furrowed. "Nothing?"

Cat nods. "If you keep calling and texting and making a fuss, you become the enemy. Thus, pushing her further into the comforting arms of Mr. UPS. If you do nothing, you give her time to think. Suddenly, rather than the bad guy, you're the reasonable, self-effacing man who's only ever wanted the best for her. She starts to realize what she's missing."

From over by the window, Ronin scoffs. The whole time we've been counseling Lee he's been silent, staring out into the night, but now he's glaring at Cat with a wicked glint in his eye, a smirk stretched across his thin lips. "Do nothing," he says, mimicking Cat's voice.

"I hardly think London's longest-living spinster is in a position to be dishing out marriage advice."

Cat whips her head around to him, lip curled. "Oh," she says, voice dripping with sarcasm. "I forgot we have an expert on matters of the heart in our midst. Do tell us what your advice would be."

Hands thrust deep into his pockets, Ronin steps away from the window. "No thanks. I'm not overly fond of telling people how to live their lives. Besides, relationships don't interest me."

"Evidently," Cat says, cutting him a scornful glare.

Davies and I exchange wide-eyed looks, as if we've just realized we're trapped in a cage with a pair of man-eating lions.

"You know," Ronin says, wagging an index finger at her, "the whole 'do nothing' advice reminds me of that night we spent together. Maybe that's your modus operandi in all walks of life, including the bedroom."

As Cat's brown-green eyes flash with anger, Lee spins around to his computer and begins typing on his laptop, and I snatch my phone, pretending to be engrossed in the home screen.

Cat lets out a high-pitched laugh. "Please, you're so used to those harpies at your club you have no idea what a real woman wants—probably never did."

"Show me a real woman and we'll ask her," Ronin retorts.

"I actually find it hilarious you're still doing this."

Ronin lets out a tiny snort of incredulity. "Doing what?"

"Razzing me because I didn't want to see you again after we slept together. For a creature who's been around since the dawn of time, you're surprisingly inept when it comes to dating. I've known five-year-olds with a better grasp of emotional maturity."

Lee Davies's fingers still on the computer keys, my phone almost slips from my grasp. This is better than *Jersey Shore*.

Ronin chuckles. "Don't flatter yourself, Catherine. I was just doing my bit for the community, giving an old dog a bone."

Cat's chair rolls backward and knocks into mine as she leaps out of her seat. The tension is so thick, they're either going to kill each other or kiss—*violently*. "If I'm such an old dog, why did you make Vincent ask me to meet you?"

I sneak a peek at the pair of them. They're a foot apart, blazing eyes locked. It's obvious they've completely forgotten Lee and I are in earshot.

He shrugs a shoulder. "I get a kick out of seeing you angry. Everyone is always so afraid of me, it's a novelty."

Cat, who is on the verge of shouting, cries, "A novelty!"

My eyes dart back to Ronin. But before I get to hear his snarky response, I'm distracted by the buzzing of my phone. I jump about two feet into the air, grabbing for it so fast it slips from my sweaty grip and slides to the floor. Lee spins in his chair and snatches it up, holding it out to me. I'm so frantic to hit the green button I barely register the fact it's an unknown number.

"Hello?"

There is a long pause on the other end. "Mila? It's Karolina from class."

My heart sinks, Lee's face dropping as I shake my head.

"Oh, hi, Karolina." Disappointment leaks into my voice.

"I'm sorry. This is bad time for you? I call back?"

The text from earlier flashes into my head. With all the drama, I'd completely forgotten I sent it. "No. Not a bad time. I can talk."

I hold a finger up to Lee and drift to the other side of the office. With all the yelling going on, I can barely hear her.

"Mila, you are there?"

"Yes, I am. Sorry, I was just going somewhere more private."

"You want to know about the life essence?"

I take a deep breath. "Yes. I was wondering if they ever change."

Karolina pauses. I imagine her examining her nails. *What makes up Karolina's essence?* I muse. Possibly Prada handbags and unsuitable men.

"The vampire man did not explain this?" There is a hint of exasperation in her Eastern European accent.

"Yes, he did, but it…" I pause, knotting a long strand of hair around my index finger. "It bothers me."

"Oh. It is woman?"

"Yes."

"And you are jealous?"

"No," I say quickly. "It's not that. There's a particular scene, a tragic incident he can't move past and it makes me wonder if he'll ever be truly happy—if *I* can ever make him truly happy. Does that make sense?"

Karolina sighs. "Life essences are different for

everyone. They mean different things. Mine is of my mother. How long ago is this tragic incident?"

I cringe. "About three hundred years, give or take."

"I see. Does he tell you he loves you?"

"No," I admit, thinking of his face right before he left, his jaw clenched so tight a pulse hammered beneath the skin. It seemed as though he was waging some inner battle, as if he wanted to unleash something important but thought better of it.

"Do you love him?"

I suck in a sharp breath. God. I do. I really do.

"It's early days," I mumble. "Very early days."

"I warn you about the relationship between vampire and human. Things are not easy. Some say it is great curse to fall for the undead."

"No shit," I mutter.

We are silent for a few seconds. Across the office, Ronin and Cat are still going at it hammer and tongs, their voices clashing with the cheering noises erupting from Davies's computer. From the sound of it, he's watching a football match to drown out the arguing.

"It's possible for the life essence to change," Karolina says. "If he lets go of the past, his life essence will change with it. But nothing is certain. There's no vampire handbook."

"No," I say grimly. "I suppose there wouldn't be."

"I wish I could help better."

I close my eyes, rubbing my temples. "That's okay. Thanks for calling me."

"Of course," she continues, "if you decide to spend your lives together, there is a way to fix age problem."

"Do you mean by me turning into a vampire?"

Karolina laughs shrilly. "Oh, Mila, no. I mean for him. To take away his immortality."

My eyes flip open, the walls and desks around me blurring. The floor seems to drop away from under me. At that moment, the shouting from Ronin and Cat reaches fever pitch.

"You're nothing but a neurotic shrew," Ronin bellows.

Cat emits a loud *ha!* "A neurotic shrew you've been pestering for the past four years."

"What?" I say into the phone. She says something, but I can't hear her over the racket. I edge toward the door, slipping out into the blessed silence of the empty corridor.

"Say it again," I say, the phone pressed tightly to my ear.

She laughs, the noise tinkling down the line like a bell. "I said, how lucky for you I am vampire witch."

I think of the card she gave me, the special talents Vincent mentioned. "Are you messing with me?" I ask, my stomach fluttering with excitement.

"No, Mila. I wouldn't do that."

I'm about to ask her to elaborate when I hear the unmistakable swoosh of the elevator doors opening around the corner of the corridor. *Vincent is back*.

"Karolina, I have to go, but I really, really want to talk more about this. Can I call you tomorrow?"

"Yes. Speak then. Bye, Mila."

We hang up. There are soft footfalls now, barely audible above the gurgle from Lee's computer, the high-pitched voices of Cat and Ronin. I slide my phone into the back of my jeans, a smile already twitching at the corners of my mouth as I hurtle along the corridor. I skid around the corner, smacking chest first into someone tall and broad.

Even before rough hands seize my shoulders, I know it isn't Vincent. A strong scent hits my nostrils—a rich, musky cologne. The knot of excitement in my tummy twists violently in fear. I stop breathing, my legs turning to water beneath me. Suddenly I'm back in the damp alley, amid kitchen waste and the lingering aroma of stale piss. My eyes home in on an open collar, a triangle of olive flesh, and then I lift my gaze, my brain joining the images together like pieces of a terrifying puzzle.

I stare into the face of David Moreau.

Without the faux charm of the bar, his features are a mask of hard lines—tight, angular jaw, broad forehead, flat cheekbones. Beneath the stark glare of the fluorescent lighting, his eyes are as hard and bitter as two black coffee beans.

He holds my gaze, his pupils dilating to slits as the scream surging up my throat dies in my mouth. My self-control leaks away as his dead eyes pierce mine.

My vocal cords are frozen. *Cat, Ronin*, I scream with my mind. *Lee. Did they even notice I left the room?*

Moreau holds an index finger to his lips, his dark eyes flashing as he yanks me by the arm along the corridor and into the elevator he just stepped out of.

I watch, numb with horror as he jabs the button to take us into the basement, to the underground garage.

When the sliding doors bang shut, he grins, a sinister, mocking smile, his teeth as white as a shark's.

"I was disappointed when you didn't call me after our date, Mila," he jeers. "Was it something I said?"

His hand clamps around my upper arm like a vise. He walks me backward until I hit the mirror, his face so close I almost choke on his cologne.

Look away, I command myself. *Look away. He can't control you.* But my eyes stay pinned to his grinning face, my body as stiff as a corpse.

"I think we'll have some fun, you and I," he continues. "There's a lot of unfinished business between us. Particularly now you're Inspector Ferrer's pet."

Under the glamour, I can barely muster a frown. Inside, however, I'm screaming like a banshee, my head throbbing painfully as I struggle to regain power over my body.

"Foolish of him to leave you unattended," he goads. "I didn't think for one minute it would be this easy. That you would walk right into my arms."

The jolt of the elevator hitting the ground floor breaks his concentration for a split second. I manage to shut my eyes as he heaves me out into the cool, stale air of the garage.

My feet shuffle across rough concrete. If I could just scream, Cat or Ronin will hear me. Surely by now they've realized I'm gone.

I wait until Moreau stops. By this point I've guessed this is more than just an escape route, that we're going to get into a vehicle. As soon as I hear him click a key fob, I take advantage of the small distraction by throwing my energy into fighting off the glamour. I think of things that have happened in the past that made me feel something—the anger when Scott ditched me, the sadness I felt when Dad moved out, the first time Vincent kissed me—drawing out memories and cramming them into my nerve endings, forcing myself into action.

The fog clears.

Without wasting a moment, I open my mouth, allowing as much air into my lungs as possible, and scream. A rattling shriek ricochets around the concrete walls. I'm so detached from it, for a second I'm convinced it isn't me at all. When I flick my eyes open, the last thing I see is Moreau's dark eyes narrowed to slits and his hand as he pulls it back to strike me, hard and flat across the face.

———※———

The first thought I have when I wake up is that I'm going to die. My skull throbs. Nausea rises up the back of my throat like bile. I feel as though I've been flung down a flight of stairs and then dragged back up by the roots of my hair. I do a mental inventory of my body, relieved to find all parts intact and fully clothed, though my side is numb from the cold concrete I'm lying on, loose stones digging into my elbow and knee.

A moan escapes my lips—a good sign, as it means the glamour has dropped. As far as good things go, however, everything else is dire. A burning sensation radiates from my wrists, and when I try to move them, I realize they're tightly bound, the searing pain caused by a thin rope cutting into my skin like a blade. I try to reach into the darkness without opening my eyes, praying I'm alone while simultaneously hoping he hasn't abandoned me, leaving me to rot in some remote dark hole.

I open my eyes to nothing but thick blackness. I screw my eyes shut again, wondering if the blow to the head has blinded me, before reopening them in an attempt to differentiate between the shades of coal black. Nothing changes. Either I *am* blind or the place where I'm tied up is windowless.

I wait for a wave of nausea to fade before slowly heaving myself into a sitting position. Right away I wish I hadn't. Not only does the pain cause a thin trickle of vomit to spill over my chin, but footsteps approach and a match hisses as it's struck. Any relief I feel at seeing the tiny flame flicker to life is eclipsed by David Moreau's face looming toward me, pale and luminous in the darkness.

I bite back a bloodcurdling scream.

"Sleeping Beauty is awake," he goads. With a spasm of horror, I realize he smells different, the scent of his cologne smothered by the unmistakable whiff of gasoline.

I turn away from the flame and he straightens, lighting what appears to be an old-fashioned gas lamp and setting it down on the ground. At first I think he's brought me to a cave. The walls of the room are rocky and uneven but set into the gray stone above are timber beams. The ground is bare, stripped of floorboards, and bone-dry.

"Did you sleep well?" he asks, dark eyes gleaming like jet in the flickering light of the flame.

"Where am I?" I demand. My voice is hoarse and slurred. It occurs to me he can't have taken me far from Scotland Yard or we would still be driving. Unless I've been out for a long time.

"Still in London," he says. "Don't worry. I've not taken you anywhere your boyfriend won't be able to find you."

As the words sink in, my eyes snag on a flash of light on the floor near my feet. There, gleaming in the orange glow of the lamp, is a large metal blade shaped like a scythe.

Moreau clocks my wide-eyed terror, following my gaze to the weapon. "Ah, don't worry about that. You'll be dead before lover boy."

My stomach churns violently and I begin to tremble. Although the air is humid and stuffy, my teeth chatter, knocking together like loose marbles in a bag. The rational part of my brain tells me to keep him talking. I recall hearing somewhere that if abducted, you should make friends with your captor, if for no other reason than to buy yourself more time.

"What's Vincent to you?"

He cocks his head to one side, frowning. "I was under the impression he knew of our connection by now. Or hasn't he told you?"

"No," I say, deciding to play dumb to keep him speaking. "I thought it was me you were after."

He laughs, and if there wasn't already enough evidence this guy is seriously unhinged, the mad cackle erupting from his mouth confirms it.

"It's so typical of your generation, Mila, to assume everything is about you." He sighs, kneeling on the bumpy ground before me. His hand goes to his trousers, and for one awful moment, I think he's reaching for his fly. The relief is short-lived, however, when he pulls a shiny object from his pocket. A knife.

My heart pounds so fast there is a rushing noise in my ears. I stare, lips trembling uncontrollably as he holds the silver blade out, shuffling backward until I hit the rough surface of a wall.

He grins, making no attempt to close the gap. "No, it isn't about you. Or about any of the other girls, really. You see, I've been waiting for centuries to get even with your beloved hero. He murdered my sister."

Even though I know about the ring and the likelihood of the connection, I'm unable to suppress a gasp. "Sister?"

I study him in the low light, searching his features for similarities to Adrienne in Vincent's essence. His thick hair is the same shade of obsidian. He has her smooth olive skin, but it's the eyes that set them apart. Adrienne's were amber, deep golden wells of emotion; her brother's eyes are as dark as a raven's. The golden hue that shone from their depths the night of our date has vanished. They are as flat and lifeless as two black holes.

"Yes. My older sister. I was only twelve years old when she died."

"Vincent didn't kill her," I blurt out. "It was an accident. He—"

I break off as he looms in on me with the blade, pressing the tip into my nose. "I'm sorry," he hisses. "I wasn't aware you were around three hundred years ago."

I swallow loudly and close my mouth.

He retracts the knife. "I *was* there, though neither of them knew it at the time. My foolish sister was so in love with him. The duke's son—her prince. Even after he married someone else, she was still just as besotted, more than willing to ruin herself by becoming his whore."

His eyes blur out for a few seconds, lost in the realms of the past.

"Adrienne was like a mother to me. Our natural mother had died in childbirth with my youngest sister and Adrienne was the eldest girl. She raised most of us. We all adored her. She was kind and gentle but capable and strong too. Fearless, really. She set her heart on your Vincent Ferrer from an early age and there was no talking her out of it. Though God knows my father tried."

It's ridiculous given the situation, but a pang of jealousy tugs at my heart. Staring into the face of Adrienne's brother bridges the gap between past and present. Although dead for centuries, Adrienne has never felt more alive.

"Vincent loved her," I whisper, instantly wishing I hadn't as Moreau's black eyes flash with anger.

"Shut your mouth," he snaps, seizing my chin roughly. "You don't kill the one you love."

Of course you do, I think. *It happens every day.*

He releases me with a shove, my head banging into the rough wall behind me. I bite my lip to keep from crying out.

"The night he came for her, I was awake," he continues, eyes narrowed. "I followed her into the garden and watched as he led her away. I was angry with her, annoyed she could be so easily led. I sometimes helped my father in the gardens of the estate, and I knew how affairs between ladies and gentlemen were usually conducted. They would walk out with chaperones. Only when a couple were married could they behave like my sister—dashing off into the trees hand in hand, the luminous glow of love shining from her face.

"I kept pace with them to a clearing, watching as he pawed at her, his filthy hands all over the place—and she with her head flung back in surrender, enjoying every second. I was about to go back to the house when her countenance changed. She screamed, stepping away from him. It was then I saw his fangs, blood snaking down her white neck into the collar of her nightgown. Adrienne ran away and he chased her. I followed them. It took me a while to catch up. I wasn't a particularly athletic child. I heard more screaming, but when I emerged from the trees, there was no sign of them at all.

"That's when I figured out where they had gone. I crawled to the edge of the cliff and looked down at the rocks where my sister lay dying, the monster hanging over her. It still stings that she died in such terror, that the image she took to the next life was of his gloating face."

Vincent would never gloat, I want to say, but I keep silent, watching the gleam of the knife as it catches the light of the flame.

"Terrified, I ran back to the house and woke up my father. When I told him who did it, he didn't believe me—the duke and his family were supposedly imprisoned in Paris at that time. Then, when I mentioned the fangs, he thought I had turned soft in the head, that my words were the foolish ramblings of a grieving child. Do you know what he chose to believe in the end? What everyone chose to believe?"

Adrienne's pale face flashes into my mind. Witnessing her tragic death in Vincent's essence was heartrending enough, but hearing this—the fallout of that tragic night—is unbearable. "What?" I ask, a tremor in my voice.

"That she killed herself. That she was so distraught at the news of her lover's imprisonment she could no longer bear it. My father declared it suicide. After all she did for us, he betrayed her memory."

A heavy silence falls. Without Moreau's voice filling the chamber, I make out the muffled rush of traffic somewhere above us.

"Vincent didn't mean to hurt her," I whisper, bracing myself against the wall. "It was an accident."

Moreau digs the knife into the loose earth as if he hasn't heard me. "Afterward, I began to doubt myself, but I knew what I saw and I set out to prove it. After the revolution ended, vampires became my obsession. I grew up and moved to Paris, determined to seek them out, to expose the monsters to the world. I chased down every lead and came up with nothing. How ironic that in the end, they found me."

He pauses, glancing up at me wide-eyed, as if realizing I'm still here. "Her name was Esme. An ancient, of course. Word had gotten around about a young man chasing vampires and she decided to pay me a visit. The rest is history."

"I don't get it," I say, voice quavering. "If it's revenge you want, why not go after Vincent? Why murder innocent people? Women with families and little brothers—just like you once were."

At once, the knife is pointed into my face. I'm so

startled, my heart spasms with fear. I lose control of my limbs again, trembling violently.

He snatches a fistful of my hair and pushes me back against the wall, aiming the blade at the space between my brows. He is so close I can smell sweat on his skin, the stench of gasoline on his fingers. "I stopped being that child the moment the ancient got her hands on me. That child is as dead as my sister. Do you have any idea what it was like? Becoming exactly like the monster who took Adrienne from us? It was my own personal hell. The only advantage was that I finally possessed the strength to end Ferrer's life—except he was impossible to find. I searched everywhere, but he'd shunned vampire society, hiding among humans like the coward he is. It was only when vampires went mainstream that I discovered his whereabouts, working for the police of all things, masquerading as some kind of hero. I even heard through an acquaintance of mine he was helping round up vampires for their part in historical crimes. Finally, I seized my chance. But I'd waited too long to merely destroy him. I wanted him to suffer first. That's when you came along."

I gulp loudly, my eyes never straying from the knifepoint.

"You are the cherry on the cake, Mila. Not killing you after our date was the best thing that could have happened. Before you, he was completely alone. I was messing with him in the professional sense, sure, but I soon realized the only way I'll ever really be able to teach him a lesson is to kill someone he cares about. When I saw you together in Leicester Square, I knew I'd hit the karmic jackpot. The next day in his car, I watched you both, too besotted to consider who might be watching. The final piece of the puzzle fell into place. You're my ultimate weapon, Mila. When I kill you in front of him, he'll know exactly what it's like to watch someone you love die—like I watched Adrienne all those years ago."

A cold icicle of fear stabs my heart. "How do you know he loves me? Maybe I'm not that important to him. Maybe it's just a fling."

He shakes his head slowly, a gloating smile on his lips. "No. He feels something for you, and who can blame him? I haven't changed my mind about you, Mila. I'm still going to be sad to kill you."

Rather than churning my insides with more terror, his words trigger a different instinct—survival. My gaze flickers from the knife to his black eyes and back again, before sweeping the room for an escape route.

The rumble of traffic pulses through the wall behind me, the distant rattle coming from somewhere above my head. The two walls on each side and the one opposite are blank, which means I'm more than likely leaning against the wall with the exit.

A tiny voice tells me it's pointless, that even if there was a wide-open door in front of me and my hands weren't tied, I would still never make it. He is a vampire, after all, and I am only human. But my survival instincts will not be crushed.

I glance down at his body and see my chance. Moreau kneels in the chalky dust, his knees on either side of my thighs. Without a second thought, I bring my leg up as fast as possible, whacking my shin into his groin. His surprise buys me a chance to duck under the knife and out from under him. On legs shakier than a newborn foal's, I slide up the wall. Glancing up, I realize there's a flight of steps running above me, a lumpy mass of shadows signaling where the staircase begins. I lurch toward it.

I manage two steps before I'm flung across the room. Hitting the opposite wall, I crumple into a broken heap, pain exploding like fire all over my body.

Moreau's shadow looms over me. "Really, Mila? What did you think would happen?"

I say nothing. Curling into a ball of misery and pain, I brace myself for further attack. Instead he crosses the lamp-lit room to the shadows at the bottom of the narrow stairs and lifts something out of the darkness. The smell of gasoline intensifies, and with a lurch of horror, I remember the strong scent on his hands as he waved the knife at me. A can of gasoline glistens menacingly in the dim light.

"I put a lot of thought into it," he says casually, as if discussing holiday plans with a hairdresser. "I decided when the time comes, I'm not going to have time to kill you myself." He twists off the can's red cap. "A lit match can do it for me. Inspector Ferrer will soon follow, don't worry. But first, I'll enjoy seeing his reaction as he watches you burn."

He lifts the can and tips it up. As the liquid begins to splatter on my body, soaking through my clothing, I finally start to scream.

Chapter 18

Vincent

I DON'T REMEMBER MUCH OF THE FRANTIC JOURNEY back to Scotland Yard. By the time I arrive at the imposing, gray hulk of glass and metal, my mouth is bone-dry, my skin whipped to ice by the wind. A long tear runs down the front of my shirt, though I have no idea how it got there.

I leap up the stairs two at a time. Until I know Mila is safe, I'm spinning on a knife's edge, dread and fury sending waves of emotion through me like a wild electrical current.

I fall into Lee's office, shoving the door open so violently it smashes into the wall behind it with a deafening thud. Cat and Ronin whip around, mouths agape. Lee jumps out of his swivel chair.

"Where's Mila?" I demand, staring frantically between them, stunned by their apathy.

Lee jabs a thumb over his shoulder to the far corner of the office. "She's on the phone."

Though I know she isn't here, I dive across the room anyway, scattering chairs and wastepaper baskets in my haste.

I glare at the three of them, their expressions rapidly turning to looks of horror as it dawns on them they've let her slip away.

"She took a phone call," Lee says, blinking rapidly. "She was standing right there."

Without answering him, I whirl around, diving back out into the corridor.

"Mila!" I yell, running the length of the offices. "Mila?!"

I fling open the door to the ladies' bathroom, but the cubicles are all empty. "Mila!"

Lee and Cat join me as I speed toward the elevators. "Why?" I demand, my fists clenched into tight balls to keep from grabbing him again. "Why did you let her leave?"

Lee shakes his head in bewilderment. "Her phone rang and she couldn't hear properly, so she went to the other side of the office. I thought she was still in the room."

Cat rakes her hands through her curls, clutching her head. "Ronin and I…we were arguing. Things got out of hand. She must have gone into the corridor."

"You were arguing?" I emit a growl before slamming my fist into the wall. "I trusted you," I say. "I trusted all of you."

Before Cat can answer, the elevator *pings*. Burke and several armed officers burst through the metal doors like rats from a sewer hole.

Burke surveys us with a tight-lipped grimace.

"Miss Hart?" he asks me.

I shake my head. "Gone." The word sticks in my throat like tar.

The backs of my eyes prickle as Burke begins barking orders at his team. "Get security on the CCTV footage immediately. Clegg, put the whole building on lockdown. Inspector Ferrer?"

I snap my head up.

"Give me your phone. I'll put a trace on her number."
He holds out his hand. "Now!"

"She could be anywhere," I say, holding out my phone
with a trembling hand. "How could I let this happen?"

Burke snatches the phone and tosses it to Clegg, who
immediately retreats into an empty office next to the lifts.

"There will be ample time later for regrets and self-
loathing, Vincent. Listen to me. Her best shot is still
you. But if you're going to let your emotions get the
better of you, she *will* die. Do you understand me?"

I briefly close my eyes. "Yes."

"Then put those away," Burke says, motioning at my
teeth.

For the first time, I realize my fangs are out.

Lee places a hand on my shoulder. "I swear I didn't
see her leave the room," he says, his eyes moist. "If I
had, I'd have gone after her. You know I would."

I shake my head. "Cat, where's Ronin?"

"Probably left," Cat says with a disgusted snort.

Suddenly he appears at her shoulder. "Not gone, actually. I was trailing his scent. They left in a vehicle. The
trail dies in the garage downstairs."

"The address was fake," I say, staring into his calm
blue eyes. "He wasn't there."

"I gathered that," Ronin says. "I can trace the person
who provided the address, Vincent, but she could be
anywhere by now."

My gut twists painfully. This isn't the attitude I need
him to have. "We're tracing Mila's phone. I don't think
Moreau will make it difficult for me to find her. This is
personal, after all, but I'll need help to get her out safely."

"I can't kill another ancient's spawn without unleash-ing Esme's wrath. You may have chosen to forget the laws of our kind, Vincent, but I haven't. I still abide by them. Well, most of the time anyway."

"I'm not asking you to kill him," I say. "In fact, I insist on doing that myself. But he's not going to let Mila run free. I need your strength and speed to remove her from the scene."

"What if she's already dead?" he asks.

My head spins. If I let my mind go to that place, I'll never make it out again. "She isn't dead. I feel it. Maybe because her blood is inside me. I've heard that can happen, can't it?"

"You drank from her," Ronin mutters. "Wonders never cease."

"Ronin. Will you come or not?"

"Yes," he says. "I won't kill David Moreau, but I will get your woman out."

As if on cue, Officer Clegg appears in the doorway waving a Post-it Note.

"Got him."

-~~-

Mila

I lie on the floor in the fetal position, knees tucked under my chin, eyes screwed shut as Moreau sits beside me, a Zippo lighter clasped in one hand.

He hums occasionally as he flicks the thumbwheel. Every time I hear the spark of the flame as it springs to life, my breath catches, black spots appearing in my vision.

"I must say, I thought he would have found you by now," he says, waving the naked flame through the air.

"Where are we?" I ask in a small voice. It's the first time I've spoken since he poured the gas over me and I screamed so loudly he slapped me across the face.

"Near Alexandra Palace. A street away from the house he visited earlier. Won't he be pissed off to know he was within spitting distance all along?"

I say nothing, awaiting Vincent's arrival with hope and dread in equal measure, consoling myself with the knowledge that if the worst happens, I'll die staring into the face of the man I love.

Moreau continues to hum, the noise unsettling and comforting at the same time. Comforting because while he's humming, he isn't killing me, and unsettling because it's a constant reminder I'm trapped here with a psycho of epic proportions.

I never could do things by halves.

When he breaks off, I open my eyes to see his features lit with eerie joy. He emits a short, bitter laugh. "I think your dashing knight might be here at last, Mila."

My stomach churns, the blood in my veins freezing to ice as Moreau scoops up the scythe in his spare hand. Over the rush of distant traffic, I hear the sound of wood splintering. I shout Vincent's name, trying to warn him about the weapon, and Moreau rounds on me, the chrome lighter catching in the glow of the gas lamp. But before he can flick the thumbwheel, he disappears, a dark blur knocking him across the room and into the rough stone wall, where he drops to the ground in a dusty heap.

Strong arms lift me from the damp floor.

Even before I catch a glimpse of russet hair and see blue eyes as cold and hard as diamonds, I know it isn't Vincent. Whoever this is smells of malt whiskey and woodsmoke; his body is hard as stone as he flings me over a broad shoulder like a sack of flour. *Ronin*.

"Hold tight, girlie," he says in a gruff voice as I'm whipped from the room. On the way up the stone stairwell, I catch a whiff of a familiar scent—the aroma of linen and aftershave mixed with something salty—like tears. But it quickly dissipates as I'm bundled out into the cool night air and set down on wobbling legs.

The streets sway about my ears. I feel as though I'm standing on a ship's deck and not on solid ground. I barely even realize I've fallen backward until I'm staring up at the stars, Ronin's powerful arms catching me mid-stumble.

"Oh, look," I say deliriously, attempting to point to the sky. "I think I see Sagittarius."

Vincent

There is no time to check on Mila as I pass by her and Ronin on the stairs, though her pulse, strong and fierce and beating through her veins like a drum, leaves me light-headed with relief. I clutch the black-handled machete, holding it aloft as I land in the dusty cellar. I've never been more ready to end the life of this psychopath.

The stench of gasoline in the room makes me sick to my stomach, as does the scent of Mila's blood, a sweet iron tang lacing the air. A dim glow radiates from a gas lamp on the floor, illuminating the fallen shape of David Moreau. I lift the machete high above my head and leap forward, swinging it in an arc toward his lolling head.

The blade strikes the floor with a *twang*.

David Moreau's laughter echoes off the walls. "So, it turns out you have friends in the vampire world after all. Can't say I'm not disappointed to lose our lovely Mila. But don't worry. I'll catch up with her soon enough."

I step closer, pointing the machete at his face as he lifts a curved blade of his own.

He motions to my blade with his. "Touché. Isn't that what we used to say in France?"

I stare into his eyes, trying to read him while at the same time searching for any resemblance to Adrienne. Aside from the dark hair and golden skin tone, there is little to mark them as relatives.

"What's Adrienne to you?" I demand.

His eyes narrow. "Sister. Witness to her murder that night you sent her over the cliff."

I flinch and he uses the momentary distraction to his advantage, swinging the crescent of the scythe sideways at my neck. I just manage to duck in time, air whistling above my head as the blade makes its vicious journey. With a burst of adrenaline, I leap through the air to the opposite side of the cell.

"No one was there that night," I hiss, inching sideways to cover the exit at the bottom of the stairs. There is no way I'll be letting him escape a second time.

He smiles, a ghoulish, tight grin, revealing sharp white fangs. "That's what you think."

"I loved her."

"You *killed* her! But I didn't come here to hear your pathetic excuses. Memory can be a curious thing, especially with lives as long as ours. Given enough time, any truth can be twisted to ease the conscience."

"How will you twist the truth in the years to come, Moreau?" I spit venomously. "To justify murdering those innocent girls?"

His jaw clenches. "I'm not as sanctimonious as you, Ferrer. I won't have to justify anything. My innocence died the night I discovered what you are. Do you know what happened to my family after Adrienne died?"

I shake my head, never taking my eyes from his beady, black eyes, fingers flexing on the handle of the machete as I wait for a slip in his concentration.

"My father stopped working. He spent his days drinking instead. Two of the younger children died of malnourishment, and I was labeled a nutcase for telling the truth about what I saw that night."

A brief flicker of guilt sparks in my gut, but then I remember the dead women—violated and torn, left to rot on the street like animals—and my resolve hardens to steel. I need to say or do something to distract him, or I will never get out of here alive.

"Fine," I say, deciding to lie through my teeth. "I'll admit it. I threw Adrienne off the cliff because she refused to become like me. I drained her dry once she was dead."

Moreau stares, impassive. "Please, you'll have to do better than that."

Just then comes the echo of heavy footfalls on the

ceiling above us. Heart in my mouth, I seize my chance and dive at Moreau, landing on his chest and knocking us both to the ground. I cling to him, one hand clamped around the back of his neck and the other clutching the weapon, but he is quick to react. He presses himself tight against me, rendering the blade useless as I stab at empty air. After one of the hollow thrusts, he manages to haul me over, switching our positions so that I'm pinned to floor beneath him. My fangs pop out as I snarl in anger, a vein in my forehead pulsing like a jackhammer. Every muscle in my body is tense as I hold him off.

My teeth are clenched so tight I prick my lip, a droplet of blood falling onto my tongue. The iron tang gives me an idea—a way of gaining the upper hand. If he loved Adrienne as much as he claims to, the image of her in my life essence should be enough of a diversion to destroy him. Without another thought, I lunge for his throat, sinking my fangs into the waxy column of his neck and trying hard not to gag as his bitter blood hits the back of my throat.

He wails as he tries to fight the vision, his fangs gnashing together like a rabid dog as he thrashes around on top of me, and then comes the moment I was hoping for—a brief pause as Adrienne's face appears in his mind. It's enough to roll him over and raise the machete high above my head.

But before I bring it down on his neck, I hear scuffling on the stairs. I lose concentration as Lee Davies of all people appears from the shadows holding a similar machete to the one in my hand. Moreau spots his chance. Blood snaking into the white collar of his shirt, he flings me across the room and into the wall.

Lee rushes toward him, weapon raised, only to be flung back like a rag doll. Moreau comes at me fast, the silver crescent of the scythe glinting in the lamp's flame like sunlight. I leap to my feet and block his weapon with mine, the clash of metal vibrating like a hammer striking iron. I spit out the mouthful of his vile blood as we strike again, metal on metal. My teeth are gritted, every bit of strength in my body going into the blade.

"The next time I capture your beloved, I won't be so much of a gentleman," he hisses, face contorted with rage. "I wonder how she'll taste when I'm inside her."

Though I try not to listen to his goading words, I lose my footing, stumbling back a few paces. Moreau's mocking laughter fills the cellar as a blade slices through the air.

I brace myself for impact. Eyes closed, I think of Mila—her smile, her infectious laugh, and the future we'll never have.

But despite the sound of metal hitting bone, a warm, wet liquid splattering my face and clothes, I remain conscious, standing, *alive*.

A hand shakes my shoulder as a voice at my ear says, "Vince," and then more desperately, "Vincent!"

I open my eyes to find Lee's anxious face staring up at me. For a wild second, I wonder if I blacked out or Lee died too, and we're both headed for the afterlife.

"He's dead," Lee cries shrilly. "Look."

I follow his wide-eyed gaze to a lumpy shadow on the ground. There, no more than a fizzing sack of dusty old clothes, are the remains of David Moreau.

"I killed him," Lee says, a hint of pride creeping into

his excited voice. "He was so busy trying to murder you, he didn't notice me creep up on him."

Blinking, I stare between the rapidly decomposing body and Lee's shiny face and back again. Then I fling my arms around my friend, pulling him into a fierce embrace.

Lee pats my back awkwardly. "Guess there's a new badass in town, eh? Watch out, ladies. London's answer to John McClane is coming to a police station near you. Fuck you, Mr. UPS. How many vampires has that wife-robbing bastard killed, eh?"

"Lee, I love you."

He steps back, frowning. "Steady on, Vince. We did the man hug. Let's not get carried away."

I chuckle. "You can forget I said that."

Lee grins. "Already have."

I kick at the clothes on the ground, sending a dust plume mushrooming up into the gloomy air. About a meter away from the rotten body is a hollow-eyed skull, the jaws frozen in an eternal scream. I shift my gaze to the stairs, knowing that when I walk out of this room, I leave the past behind once and for all. For years I've felt chained by memories, racked with guilt. Perhaps I've known subconsciously that this final showdown with Adrienne's brother was always going to happen, that I've been spinning toward it on a direct collision course for all these years.

Lee places a hand on my shoulder. "Come on, there's a young lady outside that's probably going nuts by now. Although she looked pretty cozy in the arms of your old lord and master last time I saw her. Good-looking fella, that one."

The notion of Mila in Ronin's arms is more than enough to snap me from my reverie. I whip past Lee to the stairs and speed out into the cool night air.

—◦◦◦—

Mila

For a fourth time, Superintendent Burke tries to convince me to get into a squad car, and for a fourth time, I refuse.

"I'm not leaving him." My eyes are so blurry from crying I can barely make out Ronin's face as he props me up.

We're gathered on a corner, a street over from the house where Moreau imprisoned me.

"I'm afraid we must insist on calling an ambulance, Miss Hart," Burke says, looking grave.

Ronin cuts him a snarl.

"It can wait," I mumble. There is no way I am being carted off in an ambulance without knowing Vincent's fate.

I close my eyes against another bolt of pain and rub at the deep, ugly welts left by the wire ropes around my wrists. The back of my head is throbbing from slamming into the rough wall and my face feels tight and swollen. But with the aid of my new vampire friend, I find if I stand still long enough, I can just about bear it.

"I must look like the Elephant Man," I mumble into the nook of his arm.

"Not really," Ronin remarks. "Your hair is better than his. Well, it would be without all the dirt and gasoline."

I narrow my eyes. "So, you're the ancient who turned Vincent?"

"One and the same."

"But aren't you supposed to hate him?"

He shrugs. "Times are a-changing, Mila. Besides, I was keen to meet the woman who managed to sway Vincent from his pious path."

"Has he really been that much of a killjoy these past three hundred years?"

Ronin chuckles. "Compared to me, yes." He looks down at me, copper brows pulled low, eyes like two swirling pools of ice. "Vincent is a good man. I respect him—even if I don't always understand him."

"How old are you?" I ask suddenly.

Ronin clucks his tongue. "You should never ask a vampire his age."

"Are we talking Jesus old?"

He smiles down at me. "Aye, I get why he's so taken with you. You have a spark."

"Did you ever meet Genghis Khan?" I ask, ignoring the comment.

"No," he says, "nor Julius Caesar. But William the Conqueror was a hoot."

I frown, unsure whether he's kidding or not. I'm about to ask when the gathered officers burst into sudden exclamations of relief.

I freeze. Through the gaps in the huddle comes a flash of dirty-blond hair. Then the officers part like the Red Sea and I wonder if I'm hallucinating when I see a tall, blond vampire emerge. His suit is ripped and torn, his face splattered with blood and grime. My knees almost buckle beneath me.

"Vincent!" I yell, staggering from Ronin's grip.

As soon as his eyes land on me, an intense look of relief floods his face. "Mila!"

The pavement continues to feel unsteady under my feet as I struggle toward him. A second before I fall, Vincent's strong arms loop around my waist, pressing me tightly against his broad chest.

I tilt my head to gaze up into his eyes. They seem even softer after spending the past few minutes staring at Ronin's ice-blue orbs. "You're making a habit of this," I say breathlessly.

He smiles, delicately brushing the hair from my face. "It appears so."

I open my mouth to ask what happened to Moreau, but the words die in my throat as his lips land on mine. Call it post-traumatic shock, but making out with my hot vampire boyfriend suddenly seems like the best way to deal with the terrifying events of tonight.

I'm enjoying the warm sensation of his tongue sliding over mine when a loud cough kills the moment.

Burke is standing a few feet away, a brow cutting almost vertically into his forehead. "I'm not sure this kind of behavior is entirely appropriate, considering Miss Hart is a recent victim of kidnapping, Inspector Ferrer."

We break apart guiltily. Vincent flicks Burke an annoyed glance. "It doesn't matter anymore, Superintendent, because I quit."

Burke opens his mouth but is cut off by the arrival of Lee Davies. Despite the limp and a line of blood trickling from his nose, he's smiling broadly and clutching a machete like a trophy of honor.

"David Moreau is dead, if lover boy here didn't inform you all," he announces.

Burke remains unimpressed. "Well, I guessed as much when Vincent arrived back al—"

"I killed him," Davies cuts in. He attempts to spin the machete handle in one hand but drops it instead.

Burke looks between him and Vincent, astonished. "Really?"

Vincent nods before turning back to me. "He's gone. It's over, Mila. I'm so sorry for putting you through this. After tonight, you'll probably never want to see me again."

I smile, burying my head into the warmth of his neck as he opens his jacket to wrap around me. "Like that's going to happen."

"Well, I should be going," a deep voice says at our ears. "There's a Miss World contestant back at the club who doesn't like to be kept waiting."

I'd forgotten all about Ronin McDermott.

Vincent turns around, still clutching me to him. I'm pretty sure he's never letting go. Which is fine with me.

"Ronin, thank you for getting Mila out safely."

He quirks a brow, switching his attention to me. "It was the least I could do after letting her slip past us like that. Mila, it was my pleasure to make your acquaintance."

Vincent's grip on me tightens.

"Let me know if you're ever in need of a job now you're out of work, Vincent."

Vincent shakes his head. "Not likely."

Ronin flashes me a sexy, lopsided grin before completely disappearing. I stare up at Vincent, mouth open. "Did he just go *poof*?"

Vincent smiles. "Ancients are fast creatures."

"Was he kidding about the Miss World contestant?"

"I doubt it."

I poke him playfully in the ribs. "You could get a Miss World contestant, you know?"

He leans down, placing a kiss in my dirty hair. "You are my Miss World."

I exhale slowly. For the first time in maybe forever, everything feels like it's going to be okay.

"Mila, there's something I've been meaning to say."

"Oh?" I mumble, closing my eyes against another wave of dizziness.

With impeccable timing, an ambulance veers around the corner, its flashing lights filling the street, picking out the shadows beneath Vincent's bloodshot eyes.

"Later," he whispers, watching the vehicle approach. "First, you need treatment."

I cling tightly to him, my cheek pressed against the hard lines of his chest. "You'll come with me to the hospital, won't you?"

"Yes," he says, hands tangled in my hair. "I'll never leave you again."

Chapter 19

Mila

VINCENT SQUEEZES MY HAND AS WE CROSS THE ROAD to the Royal Opera House in Covent Garden, his palm cool in mine, filling me with giddy excitement.

The weather has been unbearably humid these past few days, and even with the sun sinking below the horizon, only the slightest stir of a breeze cuts through the warm streets.

"It's a beautiful building," I murmur, admiring the majestic facade with its white columns and ornate portico. "Are you sure the box is private?"

He smiles, slowing his pace when we reach the pavement to help me up the curb. Although three months have passed since that fateful night in North London, I still suffer the occasional spasm in my lower back. Wearing heels doesn't help, but tonight is special and I want to look my best. Besides, flats really don't go with my outfit—an off-the-shoulder, silver brocade dress with a full skirt. I feel like Grace Kelly when she married the prince.

Vincent holds my fingers lightly in his, as if we are about to dance a waltz. "I'm positive. Do you really think I want to share you with anyone?"

I smirk. "Well, no. You've shown no signs of that these past few months, now that you mention it."

Smiling, he says, "Don't fret. I hear there is an excellent selection of ice cream available at intermission."

"Well, good," I tease, "because that's the only reason I agreed to come."

As I step up on the curb, he draws me close, and a familiar flame of heat licks the place where our bodies meet.

"I think there's another reason you agreed to come," he says, lips hovering over mine.

From the corner of my eye, I spot a woman in a business suit and trainers rolling her eyes in our direction as she strolls past, and I experience a weird lightning bolt moment where I realize that would have been me not so long ago.

I guess Laura and the rest of the world are right—it really *does* happen when you least expect it.

"Oh yes," I say. "The top-notch acoustics. I forgot about those."

He leans even closer, his masculine scent pulling me under faster than a riptide. "Maybe we should skip the outing and go back to that bed of yours. Maybe it's time I stopped going easy on you."

I experience several very un–Grace Kelly–like thoughts as our lips connect, my thumbs rubbing circles into his stubbly jaw as he pulls me tighter against him. Although we've had sex pretty much every day since the incident, it's been more of the intimate lovemaking kind than the wild, *take me now* variety. Though I appreciate Vincent's thoughtfulness over my injuries, I have to say, I am dying to get things back to how they were before Moreau showed up and ruined everything. Particularly the biting.

"I would love it if you stopped going easy on me. I've been asking for months," I point out.

"Begging too, at times," he says, brow arched.

I narrow my eyes. "There was no begging. Now, shall we go inside before someone tells us to get a room?"

He takes a step backward and a sudden breeze lifts a lock of golden hair from his forehead. I stare, agog for a few seconds, which happens quite often—I still can't believe he's mine.

"What?" he asks. "Did you forget your keys again?"

"No. Just thinking, that's all."

I take his arm and let him lead me up red-carpeted steps into an impressive, white marble lobby.

"It's a bit of a climb to the box. Shall I carry you?" he asks, his eyes filled with concern.

"I'm fine, Vincent. I can handle some stairs." As I loop my arm through his, I imagine how he might act if I were pregnant. From what I've seen these past months, he would almost certainly be the type to wrap a woman in cotton wool and chat to her stomach. A black chasm opens at the pit of my tummy. The more I fall for him, the more it seems to happen. I'm hoping after I've told him tonight about what I'm going to do, these dark feelings will disappear.

Vincent is as good as his word. The box is empty, four red velvet chairs with gilt backs sitting neatly in a row. I look over the balcony into a sea of red and gold below. A low hum of chatter surrounds us as people mill around, looking for their seats, a whisper of excitement on the air.

"It's really beautiful," I say, craning my neck to see

the carved dome of the ceiling, soft lights flickering like fireflies around the edges. "Like being in a fairy tale."

Vincent glows with happiness, his blue eyes warmer than a tropical sea. "I'm pleased you like it. Even if the performance is going to remind you of cats being strangled."

I chuckle as he pulls out a seat for me. "I was only kidding. I'm sure I'll enjoy every second. It's not like I'll be able to concentrate anyway, not with you here being all *you*."

He slips into the seat beside me, closing his fingers around mine. Our eyes lock.

"Mila," he says, his voice hoarse.

"Yes?" I'm so breathless the word sticks to the back of my throat.

"I love you."

Not for one millisecond do I hesitate. "I love you too."

Before there is a chance for either of us to kill the moment, the lights dim and a drumroll echoes off the walls. The heavy red curtain begins to rise.

Vincent inches his chair closer to mine. When shrill singing voices begin to cut through the air, he leans in, lips brushing tantalizingly against my hair and ear as he whispers the meaning behind each song. It is through this seductive narrative that I discover a newfound love and respect for opera. Several times during the performance, I accidentally on purpose turn my head toward him so our lips meet, his sweet tongue sliding over mine and driving me wild with desire. At the end of the first half, when the lights go up, we stare at each other for a few seconds.

"Did you really say you love me?" I ask him.

"Yes. I did. I do. Did you really say you love me too?" I smile. "Yes."

A palpable wave of arousal prickles the air around us.

He extends a hand as he rises from the seat. "I'm sure we can buy the DVD, if you want to skip the second half."

I sigh in relief before snatching his hand. "Let's go."

Like a pair of naughty coconspirators, we hurry back down the stairs and out of the building. In the car, we collide like magnets—hands and lips all over the place. When we eventually break apart, a thin sheen of mist clings to the windows.

"We need to get home," he says, his hand reaching above my shoulder for the seat belt. "Now that I no longer work for the police, I'm not so sure a public act of indecency would be easy to wipe from the system."

I reluctantly allow him to the start the engine. "Good thing there's no law against indecency in my flat. I'm ready for a lot of indecency, by the way. I'm talking torrid acts of sexual gratification in places never designed to accommodate the heat of naked skin."

He groans, pulling out onto the street, blue eyes hooded with lust. "Mila, put the dirty talk on hold or I'll crash the car."

Though Vincent's apartment is luxurious, I'm happy to be back at my flat in Finsbury Park. Thanks to kind-hearted Tom and Laura, all traces of the break-in and dead rat were gone when I finally returned home. With Lee Davies still down on his luck and living at Vincent's place, Vincent was more than happy to move in until I recovered. Which, technically, I did several weeks ago. But he hasn't mentioned going anywhere.

We crash into the flat and dive at each other. Before I know it, my dress is lying in a silvery puddle around my ankles and Vincent's shirt is nowhere to be seen, his muscles standing out against the golden glow from the window.

I drag fingers over the ridges of his tight abs, watching as he shivers, his eyes half-closed as I undo his fly and slide a hand into his trousers.

He emits a low moan before capturing my mouth in his, working on the clasp of my bra and rubbing a callused thumb in circles around my hard nipples. By the time he lifts me up and wraps my legs around his hips, my panties are soaked through.

"Oh God," he moans, carrying me through to the bedroom. "Did I ever mention your arousal is the sweetest scent I've ever had the pleasure of knowing?"

"Uh-huh," I mumble, ghosting kisses along his jaw.

He lowers me onto the bed, blond tresses falling in my face as he kisses me. With nimble fingers, he reaches down and pushes aside my lacy strip of underwear. I cry out as he parts the folds of slick flesh, arching into his touch. My back could be broken now and all I would know is ecstasy as he toys with me, liquefying my whole body until I'm little more than a hot spring waiting to erupt.

"Take your trousers off," I pant, fumbling over the zipper. In a blur of movement, he's off the bed and tossing them aside, his smooth erection springing out between us. I stroke him hungrily as he hovers above me, palms flat on either side of my shoulders.

"Bite me," I say, his thick length brushing my groin. "Do it right as you enter."

He leans down to kiss me, palming my breasts until I'm writhing beneath him.

"I've been wanting to show you for a while now," he murmurs, skimming my jaw with his lips.

"Show me what?" I whisper, closing my eyes with a shiver as he positions his slick, velvety stiffness at my entrance.

He doesn't answer, and a second later, I forget he's even spoken as he pushes inside me, his pulsing length sliding in, swelling against my wet walls.

I climax right away, whimpering as hot waves roll over me. When I eventually come back into my body, I open my eyes to find Vincent gazing intently into my face.

It's like staring up at the sun.

"When you do that, it's the most beautiful thing I've ever seen," he murmurs.

I smile lazily. "Shut up and make it happen again."

He grins, punishing me with a hard thrust. I spread my legs wide, inviting him deeper, cradling his face in my hands.

Before I have to ask, he bends to my throat, coiling my hair in one hand and gently tipping my head to expose my neck. The thrusts come harder, another orgasm building as I clench with anticipation, waiting for the bittersweet torture of his bite.

Lips brush my collarbone, fangs sharp against my skin. I moan as he presses a chain of kisses into my throat before sliding in his fangs.

"Yes," I gasp, as hot sparks of pleasure and pain hit. Then I'm tumbling down into darkness, my mind no longer my own.

I find myself not at the edge of a field of corn, but beneath a navy-blue sky, my arms wrapped around the waist of a young blond woman who is leaning against me, her hazel eyes round with fear. I'm struck by an urge to protect her and by a sudden, startling attraction that sends heat roaring through my ice-cold veins like fire. The scene shifts and I'm outside a classroom in a corridor that smells of damp books. The blond woman emerges through the door, and my heart soars as she approaches me. I am flooded with hope and fear in equal measure, all of my nerve endings firing—as if waking up after a long sleep. The corridor fades and I am holding her in my arms, my mouth fastened to hers. I am peaceful. Filled with love. I know I would do anything to make her happy.

It's only as my eyelids flutter open that I realize the woman was me. That I was the only one in his life essence.

I stare into Vincent's eyes, seeing all the love I just felt reflected back at me—deep and bottomless, like the ocean.

"That was—" I start.

"You," he says, smiling.

"But how did you know it changed?"

He kisses me quickly on the lips. "I told you once before—I know what's in my heart. I know you thought Adrienne was there because I still loved her, but really, she was there because I hadn't let go of what happened. I was hanging on to the past. Catching up with Moreau changed all of that. Though it would have changed anyway—because there's no one more important to me than you, Mila."

I pinch him hard on the arm.

"What was that for?" he asks, bemused.

"Just checking that you're real."

"Oh, I'm real," he says with a smirk, taking my hand and placing it on his hard member. "*Very* real. And I'm not finished with you yet."

I smile. Now would be a perfect time to tell him what I've decided, but all rational thought checks out as his lips seek me out, his length sliding into my warmth and obliterating all thoughts of what I was about to say.

The next morning over breakfast at my mismatched table and chairs, I decide now is as good a time as any to make my proposition.

Vincent sits opposite, poring over a broadsheet. Since quitting work, he always reads a newspaper at breakfast. He says it helps him stay in touch with what's happening in the world.

The serial killer's capture was never mentioned in the press. Vincent and Lee Davies are convinced that somewhere high up the media chain, a vampire—or at least a sympathizer—is making sure the killings never go global. The families of the victims were keen to keep their privacy too, so there is little chance of them selling their stories. To this day, my mother still has no idea what happened to me. Which, if I get my way, is how it's going to stay. I'm going to need to keep her in the pro-vampire camp, the way my life is going. For more reasons than one.

"Vincent," I say slowly.

His eyes flick up from the paper. "You want me to drive you out to that shopping place again, don't you?" he asks, quirking a smile.

"What? No. Why do you say that?"

He points at his face with an index finger. "You have that kitten eye thing going on."

"You mean puppy dog eyes, not kittens."

"On you, they're kitten eyes. Trust me."

"It's not about shopping." Though now he's mentioned it, I do need to return a dress. "I wanted to bring it up last night, but then we got busy with all the *stuff*."

Vincent's lips twitch. "Oh yes. All that stuff."

I stare into my empty mug. If I look at him, I'll get all flustered and then it's a slippery slope to Sexville. "The thing is—"

"We're moving too fast for you, aren't we?"

I flick my eyes up in surprise. "What? Are you kidding?"

"I'm sorry for burdening you with my feelings last night, Mila. I've come close so many times to saying it, but I've always stopped myself, or someone else has stopped me. I know it's only been a few months—"

I stand up quickly, the chair scraping back over the linoleum with a loud squeak, and press an index finger firmly to his lips. "No. It's not that. Last night was one of the best nights of my life. And by the way, all the other best nights of my life also involve you. This isn't too fast for me. That's the thing. I've been doing a lot of thinking and it's clear if we keep heading in the direction we're going, we'll need to address our problem sooner or later. Where we're concerned, I think sooner is much better than later."

He frowns, clearly having no idea what I'm talking about. Before I chicken out, I take a deep breath and say, "I'm going to ask Ronin McDermott to turn me."

For a moment, I wonder if time has frozen. His jaw drops, his face turning the color of parchment. The only sounds are the cars roaring along the street outside the window and the drone of a double-decker bus as it hurtles past.

"No," he says, the word coming out in a strangled choke. "Absolutely not."

I sink back into the seat. "Why not? You're going to live forever, Vincent, and I'm going to age and die. I don't want that for either of us."

"I don't want this life for you, Mila. I would never forgive myself."

"But Ronin was going to change Adrienne for you. What's so different?"

He shakes his head vigorously. "I was an idiot back then. I had no clue what I was getting myself into. You have no idea how many times over the years I've wished I'd died on the guillotine with the rest of them."

I lean forward to cover his hand with mine. "I'm not saying we should do it tomorrow, or even next year. I'm just putting it out there as a solution."

Vincent gazes down to where our hands join. "What if I told you there's another solution?"

I frown as a memory surfaces. Right before Moreau captured me that night at Scotland Yard, I was talking on the phone. I know because Lee Davies told me, though

I still have no recollection of it—concussion does that to a person, apparently. My last memory is of speaking with Lee about getting his wife back.

Until now.

I hear Karolina's husky Eastern European tones. *Lucky for you to meet a vampire witch.*

"What other solution?" I murmur, wondering if I dreamed it.

He sighs, placing his free hand over mine on the table. "When you had to stay overnight in hospital, I went back to the apartment to pack some of your things."

I nod. "You brought my toothbrush and night things and clean clothes."

"I found a card on the bed. You must have dropped it there at some point that day. It was Karolina's—the one who claims to be a psychic witch."

A hint of excitement creeps into his voice that makes me wonder where he's going with this.

"It got me thinking about vampires and their powers. I know of a vampire who was a healer in his human life. Nothing more extraordinary than those we have today, but after he turned, the power was tenfold. He could heal cuts, mend broken bones…"

"What happened to him?"

"That's the other thing. He's human now."

I screw my face up. "How?"

"He is the only person I know of who managed to destroy an ancient—his ancient. When she was destroyed, humanity returned to all her subjugates."

"Are you saying you're going to try to kill Ronin?" I ask, shocked.

He shakes his head. "No. Even if I knew how to do that, I wouldn't. He saved your life that night. I owe him more now than I ever have."

"Phew, because I don't think I can handle any more assassin trips. Besides, I did sort of like the guy." Vincent grimaces and I lean over to ruffle his golden hair. "Aw, don't worry. You're way prettier."

We both chuckle.

"So," he continues, "I got curious. Like I mentioned once before, if she was a genuine witch when she was human, those powers could be significant as a vampire. I called her."

My stomach twists. "Was I speaking to her right before Moreau came for me?"

"Yes. She spoke to you that night. I didn't want to remind you of it."

"What did she say? About her powers?"

A flush I haven't seen for a while rises in his cheeks. I recall the night we met, his shyness in the backseat of the police car.

"I explained our situation, about how besotted I am and how I hoped you felt the same."

I roll my eyes. "Duh."

He grins. "She thinks she might be able to help. Word of what happened to Logan—the vampire who turned human—has spread. Being London-based, Karolina heard about it too. When the ancient died, her venom died with her. If there was another way to kill that venom, it makes sense that humanity could be restored."

"But how? Voodoo?"

"Not exactly. There's a spell she's working on. It

involves a sort of exorcism. Ancients are more demon than human, after all. If she could rid a body of all that was demon inside it, their humanity could return."

I scrunch my face up. "What if it's dangerous? I won't let you be her guinea pig. What if it kills you?"

"That's highly unlikely."

"What if it kills Ronin?"

"Again, highly unlikely."

"This spell…what does she have so far?"

He sits up straighter in the chair. "The spell is a very old one. It involves incantations and a tub of holy water."

I arch a brow. "Are you sure Karolina isn't trying to get you naked?"

He chuckles, ignoring the question. "She also needs an object belonging to me when I was human, which is no difficulty, and a vial of Ronin's blood—which is some difficulty, but one I can work with."

"This Logan you mentioned. Is he aging?"

Vincent nods, his blue eyes swirling with hope. "He found his first gray hair a few weeks ago. Also, he has a baby son."

I sit bolt upright in my seat. Though I didn't want to believe any of this might be possible, I'm suddenly breathless with hope. "Oh, that's amazing."

Vincent squeezes my hand. "I don't want you to have to give up on becoming a mother because of me, Mila. I've seen the way you are around kids. You love them."

"Oh please, everyone loves kids. The same as everyone loves rainbows and free Wi-Fi. It's a given. None of that is as important to me as you are."

He both frowns and smiles. "I would love to be able to give you a baby one day."

An image pops into my head of the two of us surrounded by nappies, that sweet, clean nursery smell lingering around the apartment and Vincent holding a baby—our baby—to his naked chest. The idea gives me a warm, fluttery feeling in the pit of my tummy, and not just because of his naked chest.

I push the chair back and circle the table, curling into his lap. "Shall we see what she comes up with, then?" I say, burying my head into his clean-smelling neck. "But if it's in any way dangerous, we'll go back to my plan."

He shakes his head and tilts my chin to kiss me. "I love you, Mila."

"I love you too."

I always will.

Epilogue

Vincent

Three years later...

"You should probably take off your shirt," Mila says.

Her hazel eyes are as wide and innocent as a child's, a wicked grin lifting the corners of her pink lips.

I smile before gazing down at the tiny sleeping bundle cradled in my arms. "Didn't the nurse say we have to wait six weeks?"

She rolls her eyes. "Not so we can have sex, Vincent. So you can bond with him. Skin on skin, like it says in the book."

"Ah, I see." I wink at her. "Can't say I'm not disappointed though."

"Here, let me take him while you undress."

I gently transfer Louis into Mila's waiting arms. "Have you got his head supported?" I ask, preparing to slide my arm from under him.

"Yep, I think so. But go slowly."

Once the maneuver is complete, we sigh in relief. As new parents, we exist in constant fear we will accidentally injure the baby.

I get to work unbuttoning my shirt. Mila watches intently, a blush creeping into her face. As I fling the shirt onto the back of a chair, we give each other *the look*.

Six weeks already feels like forever.

I hold out my arms. "Okay, pass him back."

We go through the same process in reverse until our son is nestled cozily against my bare chest.

"Don't move," Mila insists, whirling around. "I need to get the camera."

She moves from the living room as fast as her stitches will allow, leaving me gazing into the perfect, chubby, pink face of my son.

My son. Two words I never ever thought I would earn the right to use. I reach down to unwrap Louis's blanket and lift him so we're chest to chest, our two hearts beating together. Tears prick the backs of my eyes, and my throat tightens. There is a muffled sob, though it doesn't come from me. Mila is back with the camera, tears dripping off shiny cheeks.

"What is it? No batteries?" I ask, looking between her and the camera dangling by its loop from her wrist.

"No," she says, swiping at her cheeks. "I'm just so happy."

Ah, yes. The happy hormones. They've been wreaking havoc on her emotions since she gave birth a week ago. Trouble is, I think they might be catching.

My eyes fill with moisture. "Me too. We are so blessed."

I loop my free arm around her shoulders and fold her into a three-way embrace. A tear almost spills as it hits me that I'm holding everything I care about in the world.

Mila's arms go around my waist, her cheek pressed against my shoulder, stray blond tresses tickling my skin. "Being this happy scares me, Vincent," she murmurs, her voice muffled.

I squeeze her tight. "I know. Me too."

As if wanting to get in on the conversation, Louis lets out an ear-rattling shriek.

Mila looks up at me, smiling. "Quiet time is over. He probably wants to feed again." She unbuttons the shirt she's wearing and takes him from me. I hurry to plump the cushions on the messy sofa, moving a sea of baby paraphernalia aside to make room.

Once Louis is latched on and feeding, I sink onto the sofa, my arm around Mila. "God, you're amazing. Do you know that?"

Mila grins, her freckles joining as she scrunches up her nose. "It's just breastfeeding."

"It's a miracle."

"Don't or I'll start crying again."

I press a kiss into her hair. "I love you."

"I love you too."

We're silent for a few seconds, the only noise the quiet suckling of Louis as he feeds.

"Oh, I forgot to say," Mila adds. "An envelope came addressed to you. It's from London."

"Oh?"

"Might be something from Burke. It's on the hall table."

We haven't lived in London since I quit the police three years ago, though I've stayed in regular contact with my ex-colleagues. Lee is happily married again. Just three months after she left, Sian rang him and begged to come home. He is still bragging about his vampire-killing moment of glory.

I pad through to the hallway and lift a thick, padded

envelope from the table we keep our keys on. The hand-writing is swirly and old-fashioned. Not Burke's. I tear open the seal. Inside is a blue card with a cartoon baby on the front along with the caption *It's a boy!* I open the card.

Dear Vincent,

Congratulations on becoming a father. Without wanting to toot my own horn, I think I have the potential to make an excellent godfather—the suits, the cutthroat charisma. Remember me in your deliberations. After all, you still owe me for that vial of blood…

On a different note, you will find enclosed something belonging to you. I've had it in my possession for years but didn't think to return it until now. I figure you might want to pass it on to your son one day.

Yours,
Ronin McDermott

I tip the envelope upside down, surprised when a heavy metallic object tumbles out onto my palm. A flash of gold glints in a shaft of sunlight as I stare down at the crest of my old family ring. One of Ronin's men must have taken it from Moreau's fake address the night I dropped it. I've never once stopped to think what became of it. I hold it up to the light between my thumb and index finger, its shape familiar and strange all at once. A symbol of a past best forgotten. I drop it back into the envelope and open the little drawer in the table, sliding the envelope to the back, under a pile of old bills.

Carrying the card back into the living room, I loiter for a moment in the doorway, watching the scene within—the backdrop of a messy, lived-in family room framing my beautiful Mila as she concentrates on feeding our newborn son.

A home, a family, a real life. This is the portrait I live in now, the faded relic that once hung on my bedroom wall long consigned to the dust and darkness of the attic.

One day, I will show Louis the portrait and the ring, and he will pore over them like he would some mysterious fairy tale, safe and secure in the knowledge of a happy ending. The past, after all, is behind us.

Catching me staring, Mila looks up. "What was it?"

"Nothing," I say, propping the card up amid the rows of blue and white on the mantelpiece, where it blends in with the others. "Nothing at all."

*Read on for a sneak peek at book 3
in Juliet Lyons's Bite Nights series*

Coming February 2018!

Ronin

"WHICH ONE? BLOND OR BRUNETTE?"

I lift my eyes from the amber liquid in my glass to Harper's smirking face, ghostly white under the flicker of strobe lighting, before following his gaze to the two women perched on shiny high stools at the bar.

The club is tightly packed, dozens of revelers grinding to the beat of thumping music. To call it dancing would be an insult. There is no finesse or rhythm to the heaving bodies as they sway from side to side, exposed skin glittering with sweat, arms waving wildly—drowning in an ocean of alcohol and lust.

The women Harper spotted shoot glances in our direction. Predatory stares, red lips parted like an invitation. Even if I couldn't read body language like most people read flat-pack furniture instructions, I would know their intentions in a heartbeat.

Sex.

I survey the scantily clad women with a sigh, waiting for my trouser region to wake up and smell the pheromones. My eyes feast upon their coltish limbs, buffed and bronzed beneath their short skirts, two matching swells of cleavage oozing from tight, strappy tops.

"Or both?" Harper whispers, dark eyes flashing. Though the loud thud of music mostly smothers his voice, a single arched eyebrow does the talking.

Both. Not an unusual suggestion by any means.

I'm admiring the women like a farmer on market day when my attention snags on a third woman standing a few feet behind them. A cloud of wild, curly dark hair is bending over a silver bag while a pale hand rummages desperately inside. Judging by the martini in front of her and the *tap-tap* of Paulo's fingers on the bar, she is searching for money. My throat goes dry and my knees tingle.

Surely, *she* would never come here.

A second later, I'm out of my seat and at the bar, ignoring the stares of the two women as I wedge myself into the space behind them.

"It's on the house," I say to Paulo, waiting for the dark puff of hair to lift and reveal her face.

When she looks at me, my heart crashes in disappointment. It isn't her. Though similarly built, this woman's eyes are slanted, catlike, and the color of ebony. Still, that hair. I have to stop myself from reaching out to touch it.

"Thank you," she says, smiling and ducking her head.

I take a step backward, reading her face. Unlike the females behind me, this lady is not at my club for sex. It's written in the relaxed set of her shoulders, the genuine smile on her full lips. The length in my trousers stirs. Lately, I seem to need a challenge to get off, and with that hair… If her body was arched across my desk, I would hardly know the difference between her and who I thought she was.

"Why are you here?" I ask, shifting my weight against the bar.

She blinks a few times, as if she's recently pondered that question herself. "I came with a colleague." She skims a gaze over the pulsating mass of bodies on the dance floor as if searching for someone.

Lying.

"Tell me why you're *really* here," I say.

She lets out a sigh and with a quick eye roll says, "I'm a journalist. I've been asked to write a column on alternative dating."

My brows shoot skyward. "Alternative dating," I repeat.

She takes a gulp of her martini, her hand betraying a slight tremor. My eyes track the movement like a tiger eyeing its prey. Her nerves are an aphrodisiac, a direct connection to the fangs prickling beneath my gums like knives.

"Yes, alternative. You know, BDSM, swinging… vampires."

I frown. "Isn't it a tiny bit prejudiced to consider vampires akin to sexual deviants?"

Another gulp of martini, faster this time. Her eyes dart across the pulsing room again, reminding herself where the exit is. Despite her obvious desire to flee, her voice is calmer than a church sermon on Sunday. "Not at all. There's nothing wrong with those things. They're just…different."

"What do you have on us so far?"

She jerks a little in surprise. Though, really, what did

she think I was? A solicitor, a stockbroker, a candle-
stick maker?

Her dark eyes widen. "Nothing really. It all seems…
normal."

Though it wasn't my original intention to scare her,
I can't help but lean in, closer to her ear, my lips brushing her magnificent hair. She smells of perfume and the
London Underground, a faint whiff of spices from cooking. "Stick around. Wait for the bell. Things won't be so
normal then."

"The bell?" she asks, a flash of fear lighting up her
face. "What bell?"

I grin by way of response and spin around to the
women behind me. They straighten immediately, the
brunette spilling some of her cocktail in haste.

"You should probably sponge that out before it leaves
a stain," I say, motioning to the liquid sinking between the
fibers of her tight, white top. "I have some stain remover
in my office, if you'd allow me to take care of it."

The brunette smiles. A slow, tight curl of red lips.
She steps toward me, her voice a cat's purr. "If it's not
too much trouble."

I allow my fangs to slip out over my lips so she knows
exactly what my intentions are. Like a seasoned pro, she
doesn't flinch. "Ladies first," I say, extending an arm.

"Hey," the blond cuts in. A sneer mars her sugar-
candy face. "What about me?"

Ordinarily, I would take them both, but tonight, I
need the brunette alone.

Harper appears by her side, and I watch with
amusement as her hard mask of protest dissolves at

the sight of his handsome features. "I would love to keep you company."

The Miss Piggy act is dropped. "I'm Natalie," she says, eyeing his muscular body as if he's the last sunbed by the pool.

"I'm honored to meet you, Natalie." He lifts one of her hands, kissing the back of her fingers.

Smooth bastard.

The friend taken care of, I let the brunette walk ahead of me. The stare of the curly haired journalist lasers into the back of my head. Curiosity is rolling off her in waves. I can practically hear her mind turning my words over. *Wait for the bell.*

Inside my office, I lock the door and hang back. These days, I rarely make the first move, which has nothing to do with being a gentleman and everything to do with boredom. The brunette prowls around, running red-painted nails over everything: the leather chairs in front of the fireplace, the edge of the buffed walnut desk.

"It's pretty tame in here," she says in husky tones.

I shove aside a wave of indifference, focusing on the swell of breasts beneath her tight vest. "Is it? What were you expecting? Whips and a rack?"

She hops onto the desk, knees slightly apart. "Maybe."

I watch her for a second, hands thrust deep into my pockets. *She isn't who you want,* a voice whispers in a far-off corner of my brain. *Why kid yourself?*

"You know, I've been coming here for a few weeks," she says, plucking a glass paperweight of the Tower of London from the desk and examining it. "I know you're different from the other vampires."

"Really? How am I different?"

"Older, wiser, more sophisticated—and not just because you own this place."

A buzz of warning stirs me into action. I pull myself to full height. "Turn around," I say, my voice coming out in a growl.

Her eyelids flicker, and she gulps as my fangs extend farther. "I thought you'd never ask," she retorts, a slight waver in her voice.

She spins around, fingers gripping the edge of the desk, knuckles bone-white against the lacquered wood. The sight of them gives me pause. *So pointless*, the voice in my head whispers. Shoving the thought aside, I press myself into her spine, gripping her wrists. Her hair smells of cigarette smoke and hairspray, and as I move the immaculate mane of hair from the bronze column of her neck, she shivers. Without pausing to consider if it's from arousal or fear, I scrape my fangs over her skin. The taste of chemical tan is sharp on my tongue.

"Wait," she says suddenly. "Aren't we going to have sex before you bite me?"

I grin into her flesh. Below my waist, I'm not even at half-mast. "No," I murmur. "That's not the order I like to do things."

Without further warning, I sink my fangs into her neck, the soft pop of flesh filling me with new vigor. She moans loudly, her bottom squirming against my groin, stirring me to life. I half close my eyes as my length stiffens, then I hoist her skirt around her waist and reach for my zipper. A brief glance at her startlingly white derriere affirms there are no panties to remove. As I begin to swallow her blood, I move her legs apart with a knee, bringing a hand between her thighs.

"Yes," she whimpers. "Give it to me."

I slide a digit around her slick walls, pumping a couple of times to get her good and wet before guiding my erection to her entrance. Just as I'm about to thrust inside her, I sink my fangs deeper. The slow drip of blood oozes into my mouth like an open faucet. I shut my eyes completely as her body sags, a deep, dark unconsciousness seizing her like a thief in the night. I too lose myself, surrendering to the usual fantasy—a cloud of black hair, eyes the color of sunlight on a river, and pink lips caught in a sneer that screams of hate.

—◆◆◆—

When I've taken my fill of the brunette and she's come around, I zip my fly and whirl her around to face me. Her eyes are lazy and confused, her once-perfect makeup a mask of smudged mascara.

"Look at me," I command, ducking to look directly into her eyes.

As her tired pupils try to focus, I seize her mind, waves of pulsing electrical energy passing between us like a current.

"You will leave the club and never come back. Tomorrow, you will call whoever sent you and tell them there is nothing to report. That you never saw Ronin McDermott and the club is the same as any other in London."

I hold her gaze as I lean over to push a button on the phone. My doorman, Charlie, appears in an instant.

"See the young lady gets home safely, Charlie," I say, seizing the brunette's arm and shoving her toward him. "Oh, and get her picture before she leaves. She's barred."

I notice Charlie looking at the bite marks, brows drawn. "Is she…?"

"No, I didn't turn her. The last thing London needs is more vampires. Now, get her out of here, would you?"

The brunette wobbles as she leans against my doorman, but she doesn't protest. Tomorrow, she'll wake up with a hangover and remember nothing. Chances are she'll blame it on a spiked drink. Most of them do.

After the door clicks softly behind them, I sigh, sinking down onto the edge of the desk. How many more of these informants will I have to root out? Now that vampires are common knowledge, it's only a matter of time before we're hung out to dry in the sunshine they once thought killed us.

Remembering the curly haired journalist out at the bar, I flip my wrist and glance down at the face of my Rolex. It's five minutes to midnight. I wonder if Cinderella has decided to stick around.

I slip out into the pounding noise of the club. Little has changed. Harper is sitting back in our booth with the blond straddled in his lap, sucking the face off her. Or is she sucking the face off him? It's hard to tell from this angle. I stare hard at them, forcing him to break their clinch for a second to meet my penetrating stare. I point two fingers at my eyes, indicating the need to glamour her after their fun. Who sent these girls anyway? Last I heard, the Metropolitan Police had shelved their special investigations into historic vampire crime to focus on the ones happening *now*. A wise move, considering how many human psychopaths live in this city. Vampires should be the least of their concerns.

The journalist from earlier is easy to locate. She's positioned near the exit, propped up against a gray pillar. The glass in her hand—not the shallow martini she nursed earlier—is empty. Either she's thirsty or nervous as hell. As if sensing she's being watched, her cat eyes meet mine across the room. She jerks violently when, a second later, the ringing of a bell reverberates off the walls. The noise is like a high school bell, but its meaning is much darker. A loud cheer goes up from the crowd before mayhem ensues.

Until now, it's been impossible to tell which of the revelers are vampires and which are human. Now, the difference is as obvious and jarring as a fist to the face. A dozen pairs of fangs extend, glittering white beneath the strobe lighting, as if a school of sharks have swum into the gloomy depths of the dance floor. But unlike some low-budget horror movie, no rising crescendo of earsplitting screams carve up the beat of the music. The humans succumb to their partners with little more than a satisfied sigh. Throats are offered, veins are taken, and before long, an iron tang of blood permeates the air. All the while, the music continues to pound.

My gaze beats a path between the carnage on the dance floor and the horrified expression of the journalist. Her eyes are fixed on a couple in one of the booths near the exit. A smartly dressed man in his twenties sits legs apart, head tipped backward onto the seat while a female vampire sucks at his main artery like a leech in a miniskirt. Inlets of crimson run down his pale neck, disappearing into the pastel-blue collar of his shirt.

One of my men approaches the couple and taps the woman on the shoulder. Dazed, she pulls away, as if waking up from a deep, consuming sleep, and allows my man room to hold two fingers to her boyfriend's neck. I flick my gaze back to the journalist as my worker speaks into his radio. Without anyone noticing, Charlie appears, and they carry the man's body through a concealed door at the side. The female vampire shadows them, her hands glued to the sides of her head in horror at what she's done. She disappears into the dark passageway beyond.

The curly haired woman's eyes are wider than the pool of blood left behind on the leather seat. She is frozen with fear, her skin taut and waxy under the flickering lights. She begins to move swiftly toward the narrow flight of stairs. Right before she passes out, I catch her, heaving her onto my shoulder and carrying her through the dark corridor to the exit.

Outside, amid the roar and screech of traffic pouring along the late-night street, I set her on her feet and flag down a taxi.

"Is he dead?" she asks as a black cab screeches to a halt beside us. Her once-steady voice shakes, like a toddler after a nightmare.

"I don't know," I say truthfully. "It happens occasionally, I'm afraid."

"That place is so fucked up," she mutters.

The cabbie's window slides down, and a bald head peers out suspiciously at the pair of us. "No puking in my cab," the driver says in blunt cockney tones, eyeing the female as she sways unsteadily in her heels.

I cut him an impatient glare. "She won't. Keep your hair on."

I yank open the door, but before she can climb in, I grab her elbow through her thin jacket. Her eyes flutter upward to mine.

"The club is nothing out of the ordinary," I say as a current stirs between us. "There was no bell or biting. It was just a club. Plain and simple. You didn't speak with anyone the whole time you were there."

She nods before slowly ducking into the vehicle, and I slam the door after her, watching as the car disappears into a throng of headlights. For those few seconds, standing at the side of the road, I envy her the luxury of forgetting. Of having the weight of decision taken out of her hands. I shudder, though not because of the chill in the crisp London air. I'm restless, an awful sensation of being trapped in my own skin settling around my shoulders. It happens often of late—the notion that I could pack up and go anywhere in the world and never shake it. A dark dog snapping at my heels.

Thrusting my hands into my pockets, I turn and head back into the club. Downstairs, Harper is practically inside the blond in our booth—her long legs are wrapped around his hips, ankles crossed at the bottom of his spine. His mouth is buried in her throat, a curtain of her blond hair concealing his rampant thirst from the other patrons. I shake my head with a bemused smile. He had better remember to glamour her afterward.

In my office, I buzz for Charlie. He takes a little

longer to arrive than usual, but when he steps through the door, I see why. A streak of blood stains his starched white shirt, a deep-red ribbon dropped in snow.

"The man. Is he…?"

"Alive. His girlfriend's taken him to A&E."

I arch a brow.

"She won't mention the club, don't worry. Stiven and I made sure of it."

I open the bottom drawer of the desk to take out a crystal decanter of scotch. "Drink?"

Charlie nods, a faraway gaze in his toffee-colored eyes as I line up two matching tumblers and remove the stopper.

"How long do you think we can go on like this, Charlie?" I ask as amber liquid splashes onto the bottom of the crystal.

Charlie frowns, breaking from his reverie. "Like what?"

"This." I swirl a finger around the room. "The nightly bloodlust, the accidental deaths, outsiders coming in to gape and spy."

Charlie shrugs. "It's the way things have always been done," he says simply, reaching for his drink. "We put the bell in for those who might want to leave before it gets messy."

I swirl scotch around the glass like wine at a tasting. "Aye, but times have changed. There are even vampire dating websites nowadays." What's left of my cold, dead heart flickers like a faulty bulb in my chest. "Perhaps it's time to change the way we do things."

Charlie snorts derisively. "What, try speed dating?"

Speed dating. An idea begins to unfurl in my mind.

A wicked idea. One that would definitely make a certain lady very angry.

And, as everyone knows, hatred is far preferable to indifference.

"Charlie, you could be on to something."

The image of the journalist pops into my mind, her face wan with horror. *That place is so fucked up.*

Time for a change.

For first time in a long while, the dark dog at my heels falls silent.

—∿—

Cat

WEDNESDAY MORNING, AND I'M ALREADY ON MY THIRD cancellation of the day. The deserter: Miss Belinda Pearce of St. Albans. With the four from yesterday and the three on Monday, that makes ten this week alone. Ten clients jumping ship. And it's not even eleven o'clock.

Although I could tell from her tone what she was going to say, I inject a measure of surprise into my voice. "Oh, Belinda, really? I'm so sorry to hear that. Why the change of heart?"

I minimize the internet window on my Mac and click into the accounts screen, pulling up her bank details from among the *p*'s.

There's a pause on the other end of the line. "It's just… I, er… Well, this is actually a little awkward."

"Go on."

"I'm trying something new."

"New?"

Could this be the moment I've been dreading since I started the site five years ago? Humans are finally bored of us—vampire dating is no longer *hip*. Or maybe she's realized that all the good men are taken, married to females named Fiona or Faye—women who provide healthy children, women who juggle playdates and a career and still manage to look half-decent at the end of an exhausting day.

I picture Belinda twisting her hands nervously, worrying at her red-painted lips. Despite never meeting in person, I've gotten to know her well over the past few months. She's one of those zesty, bubbly types who likes to give anyone who will listen every sordid detail of her love life. She often calls to debrief me on her dates.

"Speed dating," she says at last.

Where's she been hiding? "Oh, good for you."

"With vampires."

My smile freezes. What the actual *fuck*?

"Vampires?" I splutter.

"Yes. It's a new thing. They hold special nights at this club in Soho."

My chest tightens to cold, hard stone. "Soho?"

"Yes. Broadwick Street, to be exact."

Of course it is. I grip the computer mouse so tight, I almost break the damn thing to pieces. "Tell me more," I say in a low voice.

Belinda titters nervously. "Well, it's just a bit of fun, really. The guy hands you a number, and the ladies stay sitting—"

"No," I interrupt. "I know how speed dating works. I mean, tell me about the club. The owner."

Belinda suddenly seems to have difficulty breathing,

she's so excited. "The owner. Funny you mention *him*. Most of the women go for that reason alone. He's this hot Scottish hunk with red hair and the bluest, most amazing eyes."

I wince as an unwanted image pops into my head. Those eyes are practically burned into my brain.

"But that's not the only reason," Belinda continues.

"Really?" I ask, sarcasm creeping into my voice. "What else is he offering? A Thai massage for every hundredth customer?"

She lets out an uneasy chuckle. "No. The thing is, I heard a rumor at the speed dating. About the safety of V-Date."

"A rumor?"

"That a couple of years ago, women were murdered by a vampire using the site."

My heart drops like a stone into the pit of my stomach. If only it were just a rumor.

"Oh."

"I'm sure it's rubbish, of course, but I thought you should know."

"Yes," I say grimly. "Thank you, Belinda. I'll cancel your account today."

Without another word, I slip the phone back into the cradle, hands trembling.

"Piece of shit," I tell the empty office, and then louder for good measure, not caring if the hypnotherapist renting the space upstairs complains I'm messing with her inner chi again. "Piece of shit bastard."

Ronin McDermott.

Ancient demon. Manipulative piece of trash. *And the*

last man you shagged, a nasty little voice in my head reminds me.

On impulse, I leap from the swivel chair and grab my coat from the back of the door. I make it all the way to the top of the spiral staircase before it hits me—I'm playing straight into his hands. Me careering off to Soho is exactly the reaction he's after.

I retreat into the office, flinging my coat onto the heart-shaped sofa and raking fingers through my thick, black curls. Needing to do *something* to let off steam, I sink back into my chair and pull up an internet window, jabbing the name of the club into Google. A map pops up, along with contact details. *Bingo*. I lift the telephone and dial the number, clicking a pen like it's a flick knife held to Ronin's throat.

After a few rings, a female voice answers, silky smooth and elegant. I shove down a ridiculous pang of jealousy. "I need to speak to Ronin," I snap.

"May I ask who's calling?" Miss Moneypenny purrs.

"Cat Adair."

Without another word, she places me on hold, the theme to *Downton Abbey* tinkering down the line. Since when did Ronin associate with middle-of-the-road, Sunday-night drama?

The music plays for so long I almost hang up. But then a familiar, loathsome sound vibrates in my ear, a voice as mellow and gravelly as a whiskey on the rocks.

"To what do I owe this unexpected pleasure, Ms. Catherine?"

My fangs slip out, nearly shredding my lower lip.

"First of all—*speed dating*," I hiss.

He lets out a low chuckle. "Fancy giving it a go? I can put you on the guest list, if you like. Or are you still enjoying the single life? Lonely nights in front of *CSI*. Did you ever finish that blanket you were knitting for the Cat's Protection?"

"Screw you."

"We tried that once, remember? What am I saying— of course you do. As I recall, you hadn't made love in so long that my cleaning lady dusted cobwebs from the sheets afterward."

White-hot rage clouds my vision, but I keep my voice steady. I will not rise to his ugly bait. "Actually, I don't remember. I think I must have nodded off halfway through."

He gives a snort of derision. "You're confusing me with someone else, *mo chridhe*. No woman sleeps on my watch."

Unbidden, a shiver zigzags up my spine. "I didn't call to discuss your sexual hang-ups, Ronin," I snap, ignoring the tingle. "Though I'm sure there are plenty to keep us talking long into the night. I'm calling because I've heard the nasty rumors you're spreading about my business."

"I'm sorry to be the one to remind you," he says smugly, "but if by rumors you mean a serial killer using your site to find victims, then I'm afraid they're mostly true."

"Three years back they were true," I hiss. "If you were at all concerned about my clients' safety, why wait so long to say anything?"

A deep clunk echoes down the line.

"Did you just put me on speakerphone?" I demand.

"No. I put the phone on the desk. There's no need for

speakerphone with that foghorn voice of yours. I could probably hear you from my apartment on the other side of the river. Possibly even in Norwich." He pauses. "If there are rumors circulating about your dating service, Catherine, they haven't come from me."

"Yeah right," I mutter, before erupting, "*Speed dating!*"

I can practically hear him smirk. "Genius, isn't it?"

"No. It's not genius. It's stealing. Stealing my idea and shoving it facedown in your rat-infested, back-alley club."

"Back-alley club? We're only a few doors down from Liberty's. Hardly slumming it. Or maybe you're thinking of how it was in the nineties. The *eighteen nineties*. Admit it. That's the last time you actually visited a bar, wasn't it?"

"Not so long ago," I continue, ignoring the comment, especially because he has a point. "You were doing everything in your power to stop humans and vampires fraternizing. Now you're running social mixers. What is this? The ancient demon version of a midlife crisis?"

"I've decided to move with the times."

"Why? One too many bodies to hide? Of course, it must be hard without Logan around to mop up for you anymore."

He sucks in a breath of what I assume, at first, is anger. But then he exhales slowly.

"Are you smoking?"

"It's the only thing getting me through this tedious conversation."

"Oh, fuck off."

I slam the phone down so hard, my pen pot topples

onto the carpet. I pride myself on rarely losing my cool. But Ronin McDermott never fails to bring out the worst in me.

After I've picked up the pens, deleted Belinda's details, and ceased shaking with rage, I divert calls to my cell phone and leave the office. There isn't a hope of getting anything constructive done today. Not with the mood I'm in.

Outside, the day is bright, watery sunlight filtering through puffy gray clouds. I pick my way around sandwich boards lining the cobbled streets of trendy East London, past the coffee bars and craft shops. I remember them, like I always do, as the slum houses from a hundred years ago—families of ten to a room, children barefoot and starving, excrement and dead animals clogging the gutters. If there's one thing I've learned in my two hundred years of living, it's that human memories are ridiculously short-lived. Places change and start over in an endless cycle of birth and death, and what went before is always forgotten.

But I, and those like me, can never forget. Which is why when I reach the corner of Beechwood Street, I linger outside the door of a small beauty salon, placing a palm against the cool, red brick. I remember a small girl, bony and hollow-eyed, sitting cross-legged on the dirty threshold, a book balanced on her lap. Next to her is a bow-legged boy, downtrodden and grimy, but his eyes sparkle like stars in the night sky. When the receptionist inside notices me, I move on. Over the years, the shop has lived many lives—barbers, chemists, dentists—but while it's still standing, I will always return, will always live close by. It's an anchor to a familiar shore. By the time I reach my apartment block, I'm *grounded*.

That is, until I'm accosted by Mrs. Colangelo, the elderly Italian lady from number four.

"You're early," she says in accusatory tones, appearing from behind her door in a paisley robe. I can't remember the last time I saw Mrs. Colangelo dressed. Or outside, for that matter.

I toss her a weak smile. "I decided to work from home." *Not that it's any of your business*, I almost add.

"Probably for the best," she says, leaning against the doorpost. "There are many crazy people around at the moment. It's not safe for a young, pretty girl like you to be out alone after dark."

Like the rest of my neighbors, Mrs. Colangelo hasn't a clue I'm a vampire. Although I could tell the whole of London now if I so desired, I still abide by my old self-inflicted rules, which involve moving every ten years so no one begins to question why I haven't aged.

"They found a body on Canal Street at the weekend, you know?" Mrs. Colangelo, the eternal optimist, continues. "Badly decomposed, and that's not the worst part."

I begin to edge past her doorway, the delicious freedom of the next flight of stairs beckoning. "What's the worst part, Mrs. Colangelo?"

"No head," she says with a hint of triumph. And then, just so I'm completely up to speed, she continues, "Decapitated." She crosses herself. "Poor soul."

I frown. Decapitation is quite unusual among humans. Vampires, on the other hand...

"Dreadful," I agree, shaking my head. "Well, I have to feed the cat, so I must dash."

"We have a new man moving in next door to you. He came today to measure up."

That catches my attention. The apartment next door has been empty since I moved in five years ago. I've gotten used to having the whole third floor to myself. "Oh, who is he?"

"A musician. Young man. Unmarried. No girlfriend."

Once upon a time, I might have been excited hearing those last three sentences, one after the other. Those days are gone. Now the only part I linger on is *musician*. I sigh. Please, God, not a wretched saxophone player.

"Maybe we can have a bit of romance in our building, eh?" Mrs. Colangelo smiles, puckered lips parting to reveal a set of bright-white dentures.

I cock my head to the side. "I didn't know you were keen on younger men, Mrs. Colangelo." She begins shaking her head, but I don't let her get a word in. "But if that's your thing, go for it. You deserve to find happiness, and age is just a number, right?" Before she can utter a denial, I swivel around to the stairs. "Enjoy the rest of the day!"

She's still babbling about the misunderstanding when I slam the front door shut behind me and swing my bag into an armchair, kicking off my Louboutins and dropping about six inches in height. Designer footwear is a constant weakness. Having spent my childhood barefoot in Victorian England, being at liberty to buy shoes whenever I like is dizzying.

Wentworth the cat, who narrowly missed being hit by

a red-soled shoe, strolls over. He wraps himself around my legs and purrs like a tractor. Forgetting myself, I reach down to lift him up, making him squeal loudly and jump five feet into the air. Wentworth was a stray who hates to be picked up.

We're a lot alike, Wentworth and I.

"What happened to you, Wentworth?" I ask, crossing the room to scratch his head. "Who hurt you in your old life?"

The outburst forgotten, he stares up at me with dilated, emerald eyes. Despite the erratic behavior and occasional bit of cat vomit, he's easily the best flatmate I've ever had. For starters, he never makes me feel bad about the state of my love life—*or lack thereof*.

If someone had told me a quarter of a century ago I'd be running a vampire/human dating service, I would have ruptured my spleen laughing.

Then, about ten years ago, in the media scoop of all time, a famous Hollywood actress publicly announced she was a vampire. The day it hit the tabloids, I was down at my local 7-Eleven buying milk. There, emblazoned across the front page, screamed the headline *Vampires Exist*. At first, I thought it was some kind of joke. After all, the *National Enquirer* had been running the same story sporadically for years. But no, it wasn't April Fools' Day or even Halloween—this was the *Daily Telegraph*, and it didn't end there.

In the weeks that followed, vampires across the globe began to out themselves. The hysteria didn't last long, though. As soon as humans discovered we don't survive on blood and sleep in dirt from our motherland, everyone calmed the heck down. We became like a half sibling finally invited to the family reunion. We even got the vote.

It was during the calm after the storm that I got the idea for V-Date. Places like Ronin's club would always cater for the fetish end of the vampire dating market, but for those craving romance, there was zilch. Sex is all well and good, but it isn't what folks drive themselves nuts looking for. Love is the prize.

So, I hired a web designer and rented an office, and the rest is history. For a somewhat costly monthly fee, humans and vampires can access a database of eligible partners. I was even planning to launch a mobile app, which may have to be scrapped if my clients continue to jump ship.

Anger rises inside me as I remember the rumors doing the rounds over at Ronin's seedy nightclub. Ever since we spent that one night together all those years ago, he's been at me. He can't stand the idea of there being a woman in the universe immune to his slimy charms.

I open the kitchen cupboard and grab a latte mug, slamming it onto the counter. I didn't even find him attractive before that night.

Okay, that's a lie. It's impossible not to find him attractive. With burning blue eyes and high cheekbones, he's everyone's type. But it ends there. He's ugly on the inside. On the inside, he's Voldemort.

Like most vampires, I don't fully understand the origins of those who created us, but for me, Ronin is evidence enough that demons exist. Perhaps the worst part is that he's masquerading behind this whole bad-boy-turned-good facade. I mean, *speed dating*. What is he playing at?

I flick the switch on the coffee maker and take out a latte capsule from the huge glass jar next to the sink. I'm considering what it might take to murder an ancient when I hear a soft knock at the door. If it's Mrs. Colangelo again, I may be tempted to bare my fangs.

Abandoning the latte, I bound across the room and tear open the door, my best *fuck off* face charged and ready to go. But instead of the powdered visage of Mrs. Colangelo, I find myself staring at a T-shirt-clad chest. A *man's* chest.

I lift my gaze in confusion, meeting soft gray eyes, intelligent and kind looking, half hidden behind a pair of wire-frame specs.

Who knew midday was hunk o'clock around these parts?

"Oh," I say, pulling myself to full height—which, at five foot one and a half, isn't much. "I thought you were Mrs. Colangelo."

The hunk smiles. It's off-center, and he has a tiny chip on one of his incisors, but other than that, it's a pretty charming sight. "No, I'm Peter. I'm moving in next door. The postman put your mail in my box by mistake."

It's at this point I realize he's clutching a small wad of envelopes in his tapered fingers. *Musician's* fingers.

"Right," I say. "Mrs. Colangelo mentioned there's a new guy."

I sense her out in the downstairs hallway, earwigging. The whiff of lavender water is always a dead giveaway. "Hi, Mrs. Colangelo," I call out. "I'm meeting the new neighbor. The one you think is cute!" I catch a tiny squeal of indignation, and a door slams.

Hunky Peter bursts out laughing, eyes crinkling behind his glasses.

"That was mean," I admit. "But she's very nosy."

He continues to smile, giving me a once-over so discreet, a human woman might have missed it. Definitely not gay. "I sort of got that impression," he murmurs.

"So, Mrs. Colangelo tells me you're a musician. What sort of music will be keeping me awake at night?" To my chagrin, my voice oozes flirtation. A hot flush creeps up my neck.

"Jazz mainly. But don't worry: I have a studio on Mare Street, so I shouldn't be keeping you up."

"That's a shame," I mutter.

We stand for a few seconds, not speaking. He has lovely hair—dark brown, worn in that messy chic way that's all the rage these days.

"Anyway, I better give you these," he says, handing me the letters. "Catherine, isn't it?"

I narrow my eyes. "How did you know?"

"It's on the letters."

"Oh. Right." For God's sake. Dumb much?

He smiles. "Well, it was good to meet you, neighbor."

"Right back at ya."

He holds up a hand in farewell. "Bye."

Mirroring his gesture, I hold up my own. "See you around."

When I've shut the door behind me, I lean against it. Across the room on the sofa, Wentworth studies me through half-closed lids.

"He seems nice," I say to the cat. "Friendly."

Wentworth's eyes widen, as if to say *Who are you kidding?*

"I was not flirting," I point out. "Most people seem nice at first. It's human nature to hide all the bad stuff."

I cross back into the kitchen and flip through the mail. Most of it is junk, but a manila envelope with a red stamp catches my attention. It's from Harvey & Co. Solicitors. I tear it open, my stomach lurching as I begin to read.

Dear Sirs,

We are instructed by Mr. Aaron Leech in relation to an incident on September 8, whereby he was admitted to the hospital following an encounter with a vampire met through your dating website, V-Date.com.

Mr. Leech, who was visiting a nightclub at 66 Broadwick Street when the incident occurred, sustained injury to a vital artery and collapsed on the premises. He was taken to Middlesex University Hospital, where an emergency blood transfusion was performed.

As a result of your failure to vet the safety of the vampires using the site, we have advised our client that he is entitled to damages for your negligence. If you do not compensate our client for the sum of £100,000 by December 1, we are instructed to issue a claim in the High Court without recourse to you.

Yours faithfully,
Harvey & Co. Solicitors

Once I finish reading, I go back to the beginning and read it over and over again, my head thumping with rage each time I get to the part about 66 Broadwick Street.

Clearly not content with poaching my clients with cheap tricks, Ronin is now hell-bent on ruining me completely. Without a doubt, it was he who suggested legal action, probably to divert attention from that creepy club of his.

I stand for a moment, clenching and unclenching my fists, contemplating a joyous scenario where the ancient explodes in a puff of black smoke and is never heard of again, before snatching my heels up from the floor and shoving my feet into them.

I crash out of the apartment, and this time, when I reach the stairs, I don't turn back. This time, Ronin is going to feel the full force of my wrath.

About the Author

Juliet Lyons is a paranormal romance author from the UK. She holds a degree in Spanish and Latin American studies and works part-time in a local primary school, where she spends far too much time discussing Harry Potter. Since joining global storytelling site Wattpad in 2014, her work has received millions of hits online and gained a legion of fans from all over the world. When she is not writing or working, Juliet enjoys reading and spending time with her family. Visit her online at julietlyons.co.uk.